He Jiahong's Portfolio – Crime Suspense Series

(Revised)

The Evil in Sex

He Jiahong

8th HOUSE PUBLISHING • CANADA

About the translator

Angela Lee, MBA, had ever been worked as the Special Editor of China Wine News and Full-time Translator of translation firms. With over eight years. full-time working experience in translation, she has over 50 news published both on the newspaper and the website of China Wine News and had ever provided translation services for Shanghai Expo Summit Forum, World Rubber Summit Forum and China Rubber.

Head Note

Sex was originally a reproductive utility and an insignificant part of individual life. The Creator intended mankind to toil and suffer willingly for life continuation, so he expanded sex to cover love and mingled it with miraculous ecstasy. But such ecstasy evolved into the source of evil, for indulgence in lust is, in a lot of cases, the start of evil.

Table of Contents

The Prologue

She went into the bathroom, leaving behind a trace of female fragrance.

He walked, involuntarily, to the closed but unlocked bathroom door. Hearing the water flow, he desired to see the body in shower. Many times had he laid the hand on the door, but guilt within him pulled it back. He struggled until the sound of water ceased.

The door opened and she walked out with a pair of very thin pajamas. With slight surprise, she asked, "What are you doing?"

"Nothing." He blushed.

Having noticed his embarrassment, she smiled and walked on.

Through her pajamas, he saw an enticing curve.

She walked to the bedside and turned to him, "I have agreed to let you see my scar on the hips. Do you want to see?"

He hesitated for a second and advanced towards her.

She turned around, untied her pajamas, took off her pair of underpants and throw it onto the bed. Then she lifted her pajamas and pointed her finger to her right hip, saying, "Here, you see." She cast a glance on him, adding, "Don't touch! There is electricity!"

He was scrutinizing the dark red scar on her plump and white skin, trying to hold back. But he soon lost control of himself and touched the scar with hand. It appeared that electricity passed from her smooth skin through his arm to his heart, making it beat faster. He could not help but embraced her.

She did not resist, asking wittily, "What have you seen?"

Before she could complete the sentence, he set kiss on her lips and held her close to his chest. After a long and enthusiastic kiss, both gasped.

．．．．．．．．．．．．．．．．．．．．．．．．．．．．．．．

Having no idea how many hours elapsed, he awoke. After relishing his experience in the mind with eyes closed, he opened his sleepy eyes and saw her lying next to him. He gave her a kiss on the cheek.

She was awake, too, but her eyes were still closed. "Your bad mustache made me itch."

"Did I hurt you just now?"

She opened her eyes, seeing his earnest expression, and laughed, "That is called orgasm. You don't understand? It appears this is your first time, right?"

He nodded, putting his mouth to her ear, saying, "But now it is the second one."

"Oops, you recharged yourself so quick."

"I have a lot of energy."

"Don't boast. How much do you have?"

"Whatever amount you want!"

"I'll want whatever available in you!"

"Good, I'll let you have it!"

"Oh, you are damn good. Spare me. I don't want it now. Good brother, please…"

Both were tired after the vigorous and satisfactory love-making. They lined up on bed, closed their eyes, as if both were pondering their own stories.

She asked, all of a sudden, "You didn't have a girlfriend?"

He replied honestly, "I had one during the school years."

"How about now?"

"We parted before graduation."

"Why did that happen?"

"I'm not sure. Maybe it was a misunderstanding."

"Was she pretty?"

"Yes."

"Did you see her since?"

"No."

"But you could not forget her?"

"How to say? Well, yes. But now I think you are the woman most worthy of my love. Please trust me. I'm loving you with sincerity and will do so for the rest of my life. I can make you happy, for sure. Really! What's wrong? You don't believe me? Why are you crying?" He sat up, seeing her sobbing on her pillow, and asked anxiously.

Suddenly, she sat up, too, wiped her tears, looked at him and burst into hysterical laughter.

………………………….

Chapter 1 – The Criminal Defense Lawyer

Song Jia was a smart and beautiful girl. She put a cup of coffee in front of Hong Jun, turned in a circle lightly, then raised her right hand and spoke gravely, "I want to sit for the bar exam."

Hong Jun was a handsome lawyer with scholarly demeanor. He was just raising the cup, but now he put it down and asked, "Why?"

"People always walk their way up."

"You want job-hopping?"

"Can't I be a lawyer at your office?"

"But you are one of the rarest talented secretary."

"Probably I'm also a hard-to-get lawyer talent. Of course, I'm nothing compared to you. We are not on the same level, and your position is unshakable. I think you are the most competent lawyer in China and one of the idolized. Generally, the idolized lack capabilities, but the capable lack good appearance. I remember when I was in the middle school, my father always told me, saying I should not neglect my studies simply because I look good. And he always compared me with the handful of top students. I just said they should not look bad simply because they performed well in studies." Song Jia spoke with a clear and pleasant voice, but also with a fast speech speed.

"Exactly!" Hong Jun uttered this simple word with a deep and mellow tone. But he preferred to deliver long speeches while talking about professional topics and chatter while engaging in pleasant talks.

"That's true. Because it's hard to find a lawyer like you, people seek your help for their cases. But you are too busy. And this is where I got the idea of sitting the bar exam. If you don't agree, you can hire another lawyer."

"But few lawyers want to deal with criminal cases, indeed."

"Have you heard about the 'salvage team'?"

"What is that?"

"Those are lawyers specialized in criminal cases. No matter what kind of offense you committed, they are able to get you out, and at a cost ranging from tens of thousands to hundreds of thousands, which is clearly indicated. That is hot!"

"I'm afraid of hot things."

"So I should take the exam."

"Bar exams are not easy. Perhaps let me test you first?"

"Test me for what?"

"It's easy. This is yesterday's *Beijing Evening News*. There is a report on a traffic accident."

Song Jia came close to Hong Jun and read the news quietly, "At about 3 pm, April 8, 1995, a traffic accident took place on the side road of 3rd ring road on the west side of north Taipingzhuang in this city, in which a car hit and injured a bicycle rider and the driver escaped in his car. According to witnesses, it was a dark blue Santana. The car's front license plate, which was green, lost a big piece of coating and the last three digits of the license number were 283 or 285. We request any informed individual to…"

"Hold on! Based on this report, do you think the tail digit is 3 or 5? I give you 5 minutes." Hong Jun raised the cup and sipped some coffee.

"Is it 3 or 5?" Song Jia held the paper, made two circuits of the desk and then laid the paper on the desk. With wide-open eyes, she said, "Dark blue Santana…Well, Mr. Hong, is it your car? Oh, no, your license number is much different."

"You're wasting time!"

Song Jia put her palms together in front of her mouth, slightly frowned, as if in contemplation, and paced with rhythm back and forth. "283…285…285…283…3 plus 5 is 8, 5 minus 3 is 2. 3 multiplied by 5 is 15. 5 multiplied by 3 is also 15. But…"

"Don't procrastinate!" Hong Jun was looking at his watch.

"Teacher, can you give me some clue? Even in school exams, the teacher would set out a range." Song Jia said casually, tilting her head.

"Time is up. You should continue to be a secretary." A complacent smile appeared on Hong Jun's face.

"Ah, Mr. Hong. The time you gave me is too short. Can you extend it for 2 more minutes? Are you referring to the probability of each of the 2 digits?"

"You've chosen the wrong pathway!"

"Do you mean human's visual error rules?"

"It is not so profound. What month is it now?"

"It's April."

"This is the answer. Is it simple?"

"Oh, pardon me. What kind of answer is it?"

"Where did you pick up this phrase? It sounds like I always bully you." Saying this, Hong Jun stood up and walked to the door, "The client is coming!"

"Ah, Mr. Hong, don't interrupt our conversation."

The doorbell rang, Song Jia unwillingly opened the door. While passing by Hong Jun, she said, "I will continue to seek your advice when the client is gone."

The man who came in was in his 40s, tall and strong. His dark, dense eyebrows were almost connected together on his big, square face. His hair extended below the ears and curled forward. He was clean-shaven around lips, but the color of beard was still easily noticed. His hair at the top of the head was affected by malnutrition, presumably because there was too much hair on the face – only a few sparse strands hanging there on the bald head. His speech was almost of Beijing dialect, with a little northeast accent. The man was the general manager of an interior decoration company, and Xia Dahu was his name.

Following self-introduction, Xia said, "Mr. Hong, I came here after reading the newspaper."

Hong Jun understood Xia was referring to the report on how he went to Heilongjiang to vindicate Zheng Jianguo after Zheng was wronged for nearly 10 years. Although he was satisfied with his first case after returning to China from his overseas study, he said, "It is no big deal."

"But it is a big deal for the persons involved."

Hong Jun smiled gently. He felt that beneath the apparent relaxed expression of the guest was his enormous stress. So Hong returned to the issue at hand and said, "Now let's discuss whatever big issue you encountered."

"It's about my son. He was trading stock and it worked well, but this time he suffered a big loss and was arrested. Initially I didn't know why, but I heard the day before yesterday that the case went to the court and he was charged with fraud, as procuratorate said. I need your advice. I think stock trading is a business in which both gains and losses may take place. It might be probable to accuse him of fraud if he earned money from others, but he lost, how could this be defined as a fraud?" Can you tell why?"

"It depends. According to the criminal law, the subjective element of fraud is the purpose of illegally taking possession of public or private properties, while the objective element is to acquire public or private properties by telling lies. Therefore, whether your son committed fraud hinges on whether he cheated for illegal possession in stock trade."

"He was trading stock in the securities company. Who could he cheat? He was speculating, at most. I could not understand the charge."

"Did you get a copy of the indictment?"

"I got it the day before yesterday." Xia scoured in his briefcase and said with embarrassment, "I dropped it in my office. I was lost in the enormous amount of trouble that was haunting me recently. I will bring it to you later."

"Did the court tell you when they will open the court session?"

"They said it was next week. I'll check again."

"Generally, the court issues a copy of the indictment 7 days before the session, and you delayed 2 days. Time is really short. Do you remember any causes identified on the indictment?"

"As a matter of fact, I know nothing about stocks, so I can't understand what it says. But my son is indeed a burden."

"How old is he?"

"Twenty-one. This is an age of rebellion and trouble. In fact, sometimes I even wish I didn't have this son. Probably I could live a few years more if so."

"Maybe he was not welcome since he was born." Hong Jun said casually.

"What do you mean?" said Xia with an unnatural tone, and he looked sulky in a moment.

"Sorry, I used the wrong language." Hong Jun promptly changed the topic, "He embarked on stock trading business at such a young age, so he must be smart, right?"

"Probably he is. He got good scores in school, but somehow he fell for the stock market in high school; as a result, he failed in college entrance examination. I have an old friend who is a manager in Hongyuan Securities. My son regularly went there. Later he told me he wanted to trade stocks. Initially I did not approve, but I agreed after long-term persuasion by him and his mother. I gave him 100,000 yuan then. I said I did not expect him to get rich, and if he could support himself, I would be happy. He has been doing well in the past 2 years. He earned more than he lost, but unexpectedly, this time he lost a lot."

"How much did he lose?"

"It is hard to say. Honestly, although he is my son, I never inquire about his financial status. But I know he is extravagant. He would spent several hundred for a piece of clothing. Now he lost everything and owed money to the securities company. He is essentially a trouble-maker. Mr. Hong, I hope you don't mind my harsh language."

"Mr. Xia, I decide to accept this case. Please send me the copy of indictment as soon as possible."

"Maybe I can invite you to visit my company. I'll give you the indictment, and I also want to…" Xia was about to speak, but hesitated.

"Anything else?"

"Nothing. I just want to treat you to dinner."

"I can go, but dinner is not necessary." Hong Jun looked at his watch and stood up.

"I engaged lawyers before. They liked to have dinner with me and chat. It made communication easier."

"I would serve my customers well even if we don't have meals together. A dinner is troublesome. You'd better send me the copy of indictment this afternoon."

"OK, I will ask someone to bring it to you after I'm back to my place."

After witnessing Xia's leaving, Song Jia returned to Hong Jun's office at once, and said, in earnest, "Mr. Hong, dear teacher, please forgive my ignorance, but I need you to clarify it."

"What do you need me to clarify? Do you mean why I said Xia's son was not welcome since he was born? You are young. There are many things that you don't understand."

"Oh, pardon me. I called you teacher and you became conceited. How much older are you than me?"

"I'm 5 years older than you. We have a generation gap. Do you admit it?"

"Yes, I admit. But what generation gap? You are setting a trap for me, right? Let's go back to the original topic. What is the 283 and 285 all about?"

"What is it?"

"The license plate number."

"You haven't got it, have you?"

"I got it. You just wanted to me think hard, and then come up with 'I'm kidding you.' I'm smarter than you think, but I don't know why I always fall into your trap."

"That simply means I'm smarter than you. But today I'm not kidding you. This is a serious IQ test. As you know, Beijing government is issuing a new type of license plate, the blue one, which shall replace the old one. Plates are changed upon annual vehicle check. And the annual check is conducted according the tail digit on the license plate. If the final digit is 3, annual check shall be performed in March, at which time the plate shall be changed. Similarly, if the final digit is 5, plate change shall take place in May. It's April now, but the license plate of that car is the old one with green color, so the tail digit could only be 5 and could not be 3. Miss Song, am I kidding you? So I have to use your language, 'Oh, pardon me.'"

Wordless was Song Jia at the moment. Slight tinges of red emerged on her white cheek. Her heart was filled with admiration, as well as unspeakable love, for the lawyer, because there was another women in between – Xiao Xue, who was Hong Jun's first love in school. Song was longing for Hong Jun's love, but she did not want to hurt the woman who looked like her in appearance, nor was she willing to become the woman's substitute.

Hong Jun did not notice the change in Song Jia's facial expression because his mind was brought to Xia Dahu. He sipped some coffee, as if talking to himself. "Xia did not even bring the indictment. Miss Song, do you think the real purpose of his coming is about his son?"

"I also feel he was absent-minded. Besides, he wanted to invite you to dinner at his company. Maybe he's going after something else."

"How do you think about him?"

"He is shrewd with hidden plans."

"I feel the same thing. Apparently he is careless, but deep down he is careful. It appears that he did not bring the indictment on purpose."

"He was asking you visit his company with this excuse. Is it necessary?"

"Unreasonable things often contain hidden facts."

"Is it a dinner with plots?"

"You are too imaginative. Anyway, I have to take a look in the stock market. Have you traded stocks before?"

"Never. I dare not. I couldn't afford to lose my tiny deposit in the stock market."

"I need to learn first, but time is short." Hong Jun made a fist with his right hand and moved it in two circles clockwise in front of him, as his habitual movement to show determination.

Seeing Hong Jun was looking down at the calendar, Song Jia went out of the office and into the bathroom next to it, and turned over the plate on the door – now "Gentleman's room" became "Lady's room".

Chapter 2 – The Lost Case in the Stock Market

Hong Jun drove to Hongyuan Securities' business office and parked on the roadside. As he got off, a dark blue Santana passed him at full speed, made a swift turn and parked in front the business office. A tall and lean man went out and walked quickly into the office. Hong Jun thought, probably all stock investors were like this.

Hong Jun walked towards the office slowly. All of a sudden, he noticed the license plate number of the Santana car – 37285! Out of curiosity, he moved swiftly to the car and looked at the license plate. It was covered with mud, so he could not see whether a piece of coating was lost. While hesitating about if he should get involved in this issue, the man hurried out, opened the door and drove away. With regret, Hong went into the business office.

The expected hustle and bustle was not seen in the lobby. People were chatting in twos and threes. Two women were even knitting sweaters on the chair. Several clerks were sitting behind the counter and reading newspapers or trimming nails. Hong saw a crowd in front of the quotation display, as if listening to someone's high-profile speech. So he went in.

In the middle of the crowd, a short man in his 30s with short hair was talking with fervor, "…He always says most people earn and few people lose in the stock market and that there is a so-called '721' theory, which means among 10 traders, 7 earn, 2 break even, and 1 loses. I don't want to listen to this. It seems that I am the '1'. We can't pretend to be great at our own cost. My opinion is that a small handful of people profit from the most. Just think, there is a limited pool of money. Neither the government nor the companies add new water into the pool, so where do you make the money? Aren't you gaining from other traders' investments? Besides, the broker has a stake in it. I think the brokers are the only ones who truly make a profit, while others who claim so are probably boasting."

At this time, a middle-aged man with glasses interposed, "I've heard of an American version of '721' – in 10 traders, 7 lose, 2 break even and only 1 makes a profit."

The man with short hair said, "This is what I believe. Is the stock market a moneymaker for some individuals? Yes. Some people made a fortune indeed. I heard that some people can make tens of thousands, or even hundreds of thousands in a day thanks to "insider trading". But how many are they? How many people can get the insider's messages? Count them. The number hardly meets a few. Besides, risks are associated with big investments. There have been ample examples of failure. Say, late in the year before last, a wealthy man with surname Lin raised a loan to trade stocks but ended up with a loss of 530,000 due to sharp decline of stock prices. And he jumped from the roof of the securities company. A recent example was Xia, a VIP in our locality who also borrowed money for stock trading. He purchased a huge sum, 100,000 shares, but lost them all and was eventually charged with fraud. In brief, we are ordinary folks, so we should have an ordinary purpose. We might make a living by this, but don't expect to become millionaires."

The man with glasses laughed, "I think you probably want to become a millionaire, too. Who is content with the amount of money he has, anyway?"

"But we are self-aware. We know we are not destined to be rich, so we dare not dream big."

"There is a saying, 'He who doesn't want to be a general is not a good soldier.', or in my words, 'He who doesn't want to be a millionaire is not a good investor.'"

"Exactly," someone said in agreement with the man with glasses. "If you don't want to become a millionaire, why do you come anyway?"

"I came for daily bread," the man with short hair said. "Of course, if we are destined to become millionaire, we will not object, right?"

"Hahaha…" People's laughter added some vitality to the lifeless stock market, and even those female clerks cast their glances here curiously. When the group separated, they formed some small groups and similar conversations were resumed.

Hong Jun initiated conversation with the man with short hair, saying "You had a nice talk and that added to my knowledge."

"That was my invaluable advice," the man regained his passion. After observing Hong, he said, "Are you a newcomer?"

"Yes, I want to learn."

"You might as well prepare the tuition. Let me tell you. The stock market is a gold mine but also a trap. You might die without traces. But if you truly want to get involved, I tell you this proverb, 'Both long and short bring you benefit, but greed makes a disaster.' If you remember and fully understand this. I assure you that you will not lose in the stock market."

"But I'm still hesitating…"

"Hesitation is not good. It is the greatest weakness in stock trading. It's said the rigid cannot trade stocks. The quotation changes like a child's face, without any premonition."

"I just think it is too perilous. As you talked about the VIP Xia, how could he be charged with fraud?"

"He invested too much." The man lowered his voice, saying, "Let me tell you, he must have offended someone, who set a trap for him and he fell in."

"Can you let me know how that works, so that I will not fall for the same."

"Nowhere can I get the details. I only heard from somebody else. Someone said that was a problem in the 'insider trading', about internal conflict. Someone else said they fought for a woman. Of course these are secrets on the topside, and we are only doing the guesswork." Said the man with small hair, pointing to the ceiling.

"The topside?" Hong Jun asked, in confusion.

"The VIP room is on the 2nd floor. There are a world of gossips about them. Who knows the truth?" After saying this, the man left.

Hong Jun walked around in the securities company and was content with what he learned.

On the next day, Hong Jun reviewed the indictment. He read relevant documents at the court and then headed to the detention center to visit the defendant Xia Zhe.

Xia Zhe looked like a teenager with a foreigner's vibe. His big eyes, pointed nose, white skin and yellowish hair made him look as if he was of European descent. He was a little wild in character, but sophisticated in demeanor for his age.

Lying on the bed of the detention center, he closed his eyes, and the unforgettable scene occurred to him for another time…

It was a rare spring rain in Beijing. Rain drops carried coldness and fell from the dark evening sky. They cleaned the dry and dusty air and chased pedestrians away from streets and alleys. The streets on the north of the Imperial Palace was a little empty. Cars passed by every now and then, splashing a colorful curtain of water under the street lamps.

He was wearing a raincoat, standing under a tree beside the Tongzi River. The branches with new sprouts covered the vision above, so he could only look at the street in front through the curtain of rains. He avoided looking at the evening sky because, although not bright, the vision in front of him was without scary darkness. He used to like observing the evening sky, but what happened recently deprived him of his courage to face darkness.

Water on the road glimmered with flickering white light. He vision reached over the water and rested on the turret of the Imperial Palace. At this moment, the turret appeared to be a monster sitting on the high wall, a monster that might suddenly attack the prey below. There was some flickering light under the turret, but he could not distinguish whether it was a street lamp or home lamp.

He stared as the rainfall made a white mist before his eyes. Suddenly, the light turned red as if it was "the red in the green forest" on the quotation display. He felt as if he was in the middle of the craze of the stock market, immersed in the fanatic shouts and desperate curses of the investors.

He had not been to the securities company for many days. Since that inexplicable "accident", he started to run about, looking for any person that might help him. He used to have a lot of friends, but now there was no one to rely on. As a young man, he started to understand the meaning of the Chinese phrase "the fickleness of the world".

Yesterday, he went back home, fatigued. His mother informed him that the police was looking for him. He did not know why the police was looking for him, but he had an inauspicious premonition, mainly because of the strange anonymous letter. Maybe a disaster was approaching. He thought he had to meet Fang Qiong once again anyway. So he called and asked her to meet him here – the place where they shared unforgettable memories. What occurred to him was her petite, slim figure and her enchanting laughter.

The first time he met Fang Qiong in Hongyuan Securities, his eyes were fixed on this newly hired female clerk. It might not be love at first sight, but her appearance, figure, and temperament, especially the feminine tenderness manifest in her speech and manners, did harbor the charisma that he fell for. He had a girlfriend when he was in high school, but that seemed to be only a game. His then girlfriend was like a green fruit, fresh but maybe not tasty. But Fang was a mature fruit, irresistible, arousing his desire to taste her. He made advances in a variety of ways, but she kept a polite distance, neither accepting nor rejecting, putting him in a dilemma. He gifted her with flowers, but she smiled and put it on the table behind. He invited her to dinner, but she politely declined. He tried to send her home, but he always figured out a way to escape. Finally, he found out the right way to approach her.

He knew Fang liked dancing, so he took three months to attend a social dance crash course. Immediately after completion, he invited Fang to dance. Fang was amazed but also excited that he was also a dancer. They went into a ballroom outside of the south gate of Ditan Park. Fang liked this ballroom because of the soundness of its ground, lighting and music, and also, the grace of the people. Fang was a professional dancer but Xia only knew a few basic steps. So Fang explained the techniques for him: in standing, curl the abdomen and raise the hips, extend the limbs and straighten the back; in walking, touch the ground with the ball of feet and keep the upper torso static;

and in dancing with a partner, separate the upper and push together the lower, insert his front leg between hers, and do not separate them even in rotation. He was talented and made fast progress. But the closeness of their lower bodies often aroused biological react in him, affecting his movements. Sometimes she felt that and stared him, wishing him to focus on dancing and stay away from sexual thoughts. And he would blush, but fortunately, the ballroom light covered his face.

They danced once a week. During dancing, the fleeting of time was more vividly felt by him. The period of waiting became hard for him. He tried to make them closer but little progress was made. Every time after dancing, he invited her to dinner, but she would reject the proposal on the excuse that she had to take a shower at home. And she never allowed him to send her home. He could embrace her in the ballroom, but once out of there, no physical contact was allowed, including holding of hands. As she said, they were only dancing partners. To him, her attitude was an irresistible allure, but he was not able to get her.

One evening after the spring festival, they danced again. She was in a great mood, but a little tired. In the slow and gentle Blues music, he rested her head on his chest from time to time, and her soft breast agitated his heart. Previously she would dance to the entire tune, but on that evening, she said she was tired in the middle. While walking out of the ballroom, he held her waist, and she did not push his hand away like she did before. He attempted to invite her to dinner, and to his surprise, she did not reject him. He was filled with unexpected joy, hailed a taxi and came to Dasanyuan restaurant on the north of the Imperial Palace – surely a deluxe place, appropriate for the first dinner experience with her.

He talked a lot at dinner, particularly about his dreams and the future. He planned to become a millionaire in three years, then head south to Shenzhen and gain experience in a Stock Exchange, and finally become an investment consultant. He heard that some investment consultants in Hong Kong make tens of millions in a year. He hoped he could set up his own investment consultation company in the near future. Fang was fascinated by his talks. Charming smiles were on her face, but she seldom spoke.

After dinner, they came to the Tongzi River outside of the north gate of the Imperial Palace, and stood under a tree, face to face. He summoned up his courage and said the three words – "I love you." She was moved but said they were not a good match because she was a few years older than him, and that he should find a young girl instead. He said it didn't matter and he liked the feeling of loving a woman older than him. She shook her head and said although it didn't matter at present, it would be a problem after 30 years, because he would have retained his vigor while she would have changed into an old lady. He told her, cordially, that he did not mind what happened 30 years later, and that he would be satisfied if only he could stay with her. He held her to his chest and gave the "first kiss" on her lips. She accepted his kiss and caress, but didn't allow him to put hands under her clothes. She also put forward a condition that their relationship should not be made known in the company. He agreed, but also said he would soon enable her to leave the securities company and enjoy a better life. With affection, she said she hoped he could become a millionaire soon.

Since then, he would come to the VIP room of Hongyuan Securities every day, staring at the computer screen while thinking about Fang Qiong. He obeyed her conditions, but he would seize opportunities, when no one was around, to enjoy brief periods of intimacy with her. He decided to move fast and accelerate the implementation of his "millionaire plan", and even took the risk of overdrawing to make big investments, which led to the unfortunate "Shanghai Yansheng" incident. Now he stood at the place of "first kiss" alone, pained and confused in the heart.

The rain was coming with increasing force and thunder emerged across the sky. He raised the wrist and looked at the watch – it was 8:20. He sighed and spoke to himself in the heart, that since it was raining heavily, she was not coming. But he was unwilling to give up. At this moment, he had complex feelings for Fang Qiong. On one hand, the mysterious woman was like a puzzle, enticing him to find a solution; on the other, the woman was like a trap, seducing him to fall. He wanted to get closer to her, but there was not an access route. He wanted to leave her, but no exit was visible. He hesitated and wandered, not capable of rescuing himself from the trying situation.

Suddenly, there comes the sound of high heels knocking on the ground. He quickly turned around and looked – there was a looming figure in the east, in the misty rain. His heart beat faster and legs carried him closer, involuntarily.

But as the sound of footsteps got near, he was disappointed, because there was four feet, and two figures next to each other. He stopped his pace and returned. But the footsteps were getting closer and closer. He moved sideways to let them pass, but a female voice came – "Xia Zhe!"

He turned around but saw an unknown woman. Terrified, he asked, "Who are you?"

The young man next to her said, "We are the police, please go with us."

Xia Zhe turned and ran, and the two people ran and followed him from behind. Xia got rid of his raincoat and madly ran on the street, splashing through the waters. After a while, he thought the two persons were left far behind and felt relieved. But at this moment, a police vehicle was approaching. He stopped and looked around. Having noticed that there is no way to escape, he ran towards the police car.

"Screech…" Two copped came off even before the car fully stopped.

Xia approached them, panted and said, "Officer, there were two robbers."

But the policemen asked him to get into the car…

Xia was thinking about the excruciating question – Who sold him? Is it the mysterious Fang Qiong? At this moment, an officer opened the door, called his name and brought him to the interview room.

After self-introduction, Hong Jun looked at Xia Zhe softly. Without getting straight to the point, he said, "You became a stock market expert at such a young age. That was not easy."

"My passion in stocks started when I was in senior high school. I have an adventurous spirit. For me, high risks imply high profits. Besides, I think the stock market is the best place for a man to exert his wisdom and courage.

Later, I failed in the examination and could not go to university. So I buried myself in stock market. Of course, my play with stocks was made possible by two conditions – the money my father provided; and connections in the securities company."

Hong found that people engaged in stock trading are often talkative. "You mean Hongyuan Securities manager Lu Boping?"

"Yes, he was my father's childhood pal."

"He took care of you nicely, right?"

"In fact, the only benefit I got is the preferential rate for opening a VIP account and the convenience in routine procedures, but most of all, my father would only rest assured and give money to me if I trade stocks here at Lu's."

"But why didn't Lu help you in this incident?"

"Well, I deserve it. The stock market declined drastically and I operated incorrectly. And Lu wasn't here in Beijing. This is called 'leaking roof meets with continuous rain, and sailing ship comes across strong wind.'"

"You are still so optimistic."

Xia smiled and consoled himself, "I'm a confident person. I did not cheat anyone, so I don't think the court is able to sentence me to imprisonment. Beside, I was trained in the stock market to have such an attitude. I need to be cool, unaffected by loss or gain. If one's emotions fluctuate with his loss or gain, then he could not stand firmly, and probably he'd jump from a roof one day."

"Have you ever willingly given away money?" Hong Jun recalled this term in stock trading, which refers to buying at a high position and selling at a low one.

"Of course I did. Who haven't given away money in stock trading, anyway?"

"Why not this time?"

"I made a mistake."

"Now please talk about the details." Hong thought it was time to get to the point.

Xia reflected for a moment and said, "I'm talented in stock trading in some way. Although the stock market may kill a person without leaving any traces, the loss that took place this time was indeed not my fault. Last year, when the stock market was sluggish, only Shanghai Yansheng performed well. It was 'the red in the green forest'. That was why I thought Yansheng would go up further, so I bought 100,000 shares at a high price, 30.1."

"That was 3 million yuan. You were so wealthy."

"Nah, how was it possible? It was the broker's money."

"Overdrawing? It is a preferential treatment provided by Lu?"

"No, others may get it as well. In order to attract VIPs, many brokers allow overdrawing. Anyway, no matter you lose or profit, it is your liability, and they charge fees based on the volume of transaction. The more you trade, the more they earn. Besides, how many professional stock investors use their own money, anyway?"

"It's like borrowing chickens to lay eggs, right?"

"Yes, but there are failed instances. Soon after I bought, Yansheng started declining. Some people thought this was temporary and it would bounce back soon, but I felt something was wrong, that presumably something happened in the topside. Since I bought with the money I overdrew, I could not get stuck in it. Yansheng was still declining at about the closing time in the afternoon. So I decided to give it away. I informed the clerk of my choice. Since I was feeling depressed about the tens of thousands I lost, I signed the authorization sheet without reading it. On the morning of the next day, I saw Yansheng was still declining and felt relieved that I already closed the transaction. But when I swiped my card, I noticed the 100,000 shares I bought became 200,000. I was confused, so I asked for the record. They said I authorized a purchase yesterday. When I saw the green color spread over the entire screen, I panicked. Next it was a forced liquidation, and I lost more than 600,000 yuan. How was it possible for me to repay so much money?"

"Aren't your father wealthy?"

"That was his money. Besides, his money was held as well."

"He is trading stock, too?"

"He does not trade stock, but he trades wood. That is more risky."

"Trading wood? How?"

"He…" Xia stopped, "I don't know much about his business."

Seeing Xia didn't want to talk, Hong didn't question further. He got back to the topic, "Why didn't you fill out the authorization sheet by yourself?"

"This is a special service in the VIP room. You know, these VIPs have a lot of money but are less educated. So the clerks help them operate computers and fill out authorization sheets. They only need to sign their names."

"Isn't there a quotation when you transact? The selling rate and buying rate should be different, right?"

"That was my mistake. I just wanted to sell it, so I said I needed a transaction at market price."

"What is transaction at market price?"

"It means when the investor gives authorization, he does not give an exact price; instead, he requests a transaction at the current market price."

"Did you speak anything wrong by mistake?"

"Not likely." Xia glanced at the policeman sitting at the doorway, and said in a low voice, "I have been thinking about this in these days. I felt it was someone who put me in this situation."

"If only you can prove someone framed you, the case would be very easy. Do you have a suspect in your mind?"

"I don't know. I'm only suspecting."

"The clerk?"

"Do you mean Fang Qiong?"

"I've read the files. She did the transaction on your behalf, right?"

"Yes. It was strange. On the morning when the error came to my knowledge, I first tried to reach her, but she was not available. Someone said she went to Yunnan in the morning because her mother was critically ill. Her hometown was in Yunnan. Then after a month, I heard she was back, so I made an appointment with her. She didn't come, but police took me. These things are coincidental. But I think she might not do harm to me, although she is mysterious."

"Why is she mysterious?"

"She appeared to have a higher social position and better background than a clerk can have. She was distinguished from the team of female clerks, like a crane in a group of hens. It was not about her height, but about her character and disposition. It was said that she was a promising film actress with excellent appearance and skills although she had not played any leading role. In the beginning, someone said she came here to experience life in preparation for film shooting, but she stayed. She had been in Hongyuan Securities for 2 years, but had almost never made friends with her colleagues. Her tone in speaking sounded like she had witnessed many big events and met many prestigious persons. It was strange that she came to Hongyuan, working hard to serve customers, with little compensation and fame. Besides, she was not so young now, but was still single. Actually, she even had many pursuers in Hongyuan, but it appeared that she was so conceited that she looked down upon them all."

"Including you?"

"In fact, I was not pursuing her. I also regarded her as an elder sister, and she was nice to me. Anyway, I think it could not be her who put me into this situation."

"Then who do you suspect?"

"I suspect two persons: One is Liang Gao, the deputy manager of Hongyuan Company, who has a big mouth which is twice the normal size. People used to call him "Liang Dazui (two big mouths)". Eighty percent of his words were not trustworthy, and the remaining twenty percent shall be treated with caution. For example, if anything happens to you, he might say he can bring you to Zhongnanhai. How can you buy this? The other one is Hu Tucheng, who is also a VIP. He has a nickname "Hu Tuchong (the confused)". He has neither good appearance nor capability. He only used his father's money to invest in stock market. But this guy has ulterior motives and is always scheming to harm people."

"Why would they frame you?"

"Because of envy, I think. People are like this. If you are better than him, he would disturb you. For example, Liang always regarded me as his rival in love and expected me to have an accident. In fact, suppose I had not been there, still Fang would not have fallen in love with him. He has a wife and is not divorced. Is it possible for Fang to love him? Actually Fang dined with him simply because he was her superior. And Hu Tucheng was also pursuing Fang, but how could he get her? Besides, on the day of my 2nd buy-in, he sold out 100,000 shares of Yansheng. This incident made me feel depressed. How could I become one of the losers who released him from the transaction? It was a disgrace, anyway."

"If you hadn't buy, he could not have sold his 100,000 shares, could he?"

"Not necessarily. It depended on whether someone accepted his quotation."

"I don't understand stock trade. Suppose they did frame you, how did they accomplish this?"

"This what I have been thinking about. Later I checked and confirmed the transaction was made on the next day. I think one possibility is that someone tampered with data in the computer system, and the other possibility is that someone used Fang Qiong. But the first one is more likely to be true. Anyway, Fang Qiong is the key person to investigate is we want to figure things out. Mr. Hong, please do find her. She definitely can prove I authorized a sale that day."

"Why?"

"I remember it clearly. We even argued about this. I said Shanghai Yansheng would keep going down, but she said it hit the bottom. I said I could bet on this, but she disagreed. At last I said I could not accept her advice and then get stuck. I needed to sell them all. This was our conversation and she must remember that."

"But her depositions work against you."

"I heard that, so I want to ask her in person, but I don't have the chance." Xia paused, and said again, "By the way, there was a weird thing. I'm not sure whether it has any bearing on this case."

"What is it?"

"Just before my incident, I received a strange letter. My name was on the envelope as the recipient, and the sender name was inscribed as "See inside". After I opened, I only saw a piece of paper with printed characters, which formed a paragraph – "As man sows, so he shall reap. Let the father's debt be paid by the son and justice be fulfilled. Either he or you are facing disasters and no regret will help.""

"Can you produce the letter?"

"I tore it into pieces at the time. At first, I thought it was a mischievous joke. So many people get such weird letters anyway, some of which are in the name of Buddha or such. In my opinion, those come from people who are bored in life. But after this incident, I started to take the letter seriously. The paragraph was suggesting something and appeared to be intended for me. Probably it had a bearing on my father. It might aimed to damage my relationship with my father. I can't tell. It is strange, after all.

"How is your relationship with your father. Your father seems to not care much about your situation."

"He cares for me actually." Xia seemed to be hesitating, "that is his temperament. He does not say much, but I can feel he is good to me in the heart."

"Does he have any enemy?"

"I don't think so. He has been doing business all these years, and it's unavoidable to offend some people, but he always caters to others and is loyal to friends. People, especially his old schoolmates who worked in the countryside with him before, praise him for his goodness."

"Is the manager Lu his old schoolmate?"

"We used to be neighbors living in the same yard. When I was small, my family were more closely connected with them, but after house removal took place, we all moved and seldom met since then. But I feel my father has a complex relationship with Lu. The don't have things in common. Apparently they are on good terms, they have been old schoolmates and worked in the countryside together, but at dinner, they often compete or argue with each other. My father calls him 'Lu Buping (uneven road)', and he calls my father 'Xia Mihu (the blind)'. It's said those nicknames were fabricated when they were young. I can see that my father always wants to prove he is more competent than Lu."

"They are peers, I can understand."

"Their talks are amusing."

"Was the letter delivered to you through the post office?"

"No. Someone put it into my mailbox, right there in the VIP room at Hongyuan."

"Who put it, possibly?"

"It was hard to say. Although the VIP room was not as crowded as the 1st floor, there were still many people coming in and out."

"It is not a simply case, indeed." Hong glanced at the policeman, who was taking a nap at the doorway, and said, "Xia Zhe, I believe what you said, but some evident works against you, especially the signature on the authorization sheet, and you admit it is yours, don't you?"

"In the beginning, I suspected someone faked my signature, but I looked at it carefully. It should be mine, otherwise the skills in it would be too extraordinary to be true. Is it possible that someone made another authorization sheet and faked my signature on it?"

"Everything is possible."

"That was as wicked as the gangs. I could not have offended a gang."

"I hope it has nothing to do with gangs. But the signature is such an important item of evidence that I would ask a handwriting authentication expert to have a look. You should provide me with some handwriting samples, preferably recent ones, with your signature."

"Those are available at my home. You can ask my mother to find them."

"I will meet your father tomorrow according to my plan, and it will be just in time. Do you have any words for your father?" Hong stood up.

"Nothing. I have said whatever I should, earlier. Mr. Hong, to speak from the heart, I really want to go home to visit my mother." Xia also stood up, with a little red around his eyes.

Hong patted Xia's shoulder and went out.

Chapter 3 – The Contractual Dispute

After understanding the case details, Hong Jun found there were still a lot of issues that require investigation. So he went to the Beijing Intermediate People's Court and requested the judge to put off the court session. The judge in charge of this case is Qian Tuliang, who is in his 30s and a graduate from Beijing University's law school. He once met Hong Jun at an academic workshop on reforms in criminal proceedings system. Hong Jun delivered his speech at the workshop to introduce the American criminal proceedings system, especially the advantages of the adversary procedure and the importance of presumption of innocence, having made a profound impression on Qian. Hong Jun said he wouldn't appear in court only after a brief review of the files, an interview with the defendant and a quick check of clauses, as some other lawyers do; nor did he plan to find relationships to work things out. He wanted to clearly understand what happened in the first place. Qian appreciated that, and after obtaining the approval of his superior, he agreed to put off the court session. Qian also told him that since this case was complex, involving large amount of capital and the financial institutions, it was handed to the intermediate court, and the leaders wanted to try this case discreetly. Leaving the court, Hong Jun felt enormously relieved, because had got the time to investigate the cause and effect of this case.

Hong Jun came to China Securities Regulatory Commission to learn about regulations related to overdrawing. He came to know that despite the lack of legal bases, many securities company allowed VIPs to overdraw, because the larger was the transaction volume, the higher was their profit. For VIPs, the overdraft amount would indicate their financial strength and their relationship with the broker. But, since there was no Limit Up-Limit Down, trading on overdraft was very risky, and forced liquidation by the broker and disputes occurred from time to time. There were even incidents of suicide caused by trading on overdraft. The Commission was studying this problem, and it was anticipated to issue relevant policies next year to restrict such act.

Hong Jun also learned about "insider trading". He discovered that if an investor had access to accurate "insider information", such as the formation of joint venture by a listed company with a foreign business, or a significant change in the government's financial policies, the investor could make a fortune very easily. Hong Jun thought there were too many loopholes in this matter, and the Commission should apply stricter supervision. For example, there should be specialists in the Commission to analyze daily stock transaction records, especially large transactions, and if a insider trading was suspected, the Commission should track it to the origin. Hong Jun's interest in this problem of insider trading resulted from his vague feeling that this case likely related to insider trading while he was analyzing Xia Zhe's case materials. Besides, he heard similar rumors in Hongyuan Securities.

Hong Jun left the Commission and drove to Meihu Decoration Company located beside North 2nd Ring Road. This is the yard of a building materials company. A two-storey office building faces the large iron gate of the yard. Xia Dahu's company rented the 2nd floor of the office building. Hong Jun came to the manager office. The furnishings of the office were not luxurious, which only include an ordinary writing desk, a wooden chair, a set of sofas, a bookcase and two safes. A large Beijing map and several framed photos were hanging on the wall. All these seem to signify the owner's diligence and humility.

Having exchanged greetings, Hong Jun introduced to Xia the details of his research for the past 2 days and told him the court agreed to postpone the court session. Xia was satisfied with this and then came up with a question not related to the case.

"Mr. Hong, on the day we met for the first time, how did you know my family affairs? Did you know me before?"

"Of course not."

"then why did you say my son was not welcome since he was born?"

"That was a simple deduction. Obviously you were a school graduate. Based on your northeast accent, I figured that you had been to the Great Northern Wilderness. Xia Zhe is 21 years old this year, so he was born on

1974. As I knew, school graduates were not allowed to marry so early in those days. So I concluded that you married because you had to. Am I right?"

"Ah, your reasoning is correct."

"That must be a unique experience. I often think that in your generation, probably every person's experience could be made into a novel."

"Mr. Hong, I feel that you are very considerate. Anyway, you are different from ordinary people."

"So I ask you an ordinary question: do you think marriage life is happy?"

"Have you married, Mr. Hong?"

"I'm not married."

"Then, you have more freedom. As to happiness of marriage, honestly speaking, we did not think much, because we did not understand much, when we married. But we have been getting along very well in marriage all these years. Let me say, love is a short-lived feeling which could not last, but marriage continues for the entire life largely on inertia. People have to stay together in the absence of feelings. If they get along, that is called happiness. You will understand this after you get married."

Hong Jun noticed Xia's tone was unusual, so he changed the topic, saying, "You were a school graduate who worked in the countryside, but you founded such a large company. What a great achievement!"

"I persevere in difficulties. I know I'm not smarter than others, so I have to worker harder than them if I want to be successful. Since I returned to Beijing from Heilongjiang, I worked as a carpenter for a few years, then I did some business, and finally founded this company in 1992."

"If you are so wealthy, Xia Zhe's case should be easy to solve. If only you can repay the money for him, the charge of fraud will be rendered invalid."

"I want to help, but I really don't have that much money. I'm facing a bigger trouble."

"What trouble?"

"It has nothing to do with Xia Zhe. But if you can help me solve this, I can reward you generously." Looking at Hong's reactions, Xia continued, "Last year I got to know a foreign businesswoman with the name Sullivan. She was a Chinese American and very wealthy. Her position was the chairman of the board of a large company. And we met in a trade fair. She wanted to build a factory in China, and I hoped to create a joint venture to produce interior decoration materials. We discussed several times cordially. She even did a survey on the operation status and financial status of our company and was very satisfied. While preparing the joint venture, she even brought a deal to us – the purchase of a large quantity of wood. I figured that she was using the deal to test our capabilities. I have never traded wood, but my profession is interior decoration, so I have some acquaintances in this area and some connections in Heilongjiang Forestry Bureau. Of course, I had a stake in it. If the deal worked well, I would be able to earn at least one million yuan."

"That was a great deal."

"So we signed the contract. These months I dedicated all my energy in this business and used all my working capital. I have to make the down payment, after all. Last month, we shipped the goods to Tianjin Port, and all of the goods were manufactured in conformity with Ms. Sullivan. But the inspector she designated said the water content was non-conforming and refused to accept the goods. Another incident caused by negligence. What the hell is going on..." Xia stopped, looking at Hong, and said, "Hey, I have always been careful and have closely monitored the types and dimensions of wood, but I did not expect problem occurred in water content. If they don't tolerate this, how can I dispose of so much wood?"

"What is their attitude, then?"

"The inspector said he did not have the power to make the decision and had to ask for the chairman's instruction. Now, Ms. Sullivan will arrive in Beijing the day after tomorrow and I'm thinking about how to persuade her. Mr. Hong, you are an expert with knowledge in both Chinese and American laws, and you can speak English, so I would request your help by reviewing our contract and advising us on how to negotiate with them. You know, Ms. Sullivan does not understand Mandarin. She either speaks English or

Cantonese, but I can understand neither. We communicate through her interpreter, which is inconvenient. You have an overseas PhD degree, so you might as well join the negotiation and interpret for me. If the problem is solved, I can pay you another 100,000."

"I only handle criminal cases. You'd better ask someone else to take care of contract disputes like this."

"I understand. I engaged a lawyer before, but he was not professional and was accustomed to fooling clients."

"Let me just focus on Xia Zhe's case." Hong Jun stood up and took leave.

Xia accompanied Hong Jun to the doorway, but kept saying, "Actually for me, this business is more important than Xia Zhe's case. Though the report on newspaper, I know you are a competent lawyer who voluntarily assume responsibilities for the client. You are unlike other lawyers I met, who are only interested in money. I know you only handle criminal cases, that's why I put Xia Zhe's case before you. In fact I have been hoping you can help in my wood business as well."

Hong Jun stopped his pace, saying "So you made a false presentation."

"It's not like that. Xia Zhe's case should be solved, too, but this wood business is critical for our company's survival. If the deal works out, we can make some money and build a joint venture, but if we fail, the hope of forming a joint venture will be smashed and, worse still, our company will probably go bankrupt. You see," Xia pointed to a big photo on the wall, "this is our group photo with the foreign business after the first negotiation."

"Ms. Sullivan is the woman in the middle, right?"

"Yes."

Hong Jun walked towards the photo and checked out the middle-aged woman with photo-grey glasses. He had a feeling that he saw her before, but could not remember the details.

At this moment, the door was opened and a woman came in. She was tall and plump, with perfect facial features, but appeared to be a little rustic overall. She was wearing makeup and eyebrow decorations, which made her attractive despite her age.

Xia saw her, frowned and asked, "Why do you come?"

"I want to meet the lawyer Mr. Hong." She said.

Xia turned around, resignedly, said, "Mr. Hong, this is my wife – Bai Mei."

Hong stepped forward and shook hands with Bai Mei.

Bai Mei said eagerly, "Mr. Hong, I beg you to save Zhe. He is a good boy." Suddenly she got on her knees before Hong Jun.

Hong Jun was shocked and tried to support her with his hands.

Xia Dahu pulled up Bai Mei and said, "What are you doing? Mr. Hong is going to help to his best ability."

"No," with eyes filled with tears, she said, "I don't trust your words. You are only interested in money and care nothing about Zhe."

"Who said I don't care about him?" Xia wasn't speaking loud, but his voice was stern.

"How? Did you ask him when he didn't go home? Did you visit him when he was in jail? If I hadn't urged you all day, would you have sent for a lawyer for him?"

"These days I have been entangled in trouble caused by negligence, you know."

"I know, but our son's incident is the most important."

"Zhe was so capricious because he was spoiled by you. In the beginning, I objected to his involvement in stock market because it was too risky, but you allowed him to trade. You said we can rest assured with Lu's help. But since the incident took place, is Lu offering any help? I will settle the account with him later."

"It's useless to say this. The urgent matter at hand is how to get Zhe out."

"Yes, and this is why I'm discussing with Mr. Hong."

"I know you are not giving attention to your son, so I have to talk to Mr. Hong in person."

Hong was listening to their argument, and now he said, "I learned of the details of this case. It is complex and requires further investigation. I need handwriting samples of Xia Zhe, anything he wrote, preferably recent ones with his name. He said there are some at home. Can you find them?"

"Yes, I will look for them at home and send them to you." Bai Mei was pacified a little and sighed, "I know it is not an easy case, but Zhe was miserable. He was detained for 1 month already. That is too much for him. Mr. Hong, I heard that if he is convicted of fraud, the amount of money involved will warrant a life imprisonment. Is it true?"

"It is likely. Fraud cases are generally tried at basic courts, but this case will be tried at the intermediate court. According to law, only those cases with probable lifelong imprisonment or a heavier sentence would be in the charge of intermediate courts."

"If he is sentenced to life imprisonment, he life will be ruined. I'm afraid this is karmic reaction...No. It is not his fault. Mr. Hong, please do save him."

"I will try my best."

"But I'm still afraid, " Bai Mei murmured, "I'm afraid he could not take this."

"You may rest assured," Hong Jun said, "I met Xia Zhe. He was in a steady mood and somewhat optimistic. This experience may probably work in his favor for his life in future."

"Yes, having a rough time is just natural. We've been through this in our younger days," said Xia.

"He is different." Bai Mei was talking with Xia, but her eyes were set on Hong Jun. Suddenly, as if recalling something, she asked eagerly, "Mr. Hong, I heard that people in jail could be bailed out, can you bail out Zhe? I'd like him to stay at home. I will watch him and keep him at home."

"That was called 'recognizance on bail'." Hong Jun said. "According to clause 38 and 40 of the *Criminal Procedure Law*, those who qualify for this treatment are generally individuals who may get a light punishment, or those who may get a heavy punishment but all criminal facts have been ascertained and who will not escape from investigation and trial and are not dangerous to society. Xia Zhe probably does not qualify for recognizance on bail, unless he is seriously ill…"

"He can get out if he is sick? Yes, he is sick." Bai Mei suddenly stood up and ran to the doorway. Then she stopped at the doorway, turned around and said "Thank you" to Hong Jun.

Xia Dahu watched Bai Mei as she left, and shook his head, saying, "Since Xia Zhe was caught by the police, she went abnormal. Now I'm worrying about her more than my son. It's so unfortunate for our family to encounter this."

Hong Jun also looked at Bai Mei as she left, and smoothed back his hair with fingers of right hand – his habitual movement in reflection.

"Mr. Hong! Mr. Hong!" Hong Jun was immersed in his thought until Xia called him twice. He waved his hand and said with emotion, "One only understand the loving kindness of the parents when he raises a child of his own. Mr. Xia, I have to go, too."

Xia accompanied Hong Jun to the door, and said, "As to my suggestion, you can give it a second thought."

Hong Jun drove back to the law firm in Friendship Hotel and closed himself in the office, reflecting on the case. He knew that the best way to vindicate Xia Zhe was to prove someone had framed him. He indistinctly felt someone had set a trap for Xia Zhe, but he was not entirely sure. He could not remain focused on this issue, because the woman on the picture kept coming to his mind, especially the smile with contempt, he felt he saw it before. He sat on the chair, with eyes closed, and fingers smoothing his hair.

Suddenly, he opened his eyes, picked up the phone and rang Xia Dahu's office, "Mr. Xia, I agreed to join your negotiation with Ms. Sullivan, but as a lawyer, not as an interpreter."

Chapter 4 – The Investigation

Hong Jun thought it was necessary to learn about relevant facts in Hongyuan Securities. But given that Hongyuan Securities was the victim in this case, his research would definitely not be easy. He analyzed several target individuals and possible obstacles based on the available case materials so as to choose the optimal investigation path. Liang Gao and Hu Tucheng were suspects, and therefore not fit for investigation. The clerk Fang Qiong was a critical witness, but it would be better to obtain the company leaders' approval before inquiring of her. Lu was the company manager and an associate of Xia Zhe, so he decided to interview Lu first. He called to make an appointment, and Lu readily agreed the meeting.

In the afternoon, Hong Jun came to Hongyuan Securities at the appointed time. Again, he saw the blue Santana with license plate number "37285" at the doorway. He came to the car and saw the plate was still covered by the piece of mud. He wiped it with his foot and what he saw was the exposed part which lost its coating. He lifted his head, made sure no one was watching him, and then went into the public telephone booth and dialed the number of the law firm.

"Hello, this is Hong Jun Law Firm..."

"Song Jia, I'm Hong Jun." Hong Jun interrupted.

"Oh, Mr. Hong. Where are you calling?"

"I'm using a public telephone."

"Mr. Hong, I think you'd better buy a cellphone, the big one."

"I have a plan about this, too."

"Then let me take care of this. So why are you calling?"

"Do you remember the license plate thing?"

"Of course I remember. You are my teacher. How can I forget your instructions?"

"I saw a Santana car in front of the door of Hongyuan Securities which is very similar to the one mentioned in the newspaper. Call the traffic police and let them have a look."

"Is that in connection with our case?"

"It is a citizen's obligation."

"You are a noble person."

"Don't waste time. Please make a call."

"OK."

Hong Jun went out of the telephone booth. He did not enter the hall of the business office. Instead, he came to the guard room through the side door. He explained his purpose to the staff member there, who then made a call and said to him with a flattering smile, "Mr. Hong, our manager Lu has something to do at this moment. He asks you to wait for a while in the guestroom."

"Which floor is the guestroom on?" Hong Jun started walking inside.

"Please wait for a while. Someone is coming for you. Oh, he's coming."

Hong Jun looked back and saw a young man running downstairs. The man was wearing a black suit and a pair of sunglasses. On meeting Hong, he said only one word "Please", then turned around and let the way. On the 3rd floor, they entered an iron gate, and a young girl with a black skirt, who looked like a secretary, welcomed Hong Jun. She also said only one word "Please", then continued to lead Hong inward. And the young man with sunglasses went into the room beside the iron gate.

Doors on both sides of the corridor were closed, and quietness filled the atmosphere. The female secretary was wearing a pair of soft-soled leather shoes, which nearly do not produce a sound when touching the floor. Hong Jun was led into a reception room. The secretary asked him to wait a moment and offered to serve a cup of tea. Hong Jun waved his hand to thank her. The secretary stood at the doorway, looked outside, then turned in and said, "Our deputy manager Liang is coming."

A man with blue suit went inside and had a strong handshake with Hong Jun. He said, "My name is Liang Gao. Please sit down."

Hong Jun handed in his business card and started scrutinizing Liang, the man Xia Zhe suspected. He was in his 30s, lean and tall, with a square face, dense eyebrows, big eyes and a high nose. Indeed, he had a big mouth, which is often open, showing his neat, white teeth. From appearance, this is a shrewd and capable man. Hong Jun also discovered that he was the one who drove "37285".

Liang waved his hand towards the female secretary, who then went out and closed the door.

Liang looked at Hong Jun's business card, frowned and asked, "Mr. Hong, what are you meeting Mr. Lu for?"

"I'm Xia Zhe's defense lawyer. I want to ask for information from Lu."

"Oh, you come for Xia Zhe's case. Actually Lu does not know much about it, because he was not in Beijing then."

"So you know what happened?"

"I don't know, either. The staff members carried out the operation. Let me tell you, you should seek help from the police. They investigated, so they know the case."

"Do you know Xia Zhe?"

"I know him, but I'm not familiar with him. However, I heard that he was presumptuous and unreliable in his dealings. I advise you not to get involved in his case."

"Why?"

"He is young but tricky. Let me tell you, you are wasting your time by becoming his lawyer. It may be even worse, because you may put yourself into trouble."

"Is it really so serious?"

"I give you advice with the best intentions, but it depends on you to accept it or not. By the way, Mr. Hong, I have something else to do. So I have to take your leave." Liang stood up, hurried outside and closed the door.

Now Hong Jun was alone in the room, feeling a little distressed, but he could do nothing about it. Hongyuan Securities did not cooperate. He expected it so he was also prepared for it in his heart. He went to the window and looked at the blue Santana parked in the parking lot, thinking: "If the car caused the accident, then Liang, the deputy manager, must be the escaped driver. But how to prove that? Liang definitely would not confess. Since he hit and run, he would certainly deny the fact. If the missing piece of coating passed to the wounded bicycle rider, it will be fine, at least the truth could be proved by examining the separating edges of the piece of coating. Can the traffic police come up with this idea? Maybe the traffic policeman in charge of this case is not so responsible, or..."

Hong Jun was running wild in his mind when the doorbell rang. Hong Jun looked back and saw Liang standing at the door.

"Oh, Mr. Hong, you are still here. Lu is very busy. If you have other businesses at hand, you can do them first, then return to us later."

"I can wait."

"You are so patient. Let me tell you. Lawyers like yourself ask for trouble. I know a lawyer who always induces people to divorce. Is he wicked?"

"Speaking of wicked people, there are too many of them. Recently a man hit a bicycle rider with his car on the side road in north Taipingzhuang. He did not even get off and have a look. He just drove away in his car. That is wicked. But he was thinking he would get away from this by escaping. But there is a saying, the eyes of the masses are the wisest." Hong Jun could be harsh when he was in a bad mood, and it was implied harshness.

"What do you mean?" Liang looked at Hong Jun, stupefied.

"You don't know?" Hong laughed and looked at Liang. He thought he was smart than common people, so sometimes he could not help but wanted to show it off.

"Then...I'll take a look again. Let me check whether Lu has finished his business." Liang went out and closed the door again.

After about 10 minutes, the door opened again. The female secretary stood at the door, smiled and said, "Mr. Hong, Lu asks you to come to his office."

Lu Boping's office was very spacious. The door was directly opposite the desk, on which there was an exquisite electronic calendar and three telephones. Behind the chair was the glass window covered by a dark orange velvet curtain extending to the ground. To the left was a leather couch, and there was a pot of orchids on the wide glass tea table. A tile mural about the myth of Goddess Mending the Sky was painted on the right wall. In the wall corner between the mural and the desk was a 1m-high root carving. It was a remarkably lifelike eagle spreading its wings, which was truly astonishing for all.

Lu saw Hong Jun and stood up to warmly welcomed him. After exchange of greetings, they sat on the couch, diagonally opposite each other.

Lu was of medium height and was a little fat. His black hair was neatly combed. Wearing a pair of turtle glasses, he maintained a scholarly demeanor. His left leg was a little lame while walking, but it was only noticed by careful observers. A metal crutch was placed beside the desk.

The female secretary placed drinks on the tea table and went out. Lu smiled and looked at Hong Jun, as if waiting for the inquiries of an unwelcome journalist.

Hong Jun was observing Lu. He noticed that Lu's hands were in a slight, unnatural quiver despite his calm countenance. To ease the atmosphere, Hong decided not to mention the subject at first, so he cast his glance at the metal crutch, asking, "Mr. Lu, your crutch is special. Did you make it by yourself?"

"No, it was the gift from an old comrade in arms." Obviously, Lu was very willing to introduce the history of this crutch to people. He brought the crutch to Hong Jun and spoke with fervor, "That was on the battleground of Sino-Vietnamese War. At that time, I was the instructor of the reconnaissance company. Our commander was previously a factory worker, so he was not good at talking, but he was intelligent and skillful. This crutch was made by himself. Actually he was a bit strange, because we might lose our lives at any moment, but he had the mood to make the crutch. Later, we encountered the enemy when we were on duty. The battle was hard, and most people in our company died, including our commander. He presented this crutch to me before passing away. And the injury on my leg was a result of the battle. But I was still fortunate compared to my comrades. Later, I always kept this crutch by my side, because it always reminded me of the life in the war and those deceased comrades."

Hong Jun was appreciating the metal crutch with great interest. It consisted of 3 parts: the middle was a 40cm steel tube with turnbuckles at both ends; the upper was a short steel tube, and a spigot-shaped tree root was inserted in it as the handle; the lower was also a short steel tube in which a ball-shaped rubber plug was inserted to reduce the noise of crutch hitting the ground. Since the steel tubes were plated with chromium, they look beautiful.

Hong Jun was deeply touched by Lu's words. Although he did not like war, he always respected and resonated with the soldiers who sacrificed their lives for the country and the people. He looked at Lu's leg and imagined the scene in the woods where they were battling. His vision returned to Lu's face, but he could not see any trace of warfare on his clean and white face. So he said, "I heard that Xia Dahu was a schoolmate of yours, but you seem to be much younger than him."

"Dahu is indeed two years younger than me, but he has been taken by the allure of money. He thinks about making money throughout, so he is living a life of hard work. As a result, he gets old easily. Besides, he is conservative and dare not find new ways, so he appears older. I think if one wants to retain his youth in appearance, he needs to remain young in the mind and keep a young heart."

"How to understand that?" Hong Jun was interested.

"One should be brave enough to pursue his goals and find new ways. If one remains satisfied in his comfort zone with a stagnant mind, then his heart is already old, and his body will turn old very soon. Do you believe it? This is the principle of life. I remember there was a song, saying 'A revolutionist is young forever.' How to be young? One needs to have a revolutionary heart. A revolutionary heart means one's dissatisfaction with the present, the pursuit of new goals and the courage to think big and transform vision into reality. Mr. Hong, you have an overseas PhD degree. In knowledge, I'm nothing compared to you. Our generation was 'the corner forgotten by education'. But experience and understanding of life is not something to be learned on books. I'm practical, realistic and not inclined to pretend to be modest. So please don't mind."

"Of course I don't mind. I benefit more from conversation with you than from 10 years' reading. What new things are you pursuing?"

"A lot of things. For example, the stock market might be counted as one. I first learned about the stocks in 1987 and I was in Shenzhen then. I might be one of the first Chinese people who set foot in the stock market. Beijing people like saying 'playing with stocks', and it is similar to playing with stamps or mahjong. But there is great knowledge in stocks. Let me tell you, if you don't understand politics, you'd better stay out of stock trading. Some people think they can become stock market experts after learning some economics and finance, but that is entirely their fantasy."

"Why do you pull Xia Zhe into the stock market?"

"Xia Zhe? As a matter of fact, I initially didn't agree with his involvement in stock trading, but he was fascinated by it. And the Xias wanted my help. You know, Xia Dahu and I were childhood friends. How could I disagree? Actually I gave Xia Zhe a lot of guidance in the past 2 years. I told him that Chinese stock market was not mature yet and it was risky, so he could not covet big earnings. I did not expect that he made such a big transaction while I was on the trip. That was totally foolish. These days I have been regretting. I wish had not allowed him to set foot in the stock market."

"Xia Zhe said there was an error in operation."

"I checked it out immediately after I returned to Beijing. I also hoped it was a technical error. But the clerk's words were genuine and had positive evidence. There were computer records and Xia Zhe's signature on the authorization sheet. So I was not able to help."

"You know Xia Zhe for years. Do you think he would commit fraud?"

"Correct, I have been watching him grow up. But as I work for the company, I work for the country as well. So I have to follow the standard procedure. The determination of whether it is a fraud or not remains a legal issue. You are a lawyer, and I can't make such determination, which is in your field. But as I know, our country's legal system in this aspect is not fully developed yet. I asked others and they all said they were not sure. Certainly, if Xia Zhe could repay the money, the issue would not be so serious. Xia Dahu is capable of providing this, after all..."

The telephone rang. Lu said "Sorry" and picked up the phone in front of the office desk. Hun Jun could not hear what the other side was speaking in the phone, but he saw from Lu's glances that Lu was unnatural. Lu said in the phone, "I have a guest here, you can make arrangement accordingly and let her come here later."

The call ended, and Lu told Hong Jun, "It's tiring to be a leader. You have to handle all issues, big and small."

"Since you are so busy with your work, I'll take leave now. But I may have to bother your employees with this case in future." Hong Jun stood up and left.

"You're welcome. I'll talk to them and let them cooperate with your investigation. To speak from my heart, I also wish you can vindicate Xia Zhe." Lu Boping sent Hong Jun to the staircase of the corridor and then went back.

Hong Jun went a few steps downstairs and then slowly returned. He saw a tall woman with sunglasses coming in a hurry from the other end of the corridor to Lu's office. He felt the figure looked like Bai Mei and was a little confused.

At this moment, Liang was walking up from downstairs, asking, "Mr. Hong, what are you looking for?"

"I can't find my car key. I don't know if it was left in..."

"What are you holding in your hand?"

"Oops." Hong Jun tapped on his head and smiled with embarrassment, "I'm always doing this kind of thing. I ride on the donkey to find the donkey. It's funny."

"As long as you don't ride on another person's donkey, it will be fine. Well, don't look down upon the donkey because it may be capricious and kick you. It is not funny." said Liang, suggesting something by his words.

"You may rest assured that I don't have other fault except forgetfulness, and I have sharp eyes."

Right after saying this, Hong Jun heard someone downstairs calling "Mr. Liang", then there came the sound of rapid footsteps. The person in the guard room panted up the stairs and said to Liang Gao, "Mr. Liang, two officers came and asked whose Santana was there at the doorway. It sounded like something happened."

Upon hearing this, Liang's look became pale. He said, "Please tell them that I'm not here." Right after saying this, he glanced at Hong Jun and found it was inappropriate, then said again, "Well, let me have a look." While walking downstairs, he said to Hong Jun, "I don't like dealing with policemen. If they visit someone, there won't be good news."

Liang came to the building entrance and saw there were two policemen standing in the guard room. He went inside and said with flattering smiles, "Hello, officers, I'm Liang Gao. You are visiting me for something?"

"Does the Santana car outside belong to you?" An officer said, gravely.

"It is the company car, but I use it most of the times. My work needs it. Here is my business card. Officers, please come to my office to talk."

Hong Jun thought it was inappropriate to watch the proceedings, so he opened the door and went out. But he did not go to his car. Instead, he made a turn and walked into the business office next to him.

Today, he noticed a completely different atmosphere in the hall on the 1st floor from the one he felt last time. People crowded the front side of the counter, hurrying up to hand in the authorization sheet. People behind were shouting or swearing. And those who squeezed out from the counter were sweating all over.

Hong Jun walked upstairs to the 2nd floor and came into the VIP room. It was apparently quiet, but people's eyes focused on the computer screen revealed their anxiety and worries. With the direction of others, he found the mystery woman – the clerk Fang Qiong. Fang Qiong was operating a computer, and a young man with large belly was standing behind her, holding a tin of beer. Hong Jun stood beside and observed this "subject of investigation".

Fang Qiong was not tall, but had a well-proportioned figure. Different parts of her body, whether they were long, short, big or slim, they were all consistent with the ideal shapes. Her five sense organs, if analyzed separately, were not extraordinary, but when combined together on her tiny oval face, they look very pretty. Her skin was not quite white, but so smooth and exquisite that it felt good no matter it was covered with light or heavy makeups. Her hair was short, exposing half of her tiny ears. Every time she raised her head, she would toss her hair backwards, putting a fascinating aroma into the air.

Fang Qiong's slender fingers stopped tapping at the keyboard, and her light purple fingernails were glowing. She waited a moment and asked softly, "How do you think? Have you made the decision?"

"Bang!" The man behind her with large belly crushed the beer tin with his hand, and the beer was splashed on his necktie and shirt. He uttered the "F" word.

"Mr. Hu, it seems your vulgar language does not fit the environment here." Fang Qiong looked back at him, and spoke with a calm tone.

"Oh, sorry I forgot. Tonight I'll invite you to dinner at Pearl Seafood as my apology, OK?"

"That is not necessary." Fang Qiong's fingers started tapping at the keyboard again.

"Maybe I can invite you to karaoke tonight. I practiced singing the song *Xiao Fang* again. Surely I can sing it well."

"Sorry, I can't stand your singing voice. Besides, I have a date tonight."

"With Liang again? Let me tell you, he has a wife."

"I think you are interfering a lot."

"OK, I won't interfere. I'm just worried you are counting money for him when he is selling you."

"Oh, why are you speaking so unpleasantly?" Fang Qiong turned around and stared at Hu for a moment.

Hu immediately gave a very low bow to Fang Qiong.

Hong Jun finally found the chance to talk with Fang Qiong after closing of the stock market. He handed his business card and said politely, "Miss Fang, can you spare me a few minutes?"

Fang Qiong scrutinized this handsome man and looked at the business card at hand, then an enticing smile appeared on her dull face, "Hello lawyer, an overseas PhD, why do you want my time?"

"Miss Fang, I'm Xia Zhe's defense lawyer. I have a few questions to ask you."

Fang Qiong's smile immediately disappeared, and she said, "As to Xia Zhe's case, I have explained it to the police, you can ask them?"

"Miss Fang..."

"Sorry, I don't have time." Fang Qiong interrupted, turned around and walked away at the pace of a dancer.

Hong Jun looked at her while she walked away, and felt that this woman was indeed a mystery. He tried to sort things out but failed, and then he turned around and walked to the staircase. Just before going downstairs, he heard someone calling him from behind. Turning back, it was Hu.

"Hi, you are the lawyer? As to the case you are asking about, one person knows it from beginning to end."

Hong Jun turned around, "Yes? Can you advise me?"

Hu walked to him and lowered his voice, "You can ask for Liang Gao, the deputy manager. He manages everything in the VIP room. It's quite easy to identify him. He is the tallest one with the biggest mouth, but don't tell him I asked you to do this."

"He knows this case?"

"He knows the details, absolutely. Well, this is the insider's message, which is valuable for you."

"Thank you." Hong Jun went downstairs.

Upon exiting the business office, Hong Jun saw Liang was seeing off the police officers. He noticed that the policemen's attitudes changed a lot. They were not speaking in an official tone anymore; rather, they were laughing and talking happily like old friends. Hong Jun felt a little perturbed.

After seeing off the policemen, Liang turned around and saw Hong Jun. He was surprised for a moment, then smiled cunningly, "Oh, Mr. Hong, you have not left yet. You want to play with stocks?"

Hong Jun shook his head, "I dare not. There is extensive knowledge in stock trading."

"Nothing actually. I can tell you, the stock market is like jugglery. Outsiders see the trend, but insiders use the knack. Nothing is confidential. There is one paper layer, and once you pierce through it, you understand everything. You may have a try. Given your high IQ, probably you'll become an expert in half a month."

"If this is the case, all stock investors would become experts."

"Mr. Hong, I'm not kidding. If you are interested, just call. I can open an VIP account for you with preferential prices. I can tell you, trading stocks earns more than working as a lawyer. You can become a millionaire overnight."

"If this is the case, you would have become a millionaire already."

"I'm working here and not allowed to trade stocks, otherwise I have made a fortune."

"Then you can resign and become an investor."

"No way. I have poor techniques. I might suffer."

They talked and came to the parking lot. At this moment, Fang Qiong was going out of the company. Liang saw her and said "Bye Bye" to Hong Jun, then he went to Fang Qiong.

Fang Qiong glanced at Hong Jun for a moment, then smiled at Liang and rapidly walked to Hong Jun's Santana and put her hand on the door.

Liang said, "Fang, my car is here. Don't get on the wrong car."

Hong Jun opened the car door with his key and looked at Fang Qiong.

Fang Qiong said with embarrassment, "Oops, your cars are the same. I was mistaken. Sorry, Mr. Hong." She walked to Liang's car, opened the door and got inside.

And Hong Jun got into his car, started the engine and joined the traffic flow of after-work hours.

Chapter 5 – The Bail

In order to obtain a counterfeit hospital diagnosis certificate, Bai Mei sought help from a few friends, but none of them knew anyone in the hospital. She impatiently lamented that although she had many friends, none of them was of use to her at this moment. Suddenly, she thought of Lu's ex-wife Zhang Xiaolan, who was a doctor.

Bai Mei did not know which hospital Zhang was working in. So she went to Lu's office and was informed that Zhang was working in the internal medicine department of the Peace Hospital and that Lu's daughter, Lu Ting was also working in the hospital as a nurse. She was excited because she liked Lu Ting and Lu Ting was close to her since childhood. So she decided to visit Lu Ting first.

Bai Mei came to the Peace Hospital and saw Lu Ting in the inpatient department. Having not seen her for years, Lu Ting already grown into a beautiful woman. Slender eyebrows, big eyes, an elegant nose and an exquisite mouth ideally decorated her pinky white face. Her speech carried innocence and her smile exuded shyness. Actually, she was lively and optimistic, a lovely "sunshine girl". Lu Ting was very affectionate towards Bai Mei, calling her "Aunt Bai". Lu Ting was sad and even shed tears when she heard that Xia Zhe was framed and put into prison. She said she would certainly help, so she brought Bai Mei to her mother Zhang Xiaolan.

Zhang was a thin and weak woman from the southeast. Her face was skinny and colorless. Her eyes were devoid of liveliness, and surrounded by wrinkles. Her short hair was made loose by perming, but still appeared to be sparse. The white garment, which was regular in size, appeared too big on her fleshless body.

Zhang Xiaolan was born in a military family. She met Lu Boping in the army. At that time, her father was the political commissar of a division in the army in which Lu was serving, and she was the health worker in a regiment's medical team. A lot of young military officers were pursuing her then, but she eventually put herself in the arms of Lu. Later they got married and had a daughter, and they were transferred to civilian work in Beijing. She was a strong woman who played the role of a mother and wife at home and was highly praised in her work. To support her husband's career, she voluntarily did all the housework, including escorting the child on the way from home to the kindergarten and primary school, and vice versa. She had been doing basic healthcare work since her return to Beijing. Only after her daughter went to high school did she start her own diploma education with her spare time, until she eventually obtained an undergraduate degree and was transferred to this district hospital to work as a doctor. She had been satisfied with her life, until one day she found her husband had an affair. She panicked and suffered, but she could not accept her husband's repentance, nor could she forgive her husband's mistakes. She even felt that any criticism of her husband was unnecessary, because she was a strong woman. So she divorced her husband peacefully.

There was no patient in the clinic. Zhang was happy when she saw Bai Mei. They had not seen each other for years, and naturally they initiated discussion on a few women's topics.

Bai Mei said, "Xiaolan, you appear old. What cosmetics are you using now?"

"I don't care much about this, though."

"That is not good for you. Let me tell you, you should use a complete set of cosmetics, and the imported ones are the best. China-made products are not usable. And you need to use facial mask once in a week and go to the beauty parlor once in a month. Since we are at this age, if you don't care for yourself, you will become an old lady soon."

"I am an old lady already."

"Nah, you are only in the early 40s. People say, 'A woman is still a flower in her 40s'. Just make up yourself, and you'll be 10 years younger. Do you believe it?"

"I'm a doctor. I work for patients every day. I don't need to appear young, and if I do so, I will be laughed at by them."

"My mother is always afraid of being laughed at." Lu Ting said.

"Who will laugh at you? The foreign people use lipsticks when they are in their 70s and 80s. You'll feel very tired in life if you worry about these things. By the way, have you thought about looking for a partner, again?"

"Looking for what?" Zhang pretended to know nothing.

"Looking for a man. Many old people are in "twilight love". They say, 'Maple leaves are redder than flowers in February, and the age of 60 is better than 28.' In my opinion, you are still in the 'flower season'."

Zhang could not help but started laughing, "You are hilarious. Where did you learn about all these?"

"I watch teleplays. I have nothing to do after all. But what I just told you were not a laughing matter. If you have interest, I can help you with that tomorrow. Or in your words, I'll arrange it for you. OK?"

"Mama, Aunt Bai is right. You can consider it. The society changed, and remarriage is not a shame anymore."

"You see. Your girl is so nice. If I were not in this hospital, I would shout out 'Great understanding!' Remarriage does not have any disadvantage. Don't think of it as 'the second trial'. Since you have experience of first marriage, your second marriage would be sweeter. To tell you the truth, Dahu and I took a marriage photo last year. And when people saw it, they said it was a 'second marriage', but I found it beautiful."

"You see how fashionable Aunt Bai is!" Lu Ting said.

"I can't be fashionable. If I can see you have a nice job and a happy family, I would be satisfied for the rest of my life."

"Yes, mothers all think in this way." Bai Mei said. "We worry about our children for the entire life. And when the children don't need us, it is time for us to quit."

"By the way, Ting just told me that you visited me for Xia Zhe. How is he?"

"Oh, I was engaging in idle talks with you, but almost forgot the business at hand." Bai Mei recounted what happened to Xia Zhe.

Zhang said, "Zhe was smart and thoughtful and he was never off the track. How come that happened to him?"

Lu Ting said, "There must someone framing him."

Bai Mei agreed, "I think so."

Zhang asked, "Did you ask Ting's father for help?"

"We asked him, but he said there were policies and witnesses and he could do nothing about it."

"Then what can we do?"

"We engaged a competent lawyer, but we can't have Zhe wait in the detention center. I heard that as long as he is sick, he can be bailed out. That's why we ask you for help."

"What illness does he have?" Xiaolan asked.

"He had stomachaches before. I was informed that as long as you issue a diagnosis certificate of gastric ulcer, I can ask someone to bail him out." Bai Mei said.

"Maybe I can't, because he has never come for treatment." Zhang hesitated.

"Mama, you might as well do this to help get Zhe out. The date can be a previous one, before he was caught by the police. Even if someone looks into this, they are unable to find out." Lu Ting said.

"But we need to have the diagnosis certificate stamped over there. Will it work out if we write a previous date?" Zhang still felt it was inappropriate.

"No problem. I'll ask them to stamp the certificate." Lu Ting said.

Seeing her daughter's imploring look, Zhang picked up her pen, wrote a diagnosis certificate and handed it to Lu Ting. Bai Mei said some words of gratitude and went out of the clinic with Lu Ting. Lu Ting went to the registration office, and with the help of an acquaintance, she had the certificate stamped quickly.

Bai Mei was very happy that she got the diagnosis certificate. She came to the police station, asked a favor of some acquaintance, and handed in the diagnosis certificate. Xia Zhe's release on recognizance was soon approved and he was transferred to the Peace Hospital for treatment of gastric ulcer.

Lu Ting had been admiring Xia Zhe since childhood. Therefore, when she was at the age of awakening of romantic love, Xia Zhe became the Prince Charming in her heart. Although they have few chances to meet each other in these years, her trace of pure love remained in the heart. When she heard Xia Zhe would move into their hospital, she was so excited that she could not go to sleep. On the morning of the next day, she made herself up nicely and went to work.

At 10 o'clock in the morning, Bai Mei accompanied Xia Zhe to the admission office. Lu Ting enthusiastically ran errands and arranged bed for Xia Zhe, then she saw off Bai Mei. In the same day, she went to Xia Zhe's ward whenever she had time and always wanted to talk with him. But since there were other people in the wards, she found it inconvenient to talk. After work, she took off her white garment and came to the ward. Xia Zhe just had his meal and was lying on the bed, so she asked Xia Zhe to go for a walk outdoors.

In Xia Zhe's memory, Lu Ting was a silly little girl, but this time he found she had grown up. Since it was boring to stay in the ward, he went out with Lu Ting.

They came to the little garden next to the hospital. It was dinner time, and the garden was very quiet. They walked back and forth on a trail.

"Zhe, how come you suffer so much this time?"

"Mistakes are part of being human, just like a horse would fall sometimes. It's nothing serious. I fell, but I will stand up again."

"But I heard from Aunt Bai that you may get a life imprisonment."

"I don't believe they can give a sentence. I did not cheat. The victim deserved it. Besides, gains and losses are natural in stock trading. I lost money this time, but I can earn it back next time. Then it will be OK."

"You are taking it too easy. It is hundreds of thousands. By the way, your father has so much money, why doesn't he repay for you?"

"This is my own incident, I don't need others to cover for me. When I was locked up in the police station, I could not exert my strength. Now I'm fortunate that I came out. By the way, I have to thank you because my mother said it is by virtue of your help."

"Oh, you became so polite. You learned it in the police station?"

Xia Zhe glanced at Lu Ting, and said, "The police station does not teach this."

"What do they teach, then?"

Xia Zhe whispered at Lu Ting's ear, "They teach things not suitable for a girl to know."

Lu Ting poked Xia Zhe, and said, "Go to hell. Your mouth is dirtier than before."

"But the heart is surely good."

"Don't be loquacious. Tell me what you plan to do. Maybe I can help."

Xia Zhe's smile disappeared, and he looked at the sunset on the horizon. "I have to borrow some money to repay the debt, and then check who framed me. I can't depend on a lawyer on this matter. I have to take effort on my own."

"I heard the lawyer is competent."

"He appeared to be fine, but he has a scholarly vibe."

"Then how do you check it by yourself?"

"I'll talk with the female clerk first. She was the operator, and she must know where the dirty trick was. In fact, she was a good person, and was nice to me. I suppose it was not her who tried to harm me, there must be someone behind her. I suspect the Big-Mouth Liang. He is decent in appearance but vile in the heart. He used tricks to harm me before. And this time, I figure he played a trick on me when your father was not here. And after this incident, I asked your father a favor, but your father was too busy to help. Anyway, I can't rely on anyone in my case. I have to work things out by myself."

"What is the name of this guy?"

"Liang Gao."

"He?" Lu Ting stood still.

"You know him?"

"Of course. He was a driver who went to Shenzhen with my father. Then he stayed there until last year, presumably, when my father transferred him to work in Beijing. In those years, he visited my family far too often, like a dog. I really hated him."

"I also find him disgusting. He could not defeat me, so he set hidden traps."

"What is he competing with you for? You do not work in the company. Does he trade stocks, too?"

Xia Zhe glanced at Lu Ting and said with an unnatural tone, "Nothing, actually."

Lu Ting did not notice Xia Zhe's countenance. She frowned and pondered for a while, as if having made a decision, and said mysteriously, "Zhe, you may rest assured, let me take care of this case."

"How do you plan to do that?"

"I can't tell you for now."

Xia Zhe looked at the lovely face of Lu Ting and did not know what to say for the moment. But he was firmly convinced that he could not rely on anyone except himself. And, he believes in himself."

Chapter 6 – The Business Negotiation

At 9 o'clock in the morning, Hong Jun went into Xia Dahu's office. He was wearing a designer suit and clean shaven, and was purposely wearing a pair of sunglasses. Upon meeting him, Xia Dahu laughed, "Mr. Hong, you look like a movie star today."

"Really? When I have nothing serious to do, I will act as a movie star!"

"Then I will be a director. I heard that as long as you have money, you can shoot movies, at least act as a director. I even don't look natural while taking photos, so working as a director would be the only choice. Hahaha!"

"Mr. Xia, I will join the negotiation on two conditions: First, you may only introduce me to them as a lawyer, and nothing else. Second, you will not interfere with whatever I say."

"The second one is fine, but as to the first, I think you might as well let them know you are a PhD of Law in America."

"I rely on capabilities instead of titles. If you don't accept my conditions, I have to leave right now."

"OK, OK. I accept it." Xia found Hong Jun to be a strange lawyer, but he could do nothing about it.

Hong Jun sat on the couch and read through the wood purchase contract quickly. He found it to be standardized and flawless. He told Xia plainly, "I have never studied the *Contract Law*, nor am I familiar with wood business. I haven't identified any problem in the contract. But as a lawyer, I have a suggestion: This contract is the original. It serves as an important proof in disputes. As an entrepreneur, you should pay more attention to evidence. For example, you should make copies of the contract, and use the copies at ordinary times and keep the original securely. Once the contract gets lost or damaged, you may run into trouble."

"We do business based on relationships and credits. The contract is secondary. Besides, we sign dozens of contracts in a year. It's not so complex." Xia thought Hong Jun was changing the subject simply because he could not find any problem in the contract. So Xia dismissed the suggestion.

"Giving advice is one of my professional habits, but you have the right to accept it or dismiss it."

"Don't worry. All of my contracts are kept securely. You might as well help me consider how to negotiate."

"It concerns professional issues and I don't understand. For example, are the water content of wood, which is mentioned in the contract, and the water volume, which you said, one and the same concept?"

"We say water volume generally, but the professional term is water content."

"The 5% to 6% water content specified in the contract is really hard to achieve for you?"

"Very difficult. We are doing interior decoration in Beijing. The water content in wood required in this industry is generally about 11%. And this is the most suitable value in Beijing. But in the south, the water content is generally 15%. Of course, as specially requested, we may dry the wood until the water content reaches 8% or even 5%. But in this case, how can we dry up such large volume of wood? Even if it is all dried up, when it is transported to the port and in contact with the moisture, the water content will rise up again."

"Why didn't you put forward this problem when you entered into the contract?"

"We failed to pay attention. In China, when you conduct wood business, the types and materials of wood are of utmost importance, who care about water content, anyway? People follow the customary practice and there haven't been any problems. Had this incident not occurred, I would not have noticed this issue. I asked some of my friends in wood business, and they said they also suffered the same losses when they did wood business with foreigners. The foreign people are tough."

At 10 o'clock, the secretary came and said, "The foreign clients are coming."

Hong Jun and Xia Dahu walked out of the office and saw two women in the corridor – the one in front was older, with a pretty and lively face, and with her smile, she brought her warm greetings when she was still several steps from Xia; and the one behind was also pretty, but her facial muscles were stiff, and even her smiles appear to be rigid. If the first woman's face could be described as dynamic and warm beauty, then the second one's face was the reservoir of static and cold glamour. Both were tall and wearing big and red-rim photo-grey glasses.

Xia stepped forward, "Hello Mrs. Sullivan and Miss Chen Jingyi. Nice to meet you again. Oh, please allow me to introduce my friend – Mr. Hong, the lawyer."

Mrs. Sullivan waited until Miss Chen translated the sentence into English, and then smiled and shook hands with Hong Jun, saying, "Hello, nice to meet you."

Hong Jun patiently waited until Miss Chen translated it into Chinese, and then answered in Chinese. He spoke softly, as if he was a little self-conscious.

Xia asked Hong Jun in a low voice, "Don't you also speak English?"

Hong Jun answered, also in a low voice, "It failed me because I haven't practiced it for a long time."

"You..." Xia was trying to speak something, but Hong Jun interrupted, "Mr. Xia, shall we invite the guests to your office or..."

"Oh, let's go to the conference room directly." Xia was surprised that Mr. Hong's English was unusable. No wonder he did not want to be a translator. Maybe his PhD was faked. Times of degradation!

The conference room was not large, but delicately arranged to make it appear elegant. After the four sat down in their respective seats, Mrs. Sullivan brought a business card from her little leather bag and handed it to Hong Jun.

After receiving the card, Hong Jun apologized that his own business cards were used up.

Xia was a little unpleasant, but he did not find it appropriate to say anything. He simply asked something about the trip and then turned to the subject, "Mrs. Sullivan, according to your proposal in the facsimile, we have too subjects of discussion: one is the wood, the other is feasibility report for the joint venture. Now we discuss the wood."

"I agree with Xia. But I think the wood issue is simple. We have a contract and only need to perform the contract. Is it right, Mr. Hong?"

Hong Jun had been staring at Mrs. Sullivan's facial expression, and said hastily, "It makes sense."

Xia said, "But the wood has been transported to the port, it can't be shipped if you don't sign the papers."

"I have received the report." Sullivan said peacefully. "I know it costs a lot of money to reprocess such large volume of wood, and I sympathize with your company. But my client imposes extremely strict requirements on the water content of the wood, so I can't help much."

Hong Jun asked, "If the water content of the batch does not meet the standard, will you certainly reject it?"

"It has been made very clear on the contract." Mrs. Sullivan said firmly.

"But could you please consider our difficulty?" Xia spoke with an imploring tone.

"Since I have considered your difficulty, I have agreed to put off the delivery time, but the specifications and standards are invariable. Honest is important in business. If you couldn't do it, you should have informed me before entering into the contract. But once the contract is made, you should preform it faithfully. I don't expect my future partner to be a dishonest person."

After Miss Chen interpreted Mrs. Sullivan's words, embarrassment filled the entire atmosphere. After a while, Xia made the concession. He said, "That's fine, we'll figure out a solution."

"I hope Mr. Xia can find a solution soon, because there is a limit to the extension of delivery date. If your company fails to solve the problem within 10 days, I have to regret to consider that your company has lost the capacity to perform the contract. And your company shall be liable for all consequences."

Upon hearing Mrs. Sullivan's words, Xia got a painful look on his face.

Having observed this, Hong Jun changed the subject, "I want to hear Mrs. Sullivan's opinion on setting up a joint venture."

"Given the above situation, I think it is way too early to discuss the joint venture subject. Since we don't have sufficient trust and understanding, it is a waste of time to discuss the feasibility report of the joint venture. By the way, I have another appointment at noon."

"I totally agree with Mrs. Sullivan," Hong Jun said, "it is a waste of time to discuss the joint venture subject for now. I think Mrs. Sullivan had not the intention to discuss the joint venture subject today, is it right?"

"I don't know what Mr. Hong means." Mrs. Sullivan shifted her vision from Hong Jun to Xia.

Xia said hastily, "Mr. Hong does not imply other things..."

Hong Jun interrupted and asked, "Does Mr. Sullivan think I'm implying something else?"

"Sorry," Mrs. Sullivan stood up, looking unhappy, and said, "Mr. Xia, I don't have time to quarrel with your lawyer. If you don't have anything else to discuss, we'll take leave now."

Xia stood up hastily and said, "Please don't leave, Mrs. Sullivan, I have prepared the meal. You can take a seat for a while, and then we'll head to the restaurant and talk at the table."

"Thank you for your invitation, but I said I have an appointment. I think you also have a lot of things to do. We don't need to waste the time."

"But I have booked the table already."

"Do you need to pay for cancellation? If so, I can cover that. How much is it?"

"No, you misunderstood. I'm inviting you, so I won't let you pay."

"Thank you."

"And," Xia said, "where do you plan to go sightseeing in Beijing, Mrs. Sullivan? If you need a car and a tour guide, I can provide."

"Thank you, but I have a tight schedule, so I probably don't have time for sightseeing." Then she turned around and said to Hong Jun, "Mr. Hong. Nice to see you. Maybe I was too harsh just now. Please forgive me. I'm an irritable person."

"Please forgive me, too. I'm a new lawyer. I don't have much experience."

"You will become sophisticated. Maybe we'll have opportunities to cooperate with each other in future. Bye Bye."

After seeing off the guests, Hong Jun and Xia Dahu returned to the office. Xia complained, "Mr. Hong, I asked you to persuade Mrs. Sullivan to tolerate imperfections and accept the wood, but I did not expect you to...Alas."

"Her words make sense."

"But you can make use of some clauses favorable to us in the contract."

"There isn't any of these in the contract, so I can't help."

"But you don't need to say those irritating words. Cooperation requires a cooperative atmosphere."

Hong Jun smiled and said, "If you think you should not have asked me to join the negotiation, you don't need to pay me the fee."

"The fee is not a big issue. Actually I want you to help me with something else, too."

"What is it?"

"I know you are an expert in case investigation and have studied in America. I want you to identify the client of Mrs. Sullivan's Hongya Company. I asked them, but they said it was a business secret. According to my experience, if communication with the buyer is difficult, we'd better approach her client directly."

"What if Hongya Company does not have a client?"

"That can't be the case. They said they were purchasing for a client."

"That was on their lips only."

"You mean..." Xia fell on the couch. He was dispirited, with mouth half open, and could not say a word.

Hong Jun looked at Xia Dahu, shook his head and went out. He habitually looked for his car, but remembered that he asked Song Jia to drive it away. He was not eager to have lunch, so he strolled to the city moat.

The river was quiet, with only a few birds singing in the willow. Hong Jun stood under a willow and watched the water at his feet – the dirty water flowed gently and the reflection of the willows were torn into strange shapes by the ripples. Looking afar, some white light rose above the water surface, as if thousands of fish were sporting in the water. Breezes touched the water surface and stirred up ripples. And the tree shadows appeared to be carried far away to remote places.

Again, Hong Jun took out the business card with a trace of fragrance – Sheila Sullivan, the chairman of the board of American Hongya Co., Ltd. and the Master of Law from Northwest University.

Chapter 7 – The Equal Treaty

Lu Boping held the metal crutch – which accompanied him at all times – with both hands, and appreciated his daughter's room decorated by himself. It was two years since his divorce, and his daughter never visited him. Whenever he called, his daughter would respond with coldness. He knew that his daughter hated him, because she was firmly on her mother's side in the divorce. Sometimes he felt sorry for his ex-wife who had helped him make progress, but he had his own life philosophy, or the basis to rid himself of guilt. He believed in the law of jungle and thought that no one would sympathize with the weak, and that the strong excelled by courage and fortitude instead of unnecessary conscience. He built a successful career over these years. Although he was not a senior government official, he owned tremendous amount of capital, which equaled to power. He carefully weaved an independent 'kingdom' that did not belong to him but obeyed him, and based on the 'kingdom', he weaved a large relationship network that garnered him the society's respect and admiration.

But as he grew older, he was increasingly aware of the crisis – once he was retired or dismissed, everything he had achieved would be transferred to someone else, including the subordinates who obeyed him, the money which was under his disposal, and the luxurious lifestyle, and even the Audi auto. All of these would depart from him immediately. And what remained with him was an apartment with three bedrooms and one living room. Although such an apartment would be the ultimate pursuits for most Chinese, it could not be compared with what Lu Boping once owned.

Lu had a lot of romantic experience in his life. He didn't thought that romantic love between a man and a woman could last, nor did he believe in eternal love. Once he delivered his 'words of wisdom' in a KTV compartment after drinking alcohol – "I believe in passionate love. It takes place when people are young and impulsive, but eternal love is simply an imagination. Don't believe in the love stories in literature, because they are fabricated by mediocre authors for profit. The writer Lu Xun said plainly that love should be renewed. And this is the truth." Therefore, he often "renewed" his romantic love in his life.

He liked creating theories, because theories demonstrated his "wisdom" and "cleverness" and made him admirable. He knew some people called him "Lu Buping (uneven road)" behind his back, but he was not angry. He even used this nickname to praise himself: "I'm a crippled person, but I was not born as such. I was crippled because I was a soldier fighting for the country. As the 'uneven road', I'm different from ordinary cripples. They complain the road is uneven, but I brave the uneven road and make sacrifices for my friends."

He also had his theories regarding life. He often said that it was easier to make a living than to live. And he had a motto widespread in his circle – life is a countdown to death. He asserted that a person entered the countdown to death since he was born. And the countdown might be faster or slower overall, and faster or slower for certain periods, and maybe made zero all of a sudden. So people should enjoy lives at the moment, no matter what they were pursuing.

Sometimes he also yearned for a peaceful, warm family and an intimate father-daughter relationship. He thought only the relationship based on blood was unchangeable. So he spared a room in the apartment, and when he heard on the telephone that his daughter decided to move to this room, he felt the excitement he rarely experienced before. He knew his daughter must want something from him in doing this, but he was willing to give.

Lu satisfactorily exited his daughter's room and came to the gym next to it. He believed the human body was the foundation for all activities, so he did regular exercise. Although he had scholarly looks, he was strong and healthy. His left leg was mildly injured in Sino-Vietnamese War and the injury brought him a Second-Class Military Medal. But his legs and feet were still so flexible. He danced very well, and especially liked Jitterbug. He said only those with injured legs were able to perform this type of standard sailor dance. However, sometimes he purposely made others notice his crippled leg, and his crutch was always reminding others: "I sacrificed for you in the war. You must know this."

Lu exercised until he sweated all over. He took a hot water shower, then sat on the leather couch in the living room and started watching TV.

The doorbell rang and he rose up quickly to open the door.

Lu Ting stood outside of the security door and said in a sweet voice, "Daddy!"

"Come in, Ting. I has been waiting for you for a while."

"Daddy, your place is heavily guarded."

"This security door is not secure actually. But when I saw people install it, I installed it as well. By the way, I have given you a key, right on your bedside table. Ting, please take a look at your room. Is it good?"

Lu Ting took a look with her father, and said, "Daddy, the decoration in your place is premium. I think it is at five-star level."

"Ting, this is your home, too. I have been waiting for you to live here after decoration. I have booked meals at the restaurant, and they will deliver them here. Today is your homecoming day. We should celebrate."

"Daddy, hold on a minute. I have a condition for my living here."

"What condition? I will satisfy your wish as far as I can."

"It's simple. You should allow me to bring my boyfriend here, and in exchange, I don't interfere with your private life. No matter which woman you bring home, I promise to get along with her. This is our 'equal treaty', is it OK?"

Upon hearing his daughter's words, Lu was surprised and embarrassed. He wanted to say something, but looking at his daughter's resolute expression, he took back the unspoken words, because he knew his daughter's temper. "Ting, you have a boyfriend now?"

"Maybe he is." Lu Ting flushed.

"What is his name? And what does he do?"

"Can you first promise?"

"I have promised."

"That doesn't count. You should say, no matter who my boyfriend is, you will allow him to come and not interfere."

"What if he is a fierce tiger?"

"That is my own business."

"Your mother does not agree with your relationship?"

"Will you say it or not?" Lu Ting walked towards the door.

Lu Boping suddenly found that his daughter was similar to him in character. In his numerous negotiations, he exerted his strong will power to make the other party agree with him. So he said resignedly, "Fine. No matter whether your boyfriend is a fierce tiger or not, he can come, and I won't interfere. Is it alright?"

"Thank you, daddy."

The doorbell rang. A restaurant waitress carrying two food boxes came inside the living room and put the dishes neatly on the dining table. Right after the waitress left, Lu Ting hurriedly came to the table and said, "What a hearty dinner. I'm hungry."

"Ting, wash your hands first." Lu was in a good mood. He brought chopsticks from the kitchen and then brought two wine glasses, and said to her daughter who just came out of the bathroom, "Ting, do you drink a little wine?"

"Daddy, do you have imported wines? Let me have a taste, too."

"Do you like drinking imported wines?" Lu frowned.

"I haven't tasted them before, but I heard of them. I want to know how they taste."

"You are thinking big."

"I inherited that quality from you."

Lu Boping agreed with his dauther's words in his heart. He went to the wine cabinet and opened the door.

Lu Ting saw so many wines with foreign language labels in the cabinet and exclaimed, "Wow, so many. You bought them?"

"My friends presented them to me as gifts. Which one do you want? Pick as you wish."

Lu Ting picked the bottle whose label had a warrior on it. The warrior was a human in the upper half and a horse in the lower half and was holding a javelin.

Lu Boping laughed, "Rémy Martin – you have wonderful discrimination."

He opened the wine bottle and poured out some in each of the glasses, then sat face-to-face with Lu Ting, raised the glass and said, "Here's to Ting for her homecoming. Cheers!"

"To celebrate my father and I came to the equal treaty based on honest and understanding. Cheers!" Lu Ting contracted her brows and swallowed a large volume down, then curled her lips and said, "It was rough. Not as good as grape wine."

"Haha, you asked for it."

"Daddy, someone said life is like a glass of bitter wine. It is unpalatable but makes people drunk. Is it true?"

"Yes, it is. But life has multiple aspects for you to experience deeply. Such as this wine, you need to feel it slowly in order to develop a taste. By the way, you haven't introduced your 'fierce tiger' yet. What does he do?"

"You know him actually. Guess it."

"I know him? The doctor Feng in your hospital?"

"Nonsense. He's married already."

"Then it is the fat boy who was in your class, right?"

"Zhang Ji? He was so stupid."

"Then I'm not able to guess it."

"Let me tell you. He is Xia Zhe."

"Xia Zhe? How could you be in love with him?"

"Why? Didn't you often praise him and say he was smart, competent and would surely achieve big?"

"But now he committed a crime and was likely to be sentenced. No, no, you can't go together with him. If he is sentenced to 10 years in prison, what will you do?"

"I can wait for him. Besides, I don't believe he could commit an offense. Someone must be framing him. Daddy, he is my boyfriend, you should help him."

Lu Boping was holding the wine glass. He paused for a while and put the glass back on the table. "We can't come to a conclusion so easily. Xia Zhe changed a lot in the past 2 years. He is not the little boy you knew. I heard that he was very close to a female clerk in my company during the past 2 years. Hasn't he told you?"

"I don't care whom he was in love with, it shall be fine if he will love me in future."

"People may be different from what they appear to be, just like the imported wine, it is highly priced and looks well, but does not taste good. You are young, and you should be careful with making friends."

"Daddy, I really feel someone was framing him."

"Who do you think was framing him?"

"It probably is Liang Gao. Xia Zhe said Liang was always envious of him and made trouble for him."

"Hahaha!"

"What are you laughing at?"

"I laugh at your words. Liang is the broker, and Xia is the investor. Why should they envy each other. It's impossible."

"But, won't Liang envy Xia when Xia makes a lot of money?"

"Don't guess, but I can check it. Dear daughter, you may rest assured."

Chapter 8 – The Key Witness

The dull ceiling lamp in the center of the ballroom was rotating slowly in music. And large candles on the tables around were burning little by little in people's chitchat and laughter.

Fang Qiong was so obsessed with dancing that she would feel uncomfortable if she hadn't been to the ballroom for a few days. Tonight, she came alone to the ballroom in which she often danced. She liked the music and the atmosphere here, no matter whether it is quiet or noisy. She sat down on a couch far away from the band, lit up a cigarette, and smoked at long intervals. There were quite a few people in the ballroom at this moment. She scrutinized their dances to judge their level of proficiency as well as the relationships between partners. Most of partners here were moving in an elegant manner. Evidently they were paying attention to the dancing steps and the music. But some partners were way too intimate, as if their attention was on each other's bodies. She heard that dancing partners might become a married couple, but a married couple could not make dancing partners. Watching people come and go in pairs, she was a bit disappointed and sad, because she could not help but think of him.

She wished he were sitting beside her. She liked the feeling of placing herself in his arms, and dancing with him intimately was even more fascinating. He had a great feel of music and light steps; moreover, he always seized every chance to touch her sensitive body parts with his magical hands, enabling her to experience the burning desire. Sometimes she would feel embarrassed, but fortunately, light in the ballroom was dim. He said he was pleased to watch her face and the twists and turns of her body when she was turned on. And she liked the chemistry of getting wet. Every time after dance, she could hardly wait to make love with him. And every time they made love, he was able to put her into unbridled and intoxicating pleasure. He was truly a wonderful man. She considered herself as an experienced woman in love life, but she was willing to surrender herself to him. He was a man worthy of her heart and soul on all sides. She desired to marry him and expected a peaceful and warm family, but she also liked her affair with him which could only remain clandestine. The privacy made her feel romantic. She did not like her present job, but she was willing to give herself and suffer emotionally for the love.

She knew he would not come, but still expected his coming. So she from time to time glanced at the entrance of the ballroom. Suddenly, a familiar figure appeared in her vision. Her heart throbbed for a moment but returned to peace quickly. It was Xia Zhe.

Xia Zhe walked around the ballroom and found Fang Qiong. He said, "Fang, I have guessed you are here."

"Ah, Xia Zhe! How did you get here?" Fang Qiong looked around, as if alarmed, and said in a low voice, "You escaped?"

"Don't start, I came out according to the standard procedure – recognizance." Xia Zhe sat next to Fang Qiong.

"Oh, you scared me." Fang pressed her chest with her hand and said artificially. Then she asked in a caring way, "Did you suffer there? Did they beat you?"

"No. I behaved myself. I didn't irritate others."

"I was so worried about you when you were detained. I even asked a friend to inquire about you, but no news was heard." Fang Qiong took out her handkerchief and wiped her eyes, "I was afraid you might suffer in there."

"I did not suffer, but I learned a lot."

"You learned to be bad?"

"I persisted in my own ideology, so I was not affected by anyone else's." Xia Zhe laughed, but then he changed his tone and asked seriously, "Fang, I have something to ask you."

"You might as well dance with me first. Don't forget this is the ballroom." Fang Qiong was speaking with affection.

Xia Zhe stood up and they stepped into the uncrowded dancing floor. They danced gently to the Blues tune. Fang Qiong and Xia Zhe were physically close to each other at this moment. Her perfume and tender breasts aroused Xia Zhe's desire, and he had to try his best to control himself. After a tune, they went back to their seats. When Xia Zhe was about the discuss his subject, the band started playing "tin dance". And Fang Qiong said with excitement, "Rumba is my favorite. Let's dance again to this tune." In this way, they danced to 5 to 6 tunes before they took rest.

The ballroom was already packed at this moment. Fang Qiong was a little thirsty, so Xia Zhe bought two bottles of iced mineral water at the counter.

Fang Qiong said, "I haven't danced with you for a long time. I'm very happy today."

"Fang..." Xia Zhe wanted to say something, but he stopped because he noticed a woman with glasses was watching them in the dim candlelight.

The band was playing another tune. A gentleman came and invited the girl with glasses to dance, but she declined on the excuse that she was not comfortable.

Xia Zhe was a little unhappy, but he was helpless. He moved closer to Fang Qiong and lowered his voice, "Fang, I know you don't want to talk about the incident, but I have to mention it. I remember clearly that I sold on that day, but how come it became a buying transaction?"

"You had a lapse of memory."

"I remember we discussed before that. I said Shanghai Yansheng would fall, but you said it would bounce back. I even said I could bet on this. Right?"

"This is not what happened, I think. I remember you were hesitating about selling and buying. When it was the time to close, I asked you if you made a decision. Then you told me to 'buy in'. Absolutely, this is what truly happened."

"Was I dreaming?"

"Who knows?"

"Fang, I know you would not harm me, but I want to ask you, is it possible for someone else to enter into the program and modify the instruction after you inputted it?"

"All employees can use the program, but how's it possible for them to modify my instruction? I have told you that you said 'buy in', and I remember it clearly. Besides, the transaction was shown on the display. If there was any error, you would have told me already. I think it was either your misjudgment or a slip of the tongue. Don't think too much. You'd better think of a way to have your father wipe out the debt for you, then the court will not take further proceedings."

"Anyway, it's hard to explain. I have another question – We made an appointment on that evening to meet at the northern gate of the Imperial Palace. Why didn't you come?"

"Ah, I want to ask you about this, too. It was raining heavily and I waited for you for a long time on the street, but I didn't see you. I caught a cold after I was back, 39° high fever. I was ill in bed for 3 days. Then when I was back to work, I heard you were detained. How were you detained then?"

"What time did you get to the place?"

"I arrived late. I wanted to go there after having dinner in the company, but Liang Gao had something to discuss with me. And I told him you were in a hurry to meet me for something important. He asked where you were. I said you were at the northern gate of the Imperial Palace, which was very far. He said it didn't matter and he could give me a ride after finishing his business. But his vehicle broke down on the way unexpectedly. When I arrived at the northern gate, it was about 9 o'clock. What time did you wait until?"

"I was arrested by the police at half past eight."

"Right there?"

"Yes."

"Was it Liang Gao? He was not likely to play such a mean trick. It was possible that the police tapped my phone. They even suspected I was your accomplice at that time. Wasn't I treated unjustly?"

"I hope you weren't."

"What do you mean?" Fang Qiong said with an unpleasant look.

"If you didn't think it was unjust, I would never think I was wronged, too."

"Don't think too much." Fang Qiong set her eyes on those in the dancing floor, and her feet tapped the ground in the rhythm of the music.

Xia Zhe looked at Fang Qiong's profile in the candlelight, as if picking the right words to say, "Fang, it happened already, no matter what I say, it won't work. I can only blame my bad luck. I fell this time but I will surely stand up again. Do you believe in me?"

"What's the use of believing in you?" Fang Qiong said, without even looking at him.

Xia Zhe paused for a moment and sighed, "Fang, I felt it was tired to live in the world."

"Just dance." Fang Qiong looked at him. "When you sweat all over while dancing, you won't feel tired."

"But I'm not in the mood for dancing."

"You don't dance, then why did you come here?"

"I came here to look for you."

Fang Qiong turned her vision to the dancing floor again.

"Fang, how do you think of Liang?"

"He's fine. He took the position of deputy manager in his 30s, so he is competent."

"He and I...Which one do you think is better?"

Fang Qiong turned around and looked at him for a moment, then said, "You are jealous? You are competent, too."

"I know Liang is pursuing you..."

"I have a lot of pursuers. You are one of them."

"But Liang is a bad buy."

"He said you were a bad guy, too. All men are the same."

"You think I'm the same as him?"

"He dances better than you."

"So I'm not as good as him in your heart. I didn't expect this."

"You are sad?"

"The words you said to me before were..." Xia Zhe almost stammered.

"Those were words spoken in the ballroom. You can't take them seriously." Fang Qiong turned her vision to the dancing floor again, and said, "You see those men and women. They are close to each other and holding each other tightly, but how many of them want to live a life together? The ballroom is a performance stage. You are serious in a place where you should not. Therefore, you are asking for trouble."

"I'm only one of your dancing partners, and a temporary one, right?"

"You are intelligent to have realized this." Fang Qiong turned around to him. Her smile appeared more charming in the candlelight. She said softly, "Sir, do you want to dance again?"

"Fang, I really admire your talent of acting. Had you not left the movie industry, you might have become a movie star even more popular than Liu Xiaoqing."

"In fact, I also like acting, but I was not fortunate enough to meet a good director. Without a talent scout, the talent remains obscure."

"This is a great loss of China's movie industry." Xia Zhe stood up and said calmly, "I have always been perplexed that no matter how hard I try, you always think I'm not good enough. Now I finally understand why you think in this way. Fang, our performance is over. Good luck."

"Your look good at this moment. Bye Bye."

Xia Zhe came out to the street. The cool evening breeze touched his warm cheeks. He walked forward slowly along the road, feeling relieved in his heart, but also experiencing a bit of melancholy that is hard to dissipate.

Suddenly, a car slowly stopped by his right side. The driver was the young woman with glasses he saw in the ballroom. She rolled down the car window and said to him, "Please get on the car."

Xia Zhe was a little frightened and looked at the unknown woman. He asked, "What will you do to me?"

"Don't be afraid. I'm neither the police nor a robber, but I know you are Xia Zhe, and you are on bail. I have seen your key witness just now. I can help you. Get on the car, at least I can send you back to the hospital."

Xia Zhe hesitated for a moment, then he walked around to the right side of the car, opened the door and got inside. The car turned around and ran away quickly in the opposite direction.

Chapter 9 – The Site Survey

After hearing Song Jia's report of her work during the past two days, Hong Jun praised her, "Good job! You are good at this."

"You didn't know that until now? My 3-year study in the police academy was not a waste of time." Song Jia said, complacently.

"Then I'll give you a more difficult task – give me a cup of coffee."

"This is a task? This is wasting one's talent in a petty job." Song Jia placed the coffee in front of Hong Jun and changed the subject, "How was your investigation in Hongyuan Company."

"It went well, but Hongyuan Securities was very mysterious."

"Maybe it was because you've never been to a securities company."

"Nope. It was more like an underground organization or a gang than an ordinary company. It was scary."

"Don't scare me. Then what did you get from there?"

"Almost none. They spoke officially to me. Lawyer investigation is too difficult nowadays, and there are a world of obstacles. We can do nothing if people don't support us. When I have time, I will write another article to call on action. Currently, revision of the *Criminal Procedure Law* is under discussion. I think new clauses shall be added to protect lawyer investigation rights. Without legal protection, the investigation rights cannot be exercised."

"I think you'd better go back to Renmin University of China to teach students."

"I agree, but if I work as a teacher in college, I will not have the chance to know different kinds of people in society. Some people have loads of ill intentions, but they pretend to be honest men. What a laughing stock it is!"

"I think it is not funny. It is scary."

"These kinds of people are not scary, but the scary thing is that they are successful in society. I often think that if..."

The telephone rang and Hong Jun picked up the phone. A man said in a deep voice, "Are you Hong Jun?"

"Yes, I am. Who are you?"

"You really want to know? Baldy is my nickname. I was just released from the prison. You offended someone, do you know? Someone offered to pay me 20,000 yuan for one of your leg. You know what?"

Hong Jun looked at Song Jia, who also heard the words. Song Jia opened her eyes widely in surprise. Hong Jun asked calmly, "What do you mean?"

"What do I mean? You are such an idiot. Someone offered to pay me 20,000 yuan to break one of your leg. You know?"

Hong Jun raised his voice, "You are the idiot. Let me tell you, my leg is worth at least 100,000 yuan. You can tell that guy and ask him to pay 100,000 if he ever wants to make a deal."

"Hey, you are freaking awesome. I have to let you know I'm not kidding. My people can do anything and they know everything. Don't you own a blue Santana with license plate number 86147? If you want to keep your leg unharmed, you'd better send me 20,000 yuan at your earliest convenience; otherwise I'll guarantee that you lie in the ward within one week. Do you believe me?"

"You want me to pay to avoid a disaster? At least you should let me know the cause." Hong Jun said slowly.

"OK, I'll make it clear for you. You put your finger in another's pie. Do you know?"

"Whose pie is it then?"

"Shut up. Do you want to give the money or your leg?"

"He pays you 20,000 to have you work, and I pay you for nothing, so I should offer it at a discount – only 10,000.

"Hey, I don't want to bargain with you."

"If you want me to send money to you, you should tell me your name and address."

"Don't play tricks. And if you do, I can break both of your legs. Do you believe me?"

"Then how can I send the money to you?"

"You prepare it and bring it with you. I may ask my people to get it at any time."

The guy hung up. Hong Jun looked at the phone and laughed sarcastically before he put it down. Then he lifted his head and looked at Song Jia, and said, "How do you think? My leg is worth 100,000, not too much, right?"

Song Jia did not answer. She asked, "You're really not afraid?"

"I'm competent in all aspects. I prefer to be beaten to death rather than be scared to death."

"Don't brag. I'm afraid the call should be taken seriously."

"I think if it's only blackmail, it would be easy to handle. And if it's not, it must be in connection with our case, and the latter one is more likely."

"What should we do?"

"As Chairman Mao said, we should despise the enemy in strategy, but attach importance to them in tactics. I think we should first call the police. Even if they may not set up the case, it's good to maintain a record. Then let's see what is this guy's next proceeding. But we should also be careful, especially you. When you go to work and get off work, don't go through this building door. Enter and exit the place from the other side. And we should also check this telephone number."

"This is easy. I'll go to the telephone office and obtain a printed call records."

"That's fine. I heard there was a kind of multipurpose telephone which can display the caller number and record the call. Please buy one. And you should also buy two cellphones."

"Why should I buy two sets?"

"Each of us should have one for easier communication when there is something."

"I'm just a tiny secretary. Is it too extravagant to own a cellphone?"

"It is a job requirement."

At this moment, the telephone rang again. Hong Jun hesitated before he picked up the phone. The call was from Xia Dahu: "Mr. Hong, please come to my office right away. Something strange happened here."

"What kind of strange thing?"

"My office was burgled last night. Two safes were forced open."

"What did you lose?"

"This is exactly the weird thing – I lost nothing!"

"Did you call the police?"

"Not yet, because I'm not sure if I should call the police. I want to hear your opinions first."

"OK, I'll go there right now. Before I arrive, you'd better leave all items in the office as they are."

After hanging up, Hong Jun said to Song Jia, "Please drive me to Xia Dahu and then do your business. You can use the car then."

"You don't want me as your assistant there? I learned about site survey, too."

"No, thank you." Hong Jun said, and he walked out of the office. He was striding along, so Song Jia had to jog to follow him.

When they came to the parking lot, Song Jia opened the car door and sat on the driver's seat. When Hong Jun got on the car, she started the engine, steered the car out of the hotel yard and joined the heavy traffic on the street.

Song Jia glanced at Hong Jun, who was reclining on the seat, and asked, "Do you think the burglary is in connection with our case?"

Hong Jun did not answer.

Song Jia said again, "I think they must somehow be connected. But I also feel Xia Dahu is a shrewd person with hidden plans. And there is always something elusive behind his words. Really, I have a feeling..."

"I don't need feelings before seeing the site." Hong Jun interrupted.

Song Jia stopped talking.

The car traveled towards the east along North 3rd Ring Road, then turned south at north Taipingzhuang, and continue to travel east after entering the 2nd Ring Road. Soon it arrived at the gate of Meihu Decoration Company.

When Hong Jun rushed to the 2nd floor, Xia Dahu was pacing back and forth anxiously in his office.

This office was located in the middle of the 2nd floor of the office building. The window of the office faced south and the door was on the north, serving as the entrance to the corridor. The writing desk was in front of the window. A set of sofas was placed against the west wall, and a book cabinet and a big safe were against the east wall. There was also a small safe behind the door in the north wall. The window was almost opposite the large iron gate of the yard. There was a guard room on the east of the iron gate, and a bicycle shed was located behind the guard room. On the west side of the iron gate was a car garage. And behind the office building was a row of bungalows, which were the warehouse and the dining hall.

Hong Jun first checked the office door and noticed obvious traces of prying and pressing on the door frame beside the built-in lock.

Xia Dahu stood beside him and said, "This door was not tight. There was a big gap between the door and its frame."

Hong Jun put his hands in his trousers pockets and remained silent. He walked into the office and came to the big safe. The cabinet door was open and items within the safe were messed up. There was no trace of prying or drilling on the cabinet door and the lock was intact. Hong Jun put on a pair of white gloves and closed the door, but he found the bolt was not working. So the door could be easily opened by turning the handle, and no keys were necessary.

Xia said again, "What a bad luck! I did not tell you this on the telephone. You see the door and lock were intact, but why weren't they working?"

Hong Jun glanced at Xia and did not answer. He squatted before the cabinet door and observed it carefully for a few minutes. Then he stood up and came to the small safe behind the door in the room.

The small safe was tipped over, and its door was open and facing one side. The items from the safe was placed neatly on the ground. Obviously someone cleaned them up. There was an old leather waist belt, dark red in color and rolled up neatly, and packed in a plastic bag. It was evidently an item carefully preserved by the owner. Hong Jun looked at Xia. A faint bitter smile slipped over Xia's face, and he put away the waist belt. Hong Jun felt Xia's facial expression was a bit strange. The door and lock of this safe were also intact and undamaged. Hong Jun tried the door, and similar to the big safe, its bolt was not working. Several sofa cushions were placed under the safe, presumably to reduce the sound produced when the safe was tipped over.

Hong Jun stood up and stepped backward. He looked at both safes in surprise. He asked Xia to bring a tape and measured the dimensions of both safes carefully. Then he came to the writing desk and found there was no trace of prying. He asked, "None of these drawers were locked?"

"None."

"Was anything moved in the drawers?"

"They must have been moved."

"Nothing was missing?"

"Nothing! It was strange!"

Hong Jun went to the window, looked at the guard room at the gate and asked, "Is there anyone on duty in the guard room?"

"An old man."

"Did he hear any special sound last night?"

"I asked, and he said he heard nothing."

"He did not sleep at night?"

"He said he did not sleep. But very few night workers do not sleep at night. I can't believe him."

"Let's take a look in the yard."

Xia asked his people to watch the office, then he followed Hong Jun downstairs. They went out of the gate and walked east along the trail outside of the enclosure. On the east of the yard was the enclosure of another company, but there was a narrow lane between both yards that is leading to the north. The turned into the lane. Hong Jun observed the enclosure while walking. He stopped when he was near the outside of the bungalows behind, and noticed traces of friction made by the foot. He pointed it to Xia and Xia nodded. Since the lane led to the neighborhood on the north and was the passageway of many pedestrians, they turned back.

After entering the yard, Hong Jun and Xia turned to the back side of the office building. They noticed traces of friction made by the foot on the wall in front of the dining hall. The floor in the yard was paved with bricks and could not preserve any footprints. They went back into the office building. Upon entering the building door, Hong Jun asked if the door was locked at night, and Xia said it was not, because the building was jointly used by two companies.

Xia didn't like Hong Jun, because he felt the lawyer was putting on airs and deliberately mystifying things, but he was also amazed at Hong Jun's analyses. After returning to the office, he asked Hong Jun to sit on the couch and asked him in a way of seeking consultation, "Mr. Hong, what's your opinion on this? Was someone deliberately making fun of me? Or there is some other motive?"

"This is not mischief. I'm afraid only you can give an answer. I can only provide my opinion based on the scene. First, the perpetrator – let's call him that for now – did this for an objective I'm completely ignorant of. The route of his entering and exiting the site was clear. He climbed inside from the enclosure alongside the narrow lane on the east, then he came into the building, pried the door and entered this office. He did not come across any significant obstruction on the way. The enclosure was 2m high, which was not a problem for him, and the building door was unlocked. Besides, the lock of this office was not hard to pry. Second, the theft took place at night, because there were too many people in the day, which made it impossible for him to commit the crime."

"I agree." Xia thought all of these facts were obvious and needless to say. But he did not speak in this way; instead, he continued to ask politely, "Then how about the safes? Can you tell how they were opened?"

"This issue is complex." Hong Jun stood up and came near the big one, and said, "Common methods of opening safes that criminals use include prying, drilling, gas welding and blasting. But this perpetrator used a less common method, which I heard of from a theft prevention expert in the police station when I was in my internship. Mr. Xia, you can scrutinize the edge of the inner side of the cabinet door, have you noticed the depression?"

Xia looked towards the direction along Hong Jun's finger. There was indeed a depression. He nodded and continued to listen.

"How was that formed? Someone used force to turn the handle when the cabinet door was locked, which caused inward curvature of the strip steel used to fix the lock body; as a result, the bolt lost its function as the block pin, and the entire lock lost its effect."

"This guy must have great strength."

"Tremendous amount of strength was required to bend the strip steel, so the perpetrator needed to use some kind of tool. In fact, it was not just the strength to bend the strip steel. If we dismantle the metal plate inside the door, we can see both the bent strip steel and a cracked protection plate next to it. I guess the protection plate was made of gypsum instead of cement, so it was not strong."

"Then let's dismantle it and have a look. There are only a few screws."

"I advise you not to tamper with this"

"Why?"

"Because it's better to ask the police to do this."

"Do you mean I should call the police?"

"Exactly. Although you did not lose anything, prying a safe constitutes a crime by itself. And the perpetrator might be an experienced criminal who is expert in prying safes."

"You mean I must call the police?"

"Not you must, but you should. This is my advice as a lawyer, unless you have special reasons to preclude police intervention. If that is the case, it indicates you know the purpose of the perpetrator."

"I really don't know."

"Maybe you are just guessing or worrying. Since you asked for my advice, you should tell me everything. As a lawyer, I'm obliged to keep secrets." Hong Jun looked at Xia's eyes, but Xia's vision fell onto the writing desk. After a moment, Hong Jun asked again, "There wasn't anything precious in your safe, indeed? Cash or securities?"

"None."

"Was there any thing or document that you don't want others to see?"

"All of them were company documents. There wasn't any personal item. And I have told you nothing was lost. I have checked them?"

"Is the old waist belt which you just put away precious?"

"Precious? No, no. It is an ordinary waist belt which I used during the Cultural Revolution. Young people liked to use this type of belt at that time. It was called 'army belt' and was used in the military. I was reluctant to throw it away during all these years, because it carried my past. It can be said that the belt recorded the pursuits of our generation in our youth as well as our disappointments."

"Maybe it could make an antique. When I was in America, I heard someone auctioned a waist belt for 100,000 dollars. It was incredible."

"I'm afraid my belt could not even be sold at 10 yuan." Xia sighed. "But it has nothing to do with this case. You don't need to waste your energy on it."

Hong Jun came to the small safe, pondered for a moment and said, "It was strange, indeed. Based on the scene, the perpetrator was obviously searching for something. He put so much effort in this but did not take anything away. Maybe he hadn't found it?" said Hong Jun, as if to Xia and to himself. "There was another question – why did the perpetrator tip over the small safe? It took great trouble to do that."

After Hong Jun left, Xia sat on the couch and looked blankly at the small safe lying on the ground.

Chapter 10 – The Accomplished Theft

After leaving Meihu Decoration Company, Hong Jun took a taxi to Hongyuan Securities. On the way, he was trying to divert his attention from the scene of burglary to Xia Zhe's case, but the two safes frequently appeared in his mind. After getting off, he went directly to the VIP room on the 2nd floor of the business hall.

When he reached the upstairs, a poker-faced guard held out his hand to block him and asked him to produce his ID. He asked why. The guard said something was lost there recently and the leader demanded enhanced security. Hong Jun said he was a lawyer and was asking for information, and that their manager Lu Boping had approved it. The guard said that Lu did not bother with these trifles and these were managed by the deputy manager Liang. Hong Jun said he wanted to see Liang. The guard spoke some words to the intercom and then asked Hong Jun to wait in the guard room nearby.

Hong Jun stood alone in the guard room. With doors closed, he once again had the feeling of being locked up. Ten minutes passed but no one came. He opened the door and saw the guard was there, so he asked when Liang would come. The guard said it would take some more time and asked him to get inside. The door was closed again. Still, no one came after another 10 minutes. Hong Jun could wait no longer. He opened the door and walked out again. The guard said Liang would come very soon and asked him again to wait inside. Hong Jun said he would not wait further and he tried to leave. But the guard forbid him and said Liang was informed already. Hong Jun said angrily that they did not have the right to restrict his freedom, and that if they didn't allow him to leave, he would accuse them of unlawful detention, which was a crime. But the guard said since he came without permission, he could not leave so easily.

When both were in disputes, Liang came with quick steps. When he saw Hong Jun, he put on a false smile and said, "Ah, Mr. Hong. You came here to ride on someone else's donkey?"

Hong Jun swallowed and said while frowning, "Mr. Liang, I came for information, and it was approved by your manager Lu."

"It's OK for you to investigate, and we'll try our best to support you. But you'd better inform us first. You can talk with anyone. If you don't let us know beforehand, misunderstandings may occur. And it will be troublesome if any accident takes place."

Hong Jun felt Liang's words carried some threat, so he laughed disapprovingly, and said, "Fine, I want to talk with Fang Qiong now, is it OK?"

"Of course. I'll lead you there." said Liang. He turned around and walked towards the VIP room.

Hong Jun looked at the guard, took and deep breath and followed.

There was a door in the VIP room connecting the office area of the security company. Liang led Hong Jun to the employee lounge and then sent for Fang Qiong, and said, "Fang, Mr. Hong came to ask for information from you. You can discuss freely."

After Liang got away, Hong Jun said, "Miss Fang, excuse me."

Fang Qiong smiled and said, "Mr. Hong, when you came last time, something was bothering me. So, if I was not considerate in speech, please forgive me."

Hong Jun did not expect her dramatic change of attitude, so he said hastily, "Never mind, I was annoying you on that day, please forgive me, too."

"You words are so pleasant."

"I'm a lawyer, I make money with the tongue."

"You are telling the truth."

"This is the significant difference between a lawyer and a fortune teller. Both make money with the tongue, but the lawyer tells the truth, but the fortune teller tells lies."

"Then what truth are you going to tell me today?"

"I want to ask you a few questions."

"Then please sit down."

After taking the seat, Hong Jun asked, "Fang, did you operate the two transactions of Xia Zhe in relation to Shanghai Yanshen stock?"

"Yes."

"He said the second one was selling, but why was it made a buying?"

"He had a lapse of memory. He said he was buying at the moment."

"Did he discuss the trend of Shanghai Yansheng with you before he decided to sell or buy?"

"I can't remember, it seems he said Yansheng was going to bounce back after hitting the bottom."

"You didn't help him analyze the trend?"

"No. My job description only includes operating and receiving orders. I never give advice to the customer. Besides, analyzing stock trend requires professional knowledge, which I don't have. How can I make irresponsible remarks?"

"Did you know he was overdrawing?"

"Yes, I knew, but the company allowed it and he had guarantee." Fang Qiong noticed Hong Jun was observing her from head to toe while she was speaking. She was surprised and asked, "Mr. Hong, what are you looking at?"

"It seems that I saw you somewhere." Hong Jun said in earnest, "Fang, have you ever acted in a movie?"

"Yes? Which movie did you see me in?" Fang Qiong raised her eyebrows.

"Let me think...it seems to be a movie about student movements before liberation. That's right! It is *The River of No Return*. You acted a female student with short hair, who was shot dead by the enemy in front of a procession, right? You didn't appear often, but your performance was impressive."

"I didn't expect you have such a great memory." Fang Qiong said brightly.

"It's my supernatural skill. I retain everything necessary forever and forget everything unnecessary immediately. Why did you leave your career as an actress?"

"I studied finance and accounting, while movie acting was my part-time job. Of course, I did not meet a good director." Fang Qiong said with regret.

"It's a pity. There are so many movies and TV dramas today. Do you want to have a try?"

"It's too late for me to work in the show business at my age."

"Not necessarily. The acting circle in China lacks mature women who are both skillful and competent."

"That's right. There are very few truly talented actresses in China."

"Why don't you join the competition?"

"There is some personal reason behind my disinclination to join the show business."

"Because of love?"

"How do you know that?"

"I guessed it from your voice and expression. When you were saying this, your voice became softer, your mouth corners were curled upward, and your upper eyelids sank. Generally these signs indicate sweet memories."

"You have supernatural skills indeed."

"There are times when I guess wrong."

"Hahaha," Fang Qiong laughed and said, "it's a pleasure to speak with you."

"Speaking of love, I thought of a question. Do you mind my asking it?"

"Please ask."

"Are you single?"

"Yes."

"Is Xia Zhe your boyfriend?"

"He is only one of my pursuers."

"You have more than one pursuers?"

"If former ones are included, my pursuers are as many as the number of people in an reinforced platoon."

"Which pursuer do you have here except him? On that day, I found the deputy manager Liang was interested in you from the way he spoke to you."

"He is also one of them. And the large belly guy you saw on that day is pursuing me, too. His name is Hu Tucheng, and others call him 'Confused Hu'. Why are you asking this? Are you trying to spy on the 'rivals'? Hahaha, are you married?"

"I'm not married."

"Do you like dancing?"

"A little."

"That's great. Let me see you dance someday. Considering your figure and temperament, I'm sure you can dance very well."

"I also want to appreciate your dance."

"Do you have time tonight?" Fang Qiong suddenly switched to English, although her pronunciation was not quite good.

Hong Jun was a bit surprised and replied with English, "Sorry, I have an appointment tonight. You can speak English?"

"I'm studying English. I don't speak well. Can I learn it from you in future?" Fang Qiong smiled and switched back to Chinese. She said, "I know you are busy. Well, I give you a business card, and my pager number is on it. When you have time to enjoy, just call me beforehand. We can dance while practicing English."

Hong Jun accepted the business card, stood up and said, "Fang, pardon me for taking up your time. Thank you."

"You're welcome. I don't work hard, anyway."

Hong Jun and Fang Qiong went out of the lounge and parted as if they were friends.

The telephone rang as soon as Hong Jun walked into his office. He picked up the phone and heard Xia Dahu speaking.

Xia said in haste and with embarrassment, "Mr. Hong, something in the safe was lost, indeed."

"What have you lost?"

"The contract."

"The wood purchase contract?"

"Yes, it is."

"How did you discover it was lost?"

"Soon after you left, the police came. After surveying the scene, I checked the items in the safe again clearly and noticed the contract was missing."

"Why didn't you notice that in the morning?"

"I was in a hurry, so I did not check things clearly. The contract and relevant materials were put in a big envelope. I cast a glance and saw the presence of the envelop and things it contains, so I did not check it carefully. I was careless."

"Was the safe door dismantled? What did the police say?"

"They dismantled it. It was exactly in the same state as what you said. I told them your analysis before they dismantled it. And they said you were amazing. Before leaving, they said they would set up the case and asked me to report to them upon occurrence of any events. But I felt they were not taking this seriously and were fooling me."

"Have you seen Mrs. Sullivan again?"

"No. I called several times but it was Miss Chen who received the call. She said Mrs. Sullivan was very busy, and that if we can solve the water content problem of the wood, then we can appoint another time for meeting. I have been running around for this these days. I even met my supplier and tried to find a solution. I think if things don't work out, I may return the goods or dispose of them, but even this is very difficult. This batch of wood was manufactured as per Hongya Company's requirements which contain weird specifications and dimensions. For others, the wood is not usable. It's such an unfortunate event. Now the contract was stolen and I'm not able to explain myself to either party. I feel I have fallen into a large trap. Mr. Hong, your advice on that day on the necessity to safeguard the contract was correct indeed. I regret I did not accept your proposal. Now I don't even have a copy. What should I do? I need your help."

"Mr. Xia, I will try my best."

After hanging up, Hong Jun turned his chair towards the glass window, and looked at the trees with sprouts. His fingers started 'combing' his hair again.

Xia's words were a little suspicious to Hong Jun. He thought, was it possible that Xia used this theft case to make up a story of a stolen contract? But he also felt the probability of Xia's doing so was very small, because he did not see any benefit on Xia's side in such kind of deed. Although the contract clauses worked against Xia, the contract served as the basis for his purchase of wood from others. If the contract was missing, then his agreement with the supplier would be suspicious of fraud. Based on this, Xia's contract was stolen indeed. But why didn't he notice this? The wood transaction should be his most important business at the present moment, so the contract should be his primary object of attention when he discovered the safe was forced open, but it was not the case. Why? An reasonable answer is that he had something he cared more about in the safe, or an item he was more afraid of being stolen. What was it? Was it the old waist belt?

Hong Jun's reasoning had to come to an end, so he started another line of reasoning – who would steal the contract? The first suspect he could think of was Mrs. Sullivan, because she established a condition in the contract that the other party could never meet. From the perspective of law, the contract was flawless, but an insider could discover that the water content of wood specified in the contract was not possible to be achieved in China. Therefore, she was suspected to hold malicious intentions at the time she signed the contract. If this was the case, she definitely did not wish the contract to be in Xia's hands. But she would not pry the safe by herself, and Miss Chen was not capable of this, either. Then who was the burglar?

Hong Jun did not want to be involved in the dealings between Xia Dahu and Mrs. Sullivan, but he found himself gradually dragged into this quagmire and he was unable to stop. So he decided to meet this mysterious woman. Meeting her was also the desire of his heart, because he want to solve the mystery of "Mrs. Sullivan".

Hong Jun obtained Mrs. Sullivan's telephone number through the service counter of Shangri-La Hotel. When he got through, Miss Chen answered the phone. Hong Jun spoke with a perfect American English accent, "Hello, may I speak to Mrs. Sheila Sullivan? Please tell her I am her schoolmate from the law school of Northwest University. I'm Jon."

Soon he heard Sheila's excited voice, "Hello, Jon, how are you? I'm happy to hear your voice again."

"I'm fine, Sheila. How are you?" Hong Jun switched to Chinese.

"I'm doing good, too. How do you know I'm here?"

"I have supernatural power."

"Really? Something like reading texts with the ear. Then let me see."

"You are the chairman of the board of a large company, do you have the time to meet nobody like myself?"

"You are too humble. Do you have time today? Let me treat you."

"Are you doing this to repay your debt to me? I said I could always remember things people owe me."

"But I did not forget it, either. Jon, can you come here at five?"

"OK, Sheila, I'll come on time."

"OK. I'll wait for you in the lobby."

Hong Jun put the phone back to its seat, but his vision lingered there for a long time.

Chapter 11 – The Extraordinary Pair

Hong Jun entered the lobby of Shangri-La Hotel from the east entrance. He looked around and did not see Sheila, so he went to a couch nearby and listened to Beethoven's masterpiece Für Elise played by a pianist while looking at the courtyard-type garden with Chinese characteristics outside the tall glass window on the east of the lobby.

At five o'clock, Sheila went out of the elevator. She was wearing a rosy cheongsam.

Hong Jun put on photo-grey glasses and came to her.

Sheila was looking for Jon with her past memory, and when she saw Hong Jun walking towards her with a smile, she was surprised for a moment, then she came to him and said warmly, "Ah, it's you. I felt you were familiar on that day. It has been six years since we separated from each other. Time flies. You still look so good, young and graceful. I said in those days that I wanted to see how you would look when you shaved your beard, but you did not satisfy my desire."

"That was not my fault, mainly because you didn't want to see it anymore." Hong Jun smiled, "I recognized you as soon as I met you in negotiation, and I felt embarrassed. Fortunately you forgot me and did not recognize me, so I did not mention it and continued with the negotiation ."

"I didn't forget you, but I didn't expect it was you. And you changed a lot. You shaved your beard and put on glasses, and you didn't know English. Nice camouflage."

"You are the same. You pretended to not understand Mandarin. We are birds of the same feather, and this is what you used to say. By the way, why did you pretend to not understand Mandarin?"

"You don't know. We need to disguise ourselves in business so that the other party does not know our details." Sheila suddenly took back her smile, and asked solemnly, "Are you meeting me today as an old friend or as Xia Dahu's lawyer?

"Of course it's the former, because I'm off work already."

"Then we can only exchange friendship and cannot discuss business."

"Whatever you like to talk about, I can talk with you. The guest should suit the convenience of the host."

"Then you cannot switch roles with me. OK, let's talk in the restaurant. I ordered a western meal without asking you, because I want to find the feeling of the old days. By the way, should I call you 'Jon' or "Mr. Hong'?"

"Just suit yourself."

"So I will call you 'Jon', it feels familiar."

They went to the western-style restaurant on the 1st floor and took seats next to the window. After they sat down, Sheila looked at the red gallery and green lawn bathed in golden light of the sunset through the window and said with emotion, "It is rare to be blessed with a garden like this among all the tall buildings. And in a hectic life, sitting together with a friend, drinking, and chatting in a relaxed atmosphere is also a rare thing."

"You are still so philosophical. By the way, I remember you said you dreamed to be a poet when you were small, right?"

"Did I tell you? Maybe I did. But later, I did not want to be a poet anymore, because I didn't want to commit suicide, especially on railway tracks."

"Do you mean the poet Hai Zi? He also studied law in university, but he killed himself on railway tracks at the age of 25. It's such a pity."

"Exactly. Even if he decided to commit suicide, he should not have done that on railway tracks. He should have jumped into the river as Qu Yuan did. He seemed to have written a poem entitled 'Water Surrounds Qu Yuan'. In fact, I had suicidal thoughts before, and I attempted suicide in the way Qu Yuan did." Sheila squinted her eyes, as if absorbed in memory.

"What happened then? You couldn't swim, right?" Hong Jun had been trying to uncover Sheila's life mysteries.

"Ah, yes. I was saved by someone. He was a good person and an unsung hero. I'm not able to repay him in my life."

"Was he dead?"

"No. Ah, I don't want to talk about this now. It will reduce my appetite. I want to tell you, I'm different from Hai Zi. He said, 'May you be happy in worldly life, but I only wish to face the sea and enjoy the blossoming flowers and warmth in spring.' However, I'm thinking in the opposite way. I only wish to face the worldly life and enjoy happiness."

"You have realized your wish." Hong Jun looked at Sheila's face and said.

"Jon, don't keep looking at me that way. I'm embarrassed."

"I'm thinking something is missing on your face."

"Five sense organs are there. What is missing?"

"I remember you had a large mole on the face, right?"

"Ah, yes. It seems that you have kept me in the heart. Do you like it? Unfortunately I removed it."

"Why?"

"It's said the mole may cause cancer. Do you think I'm ugly now?"

"No, you are as beautiful as you were in the graduation ceremony."

"Really? I haven't changed into an old lady?"

"What a joke! But I have been unable to guess your age. You might want to be my elder sister and I can accept it. As Mr. Liu Shaoqi said, 'Lose small and win big.'"

"Did you win it?"

"Guess it."

"Then you can continue to follow your feelings."

The dishes and drinks were served. They held glasses and toasted each other's happiness and health. After tasting the courses, Sheila inquired, "Jon, how did you spend all these years?"

"After graduation, I worked in a law firm in Chicago for 2 years, then I returned to China."

"Why didn't you stay in America? I guess I'm neither the first one nor the last one to ask you this question."

"I wanted to do something for myself back in China."

"Wasn't it good to be a lawyer in America?"

"There were too many lawyers in the US, but China did not have enough. Even Americans wanted to 'export' lawyers to China. I couldn't wait until the day American lawyers occupy Chinese market, so I transferred from overseas to domestic."

"I think it was because you were afraid of becoming the test subject of 'new drugs'"

"What?"

"Americans suggested using lawyers instead of rats in new drug experiment – because there were less rats than lawyers."

Hong Jun laughed, too. "It seems that everything went well with you all these years."

"Went well? I just married a rich and old man. After he died, I inherited his money."

"You are the chairman of the board of Hongya Company. What business does your company conduct?"

"We conduct US-China trade. You know, law professionals have two career choices if they want to make achievements in the US: one is immigration business, and the other is US-China trade. My first job in Washington after graduation was about immigration. Later when I had money, I transferred to trade industry."

"What kind of trade do you do? I heard that clothing processing industry has a big market."

"We are doing business in clothing and toys."

"Why do you conduct wood business this time?"

"I go for anything profitable. Ah, are you spying for Xia Dahu?"

"I was just asking it casually. By the way, do you still believe in Christ?"

"You are forgetful. I told you earlier that I didn't believe in Christ. I was straightforward, but you beat around the bush to scold me."

"How could that happen?"

"Oh, you look innocent now. Is it camouflage?"

"I really can't remember I scolded you."

"Well, you first said I was a dog, then said I was a donkey. I was scolded many times in my life, but no one could do that as skillful as you did, which I could not forget in my life."

"Really? It corresponded with the common saying – 'Making a masterpiece by accident.'"

"We quarrel whenever we meet, maybe this is the destiny that ties us together. Although we only had a couple of one-night stands, I always felt destiny tied us together. Jon, I had relationships with many men before, but only you were my true love, although our relationship was short. But as expert says, true love lasts only a short time, which does not exceed 100 days. So let's drink to our destiny and love." said Sheila. She raised the glass filled with red wine and clinked it with Hong Jun's glass, then she drank off the wine.

Hong Jun drank the glass of wine as well, and said, "It seems that your drinking capacity increased a lot. I remember when we dined in Washington, you flushed after drinking only a little."

"That was intoxication caused by myself instead of the liquor. Besides, it was also because I had been aloof from liquor for a long time. I used to cut expense on eating, how could I use the money to buy alcohol?"

"You have a lot of money now. By the way, how did you meet the millionaire?"

"Thanks to God. Mr. Sullivan was a pious Christian. Maybe he did some immoral things to make money when he was young, so he worked hard to engage in charitable activities in his old age, presumably for redemption. His sister introduced us to each other in a church. Miss Sullivan, for whom we delivered the vehicle, was his sister. He saw I was in need, so he asked me to move to his home. He provided food and accommodation for free, but please don't think he was kind. He did not want money, but wanted something else. Now that I told you this, please don't be envious. So, cheers!" Sheila drank another glass, and her eyes were getting red.

"So you made the right choice of feeding on 'Christ'. You won the bet."

"It was not a total bet. There is an ancient saying, 'To know oneself is true knowledge.' I analyzed my conditions on all sides – I was not stupid, but I lacked perseverance, so I could not achieve success by hardworking. I was beautiful and not old, so I probably could make use of this 'capital' left to me by my parents. Mr. Sullivan did not have children, and his wife was dead. There was only him and two servants at home. So we got married quickly. Later he had liver cancer and bequeathed me his entire estate. I was living a tragic life, and it was Christ who gave me a rebirth. So I thank God even if I don't believe in him. Ah, my lord, please forgive me, amen." Sheila said and made a cross in front of her chest.

"You started to believe in God already."

"Sometimes I wish I could believe in God. In any case, having faith in God is better than believing in money. God ultimately advises people to do good, but money drives people to evil."

"Don't you love money?"

"That's why I can't believe in God." Sheila took a gulp of alcohol and added, "In fact, I don't like money, but I need it to help me achieve goals in life."

"Can't God help with that, too? Aren't Christians saying, 'My almighty lord'? Why don't you implore God to help you achieve goals in life?"

"God is too busy and does not bother with my trifle. If he helped us with everything, he would be exhausted. Please forgive me, lord. Amen." Sheila made a cross again.

"Can I help you?" Hong Jun asked cautiously.

"No, you can't. You are very smart, but too virtuous. You always want to do good. So you can't help me."

"You want me to be an asshole?"

"No. There are too many assholes in the world already. It's useless to add another. Beside, humanity will not be too unfortunate when there are good people like yourself. Well, let's not discuss heavy topics like this. We can talk about some light topics."

"OK, I have said the guest should suit the convenience of the host."

"Jon, it seems that you are working alone, right?"

"I'm searching for a partner."

"I'm not talking about the law firm partner, I mean a life partner."

"Isn't this more fashionable?" Hong Jun asked in reply while looking at Sheila's red cheeks.

Sheila took another gulp and did not answer Hong Jun's question. She said in a relaxed mood, "Many things in life are transient. You should enjoy what belongs to you. You see the branches outside the window. They are lovable for their green tender leaves, but when they wither and turn yellow, who want to see them once more? I read a book written by Gorky, the *Foma Gordeyev*, there is a splendid paragraph. I remember it till now – 'Cherish your youth! There is nothing better or more precious than it in the world. Youth is like gold, which helps you realize all your dreams.' Jon, I give you this sentence: Cherish your youth! Time is merciless. One becomes old overnight and death approaches unknowingly."

"Sheila, you should really become a poet. You are wealthy now, and free from anxiety. Why not write poetry?"

"No poetry comes out in the absence of anxiety. Well, let's just drink. Poets drink a lot. Li Bai wrote hundreds of poems while drinking." Sheila raised her glass again.

"You have drunk a lot. You'd better stop."

"There is an ancient saying 'Wine is never enough in front of a good friend.' I haven't drunk so freely like this for many years. Jon, I have been considering you as my 'male confidante' and the only person to confide in. I like drinking but I'm not addicted to it. When I'm happy, I can drink every day, and when I'm not happy, I can refrain from it for half a year. I drink for intoxication instead of health care. When you have swallowed certain amount of alcohol, you feel you are in heaven, and you forget all anxiety and worries. Intoxication is really a fantastic life experience."

Hong Jun looked at Sheila and suddenly felt the woman was no longer young. Luxury cosmetics and elaborate skincare could cover the age on face, but were not able to wipe out the turbulent past of one's heart.

When Hong Jun went out of the restaurant while supporting Sheila with his hands, Sheila was walking with drunken steps. Hong Jun escorted her home. After entering the bedroom, Sheila lied on her bed and looked at Hong Jun with drunken eyes.

Hong Jun said, "Sheila, where is Miss Chen? Do you need me to send for her?"

"She stays next to my room, you don't need to call her."

"Please take a good rest. I have to go. I will call you tomorrow."

"Please don't leave. I have been regretting. I should not have rejected your request at the night we broke up. You were a decent man with self-respect, so you normally didn't implore others. But you implored me at that time, and I rejected. I should have accepted your request, but I was afraid if I accepted your request, I would not have had the determination to break up with you. Do you know I was driving away with tears. I can say no more, Jon. Now I can give it to you as repayment for what I owe you. Only once."

"Sheila, you are drunk."

"I'm speaking from my heart after getting drunk." Sheila closed her eyes. "Do you think making love with the counter-party goes against your professional ethics? Well, please mind your own business. Xia Dahu is suffering from his own actions. He should repay for his misconduct and be punished. Well, I hate him, and I want him to go bankrupt and be left alone by his wife and children. I want him to suffer, regret, and...This is karma. Well, Jon, you can go. I'm tired, really tired. I have to...sleep now. Sleep. May lord bless..."

Sheila spoke more and more slowly and softly. She went to sleep.

Hong Jun stood at her bedside, and looked at the sleeping woman in silence. He thought Sheila's serene countenance could reflect her nature better. He felt there was something behind Sheila's words, but he could not guess it.

Suddenly, a girl's voice came from behind, "Mr. Hong!"

Although it was a soft voice, Hong Jun was startled. He turned around and saw Chen Jingyi smiling and standing behind him. He was puzzled that Miss Chen came in even if no one opened the door for her.

"Mr. Hong, do you want to have a soft drink?" Chen Jingyi looked at him with a weird expression in her eyes.

"Ah, OK." Hong Jun was a little nervous.

"Coke?"

"OK."

"Then please sit down in the living room." Chen walked without producing a sound. She took out a tin of coke and put it on the tea table.

Hong Jun came out and sat on the couch. He thanked Miss Chen, opened the coke and took a gulp of it. The cool and sweet drink restored his mood. Chen was sitting on the couch opposite him and looking at him quietly with a smile on her face. He felt the atmosphere was a bit embarrassing, so he asked, "Where are you from, Miss Chen?"

"You have a sharp perception, can't you tell where I'm from?" Chen spoke with a stress on the phrase "sharp perception".

"It seems you are not from Beijing, but your Mandarin is perfect. I can't tell."

Chen smiled elegantly, "I was born in Taiwan, but my parents were from Beijing."

Hong Jun wanted to ask something but he felt it was inappropriate. Besides, it seemed that something elusive was hidden behind Miss Chen's smile, so he took leave.

On his way home, Hong Jun's mind kept wandering to the other side of the earth – he recalled his two journeys with Sheila, which brought him not only unforgettable happiness in idyllic and picturesque attractions, but also scary and perilous experience...

Chapter 12 – The Asexual Cohabitation

In the summer of 1988, Hong Jun left his hometown and began his overseas study in the law school of Northwest University in Chicago, Illinois, USA. His life of hard work started. Before going abroad, he had no doubt of his proficiency in English, but after arriving in America, soon he found he had a lot of difficulty communicating with the local people. In China, the foreigners' English was easy to understand, but only when he came to America did he discover all the fast speech and murmuring of English language. Maybe as soon as the foreigners were in their own county, they were not quite patient in talking with you. Furthermore, studying abroad was different from traveling or visiting a family member. Since his major task was to complete school work, he had to overcome obstacles in academy study, including getting familiar with the literature retrieval method in the library of American law schools.

Hong Jun came across difficulty in his first search in the library for information. Although he studied some BASIC language in China, he knew almost nothing about the computer-based retrieval system. When he sat in front the computer, he gradually entered into the book retrieval system by his cleverness and turned out the introduction of a book, but he could not return to the catalog in any case. He tapped a few keys, but the computer did not work as intended. And he dare not tap every key on the keyboard. When he heard other people tapping on the keyboard with high speed and proficiency, he was very anxious, but he still pretended to be in a state of reflection.

At this moment, a gentle voice came from behind – "Do you need help?"

Hong Jun turned around and saw a Chinese girl standing behind him. She was slim and pretty, and had a distinct black mole on her chin.

Ever since Hong Jun came to America, the people around him were all Americans, so he felt familiar when a Chinese girl appeared in front of him. He plainly admitted his ignorance in computers. The girl helped him return to the catalog, and then patiently explained to him the procedures and tips of operating the computer-based retrieval system. A feeling of warmth arose in Hong Jun's heart, but the girl left before he even had a chance to say 'thank you'. After a while, the girl brought him a *Library Guidance* with an introduction to the computer system, then left hastily.

At the lunch break, the law school building was very lively. Students were everywhere in the restaurant and the lounge. They were talking enthusiastically while having simple lunch. Some of them sat on the ground, and some lied on the carpet. Some even put their feet on the couch back or the tea table.

Hong Jun bought a tin of coke and a sandwich in the underground restaurant, then searched for the Chinese girl in the crowd. But he could not find her after walking around. Feeling disappointed, he went to the library on the 2nd floor. It was quiet at this moment. He went inside through the passageway between the bookshelves.

The law school building was located beside Lake Michigan in Chicago downtown. Sofas were placed under the large glass windows at the end of the library. If one sat on a sofa there, the boundless lake would enter his vision.

Hong Jun walked to a sofa. When he was about to sit down, he noticed someone sitting on the sofa in the southern corner. Although he could only see her back, he felt she was the girl he was looking for. He walked to her and knew he was correct. So he warmly greeted her, "Hello, thank you for your help this morning. My name is Hong Jun, and my English name is Jon."

"You're welcome. That is my job. My Chinese name is Han Xinyun and the name I use here is Sheila." The girl was holding a large cup with instant noodles.

"I guess from your accent that you are from Beijing, is it right?"

"Ah, yes, are you from Beijing, too?"

"Then we are from the same city. I graduated from the law department of Renmin University of China. Which university did you take your undergraduate education?"

"I was in the English department. Later I studied law by myself."

"It was not easy for you. How long have you been in here?"

"More than a year. I study LLM."

"LLM in America takes shorter to study than in China, it seems the length of schooling is only one year, right?"

"One year is for those who learn fast. I'm in the second year and I hope it will be the last. Jon, are you studying JD? It takes 3 years and is more difficult."

"Chinese people consider JD to be Doctor of Law, but I think JD is very different from the doctor program in China. It is similar to an undergraduate program. But I find it difficult to understand classes. I can't follow. I have been thinking I'm smart, but I find myself quite dull among the American students. Maybe it's because of my poor English."

"It's not just about the language. The teaching method also plays a role. American professors use the Socratic method. They often ask students questions and use judicial precedents. You are not accustomed to this approach, that's why you find it difficult."

"That's true. Chinese teachers focus on the system of knowledge, like item one, two, three, and sub-item one, two, three...It is very clear and easy to memorize, but American teachers jump from here to there and there is no system. I often feel confused after a class."

"Let me tell you, you should make preparations before a class when you study here, especially the judicial precedents, you cannot wait till the teacher completes and then go over textbooks. Actually those American students are not as smart as you. You should trust your capability."

"Thank you for your encouragement. I have suffered a series of setbacks since I arrived in America. Sometimes I even doubt whether I'm an idiot, because it seems I know nothing."

"I can understand. Many things were not heard of in China, so we should learn them from the beginning." Sheila yawned and then said sorry.

"Are you tired? Maybe you should have a rest?"

"It doesn't matter. I speak English with Americans every day, now I can take rest by speak Chinese with you."

"Are you working in the library? It's hard for you to study while working."

"What can I do? You earned a full scholarship, right? That's much better than me. I earned a half scholarship. I don't need to pay the tuition but I have to make money to cover living expenses. In fact, I'm fortunate to have found this job in the library, which is far better than washing dishes in a restaurant."

Hong Jun looked at Sheila, and the desire to give her loving protection naturally arose in his heart.

Since then, Hong Jun often came to the place at lunch break. He would chat with Sheila in a relaxed mood. When Sheila was not there, he would gaze at the great lake beyond the window. He noticed that Sheila never talked about her family or her past, and she ate only one bag of instant noodles every time. He bought sandwiches for her but she declined. She said accepting other people's help was her last resort. But later he received Sheila's call for help unexpectedly.

Hong Jun was living in the city of Evanston, which was 20 miles north of Chicago. Situated beside Lake Michigan, Evanston had a population of 50,000 and had a beautiful environment. Since it was the location of Northwest University's main campus, there are many university students here, making it a "university town". Through a friend's introduction, Hong Jun was able to live in a three-story attic of an American professor.

It was Christmas Eve. Hong Jun's landlord was a Jew, who did not celebrate Christmas, but many neighbors decorated the front side of their houses with festive colored lamps, and installed gift-loaded Christmas trees in their lobbies. In the festival of family gathering, Hong Jun sat in his tiny room less than 10 square meters and tried to dissipate his loneliness by reading.

Suddenly, the telephone rang. He picked up the phone and it was Sheila.

Sheila was speaking, and her tone revealed her urgent need, "Jon, can I stay for the night in your place?"

"Hmm..." Hong Jun looked at his tiny room.

"I was kicked out by my landlord. It is so late and I don't have other friends, otherwise I would not bother you with this."

"No problem." Hong Jun wanted to protect her, as a man.

After hanging up, Hong Jun cleaned up the room, then he put on his down jacket and went to the subway station to pick up Sheila.

It was cold in the winter of Chicago. Hong Jun paced back and forth at the subway entrance. Sheila finally came. Hong Jun helped her carry the handbag and they went home side by side. Maybe because of cold, they did not speak with each other on the way.

After entering into Hong Jun's room, the warm air invigorated them. Hong Jun performed his duty as a host, and Sheila took what he offered. She said, "I have nowhere to go today, so I have to ask for your help."

"Why did the landlord kick you out?"

"The landlord is a rascal. He is a single old man, a Chinese, who profess to be a pious Christian, but he is very mean to people. The tenants are all from China mainland and often work for him. But he often calls us together and says we are 'ill-mannered', 'uneducated', 'inferior' and 'unteachable'. He often threats to expel us all. He charges a cheaper rent so we tolerate him. Chinese people are tolerant, especially we live under someone's roof. Last Friday he ordered us to move away within 2 weeks, but tonight he asked us to move all of a sudden. This is the Christmas Eve. We tried to reason with him, but he sent for the police. Of course the police was on his side. Finally he said we could move our belongings tomorrow but we must leave today. I knew he just wanted us to beg him by going down on our knees. But we were not spineless, so we had to take shelter in the places of our relatives or friends. You know only you and I are Chinese in the law school, and I don't have any other friend, so I have to call you. Thank you very much, Jon; otherwise I will be frozen terribly outside since it's so cold." Sheila said with red eyes.

Hong Jun said hastily, "You're welcome. We are all Chinese. The difficulty is that my room is too small. Sorry for that."

"Even this is larger than mine." Sheila smiled bitterly, "People in China might think we are enjoying life in America and making great money, but who knows our hardships? Maybe men live better. One day when I was walking on the street, an American came to me and asked if I wanted to have some fun in his room, and that he could pay me. I was angry at his words and cursed him in Chinese. Although he could not understand Chinese, he figured out what I meant. Guess what he said? He said, 'Aren't all female Chinese students doing this?' That was totally bullshit."

Hong Jun was surprised that such a quiet girl could use vulgar language. He looked at Sheila's emotional facial expression and did not know what to say, but Sheila's contemptuous smile made a profound impression on him.

Sheila realized this and said with embarrassment, "Sorry, I was a worker before, and occasionally I use the workers' vulgar language."

In fact, Hong Jun was not averse to Sheila's words. He even liked Sheila's tone and expression while she was speaking. "Hi, it is indeed not easy to study abroad. Both Americans and Chinese here discriminate against us. On that day, I went to the Chinatown to buy things. When I asked the price in Chinese, no one answered."

"You must have been using Mandarin."

"Exactly."

"Chinese people are miserable. We live under the roofs of Americans, but we envy each other and discriminate each other. Well, if you meet a Chinese in future, you'd better use English. The better you can speak English, they more respect they'll give you. Or you can use Cantonese. Anyway, in the Chinese people's circle in America, those who speak Mandarin are looked down upon by the most."

"Why?"

"Because we the the poorest."

Hong Jun fell silent. After a moment, he stood up, took out a bed sheet and a blanket, and rolled them out on the carpet next to the small desk. Then he said to Sheila, "You can sleep on bed, please take a rest early."

"Then thank you for sacrificing your own convenience." Sheila smiled elegantly and went to the bathroom.

When both of them lied down, Hong Jun turned off the light, but he could not go to sleep even after a long time.

When Hong Jun woke up on the next morning, Sheila had finished washing herself. Hong Jun got up and put on his clothes. Sheila sat on the bedside and asked him gently, "Why do you treat life so seriously after you came to America?"

Hong Jun said while folding his blanket, "Only when you treat life seriously will life does the same to you."

"Thank you, Jon, really."

"Why?"

"Because you are a good man."

Hong Jun rolled up the bed sheet and blanket together and threw them onto the bed, and said, "I'm used to it."

Sheila took out a small dressing case, and said while applying lip paints, "You are not old, but why do you keep the beard. You look like a foreigner."

"I'm observing their customs, and I'm doing so to save money."

"How old are you?"

"Twenty-five. And you?"

"A woman's age is a secret. I won't tell you. But I could be your elder sister."

"It's my pleasure. I'm blessed to have an elder sister in America."

"I will also be happy to have a younger brother like you."

After washing himself, Hong Jun asked Sheila where she planned to move. Sheila said she could first live in the school's temporary dormitory. The long-term dormitory's monthly rent was 400-500 dollars, which was too expensive. Temporary dormitory had 3 students in one room and its monthly rent was

150 dollars, but only new students could live there, and they were only allowed to live for half a month. Since Sheila was in temporary difficulty, the school should allow her to live there.

The day was Christmas. Sheila made several calls before she could reach the school's dormitory management. After obtaining their approval, Hong Jun started helping Sheila to move. When they went downstairs, they came across the landlord lady, but Americans were not surprised by things like cohabitation, so she simply greeted them and left.

Sheila was living on the border between Chicago and Evanston. It was a long and narrow three-story yellow building located beside a rectangular four-story white building, like a piece of butter pasted on a large piece of bread. The building looked worn out but was clean inside with a carpet. Upon entrance, he saw a small blackboard with the words "Wipe out mud on the shoes before you enter." The door on the 2nd floor was opposite a staircase, and on the right was a long and narrow corridor connecting the back side. Sheila's room was on the 3rd floor. The staircase was old. It squeaked when people stepped on it, as if it might collapse at any moment. Sheila's room was indeed small. A single bed, a desk, a cabinet and a wooden chair filled the entire space. There was a window facing the east, but it was so close to the opposite building that one would feel he was in the twilight even during the morning hours.

Shela packed up her belongings. When Hong Jun carried the suitcase downstairs, he really wanted to see the true colors of the "old Christian", so he purposely stamped on the staircase and made a loud noise, but the old guy didn't appear. When he was at the door, he looked back towards the long and narrow corridor on the right side of the staircase in a bit disappointment, and he felt a pair of eyes were watching him from a dim room.

Hong Jun and Sheila came to the dormitory of the Northwest University by car. After completing the procedures,they came to a room on the 8th floor. It was a large room with a clean bathroom, three beds, three wardrobes and three writing desks, and Sheila would live alone there.

Sheila looked around and said happily, "Wow, the room is great. If only they allow me to live here for a long time!"

"That's true. It's such a big room with nice condition, and it costs only 150. I think they will not kick you out, because no one else lives here."

"I hope so. The only drawback is that there isn't any place to cook. Maybe I should buy that microwave oven."

"What microwave oven?"

"Didn't you see the piece of paper beside the elevator on the 1st floor – "An used microwave oven for sale, 80 bucks."

"It's better to study in China, because meals and accommodations are free."

"Then why did you come to America? Just for keeping your beard? Well, Jon, we'd better think about something realistic. You helped me a lot. How can I reward you?"

"You can owe me that for now."

"I have a poor memory, especially, I can't remember things I owe others." Sheila said, in earnest.

"I have a good memory, especially, I remember things people owe me very well." Hong Jun also said in earnest.

"We are birds of the same feather, and we are sister and brother." Sheila laughed. She calmed down after quite a while, and said, "I haven't been so happy for a long time. I'm really so glad today. Have you been to Sears Tower? Let's go there together."

In the afternoon, Hong Jun and Sheila climbed up the tallest building in the world – Sears Tower. When they stood on the indoor platform 406 meters to the ground and overlooked the surrounding buildings, they felt everything below had become small.

Sheila looked out to the skyline in the sunset and uttered a poem gently, "People say the sunset is the end of the world; you can see the end of the world, but you can't see your home."

Hong Jun looked at Sheila's intoxicated countenance and asked, "You like poems, don't you?"

"When I was a kid, my dream was to become a poet, and my father also hoped I could become a writer, but I failed him. I feel sorry for him."

"What does your father do?"

Sheila glanced at Hong Jun and said, "American people don't like to inquire about other people's privacy, you didn't learn it, yet?"

"One's habit cannot be changed overnight. For example, I live in Professor Rawson's home. Every time he comes to my room, he knocks at the door, even if the door is open. I don't think it is necessary. He only needs to say hello."

"Americans have a lot of strange habits. On one hand, they are picky about food. They always complain Chinese people put too many oil in stir-fried dishes and the dishes are salty and unclean. On the other hand, they never wash their hands before eating, and they lick their fingers when they turn pages of a book or speech draft. Furthermore, they dare to drink cold milk in the fridge even in the morning in winter. I would feel stomachache even at the thought of this, but they don't mind. Do you think this is strange?" Sheila was speaking loudly as if no one was hearing. Fortunately, people around didn't know Chinese.

"Americans are strange, indeed. They eat uncooked vegetables like rabbit does. Occasionally they half cook vegetables in the pan. They don't eat so much salt, indeed. I doubt that their hair color, which is not black, is caused by insufficient intake of salt."

"It's likely. You might do some research and write a thesis. Americans have weird table manners. They may be casual in one way, but they have specific rules of holding the knife and fork, and they don't make a sound while drinking soup, until they have put the soup into the mouth with a spoon. They may be careful in one way, but they lick their fingers or blow their noses at dining tables. And they are not embarrassed for their behaviors."

"Exactly! Sometimes I feel embarrassed for them." Hong Jun agreed, "I heard there is a law in Connecticut requiring that a restaurant has to designate a zone which allows nose blowing and a zone which forbids that. Both their habits and laws are strange."

"When you spend a long time here and see it enough, you will be accustomed to it. Maybe after a few years, you will lick your fingers at tables, and you might be criticized after you return to your hometown." Sheila laughed.

"Not so serious, but I think Americans have a good habit of throwing things away. Chinese people don't like to throw things away. We keep even needles, threads, and pieces of cloth for possible future use. But Americans throw everything away. Last week my landlord lady asked me to help her move a large sofa to the garage at the back. It was almost new, but was thrown away like garbage. But the driver of the garbage truck found it troublesome, so he did not accept it until Mrs. Rawson gave him a 10-dollar tip. It was not troublesome actually, because the garbage truck was equipped with a lifter and a pulverizer. It does not require any human effort to carry the sofa."

"There is a 'garbage sculpture' in Chicago, which was made by pasting all kinds of garbage together. You haven't seen it, right? It's special. And there is a 'auto sculpture' made by threading 7 to 8 scrapped automobiles onto an iron column. It is also worth having a look. Some people say Americans belong to a race which like throwing things away, but in my opinion, the American people like the new and hate the old."

"It makes sense." Hong Jun gazed at the boundless lake on the east, and said as if he was absorbed in thoughts, "Liking the new and hating the old is not necessarily a bad thing."

"Exactly, in a sense, our free talking at this place is a result of liking the new and hating the old. Am I right?" Sheila looked at Hong Jun, who seemed to be immersed in his thoughts.

"Jon, what are you thinking about?" Sheila poked Hong Jun.

"I think maybe we should go home."

"Go home? We are vagabonds. Where is our home?"

"If a man has aspirations, his home is everywhere."

"Unfortunately I'm not a man. Well, let's go back to the dormitory, if not the home. You go to the men's dormitory and I go to the women's. So we are feeling better by thinking in this way. Right?"

Thus, the pair descended from Sears Tower, went to the subway station and got on trains running in different directions.

One day before the new year, Hong Jun received a call from Sheila again. She said the Water Tower Place had discounts and asked him to go shopping together. People miss their relatives at the new year. Hong Jun could not concentrate on reading, so he agreed. They met each other at the mall entrance and walked into the mall side by side.

The mall was very lively with a lot of people and noise. Hong Jun was a little disoriented because it ws his first time to visit large shopping malls. But Sheila was a regular visitor. She kept introducing goods to Hong Jun and helped him to make choices. Finally, Hong Jun bought a pair of jeans and a leather jacket. Sheila seemed to like a dark green skirt. She looked at it several times and put it in front of her body to check the size. Hong Jun said she could try it on. Then sheila went into the fitting room. When Hong Jun saw Sheila wearing the skirt, he was instantly attracted to her. In the past, Sheila looked beautiful and energetic in a pair of jeans and a sweater, but now she manifested a woman's glamour. Sheila stood in front of the mirror and looked at herself from different angles, and she was very satisfied.

Hong Jun said, "You look beautiful in this skirt. You can buy it."

Sheila sighed and said, "Yes, I need to find a job in the next semester and go to interviews, so I need a skirt like this, but it is too expensive. Even the discounted price is 59 dollars, which is half of one month's living expense for me."

Hong Jun calculated it in his mind and said, "I can pay that for you as my new year gift, sister."

Sheila looked at Hong Jun in earnest, and said, "Thank you for your kindness, but I can't accept it. I'm not inclined to owe people money."

"It's a gift. You don't need to repay me."

"Then it will be worse because it will make a debt in my heart. Let me buy it by myself." Sheila seemed to have made up her mind. She picked another skirt which was red from the clothes hanger and went into the fitting room.

Hong Jun waited quite a while before he saw Sheila again, but she did not put on the red skirt. Instead, she was wearing her own clothes. Hong Jun asked, "Did you try it?"

Sheila said gravely with simple words, "I tried it. It's not good."

"I agree. It is far from the green one."

"Let's go." Sheila put back the red skirt and picked up the green one. Then she went to the exit.

Hong Jun followed her, but he felt Sheila looked a bit strange. After checking out at the counter, they went rapidly out of the mall. When they came to the street, Sheila laughed suddenly.

Hong Jun asked her in confusion, "What's up? Why are you so happy?"

Sheila said complacently, "Do you know how much I paid for the skirt?"

"Isn't it 59 dollars?"

"Let me tell you. I only spent 29 dollars."

"Really? I didn't hear the cashier gave you a discount."

"I gave myself a discount."

"How did you offer yourself a discount?"

"This is a business secret. The skirts I saw over there were similar in style, but varied greatly in prices. The green one was 59, but the red one was 29. I found the price tags on the clothes could be taken off. So I switched them in the fitting room. So I only spent 29. You see? How smart I am!"

"You are unscrupulous. You will get into trouble if they find it out."

"Let me tell you, Americans are simple-minded. They can't even think of this trick."

"But..."

"But what? Do you think this is not good? Well, this is the wisdom of Chinese people. If you are not willing to share my happiness, you can pretend you don't know. By the way, tomorrow is the new year, I can treat you with dumplings. I'm still living alone in my room and there is a public kitchen in the same floor. I can cook dumplings there. You can come at 10 tomorrow morning. I will prepare the tools for making dumplings, and you will buy a bottle of red wine. Let's celebrate it together."

On the next day, Hong Jun and Sheila spent a happy new year.

When the semester began, Hong Jun and Sheila was again immersed in their ordinary lives as students. Sometimes they came across each other in the law school building, but they could only greet each other or exchange a few words because they both have a tight schedule.

Chapter 13 – The Romance

On the evening before the spring vacation in 1989, Hong Jun received a call from Sheila again. Sheila said she joined the Christian church and hoped Hong Jun could attend her baptism as a family representative. And it was a "religious journey" to Ohio free of charge. Hong Jun was not interested in religion, but he had not traveled to far places since he arrived in America, and this was a nice chance – it was free and during the spring vacation. So he agreed.

On the afternoon of that day, Hong Jun took a coach together with Sheila and 20-30 Chinese people who spoke a Chinese dialect which he did not know, and left Chicago. He relaxed his mind and appreciated the scenery outside along the way – the vast fields and scattered cottages were a sharp contrast to a city full of skyscrapers. He had a good impression of the splendid natural environment of America.

At 7 o'clock in the evening, they arrived at the destination – a motel in the suburb of Toledo. It was said that the owner of the motel was a member of the church.

A general meeting was held on the morning of the next day in the large restaurant of the motel. Nearly 200-300 Chinese followers from across north America sat on rows of chairs, and there was a platform in the front. Hong Jun felt the arrangement was more like that of a workshop or a lecture than that of an religious activity. Before the meeting, every person was issued several paper sheets with printed Biblical song lyrics. Then a host came out and announced to everyone the accommodation costs of the activity and encouraged everyone to put their donations in the donation box at the door when they rested. Since the lecturer hadn't arrived, the host taught everyone to sing the Biblical songs, and then they started "alternate singing" – the female followers sang once, male followers sang once, then it was the turn of New York and Toronto followers, consecutively. The atmosphere was very lively, like in a party.

The two lecturers finally came. They were both in the 50s and talked in a casually manner. There was neither the artificial preaching tone nor the solemn demeanor of holy missionaries.

The first lecturer spoke about why people should believe in Christ. He was eloquent and speaking continuously with strict logic. He quoted a lot of Biblical language, but his main idea was that if one did not believe in Christ, his life would be spiritually vacant. For example, you were happy when you just obtained a master's degree, but you would soon feel vacant again. Then you enrolled in a doctor's program, and felt happy when you were granted the doctor's degree, but the vacancy would fall upon you soon. The same applied to making money. You might be happy for having earned 100,000 dollars, but vacancy was disturbing you, and you started making more money. Even if your wealth reached 1 million or even 10 millions, you still could not get rid of the feeling of emptiness. Therefore, the only way out was to believe in Christ and observe his teachings, and wait for his advent, and then you could truly enjoy the happiness of life.

The second lecturer delivered his speech in a totally different style from the first one. He combined theory with practice. His subject was how to understand several paragraphs in the Bible. According to his explanation, believing in Christ means to enjoy Christ, or to derive material abundance and spiritual happiness from the lord, or in common language, to "feed on Christ". Such an explanation was highly praised by the followers, because many people were exclaiming "Amen". This lecturer was indeed a talented stand-up comedian. He interspersed his lecture with jokes and small stories, which caused everyone to laugh. And when he came to the splendid parts in his lecture, he would ask the followers, "Will you say Amen?" Then everyone would shout "Amen", which made the meeting very lively.

After the lectures, people delivered their impromptu speeches to share their experience and understanding in Bible study. They were very eager to speak, but mostly on how they studied Bible conscientiously and how they did self-reflection. A follower even vividly described how he heard the Christ's voice, and people were so excited to hear about this and exclaimed, "Amen."

Hong Jun thought if the follower was telling the truth, it simply meant he should be examined by a psychiatrist for symptoms of hallucinations.

All the speeches that followed were in the same pattern. People expressed their gratitude and love for Christ with simple words, or more accurately, stood up and led people to shout "slogans". Some people were too excited or unaccustomed to speak in public, so they would deliver incoherent speeches, but people didn't care what he spoke. As long as someone was speacking, they would shout "Amen". What a lively atmosphere!

Sitting in the venue, Hong Jun was curious about the scene and also familiar with it. It was unexpected that a religious activity took such a lively form, but it reminded him of the activities in cultural revolution – "Let everyone sing the revolutionary songs", "Creatively study and apply Chairman Mao's writings" and "Show your loyalty to Chairman Mao". He found the prayers chanted before meals, and in the morning and evening similar to revolutionary people's "morning requests and evening reports" chanted before the great leader Chairman Mao during the cultural revolution. Although he had not personally witnessed the age, he was familiar with it by what he heard. At this moment, he did not know whether it was coincidence in history or imitation by people. He could only feel sorry for the "common nature" of all humans.

After lunch, Hong Jun met Sheila in the yard. He said he did not want to hear the "exchange of experience" in the afternoon and he wanted to take a look in the farm. Open fields were everywhere, but there were several houses nearby which looked like farms. Sheila also found it boring to shout slogans, so she agreed happily.

It was a family farm, indeed, which consisted of a beautiful house and several tall warehouses. They saw an old man at his 50s and a young man fixing a rubber-tyred tractor in front of a warehouse. They greeted them and told them about their journey. The old man was very glad to hear that they were from China. He warmly led them to visit the feed storage and pig farm, and introduced the situation of the farm. The young man was the son of the old man. He was already married and did not live there. They co-operated the farm which was about 300 acres and kept hundreds of pigs. Most jobs were done by themselves, and they only hired short-term laborers in busy farming seasons.

After visiting the farm, the old man warmly invited Hong Jun and Sheila to take a look in his house. It was a bungalow with 7 to 8 rooms. Only he and his wife lived there. The floor was covered by a carpet, and all the furniture was beautiful and modern. And there was a piano in the living room. The old man said he was uneducated and his son did not get a college education, either, but he was happy with his life. And his only worry was whether the harvested food and grown pigs could be sold out. His wife warmly served the guests but seldom talked. She just smiled and listened to her husband speak. The custom here seemed to be different from the city. And the old man told them that farmer settlements have disappeared in America, and all rural areas were comprised of family farms like this. Before separation, the old man took off his work clothes and took a photo with Hong Jun and Sheila, and said he hoped the friendship between Chinese and America people can last forever.

After leaving the farm, Hong Jun and Sheila went back along the village road.

The red sunset created a peaceful atmosphere on the vast fields, it seemed the running vehicles on the highway far away had slowed down. In a fast paced and competitive society like America, such a scene is the rarest enjoyment.

They both slowed down and stopped, and stood on the roadside close to each other. They gazed at the horizon on the west and did not speak, as if they feared language would destroy such a happy experience.

After a long while, Sheila asked Hong Jun softly, "Jon, do you believe in God?"

"I don't believe in him, do you?"

"I don't, either."

"Then why did you join the Christian?"

"Because I want to feed on the Christ."

"It seems you agree with the second lecturer's opinions."

"I think the first one is more reasonable. He said humans should not have too many desires, because desires cannot be satisfied and will drive people crazy. And people cannot be without desire, either, because people without desire will feel vacant and bored, with no pain and no happiness. In the secular society, people are often tortured by desires and emptiness and wander between the two. They are either burned in desires or frozen in emptiness. They only way out is to believe in God, and only in this way can they get rid of the burning desires and freezing emptiness. If we ponder over his words, we'll find they make sense."

"Isn't this as good as accepting the point of view of Christianity?"

"It's different. I'm a materialist cultivated in the education of the Communist Party. It's not possible for me to believe in God. To be honest, I joined the church for a material purpose."

"You are always speaking profoundly."

"It's not profound at all. I can tell you. As Chinese students, if we want to establish our positions in American society, we only have three choices: the first is to be a conscientious student and employee; the second is to speculate in politics and trade; the third is to seek a suitable marriage partner or join the church. For me, the first path is too difficult; the second is too mean; only the third is suitable for me. It requires chances to seek a suitable marriage partner, but joining the church can improve life and bring about opportunities, so I decided to be a Christian."

"You are not afraid of God's punishment?"

"God only exists if we believe he does. I don't believe in God at all, how can he punish me? Jon, why are you staring at me that way, as if I'm a monster? In fact, I'm not worse than common people, but I don't cover my dirty inner world and pretend to be noble, like many people do. I like frankness and hate hypocrites. I remember a Russian writer's magnificent words: 'If this could make everyone disclose all of his secret thoughts, including those he dare not speak of and is not willing to tell, and those he does not want to tell even his best friend or even admit by himself. If he disclose all of these without hesitation, this world would be filled with filth and suffocate everyone.' What are you laughing at, Jon? You don't agree with him? Maybe you think there are noble things in the world, or love is a noble affair. You are wrong. Love is only a small episode in life and a way of connecting people together. Don't people in love want something from each other to satisfy their selfish desires? You see how frank I am. Although our relationship is similar to roman, I have never thought about pretending to be a lady. What do you want to say?"

"I want to say...I'm fortunate that I'm not in love with you."

"Haha, I'm happy you learned to be frank as well. We are birds of the same feather, again. But in future, you might regret not having been in love with me. Then you will regret not having kept me to your side."

"A chain made of sausages cannot keep a dog locked."

"What did you say?"

"A man cannot prove to a donkey that it is a donkey."

"Haha, Jon, I like your humor. Haha." Sheila laughed and stooped.

The sunset was covered by a gray cloud, but decorated the border of the gray cloud with colorful rays.

Hong Jun and Sheila went to the motel. They chatted and laughed all the way, as if they had not had a conversation about the soul. When they returned to the motel, the followers had started the prayers before dinner.

On the morning of the next day, baptizing ceremony for new followers would be held in the indoor swimming pool of the motel. Sheila was wearing a light blue outfit similar to the pajamas. When she saw Hong Jun, she went to him in quick steps and held his hand tightly. She seemed to be excited and nervous. Her body was quivering but she did not speak anything.

The ceremony began. Sheila walked slowly into the swimming pool in solemn music, until the water came to her chest. Two male followers standing in water followed the instructions of the host at the pool side to press Sheila's head backward into the water, and then lifted her head up, as an indication that Christ had given her a new life. Now the followers at the pool side shouted the slogans loudly and exclaimed "Amen".

Hong Jun walked out silently.

After a month, the law school of Northwest University held the year's graduation ceremony in the Navy Pier Auditorium beside Lake Michigan on the east of the urban area of Chicago.

Teachers and students of the law school and the graduates' relatives and friends from across America and even the world got together in the same place. The graduation ceremony was solemn and lively, especially when more than 200 graduate students stepped onto the platform upon announcement of their names, and their relatives and friends stood up and applauded.

After the graduation ceremony, coaches transported the teachers, students, and guests back to the law school.

Balloons and colorful ribbons were floating in three buildings of the law school, which were connected together by a corridor. It appeared to be a big festival. The law school prepared the buffet. The teachers, students and their relatives and friends were holding dishes and glasses. They were sitting, standing and walking. The sound of chatting, laughing and cheering were heard everywhere. And the students who wore casually in ordinary times changed their attire – men in suits and women in fashionable dresses.

Sheila was wearing a rosy cheongsam, which added glamour to her slim figure. And such a special dress made her the object of attention. Presumably she drank a lot of wine, because redness emerged in her originally white cheeks and her watery eyes appeared delicate and attractive. She was very busy, and Hong Jun took quite a lot of effort to find the chance to talk with her beside the staircase in the hall at the 1st floor.

Hong Jun raised his glass and walked to her, "Sheila, congratulations to you for getting the Master of Law degree."

Sheila clinked glasses with Hong Jun and sipped a bit wine. She tapped her upper chest with her left hand as if she was expelling fatigue and stress from her body. "Thank you. Although a master degree is not some great achievement, I have completed my overseas study anyway. My suffering paid off. I should be happy, but my feeling today is complex. I feel as if I'm attending a wedding ceremony or released from prison. It's indeed strange."

"Are you married?"

"Do you really want to know?"

"Just asking."

"Then I won't tell you."

"I...really want to know." Hong Jun flushed a bit.

Sheila smiled gracefully, "I only had a relationship but did not have experience in bed. Are you satisfied?"

Hong Jun flushed more heavily and didn't know what to say. He unexpectedly asked a question that flashed in his heart, "You were in prison?"

"What are you talking about?" Sheila took back her smile.

"Nothing, just right now you talked about the feeling of being released from prison, so I thought...please don't be angry." Hong Jun said incoherently.

"Oh, I won't get angry." Sheila smiled again, charmingly.

Hong Jun changed the topic hastily, "Have you found a job?"

"Nearly." Obviously Sheila was not interested in this topic.

"Sheila, you are beautiful today." Hong Jun tried to find things to talk.

"Thank you. You regret it?"

"Regret what?"

"You forgot it. I said you would regret not falling in love with me. There aren't many chances in life, but you allowed them to slip away. I hope you can seize chances in life next time. Cheers."

After toasting, Sheila was called away by a student.

Hong Jun looked at Sheila blankly while she was leaving. He stood for a long time before he went towards the long corridor connecting the old building and new building of the law school. He stood in front of the large glass window and looked at the garden enclosed by the old building and new building. There was a large bronze statue in the shape of a hand in the middle of the garden. Some students in academic clothes were taking photos in front of the statue, and some students were sitting in circles on the lawn and drinking, chatting and laughing.

Hong Jun had never felt so lonely and so desperate for love before. He closed his eyes, but Sheila's figure appeared again in his mind. He sighed, rubbed his eyes and took out his purse. Then he took out a photo from the inter-layer of the purse. He gazed at the girl on the photo who was smiling and looking at him, and said in his heart: "Xiao Xue, how nice it would have been if you had come to America and studied together with me. It has been three years since we broke up. How are you doing now? Are you married? Are you happy?..."

Chapter 14 – The Inadvertent Intrusion into the Customs

The summer vacation in America was very long. It lasted 3 months. Hong Jun decided to work part-time in the vacation, so he started to seek opportunities since mid-May. He saw an attractive recruitment ad in a local newspaper: a company was recruiting bilingual people, including Chinese, with decent pay. He found himself suitable for this job, so he decided to apply.

It was a kitchen ware manufacturing company headquartered in west Chicago. A man who claimed to be the deputy manager accepted Hong Jun's application form and introduced to him the company's business performance. Then the man asked some personal questions and officially told Hong Jun that he was hired but he needed to accept three day's training. Hong Jun asked about the nature of his job, and the man said the job was to communicate with customers who did not know English and therefore required strong bilingual proficiency. Hong Jun thought he was competent to carry out the "translation" work. He wanted to ask about the compensation, but hesitated and did not ask. He paid 40 dollars as the training fee.

On the morning of the next day, Hong Jun spent one hour in the subway and came to the company for training. There were more than 20 trainees, most of whom were south American immigrants of Spanish origin. He heard for a while and finally understood the job was to promote the company's products door to door. He needed to identify potential customers who were mostly Chinese people without English language capacity, and his compensation would depend on his sales performance. He could not accept such kind of job, so he quit the training session, and the 40 dollars were paid in vain. After leaving the company, he felt he was cheated, but he could do nothing about it.

In the evening, when Hong Jun was scouring through the newspaper, he received Sheila's call.

"Hello, Jon, I have a chance for you again."

"What chance?" Hong Jun was a bit confused.

"Let me ask you first, have you got a driver's license?"

"I have got it. It will be pity if one does not learn driving in America."

"Have you been on the highway?"

"Yes, last week I went to Milwaukee with my friend. And I drove all the way in the round trip."

"That's great."

"Nothing. It's only a simple skill."

"I'm not praising you. Jon, I have a wonderful opportunity for you. You can take a trip to the east coast."

"What opportunity is it?"

"One of my friends will move to New York. She has a car but she does not want to drive there. She is old and can't drive so far. She wants to find someone to driver the car to the place. She will pay 800 dollars, including oil cost, highway cost and the driver's expense of returning home. And she will cover meals and accommodations of the driver in New York."

"Why don't you go?"

"I will go there, too. But you know, I seldom drive although I have a driver's license. Besides, it's better to have two drivers to drive alternately on such a long way."

"What time?" Hong Jun asked again.

"Just drive the car to New York in this weekend. Will you work in the vacation?"

"I'm looking for a job. A friend told me a restaurant is recruiting people, but the work will start in the next month. If I can't find a suitable one, I will do dish washing."

"Our ancestors said, 'No pains, no gains.' Now that you have time at this moment, you can go with me to send the car to New York. This is also a way of making money. I have applied for a job in Washington and I have to go for the interview. I plan to drive the car to New York first, then hire a car in New York and head to Washington. And go back to Chicago at last."

"Is it alright?"

"It's alright. I have asked about everything."

"This is indeed a nice chance. I have been wanting to visit New York. And it will be even better if we can take a look at Niagara Falls."

"Your desire is insatiable. But I can talk with the owner, maybe she can agree with it. So how's your plan, Jon? Will you go?"

"Of course!"

"OK, then we'll use the 800 dollars on the way. If it's not enough, I will pay for the rest."

"Then you'll lose."

"It doesn't matter. I'm like your elder sister. Additionally, you should drive for the most part. Let's decide it."

"It's a deal." Hong Jun was very happy.

"Please wait for my call." Sheila was happy, too.

After hanging up, Hong Jun sat still for quite a while, then he took out the photo of Xiao Xue from his purse, wrapped it up with a clean, white handkerchief, and placed it inside an envelope. He put the envelope into his suitcase. After zipping and locking the suitcase, he gave a sigh of relief.

On Thursday, Hong Jun and Sheila started their journey. It was their first tour to the east coast, and they were driving by themselves, so they were very excited. The set off at the dawn. The car was a German Benz which had a past driving distance of only 20,000 miles and could change speed automatically. Hong Jun had test driven it once, so he was relaxed and confident in the driver's seat.

There were very few cars on the highway. They passed through downtown Chicago from north to south, and then drove fast along No.94 highway at the southern end of Lake Michigan towards the rising sun. Tall buildings were left behind and the vast fields appeared on both sides of the road. Sheila excitedly talked about a variety of topics like a girl in an outing, and expressed her heartfelt praises of the roadside scenery.

At 4 o'clock in the afternoon, the arrived in Buffalo, which was about 30 miles from the large waterfall. One of Sheila's god sister taught in the Buffalo school of State University of New York. She agreed to accommodate Sheila and Hong Jun in her house. Hong Jun drove the car into a gas station at the roadside. After refueling, he took out the map to check the driving route. One would not get lost on the highway while driving in America, but he should be careful after entering the urban area, and the most important thing was to find the accurate exit of the highway.

Hong Jun had driven for nearly 10 hours. He was a bit tired. Sheila felt sorry for him, but she could do nothing but encourage him. Hong Jun drank a tin of coke and returned to No.90 highway. After a while, he turned into No.190 highway and drove westward into downtown Buffalo. Sheila held the map and looked at the road signs while checking out the map in order to find the exit of the Post Avenue.

It was the off-work rush hour. There were many cars on the highway, and sometimes they could only drive slowly. The road ahead was under maintenance so they followed the traffic to the alternative road. When they estimated that they were near the Post Avenue, they came across a highway toll station. They were used to seeing such kind of toll stations. Some stations charged fees manually, and some automatically – if you put the coins in the basket of the charging machine, the bar would rise automatically. Of course, you could put more than the required, but could not put less.

Hong Jun drove the car in the queue to the toll gate. After paying 1.25 dollars of highway fee, he asked the toll collector in blue uniform, "Can you tell me the way to the Post Avenue?"

"What? The Post Avenue?" The toll collector was surprised.

"Yes, the Post Avenue." Hong Jun repeated.

"Sir, you have passed it. This is American border. In front of us is the Peace Bridge leading to Canada." The toll collector looked at the long queue of cars and blew his whistle.

Hong Jun was panic-stricken. He wanted to back the car up, but there was a long queue behind. The toll collector knew his intention and said to him calmly, "Sir, this is a one-way road."

"What can we do?" Sheila leaned closer and asked through the car window.

"Ah, Miss, if you don't want to take a trip in Canada, you can get around to the border entrance on the other side, and enter America again." The toll collector said in a relaxed tone.

"But we don't have the visa." Sheila said anxiously.

"Ah, then you will be in trouble. But you have no choice but to tell your stories to the customs officer on the other side and try your luck."

The cars behind sounded the horns impatiently. Hong Jun drove the car out of America resignedly and turned around before the Peace Bridge and drove to the entrance on the other side. Many vehicles were waiting to cross the border and there was a long queue in each checkpoint. Hong Jun directly parked the car beside the checkpoint, got out of the car and went to a customs officer who was inspecting the entering vehicles. He told the officer how he got lost, but before he could speak more than a few words, the officer asked him to drive the car to the end and wait in line. Hong Jun did not know whether the officer understood what he meant, but he could not explain further. He had to get back into the car, drive to the end of the queue and wait in line for entrance.

When they finally made it to the checkpoint, Hong Jun parked the car and got off. He told his story to the poker-faced officer as lightly as possible. The officer heard it casually, then he went to the rear, asked Hong Jun to open the trunk and examined the luggage. Sheila came out at this moment and helped Hong Jun to explain the incident. After examining the car, the officer asked them to produce their passports and visas. Hong Jun and Sheila took out their IDs and handed them to the officer.

The officer held these documents and went into a small house beside the checkpoint. After examining the documents, he asked, "Who will you visit in Buffalo?"

Sheila said, "We are visiting Marian House. She is the professor of Buffalo school of State University of New York."

"Good. Please call Professor House and ask her to come." The officer said with an irrefutable tone. Then he asked the vehicles behind to back up a little so that Hong Jun could drive backwards and park the car on one side.

Sheila had to call Professor House, but no one picked up the phone in the office or at home. She suddenly remembered Professor House said she had something to do tonight and had told her where the keys were placed. Sheila hung up and told the situation to the officer. The officer looked at Sheila suspiciously and said, "Too bad. It's your bad luck. You have to wait here until Professor House got back home."

Sheila got back into the car in frustration and said to Hong Jun, "It's all your fault. You did not even know you were driving the car out of America."

Hong Jun did not respond. He leaned his head on the back of the seat and closed his eyes.

Sheila looked at the fatigued expression of Hong Jun and felt she was a bit harsh. So she said gently, "Jon, I'm not blaming you, I just feel our luck is extremely bad. I don't know how long we will wait here."

The night fell slowly. Cars waiting to enter were less and less. Sheila called a few more times, but she only heard the beep sound from the phone.

At about 8 o'clock, the officer was off work. A young man took his post. Sheila noticed the man had a kind look, so she walked to him and explained to him their situation and difficulty. The officer listened to her with great interest and laughed. Then he checked their passports and visas and allowed them to pass the border.

Hong Jun and Sheila drove into the customs happily and identified the Post Avenue at the intersection ahead. Later they found the home of

Professor House. Sheila found the keys according to Professor House's instructions, opened the door and entered.

After dinner, Hong Jun took a shower and went to sleep.

Sheila was watching TV and waiting for Professor House's return.

Chapter 15 – The Baptism in the Storm

On Friday, after having breakfast with Professor House, Hong Jun and Sheila drove straight to the Niagara Falls. The passed bridges and islands and appreciated the picturesque scenery on both sides. After 30 minutes, they arrived in the parking lot on the Goat Island of the Niagara Falls State Park.

There weren't many tourists at this moment, and hundreds of pigeons and water birds were playing on the lawn. If one looked forward, he could see the beautiful blue sky and green grasses, as well as water torrents with glaring sprays in the sunshine. Immersed in such a beautiful natural environment, they felt completely relaxed and happy.

After leaving the parking lot, they went west along the island trail. After passing a stone arch bridge in the shadow of green trees, they came to the delicate Sisters' Islands, which was filled with bizarre stones. Standing beside the island, he saw from a distance some white smoke rising slowly behind the woods on the west.

Sheila pointed to the white smoke and asked, "What is it?"

Hong Jun said, "Maybe it is a factory."

Sheila sighed, "There is air pollution in such a beautiful place. What a disaster!"

But after they left the Sisters' Island and went west for a while, they found they were wrong – the white smoke was not from a factory chimney, but from the large waterfall.

The water mist stirred up by the waterfall rose slowly into the sky and was transformed into thin clouds, which moved northeast with the wind. They looked up towards the sky and sometimes felt small drops of rain falling on their faces. He did not see the waterfall yet, but felt its power from the cloud-forming spectacle.

Continuing westward, they gradually heard the deep and continuous roaring. The asphalt road and the flowers and trees on both sides became wet. They both quickened their paces.

After coming to the southwest end end of Goat Island, they finally saw the magnificent Niagara Falls. The waterfall consists of two parts: on the left was the Horseshoe Falls in Canada, and on the right was the American Falls in America. Since they could only see the profiles of both waterfalls, they decided to take a boat to Niagara River to view the great waterfall from the front side.

The reached down to the dock. Each one of them took a blue raincoat, and they boarded the "Maid of the Mist" boat with dozens of tourists.

After leaving the dock, the two-story boat turned the nose and sailed countercurrent to the center of the annular Horseshoe Falls. The water curtain as high as 50 meters hung down from three mountain tops. The pond water was slapped and made turbulent by the waterfall, and produced tremendous amount of mist. Seeing such a splendid waterfall, people were naturally touched by the miracle and magnificence of nature, and felt the humanity's tininess and fear. The boat kept sailing towards the waterfall, as if testing the tourists' courage, until people could see the cliff behind the water curtain and could not hear the grumbling of boat engines.

Sheila leaned herself close to Hong Jun's chest. She held the railings of the ship with one hand, and Hong Jun's sleeve with another, and nervously looked at the boat nose which was cutting through water waves. She said with quivering voice, "Why are we continuing forward?"

Hong Jun looked at her panicking expression and laughed, "In fact the boat is not going, it is the illusion caused by water flow. You will know this by looking at the mountains."

Sheila looked to both sides and calmed down a little. She then looked back and saw a rainbow hanging on the mast of the boat. She exclaimed with excitement, "Wow, the rainbow!"

Hong Jun looked back and saw the rainbow was in front of them. It was so clear and colorful and matched perfectly with the white Rainbow Bridge crossing the Niagara River far away. He could not help but praised, "Niagara is so beautiful!"

After getting off the boat, they had lunch and went onto the viewing deck at the riverside by elevator. When they overlooked the great waterfall from the high deck, the water curtains appeared to be static and lost their shocking power. And they seemed to have rediscovered their self-confidence as humans, which was lost at the foot of the waterfall. Looking down, the riverside tourists were like ants and boats on the river were like leaves, which was another amazing phenomenon.

Sheila asked, "I like watching the great waterfall from a distance."

"Why?"

"Because I feel safe when I'm far from it. Don't laugh at me, Jon, actually I have been afraid of water since I was small."

"Do you know how to swim?"

"No."

"No wonder you were so nervous in the baptizing ceremony. I remember you were shivering all over when you held my hand. I thought you were afraid the Christ did not give you a new birth, but you were actually afraid of water."

"I'm really afraid of water. Jon, do you think my appearance on the boat was funny?"

"No, I think you were lovely."

"Really? Why do men love weak women instead of strong ones?"

"I did not say so. In fact I also like strong women, but..."

"But what? But a woman should behave like a woman, right? I heard this many times. Why should women speak softly and be little birds? I know you men hope women were weak so you can treat them as toys."

Hong Jun looked at Sheila in surprise, and said, "Sheila, what's wrong with you? Why are you so excited. I did not say anything."

Sheila did not answer. Her cheeks which became red due to excitement gradually recovered to normal cover. She looked at Hong Jun for a while, then said in embarrassment, "Jon, sorry. I'm easily agitated. I'm not sure what stimulated me. It comes and goes, and I can't control myself. Maybe my scar in the heart is too deep."

"You were bullied by someone before?"

"I don't like to recall the past. The verse 'Let bygones be bygones' applies to my situation perfectly. Jon, don't be angry. I was not attacking you. I know you are different from other men, and you are a rare gentleman. I feel safe with you, but I also feel tired to be at your side. Sometimes I wish you were a man like everyone else."

Hong Jun thought about Sheila's words. He recalled Xiao Xue and a bitter feeling arose in his heart. He had to overlook the skyline on the west.

"Jon, are you still angry with me?"

Hong Jun shook his head and said, "Since you were not attacking me, why should I be angry?"

"Then...where should we go? Jon, aren't you the tour guide?" Sheila picked up her usual teasing tone again.

"We should go to the 'storm platform' under the waterfall and have a look." Hong Jun pointed to the yellow figures at the food of the American Falls, and said, "However, if you are afraid of water, we'd better not go there."

"No, we traveled a long way to arrive here, how can we miss the opportunity? I just said you are a gentleman, so I 'sacrifice myself for the gentleman.' Besides, I want you to feel the loveliness of myself again."

Hong Jun and Sheila descended from the viewing deck and returned to Goat Island. They put on yellow raincoats and linen shoes in the changing room, took the elevator down to the "wind tunnel", and followed the tour guide to the foot of American Falls with a dozen of tourists. Then they walked towards the bottom of the waterfall along the curving trestle. When they looked upward, they saw white colored water coming down with great force.

And the miraculous nature created numerous rainbows by the side of the waterfall.

Sheila followed Hong Jun and tightly held his hand, as if she was afraid she would slip down into the fathomless dark water below. The finally came to the "storm platform".

Water fell from the top and slapped a large stone, then splashed onto the wooden platform which was a few square meters in size. Hong Jun and Sheila stood side by side on the platform and felt as if they were in the storm.

Sheila unconsciously leaned her body close to Hong Jun, and Hong Jun opened his arms and embraced Sheila. They stood there silently. In fact, even if the spoke, they could not hear each other. When the tourists left one by one, they also went off the "storm platform", and returned through the trestle. When the "storm" was left far behind, they stopped and looked back.

Sheila asked Hong Jun with great interest, "You guess what I was thinking about on the platform?"

"The storm." Hong Jun was a bit absent-minded. It seemed he was relishing the feeling of embracing Sheila just now.

"You are too unimaginative. Let me tell you. I thought about *Wedding on the Execution Ground*. Did you watch the movie? At the moment, I was fully at ease, as if I was facing death unflinchingly. Did you have the feeling of attending a wedding ceremony?"

"I think it will be more appropriate to name it 'the baptism in the storm'. This is more interesting than the one in the swimming pool, right?" Hong Jun dare not continue with the topic of wedding ceremony, because he was contradictory in the heart."

"If this is baptism in water, this is my fourth time." Sheila sighed and seemed to be a bit disappointed.

"What are the prior two times?" Hong Jun was even more interested in Sheila's past.

Sheila did not answer him. She turned around and walked to the elevator. The tour guide was hailing tourists. And Hong Jun followed Sheila.

When they were lifted to the ground by the elevator, Hong Jun and Sheila went to the changing room to return the raincoats and linen shoes. They put on their own raincoats and shoes and went to the parking lot along the path on the island.

In the parking lot, they sat side by side on the grassland at the riverside, and appreciated the beautiful scenery around. Clear water was flushing smooth cobbles. Warm spring wind was swaying tender branches. Sheila leaned her body on Hong Jun's shoulder. Hong Jun glanced at her, and wanted to say something but stopped. Sheila glanced at Hong Jun and smiled gracefully.

The sun was setting in the west, and they drove on the way back to downtown Buffalo reluctantly.

Chapter 16 – The Escape from Death

On the morning of Saturday, Hong Jun and Sheila left Professor House and drove south to New York city. In order to appreciate the natural beauty of the mountains and villages in northern New York and save the traffic cost, they decided to travel on a small road and take the shortcut instead of driving on the highway.

Having exited downtown Buffalo, they went east along No.20 highway. The road was not wide but very flat, and there were few vehicles, so they could keep their speed at 50-60 miles.

At 9 o'clock in the morning, they turned into No.63 highway, refueled the car at the oil station, and went to the toilets at a small restaurant nearby. The restaurant was not an upscale one but very clean. The seats around a dozen tables were all occupied. Most of the diners were residents nearby. They were either chatting or reading newspapers in a carefree manner, which contrasted sharply with the lifestyle of city dwellers who rushed through work and entertainment.

When they were on the way again, the villages on both side of the road became less and less and were substituted by green forests. This was Appalachia plateau. The highway passed through the mountains, sometimes on the peak, and sometimes in the valley. The weather was fine and the landscape was beautiful, and no other vehicles were seen on the flat road. Hong Jun and Sheila both felt very comfortable. However, they soon turned into No.390 highway, and the number of vehicles was increasing. Then they entered No.87 highway through No.17 highway, and reached the northern suburb of New York at four p.m. After taking rest at an oil station, they drove towards Manhattan in high spirits.

Driving in New York was difficult. Hong Jun and Sheila entered Manhattan along with the stop-and-go traffic. They also hoped the the car slowed down, because in this way, they could have more time to check out the map and road signs. New York people did not like to give way to each other in driving, they squeezed in every gap and space, and sounded their horns from time to time.

Hong Jun adhered to the driving principle of "safety first" and "stopping for 3 minutes instead of competing for one second", but his action only invited a lot of horn sounds from behind. The passed through the Central Park and drove into a one-way street that allowed only one car to pass – cars had filled both sides. Hong Jun stopped and went again and again along with the fleet, and some cars often overtook him and came in front of him. Hong Jun was not in a hurry, but people behind kept sounding their horns impatiently.

Hong Jun saw in the reflective mirror that the driver behind him was a black young guy. The guy judged from their license plate that they were not locals, so he sounded the horn, waved his fist and shouted.

Sheila saw it and said gently, "I hope this guy won't take out a gun."

After quite a while, they reached the intersection ahead. Hong Jun turned left, and the guy stamped on the accelerator and overtook them on the right, and shouted curses from his open window which both Hong Jun and Sheila did not understand.

Near the night, Hong Jun and Sheila finally came to the Queens District in the Long Island and found the new home of the car owner. The owner was an old nun named Margaret Sullivan. She inspected the car and was very happy. Then Hong Jun and Sheila had a fancy dinner at her invitation.

Hong Jun and Sheila completed the main task of the journey and felt exceptionally relaxed and pleasant.

On Sunday, the pair decided to visit downtown New York.

In the morning, they took the Long Island train from Queens to the junction train station in Manhattan, then they took the subway for Battery on the southern end of Manhattan Island. They had made sightseeing plans on the travel map. Now their first destination was the Statue of Liberty.

When they came out of the station, it was drizzling. It was still early on that day, so few people were on the street. They walked hand in hand, like lovers, through the street park to the dock. There were already a lot of tourists waiting to board the ships. And many vendors were selling all kinds of souvenirs and food. They bought the tickets, waiting for a while and boarded the sightseeing ship bound for the Statue of Liberty Island along with the tourists.

The drizzle came intermittently. They stood on the upper deck and allowed the wet breeze of New York Bay to touch their faces. Looking at the obscure Statue of Liberty in front of them and the World Trade Center whose top was covered by rain fog, they were both excited and melancholy, because this was not their hometown.

After getting off at the Statue of Liberty Island. They went in the rain to the Statue of Liberty. They first visited the American Immigration Museum built at the foot of the statue, then climbed up towards the head of the statue along the winding staircase.

The winding staircase was wide enough for only one person to pass and was a one-way route. Those going upwards and downwards could see each other face to face but could not get close to each other. They could only exchange a few words of encouragement. Sheila walked in the front and Hong Jun followed. Sheila went and stopped now and then, so Hong Jun used his hand to push Sheila from below. They climbed about 300 steps and finally came to the head of the Statue of Liberty. They panted.

No one was there at this time. Sheila said she was very tired, so she leaned her back at Hong Jun's chest and closed her eyes. Hong Jun surrounded Sheila's waist with his hands and smelled the aroma of her hair. Sheila's hair was rubbing his cheeks, making him itch in the body and heart.

Tourists came from below. Hong Jun pushed Sheila and said it was time to go. They took turns to lean on the gemstone-shape window at the crown and looked into the distance, but gray fog filled their visions. They looked at the unaesthetic copper plates and angle irons around and commented on the handwriting of "I was here" left by the tourists on the angle irons. Then they walked downwards from the other side of the winding staircase. Hong Jun walked in the front this time. He pulled Sheila's hand and looked back at her now and then. Sheila was smiling happily.

After returning to Manhattan, they ate a simple lunch in Chinatown. Then they visited the Wall Street and the Broadway Avenue, took a look at the United Nations Headquarters and the Empire States Building, and amused themselves in the Central Park. As late as 7 o'clock in the evening, they arrived in the Queens District by bus. When they walked towards the home of Ms. Sullivan, Hong Jun's arm naturally held Sheila's waist.

On the morning of Monday, they left Ms. Sullivan and came to Hertz Auto Rental Company to take the car they reserved. They booked an ordinary car, but such cars were not available at this time, so Hertz Company had to rent a Ford deluxe sports car to them at the price of an ordinary car. It was a pleasant surprise.

Since it was Monday, there were many vehicles on the road. They have heard much early that the highway in Long Island was the "longest parking lot in the world", and now they experienced it personally. It took them more than one hour to drive from the Queens District to the Verrazano Suspension Bridge on the southwest of New York.

The double-layer suspension bridge with a span of 1,298 meters was indeed magnificent, and it was thrilling to drive on the bridge floor which was 60-70 meters above water. But the toll was expensive – 6 dollars, which was the highest in this journey.

After entering New Jersey, they turned to No.95 highway from No.495 highway, then they went on No.9 highway. Near noon, they came to the Atlantic City on the Absecon Island.

When they got near the urban area, they saw large billboards with gambling city characteristics on both sides of the road, which signified the prosperity of the gambling city. But after entering the downtown, they only found deserted streets and ordinary buildings. And there were even ruins in some places, which were similar to the slums area. They were a bit confused. Was this really the well-known Atlantic gambling city?

Hong Jun parked the car at the roadside. They checked out the map and made sure they were not in the wrong way. So they drove along.

After more than 10 minutes, they came to the shore. It was almost another world. Wide sky-blue sightseeing vehicles were connected together in fours and fives and running on the wide avenue with tinkling sounds. Large recreation facilities on the flat shore were situated between the sea and the sky and looked like departing warships. Tall and colorful buildings with bizarre shapes were shining in the sunshine like palaces in the fairy tales. However, the most characteristic elements were the people – they wore all kinds of clothes and had different skin colors, and they were fully at ease.

Under the direction of others, Hong Jun and Sheila came into the most luxurious casino in the Atlantic City – Trump Taj Mahal, which integrated gambling, accommodation, dining, shopping, and entertainment. And its luxury overshadowed all first-class hotels and restaurants in the world. The central hall on the first floor was similar to a large self-service shopping mall, but the items on colorful counters for customers to pick up was all kinds of gambling machines, or called "slot machines". Surrounding the central hall was a circle of corridor, and out of the circle was some small gambling halls which offered roulette, pokers, and horse races.

After walking around, Hong Jun and Sheila decided to try their luck on the slot machines in the central hall. They exchanged for tokens with 20 dollars and started playing on a machine.

After half an hour, Hong Jun lost all the tokens to the slot and Sheila's tokens had almost run out. Hong Jun stood behind Sheila and waited for her to lose all the gamble fund.

However, when Sheila pushed the handle for the last time, with a loud nose, the slot machine threw up a large pile of coins. Sheila excitedly jumped and asked Hong Jun to collect the "spoils" for her – 228 dollars in total!

The exchanged the coins into dollars and went out of the casino excitedly.

When they came to the parking lot, Sheila was still very excited. She insisted on driving the car. Since there weren't many vehicles on the street, Hong Jun agreed.

After leaving the gambling city, they drove west along No.42 highway. Cars on this road were even fewer. They could hardly come across one. Sheila was relaxed and happy. She increased the speed gradually from 40 miles to 60 miles while humming songs happily.

After driving for a while, Sheila noticed a green van was following her closer and closer. She turned into the lane on the right so that the van could overtake them, but the van turned into the right lane as well. She speeded up to get rid of the van, but it followed her closely. It seemed that driver behind was deliberately joking with them. When she drove fast, the van behind was fast, too. And when she was slow, the van slowed down as well. When she changed the lane, the van did the same. There were several times when the van almost crashed into their car, and Sheila cried out in fear.

Hong Jun looked back at the van behind, and said to Sheila, "Focus on driving, don't worry about them."

Right after saying this, they heard a loud bang, and their car shook heavily – the van crash into the back of their car. Hong Jun said angrily, "This is crazy! Park at the roadside."

Sheila parked the car at the roadside. Hong Jun said, "Don't get off, I'll take a look." He opened the car door and got off.

At this moment, the van also parked at the roadside. Two black young men went out. One man was tall and the other was short. Hong Jun went to the back of the car and checked out the bumper. He saw a little trace of collision that was not so obvious. Then he went to the side, stooped and saw a less obvious depression at the crashing point. He said to the black guys who were walking towards him, "How are you driving? It's so dangerous."

The black guys went to the back of Hong Jun's car and looked at the trace of collision. The short guy laughed, "Just a gentle kiss. Nothing serious. But our car is damaged."

"That's your responsibility." Hong Jun looked at the Toyota parked several meters from him, and said with confidence.

At this moment, the tall guy took out a gun and pointed it to Hong Jun. He sneered, "If you want to leave here alive, you should give all your money to us."

Hong Jun was stupefied and realized this was a robbery. He asked, "What do you mean? What did you say?", but in the meanwhile, he was thinking about strategies.

Suddenly, the car moved and swiftly rushed backwards. The black guys were hit by surprise and fell to the ground. And the tall guy's gun flied away.

Sheila said, "Go!" Hong Jun quickly got onto the car. Sheila pushed the accelerator, and the car ran forwards quickly. Hong Jun looked back and saw the black guys picked themselves up, and the tall guy picked up the gun and shot twice towards their car. Then the guys ran to their green van.

Hong Jun turned sideways and looked at Sheila. Sheila was very calm. She held the steering wheel tightly, closed her mouth, and stared at the road surface ahead. The car was running on the isolation line of the lane with a speed higher than 100 miles. And the green van was left far behind and disappeared.

Sheila gave a sigh of relief and her foot pressing on the accelerator was lifted a little. After a while, they saw a vehicle in front of them. Sheila hastily slowed down, but they still overtook the vehicle on the left, and the driver of the vehicle hastily shunned them to the right.

Hong Jun looked back and said, "Driver slower."

Sheila slowed down to 65 miles, but whenever there was a vehicle ahead of them, she speeded up and overtook it. They drove in this way for half an hour. Suddenly, Sheila saw in the reflective mirror that the green van was catching up with them, so her relaxed nerves got tense again. She asked Hong Jun, "Is it them?"

Hong Jun looked back and said "Yes."

Sheila's foot pushed the accelerator again, and they got rid of the green van again, but Sheila kept driving in high speed. They were presumably approaching some town, because there were more vehicles on the road, so Hong Jun helped turn on the "double-turn light" to warn the vehicles ahead to shun them. They kept overtaking vehicles, but when they speeded underneath an overpass, a police car's siren was heard from behind.

Sheila saw a police car with flashing light coming from behind in the reflective mirror, and cried, "Too bad. We have speeded. What should we do?"

Hong Jun said, "Slow down and park at the roadside. We need the police."

Sheila parked the car at the roadside. The police car parked in front of them. Two white men in police uniform came off. Hong Jun and Sheila wanted to get off the car, but the police told them to stay inside and wanted to see Sheila's driver's license. Sheila took out her driver's license while narrating what happened. The police heard her narrative with uncertainty, and a policeman even went to the back of the car to see the trace of crash.

Hong Jun was sitting there and did not speak. He kept looking backwards, and when he saw the green van coming out of the overpass, he told the police in a hurry, "See, this is their van."

A policeman stood at the roadside and signed to the green van to stop. But the green van speeded up and ran away, putting the two policemen in a frenzy.

Hong Jun asked the policemen, "Why don't you ask your headquarter to intercept the vehicle?"

A policeman shrugged and said, "It is Pennsylvania ahead of us. Pennsylvania is not our jurisdiction, so the headquarter can do nothing about this."

Hong Jun asked again, "So you just allowed them to run away? And our car was hit by them for nothing?"

The policeman said disapprovingly, "I think you should be happy with your luck. A similar case took place last month. It was also crashing and robbing.

And the victims were a couple on a trip, presumably Germans. But they were robbed and the husband was beaten to death. Young man, you should be grateful to God for giving you a beautiful and resourceful wife. If it had not been for her, you probably could not talk with me like this.

Hong Jun was wordless.

Sheila told another policeman, "What should we do? Will they wait for us ahead?"

"It's hard to say." The policeman said.

"What should we do? They have a gun." Sheila wept.

"Where are you going?" The policeman asked.

"Washington." Sheila said with sobs.

"Don't worry, madam. We can escort you for a while. Philadelphia is near us. We drive in front, you stay behind. There are many vehicles in Philadelphia and you will be safe. But remember to enter Philadelphia first, then change the route to head for Washington lest the guys know your destination. You know, they took a beating so they won't let you go easily."

Hong Jun and Sheila exchanged their seats and went on the way behind the police car.

Hong Jun said the two policemen were good people.

Sheila said, "So there are good people in the world, indeed."

Hong Jun followed the policemen's advice. He first entered downtown Philadelphia, then turned back to No.95 highway and drove south. Since they were not sure whether the danger was eliminated, they were not in the mood for sightseeing or talking. They crossed the Delaware River Bridge and headed southwest through a corner of Delaware into Maryland. Then they passed through downtown Baltimore and arrived in Washington City located between Maryland and Virginia before the night.

They were extremely wary of the green van all the way, but they did not see it since.

Chapter 17 – The Mature Woman and Innocent Man

After driving into the urban area of Washington, Hong Jun and Sheila took some effort and eventually found the Kurti Hotel in the northern suburb of the city before it got dark.

Sheila reserved only a double room to save cost. After all, they were almost brother and sister and it was not the first time they stayed together. They checked in at the counter, parked the car in the underground parking lot, and then came to their room on the 8th floor.

This guest room was 20 square meters. On the left were two single beds lined together, and the beds were separated by a lighting control table similar to a bedside cabinet. On the right were a row of short cabinets and a TV. The door was directly facing a large floor-type glass window, and a writing desk and a pair of sofa chairs were placed against the wall beside the window. On both sides of the door were the bathroom and large wardrobe, respectively.

After entering the room, Hong Jun and Sheila put down their luggage, and let go of their tension, fear, and fatigue on the way. They sat on their bedsides face to face and looked at each other in silence. After several days' journey, especially the dangerous experience, they had many words to say to each other, but they did not know where to start.

Hong Jun looked at Sheila's expression of encouragement. He stood up, walked to Sheila, and held her hands.

Sheila stood up, too. She raised her head slightly to gaze at Hong Jun's eyes.

Hong Jun said with emotion, "Thank you, Sheila!"

Sheila quivered and leaned to Hong Jun's chest.

Hong Jun held her, but he quickly felt her body was shaking heavily and heard her crying. He was a bit worried, and asked her gently, "What happened to you?"

"I...I'm fine." Sheila sobbed and raised her head. Tears were on her face, but she smiled happily. Her look exuded expectation.

Hong Jun's heart throbbed. He lowered his head and kissed Sheila's cheeks and lips gently.

Sheila closed her eyes.

Hong Jun lifted his head as if waking from a dream. He pushed Sheila's body away and said in panic, "Sorry, I should not..."

Sheila looked at Hong Jun affectionately and said gently, "Why are you saying this? No matter what you do to me, I won't blame you. Romance between a woman and a younger man feels so good, really!" Sheila half-closed her eyes, as if relishing the feeling just now, and as if awaiting something.

Hong Jun stepped back and smiled naturally. He said, "Now we should eat. Are you hungry? I'm seriously hungry."

Sheila sighed, "OK, let's have meals. I can treat you today. Just tell me whatever you want to eat. I won 200 dollars, anyway."

They came to the restaurant downstairs. The restaurant was not big, but was elegantly and nobly decorated. Under the central splendid pendant lamp were several large dining tables, which were surrounded by small compartments. In every compartment, there was one lotus leaf-shaped dining table, and on three sides of the table were sofa chairs with shapes matching the dining table. On the table was a pair of golden candle holders with two thick red candles burning without smoke. Metal wall lamps were hanging on both walls, which have the styles of European palace accessories. There weren't many people in the restaurant, and they were eating and talking in low voices, as if afraid of overriding the piano's light and melodious tunes.

A waiter in red and white led Hong Jun and Sheila into a compartment. After taking their seats, Sheila ordered two dishes skillfully, and asked for two glasses of red wine. After the waiter left, Sheila picked up a piece of bread from the basket on the table, cut off butter with knife, smeared the butter over the bread, and then ate the bread with relish.

Hong Jun ate a piece of bread, too, and then wiped his mouth with napkin, "You surely often went to the restaurant when you were in China?"

Sheila nodded with a smile and did not speak.

The waiter soon served the wine and the dishes.

Sheila raised the wine glass and said to Hong Jun, "There is a saying, 'Good luck must come to you soon after escaping the risk of death'. Let's toast our happiness in future."

Hong Jun raised his glass, too, "Thank you for saving my life. Cheers!"

Sheila took a gulp of wine, and red clouds floated on her cheeks quickly. She said, "We go through thick and thin together. Why do you always keep a polite distance?"

"It's not about politeness. I'm grateful for your help indeed. Really, you were very calm and reacted quickly. In such a situation, an ordinary woman might tremble in fear."

Sheila took another gulp and said, "When the Negros came, I just knew they were holding malicious intentions, so I was prepared. I had more experience dealing with such people. To tell you the truth, I have witnessed a lot of such situations. When I was in Beijing, I saw all kinds of rascals and rogues. And there was a scar left by a striking knife on my hips. If you don't believe it, I can let you see."

"I dare not look at it." Hong Jun said hastily.

"What are you afraid of?" Sheila flushed.

"I'm afraid...I might be dizzy."

"Why weren't you dizzy just now?"

"Just now? When?"

"When you were kissing me. Jon, why do you always pretend to be ignorant? Don't you have any true love for me? Am I not worthy of your trust?"

"Sheila, please don't misunderstand. I just feel..."

"Feel what?"

"We don't understand each other fully."

"Love requires such feeling of ambiguity. If both persons understand each other completely, the feeling will be lost. Do you believe it?"

Hong Jun avoided Sheila's vision, as if murmuring to himself, "Actually we have lived together already."

"Then why are you afraid of?"

"I don't know what the tomorrow will be like."

"The tomorrow? Won't you know it the day after tomorrow? Why do you think so much? You can follow your feelings." Sheila emptied the glass and looked at Hong Jun with moist eyes.

Hong Jun drank up the wine, too.

After dinner, Hong Jun and Sheila returned to the room. Hong Jun went into the bathroom and was about to urinate when Sheila opened the door and came in. She said, "Man, please go out."

"Why?"

"Because this is the lady's room."

"Who said it?"

"I said."

"How come?"

"Because I cannot hold myself."

"What are you holding from?"

"Go to hell. I want to urinate."

"I came in first."

"You want to see a girl urinate? Bad boy!" Sheila pushed on Hong Jun's chest gently.

Hong Jun took the chance to embrace Sheila and said, "You are breaking the rule, let me kiss you once more."

"No, I almost pee in my trousers now. Good brother, go out quickly, and I will let you kiss me to your heart's content. OK?"

Hong Jun exited the bathroom and went to the window. He saw the moving lights in the three-dimensional parking building facing him while thinking about the woman in the bathroom.

Sheila came close to Hong Jun and kissed passionately for a while.

Hong Jun was already overwhelmed by desire, but Sheila seemed to be absorbed in thought.

After a moment of silence, Sheila asked gently, "Jon, do you think I will succeed in tomorrow's interview?"

Hong Jun looked at Sheila's eyes and said, "I have faith in your capability."

"I really hope I can get this job, because this job can provide me with security. I'm very tired. I really hope I can live a peaceful and carefree life. But the human proposes, and God disposes. I hope God won't be too harsh on me. OK, it's time to go to sleep. Now it's the second time for us to stay together, but we are doing so in name only. Jon, you can take a shower first." Sheila slowly drew the curtain.

Hong Jun did not speak. He took out the undergarment for change, and went into the bathroom.

After the shower, Sheila went into the bathroom, too.

……………………………..

Chapter 18 – The Arcane Book

On the morning of Tuesday, Hong Jun and Sheila took the subway for the urban area of Washington. Then Sheila went for the interview, and Hong Jun visited the White House.

At noon, Hong Jun came to Dupont Loop Intersection as appointed. When he went out of the subway station by escalator, he saw Sheila already waiting at the roadside.

"How was the interview?" Hong Jun walked to her and asked in concern.

"Not too bad, but I always feel good after examinations." Sheila smiled.

"What did the boss say?" Hong Jun asked further.

"He asked me to go home and wait for their notification. Who knows? Let's not discuss this now. How was your visit to the White House in the morning? Did you get a taste of how the president feels?"

"No, but I think the president may be bored. Suppose I had the chance, I would not want to become one."

"Forgot it. When you cannot eat the grape, you say the grape is sour. Chinese people are all like this, especially men like you."

"You are criticizing a large group of people."

"Not large at all, because we accepted such education when we were small."

"This is profound."

"Is it? Let me enlighten you." Sheila shook her head and said in a thoughtful manner, "Do you remember the tongue twister we learned in childhood? It is the teaching of Confucius and is known to all. You can't recall it? You're dull. I find that you react too slowly sometimes. I made things clear but you didn't react. Well, let me tell you. Remember, this is Confucius' words.

He said, when you eat the grape, you don't say the grape is sour, but when you don't eat it, you say it's sour." After saying this, Sheila laughed.

"You can't make things up." Hong Jun laughed, too.

"Who don't make up things?" Sheila took back her smile, "Didn't I tell you not to be serious with me? But you appear lovely when you are serious. I like to act according to circumstances, and this is required in American society."

"You always act, so I don't know the real you."

"Life is like this. You can carefully analyze people around you, including the most intimate friends, and of course your first love. In fact, they are all acting and wearing masks. The difference is that some people wear masks to please or cheat others, and some do so to protect themselves. Jon, don't be frustrated. Life is like this, and this is not bad. If genuine and ugly faces are all around us, we will not have appetite even in front of delicious food. Let's go, dear brother. Let's satisfy the fundamental desire of humans." At this moment, Sheilas had a sense of achievement, because she not only completed the interview, but achieved Hong Jun's love.

Hong Jun walked to the pizza shop on the northeast corner of the intersection. He was both happy and confused. He felt Sheila was a lovely and mysterious woman. If every woman is a book that is hard to understand, then Sheila might be an arcane one. He devoted his love and obtained hers. But can he understand her? He was not sure, but he decided to read the "book" carefully from page to page.

In the afternoon, they first came to the Capitol Hill. Because of maintenance, the Statue of Liberty on top of the Capitol was moved to the square outside the east gate. This was a 4m handsome bronze man in robe who wore a crown and held a sword. The statue had been situated high above ground, but today it was close to everyone. All tourists fell over each other to have a look and take a photo with it. The Capitol was open to the public, and tourists only needed to pass the security check entrance.

Museums in Washington were well-known in the world and free to visit. Hong Jun and Sheila looked around casually and were filled with emotions. Especially, when they saw the precious Chinese antiques in the history museum, they could not hold their excitement. On one hand, they were proud for the splendor of Chinese history and culture; on the other hand, they were sad that Chinese antiques ended up in another country.

Hong Jun said, "Numerous Chinese antiques ended up in the hands of foreigners. Not to mention the history, many antiques are still smuggled abroad even today. I know an American in Chicago who is very wealthy and likes collecting Chinese antiques. He travels to Hong Kong twice each year to buy several boxes of antiques smuggled from China."

"Hi, we are poor people. We have to sell whatever our ancestors left to us." Sheila said bitterly, "I think it's such a pity to allow smugglers to make all the money. It's better for the government to conduct antique export in an organized manner. They can set up an antique export corporation specialized in excavation, purchase, and export of antiques. Didn't the Middle East countries get rich by exploiting the underground petroleum? Maybe our country can accomplish the 'Four Modernization Goals' ahead of schedule by exploiting the underground antiques."

"Your idea is really..."

"Really great, right?"

"Really wicked."

"Jon, you can't criticize me like that, because there are many people more wicked than me. For example, digging ancestral graves is a very wicked thing. Today, urban residents don't care about ancestral graves, but when you go to villages, you'll see they value ancestral graves more than their own lives. If you plan to dig a family's ancestral grave, they will fight with you. But our country openly dug the ancestral graves of the people, and they exposed the bodies for people to see. Are they wicked? I can tell you, they will suffer from karmic reactions. Some people said Xingtai earthquake is caused by digging the Ming Dynasty Tombs, and Tangshan earthquake by digging the Mausoleum of the First Qin Emperor.

"Didn't you say you are a materialist who don't believe in superstition? Why are you interested in such kind of saying?"

"This is not superstition. This is called, 'What goes around comes around.' I firmly believe in this rule." Sheila said with a contemptuous smile.

Hong Jun looked at Sheila in surprise. He liked to study people's character, but he could not figure out Sheila's personality. He did not want to debate with her, so he kept quiet. Sheila's smile warmed up from coldness, presumably she did not want to discuss the topic, either.

The sun set and lights went on. Hong Jun and Sheila walked back to the hotel in weary steps. When they were near the entrance, Hong Jun saw a green van parked at the roadside. He said casually, "Why is this van the same as the two guys'" But they did not pay attention, because they did not expect the black guys could follow them to this place.

Hong Jun and Sheila did not fetch the key at the counter of the hall after returning to the hotel. They went around to the entrance of the underground parking lot and walked downward. They could not eat in the restaurant every day, because they could not afford it. Today, they decided to get some prepared food from the car and have a convenient meal in the room.

It was dark in the parking lot, and they walked towards the location of their car. Suddenly, Hong Jun saw a flashlight in front of them. He alertly pulled Sheila, and they started to walk lightly. After passing several rows of cars, they saw their white sports car, but two persons were walking beside it. The tall and short figures showed they were the black guys who tried to rob them. So they retraced their steps quietly.

After exiting the parking lot, they hid behind the woods on one side of the road. Sheila said, "How can they find here? What should we do? Shall we call the police?"

Hong Jun thought for a moment and said, "I think it is not necessary, because they are in our vision and we are not in theirs. The situation is favorable for us. Besides, even if we ask the police to come, we can't prove to them they guys tried to rob us; instead, we may get into trouble. Let's wait for a moment and see if we can find a chance to get rid of them."

At this moment, the black guys went out. The tall one was limping, maybe because he was hit by Sheila's car. They did not exit the parking lot. Instead, they passed through the glass window inside and went into the hall of the hotel. Hong Jun and Sheila walked there, stood in the shadow outside the glass window, and looked into the hall. They saw the black guys walking towards the counter.

Sheila said, "I'll get inside to hear what they are doing."

Hong Jun said hastily, "You can't. It's too dangerous."

"It doesn't matter. I was sitting in the car, and they did not see my face clearly." Sheila opened the door and came in.

There were many people in the hall. Some were new guests and some were tourists who just had dinner. Standing outside the door, Hong Jun closely watched the behaviors of Sheila and the two black guys, and was prepared to rush into the hall at any moment.

Sheila casually went to a sofa near the counter. She picked up a handy magazine to hide her face. She attentively listened to the conversation between the black guys and the hotel clerk:

"...we knew each other on the way. He said his name is Zhang, but I forgot it. You know, Chinese people's names are hard to remember. They seemed to be tourists from Taiwan." The short black guy said.

"How do you know they are here?" The hotel clerk was a white young woman.

"Their cars are in the parking lot. We had lunch together yesterday, and they left an important item in our place. We want to bring it to them." The tall guy said.

"OK, let me check. They checked in yesterday?" The female clerk tapped the keyboard. After a while, she said, "It should be them. They man's surname is Hong, and his given name is Jon. They live in Room 814."

"Thank you." The black guys turned around and walked towards the elevator, but the female clerk stopped them, "Where are you going? They are not in the room. They went out and had not returned yet. You see, the key of Room 814 is still here."

The black guys stopped and hesitated. The female clerk said, "You can put the item here and leave your telephone numbers. I can give it to them when they return. No problem."

"No, don't bother. Let us hand it to them by ourselves." The short guy said.

"Miss, can you check when they will leave? So we can decide whether to bring it tonight or tomorrow." The tall guy said.

The female clerk looked at the computer screen and said, "They will leave tomorrow."

"Thank you very much. We will come back soon, but please don't tell them, because we will give them a surprise. Maybe they will give us some gifts. They are driving such a deluxe vehicle and must be rich." The black guys smiled and left the counter. They looked inside at the door of the restaurant and exited through the main entrance.

Sheila calmly went to the side door to the parking lot and found Hong Jun. They stood in the shadow beside the door. They were relieved when they saw the black guys went on the green van and drove away.

Sheila recounted the conversation she heard briefly to Hong Jun, and said, "We have to go now. It will be troublesome when they come back."

"OK." Hong Jun nodded.

They came to the counter of the hall. Hong Jun received the key from the female clerk and asked, "Can we check out now?"

"Aren't you leaving tomorrow according to the your reservation?" The Miss asked.

"But we have some urgent business and must go back to New York tonight." Hong Jun said.

"Of course you can check out, but we can't return tonight's room charge, because it has passed 6 o'clock." The Miss said.

"It doesn't matter. We will pack things up and check out."

"Sir, two black guys wanted to see you just now. They said they were your friends."

"OK, I know. If they come again, just say we are back in New York."

Chapter 19 – The Horror in the Mountains

Hong Jun and Sheila went back into the room. They packed their luggage in the fastest speed, went downstairs and completed checking-out procedures. They felt as if running out of the deathtrap when they drove away from the hotel.

There weren't many cars on the street. Hong Jun drove north and entered No.495 highway which surrounded Washington, and drove west. Then he turned into No.270 highway and left Washington. They drove northwest for more than one hour before they parked and had dinner at a gas station.

After dinner, they resumed the journey. They turned into No.70 highway in Frederick, and after two hours' drive, they turned into No.68 highway and drove westward along the narrow valley in Maryland which separated Pennsylvania and West Virginia.

Now they were in the northern end of the Blue Ridge Mountains, which were high and steep with dense forests and deep valleys. The No.68 highway sometimes rose to the mountain top and sometimes passed through deep valleys. It was dark all around, and only the light of their car provided a small field of vision.

Sheila was snoring softly.

Hong Jun tried his best to open his fatigued eyes and stare at the dim separation line on the road ahead, and he mechanically held the steering wheel. He felt his brain was not listening to his orders – when the car climbed to the mountain top, he would subconsciously consider the stars in the sky as the taillights of automobiles in front, and when he drove down the valley, he could unconsciously consider the woods on both sides of the road as houses. He was really tired. Once in a dreamy state, he almost rushed into the woods. He was shocked and realized he could not drive anymore, so he drove the car into a rest area at the roadside.

When the car was fully stopped, Sheila woke up with a start. She opened her sleepy eyes and asked Hong Jun nervously, "The car broke down?"

"No, I'm too tired. I have to take a rest." Hong Jun leaned his head on the seat back and closed his eyes.

Sheila looked at Hong Jun and said, "Honey, you are tired." Her voice was filled with regret and tenderness, "You might as well sleep on my seat and let me drive."

"You are tired, too. Besides, there isn't a quality visual field at night, which is dangerous for driving. I think it is safe here. They won't catch up with us. Let's sleep, and set off in the morning." Hong Jun put out the engine, lifted up the windows, locked the doors, put down the seat back, and lied down. Soon he fell asleep.

Sheila sat beside him but lost her sleepiness. He looked at the dark forest around and the road which was vaguely seen in starlight. Everything was quite, and only Hong Jun's even breathing could be heard. She closed her eyes but opened quickly, as if she was worried some danger might fall upon them all of a sudden. She looked around, but all around her was stillness, as if there was no life on earth, and only the stars in the sky were blinking.

Suddenly, she discovered some flickering light in the woods behind her, but when she fixed her eyes on the light, it disappeared. She thought it was her illusion, but shortly afterwards, she saw the light again, which flashed across the horizon. A sense or horror arose in her heart. She wanted to wake up Hong Jun, but when she held out her hand, she hesitated and took it back.

The light appeared again, as if behind the hill far away. After a while, a pair of car lights appeared in the hill, and she was relieved. But when she saw the flickering light coming near, another kind of fear emerged in her heart. The car lights moved faster and faster, and finally passed them as quick as a flash, and then slowly disappeared in the woods in front.

Sheila twisted her body and lied back on the seat. Her eyelids got heavier and heavier, and she closed her eyes. Without knowing the time that elapsed, she was awakened suddenly by a sound, and when she opened her eyes, she saw a black figure leaning on the window beside her. She exclaimed in horror.

Hong Jun was awake and sat up suddenly. He was about to ask when he saw in the dawn an animal as tall as a man outside the window. "Bear!" He shouted, and promptly turned the key to start the engine, and then turned on the light.

The sudden sound and light scared the black bear. It fled into the woods in a hurry.

Sheila pressed on her chest and was not yet recovered from the fright, "I was really scared just now."

"So the hero lost to a black bear." Hong Jun laughed.

"I was so scared but you are laughing." Sheila curled her mouth.

"Sorry, don't be angry. I don't mean it." Hong Jun stuck out his head and kissed on Sheila's lips.

"I hate your beard. Really, I want to see how you look when you have it shaved."

Sunshine appeared on the east horizon. The fragrance of trees, flowers, and grass permeated the fresh air. The woods were quiet, and bird songs were occasionally heard.

Hong Jun stood beside the car and moved his stiff limbs, and took several deep breaths. He felt very cozy. When he returned into the car, he adjusted the seat back, looked at Sheila who seemed to be absorbed in thoughts, and drove on the way.

There was almost no vehicle on the mountainous highway. Hong Jun's right foot pressed on the accelerator, and the speed soon reached 80 miles. He knew he was speeding, but he wanted to drive longer when few cars were on the road, so that he could arrive in Chicago before the night. Meanwhile, he was sure the police would not patrol in the mountains so early.

They have already identified a shortcut before departure – on No.68 highway, there was No.40 road, which led directly to the No.79 highway they were about to drive on, and thus eliminated the need to go around south to Fairmont in West Virginia.

When the sun rose on the east, they could see the road sign of No.40 road, so they got off the highway and drove into the mountains through a flat but not wide road. After more than 10 minutes, they arrived in a beautiful mountainous town.

The town was built on a flat sloping field in the mountains. Small buildings with pinnacles which were in mixed colors – red, white, and yellow – were scattered on the mountain slopes covered by green trees. They made people think of fictitious lands of peace. Neat streets in the center of the town and the wide and bright show windows on both sides gave people a modern city impression. The morning fog in the sun brought a sense of harmony to the town. And the melodious chimes of the church reverberated in the silent valleys.

Hong Jun spontaneously slowed down the car, as if afraid of waking up the town's sleep. Both he and Sheila were affected by the town's atmosphere. They quietly appreciated the landscape through the open windows.

When they came to the intersection in the center of the town, the red light was on. Although no cars were around, they still waited. Because he had to observe traffic rules, and more importantly, he needed to determine the driving direction – the No.40 road sign was absent, and there were only two names: Jackson Road and Washington Road. The green light went on, and he decided to drive straight.

After leaving the town, the road became narrower and narrower. On both sides of the road was beautiful and uninhabited forest. They drove past two mountains and came into a mountainous basin. Despite the unparalleled beauty of the meadow surrounded by the mountains, they were not in the mood to appreciate it, because the asphalt road led them to a cottage, and further in front was an earthen road.

The cottage mainly consists of two red houses and two tall cylindrical barns. Hundreds of yellow cattle and a dozen of black and white cows were kept in the fence.

A gray car and a red pickup truck were parked in front of the house. Beside the pickup truck, there was an old man in a hat with curling brim, a lattice shirt, and a pair of strap-type worker's trousers who was loading the truck. Hong Jun decided to ask the way, so he parked the car at the roadside.

Hong Jun and Sheila got off and went to the old man. After greeting him, Hong Jun asked, "Could you please tell me where No.40 road is?"

The old man smoothed out his tidy white beard and asked, "Where are you going?"

Hong Jun said, "We are going to Chicago."

The old man laughed, "Then why do you come to the mountains? You can just drive along the highway."

Sheila said, "We discovered on the map that No.40 road is a shortcut, and heard that the landscape here is beautiful, so we came in. But we didn't expect we got lost."

"I haven't heard of No.40 road. Are you looking for Jackson Road?"

Hong Jun knew American roads generally have a name and a number, but local people often use the names, and outsiders use the numbers. He fetched the map from the car, but there were only numbers on the map. He could not see the names.

The old man looked at the map and said, "It seems No.40 road is far from here. OK. Since God brought you to my home, then please have breakfast with us." After saying this, the old man turned around and walked to the door without waiting for Hong Jun and Sheila's answer. He called out, "Cathy, I tell you a piece of good news – two guests are going to have breakfast with us." After opening the door, he turned around and said to Hong Jun and Sheila, "Come on in."

Hong Jun and Sheila walked inside with the old man.

After entering the house, they passed through the hall and the living room and came to the bright and spacious dining room. Inside the dining room, there was a rectangular hardwood dining table covered by a clean and white cloth, and a pot of flowers was placed in the center of the table. The old man sat at the internal end of the table, and asked Hong Jun and Sheila to sit on the left side. He said, "I'm Richard Eastman. You can call me Dick, but I don't know your names yet."

Hong Jun and Sheila told the old man their names and introduced themselves. Mr. Eastman said, "I just guessed you were Chinese and not Japanese, otherwise I won't invite you into my house. China is a miraculous country. When I was small, my father told me if I dig a hole deep enough, it will reach China. And later I went to China, indeed. But I did not go there through the earth; rather, I flew there. It was during the World War II when I served in the air force. You see, I went to China even before you. Haha!"

At this moment, a kindly and healthy old woman came in from the kitchen and was holding a dish, knife, and fork. Mr. Eastman said, "This is my wife, Catherine, and this is Jon, this is Sheila, guests from the other side of the earth."

Hong Jun and Sheila stood up to greet Mrs. Eastman, and then Sheila helped with her in the kitchen.

Mrs. Eastman said to Hong Jun, "Cathy is as fat as a cow now, but she had a very beautiful figure when she was young. Let me tell you, Jon, you can't let your wife eat too much or sleep too much, otherwise she would be as fat as Cathy. Do you know?"

"We are not married yet." Hong Jun said.

"Ah, I know. Young people today are different from us. They don't marry and men call their women 'partner' instead of 'wife', right? The world changed. Men used to cohabit with women for marriage, but now they cohabit because they don't want to marry. This is inexplicable."

Hong Jun smiled and did not know how to answer.

Mrs. Eastman and Sheila put oatmeal, milk, baked meat strips, bread, butter, and jam on the table. Mrs. Eastman sat on the right side of Mr. Eastman, and Sheila sat beside Hong Jun. While eating, Mr. Eastman asked his wife if she knew No.40 road, and she did not know. After the meal, Mrs. Eastman made several calls in the kitchen and finally understood Jackson Road was No.40 road.

Hong Jun and Sheila were very grateful for their help. Sheila fetched a silk turban embroidered with giant pandas and presented it to Mrs. Eastman. The old lady was very happy. She went into the room and brought a unique gift – an item made by branches which was similar to a battledore. Its oval ring was tied with many cowhells irregularly, and a crude, translucent "gemstone" was fastened in the center.

Mrs. Eastman said to Sheila, "This was made by myself and was called 'dreamcatcher'. You can hang it on the window of your bedroom. Then nightmares will leave you, and happy things in your dreams will become the reality. Sheila, I sincerely with you happy."

Sheila received the "dreamcatcher" and embraced both hosts according to the American custom, and they kissed goodbye.

Mr. Eastman said he would go to town to deliver milk, so he could send them for a while. Hong Jun drove the car and followed Mr. Eastman back to town. When they were near the intersection in the center of the town, Mr. Eastman stopped at the roadside and signed to Hong Jun to turn right at the intersection. Hong Jun and Sheila waved thanks to him and drove away.

At this moment, the town already woke up from slumber. Now there was moving traffic and pedestrians who were not as rushed as city dwellers on the street. Hong Jun said with emotion, "This is a wonderful place. The scenery is beautiful, and people are nice. If I have a chance to choose the place of residence, I will choose here."

Sheila agreed, "Yes, people here are much cuter than those in New York."

Soon after they left the town, they finally saw the No.40 road sign again. They felt at ease and continued westward.

Hong Jun drove for another half an hour, yet he did not see the road sign of Uniontown. However, he saw the signs of road maintenance. He suddenly cheered up and said, "It's not easy. I finally see people."

Since half of the road surface over a long distance was occupied for maintenance, the two-way road was made into a one-way lane. Each worker holding an intercom stood on one end of the road section, commanding the vehicles on both ends to enter the one-way lane in turn. When Hong Jun drove through the section to the other end, he stopped the car next to the commanding worker, rolled down the window and asked, "Can you tell me how far Uniontown is from here?"

"What? Uniontown? It's still far." The work thought for a moment and said, "You can drive about 30 minutes, and turn left at an intersection. You will enter No.68 highway. You should drive west on No.68 highway and try to find the road sign of Uniontown, or ask someone else."

Hong Jun was confused, but he drove back to No.68 highway according to the worker's direction. According to his intuition, they left No.68 highway in the morning, then made a circle in the mountains in the north, and drove south back to No.68. It was a long distance, but they did not make a lot of progress westwards. He finally found the answer at the gas station. The No.40 road was connected to No.68 highway at multiple points, and whenever there is a town in the mountains, No.40 road would extend out into the town; therefore, it was also called "sightseeing road".

Hong Jun consoled himself, "We took a trip in the mountains, so the journey has not been made in vain."

Sheila said, "If we always do this, we won't get back to Chicago until Christmas."

Hong Jun did not speak. He sang softly:

Oh baby don't you want to go

Back to the land of California

To my sweet home Chicago

Now one and one is two

Two and two is four

I'm heavy loaded baby

I'm booked I gotta go...

This was Appalachia plateau. The mountains were high but slopes were gentle, so many roads were built on the mountains. Weather change was fantastic. Once they saw dark clouds in front, as if a heavy rain would come, but when they got near, they only felt several big rain drops falling sparsely. The car was running on top of the mountain, and white fog filled the valleys on both sides, which gave people a thrilling experience. Suddenly, wind made a gap in the dark cloud, and a ray of sunshine came down, decorating the fog ocean with an expanse of golden light.

Hong Jun and Sheila cannot control their admiration of the nature's magic and beauty. They knew they could not get back to Chicago as per the original plan, but they accepted the delay, because they were not in a hurry to put an end to this beautiful journey.

At 5 o'clock in the afternoon, they found a motel named Lennox more than 10 miles east of Columbus, the provincial capital of Ohio. After checking in, they drove out and purchased hamburgers, chips, and drinks at a "non-get-off" fast food restaurant. Such a fast food restaurant was specially designed for drivers. When you drove to the price board behind the restaurant, a waitress would ask you what you wanted to buy in a loud-speaker, but you could not see her face. After telling them the food you wanted in the car, you drove to the first window on another side to make payment, then to the second window to pick up your food. In the entire process, you did not need to leave the driver's seat. If the food you bought could not be prepared immediately and there were other cars waiting behind, the waitress would ask you to drive into the parking lot nearby. When they prepared the food, they would deliver it to your car.

After returning to the hotel and having dinner, Hong Jun and Sheila took a shower. Both of them felt relaxed all over the body, as if the fatigue and tension of these days were all washed away by the water.

Tonight, they held each other and went into sleep.

Chapter 20 – The Distressing Farewell

On the morning of Thursday, Hong Jun and Sheila continued west. They passed through Columbus and went into Indiana along No.70 highway. It was central American plain, and on both sides of the road were boundless farmlands and grasslands. After entering the urban area of Indianapolis, the provincial capital of Indiana State, they turned into No.65 highway and drove north to Lake Michigan, and then into No.94 highway, and drove northwest into downtown Chicago. It was 4 p.m. in the afternoon already. They were excited and hungry, so they drove to an "old village cafeteria" on the west of Chicago and had a large meal.

After dinner, Sheila said to Hong Jun, "Jon, the song I heard you sing on the road – Sweet Home Chicago – was interesting. It was Blues. Do you know? Although the Mississippi River Delta was the birthplace of Blues music, the Chicago Blues was very popular, even more so than the Delta Blues. Have you been to a Blues bar? Not yet? It's a pity. How can you study in Chicago without listening to Blues? I can take you to a well-known Blues bar, which is not far from my previous place. I can treat you, as my thanks for your help." Somehow Sheila's tone carried a bit of sadness.

"Sheila, why did you become distantly polite to me? If we have to say 'thanks', it's me who should thank you, because you saved me in the critical moment, and provided me with the opportunity of free traveling. And the whole week was my happiest time since I came to America."

"Then let's put a perfect end to the happiest time."

"What do you mean" Hong Jun looked at Sheila in surprise.

"I don't mean anything. I mean...I probably will work in Washington, so we have to separate." Sheila looked out through the window.

"It doesn't matter. We can keep in touch by the phone. I can visit you in Washington, and you can see me in Chicago. Traffic in America is so convenient. Don't you trust me? I love you sincerely and have no other intentions."

"Yes, the love is pure, so much so that I dare not preserve it, for fear of polluting it." Sheila spoke in a low voice, as if to herself. At this moment, she had conflicting thoughts in her heart, because her feelings for Hong Jun was complex. In the beginning, her relationship with Hong Jun was an interesting act, at most it added some tinges of romance to the dull and depressive student life abroad. But by living together in these days, she was drawn deeper and deeper to Hong Jun, and it was a kind of love transcending carnal desires. She found Hong Jun had a special kind of charisma that she did not find in all men she was in a relationship with. The charisma strongly attracted her and made her want to love at any risk, even at the cost of abandoning her life beliefs and pursuits. However, she was persuaded by reason that she could not indulge in love because there was a world of differences between them and they would not have a happy ending. She kept warning herself: You must end the relationship decisively, otherwise it will be too late. This is probably the only relationship which can be called love in your life, and if you cherish it, you have to end it. You don't want to hurt Hong Jun, so you have to break up with him immediately, because the longer you stay with him, the more you will hurt him. You have to part from him as soon as possible and as thoroughly as possible.

"Sheila, what do you exactly want to say? Are you worried I will deceive your feelings?" A look of confusion appeared in Hong Jun's eyes.

Sheila saw that, so she raised her voice, "Jon, don't think too much, let's go. I'm familiar with the traffic here. Let me drive for you and you can take a nice rest."

Sheila drove to Fullerton Avenue on the north of Chicago. She parked the car and led Hong Jun to a bar. The entrance ticket was 8 dollars for each. It was the first time for Hong Jun to visit such a place, so he looked around curiously after coming in.

The bar faced south. It was 7-8 meters wide from east to west, and 30-40 meters long from north to south. A thin, long oval counter was situated beside the door at the east wall. Within the counter was a tall wine cabinet and the workplace of bartenders. A row of rotating high chairs was placed outside the counter. On the north of the counter were several square dining tables, and further north was an empty area of ground, in the center of which was a small stage similar to a boxing stage. At the west wall was an array of wooden stands like those in a stadium, and a row of square dining tables were also placed beside the stands. It was dim in the entire bar, and only the light on the small stage was bright. There were many people sitting in the bar at this moment. Hong Jun held Sheila's hand, squeezed though to a dining table inside and sat down.

The performance started very soon. Three bandsmen went onto the stage. One of them played electronic organ, and two played electric guitars. One of the guitarists was white. After a short opening speech, they jointly played a tune that was strictly rhythmical and highly appealing. After the joint performance, they took turns to show their unique skills, including performance skills, postures, and countenances. The white guitarist was not only skillful, but also had a humorous look. Especially, his long lip beard danced to the music and attracted the applause of the audience.

Hong Jun was about to ask Sheila why there was only playing and no singing when a tall and stout black man in his 50s stood up beside the dining table at the east wall. He was wearing a less fitted suit and carrying on his shoulder a yellow "grenade bag". But the bag did not contain any grenade. In the bag were harmonicas of different sizes. Probably he was a famous singer, so the entire bar was filled with applause when he went onto the stage. His singing was wonderful. Sometimes he used high pitch and loud voice, and sometimes low pitch and hoarse voice. He was immersed into the song, which can be seen from his expression. He was in one occasion like weeping, and in another intoxicated. Hong Jun could not fully comprehend the lyrics, but he knew the song was obviously a sad melody, and he was soon overwhelmed. Hong Jun did not understand why the man's singing was so appealing.

All seats at the tables were occupied, and late comers had to sit on the stands at the west wall. Several female bartenders in tight top and miniskirt were squeezing here and there in the audience. They occasionally received cash from the audience, put it into their wallets, and brought alcoholic drinks from the counter. Since the musical sounds in the bar smote upon the ear, all of the bartenders wore earplugs and seldom spoke. They communicated with the audience and counter clerks with mouth shapes and gestures. And their gestures were very graceful. Especially when they asked the counter clerks to prepare drinks, their gestures were like dancing movements, which were very impressive to Hong Jun.

When the black singer took out harmonicas of different sizes in turn to play on them, the entire performance reached its climax. Many audience stood up and danced to the music, and the scene in the bar was like a carnival.

After leaving the bar, Sheila drove Hong Jun back to Evanston. Hong Jun excitedly talked about his feelings in the bar, but Sheila talked very little. She seemed to be focused on driving or immersed in thoughts. When the car arrived in Hong Jun's residence, Sheila carried Hong Jun's luggage into the porch, and silently stood in front of Hong Jun.

Hong Jun held Sheila closely in his arms and kissed her lips enthusiastically. An impulse arose in his heart, and he said sincerely, "Can you come into my room?"

Sheila understood his intention, but she gently pushed him away, and said, "No, please. Let's separate right here."

"Separate? Why?"

"We are unfit for each other."

"The age is unfit? Didn't you say it was nice for a woman to be in love with a younger man?"

"It's not about the age."

"What is it, then?"

"The thing is, we are different creatures. I have thought carefully, you are a good person, and I am a bad person. I wanted to be a good person before, but I changed my mind and decided to be a bad person for the rest of my life. Don't stare at me that way, it's scary. I'm telling the truth. Of course, I won't hurt others for no reason, and I won't hurt you. You may rest assured. But we cannot live together. Just think about it. You want to be a good person, and I want to be a bad person, how can we live together?"

"But we have already lived together."

"You mean making love? You are too serious. I said I like acting. Now I can tell you men are tools of sensual enjoyment for women. You don't want to hear this but this is the truth. Actually many men also think of women as tools of sensual enjoyment, or in other words, tools to satisfy sexual desires. The women should have the same rights. Of course, making love with you enabled me to feel the passion of love, and I like such feeling, but this is not my pursuit. For me, making love is not true love. When love making is finished, love is finished. I don't want to make things so clear and unpleasant, but I must let you know I'm not the woman you want. I'm not the woman who can give you happiness in life. We have to break up thoroughly. Bye Bye!"

Sheila's eyes brimmed with tears. She turned around suddenly, went out of the porch and ran to the car.

Hong Jun followed for a few steps, then he stood at the roadside and watched the car's taillight disappear at the corner of the street.

Since then, Hong Jun never saw Sheila or heard from her. He called up her residence but only heard the voice: "The number was canceled." He used to expect Sheila's call, but his expectation was eventually worn out by ruthless time. He even dreamed about Sheila, but he did not have the "dreamcatcher" to transform good dreams into reality. Once again, he suffered the disappointment and confusion of love life, and he increasingly missed his hometown and relatives. He often repeated the sentence said by an overseas student in the Spring Festival Entertainment Party organized by the consulate: "We are all dreamers, and when the dream left, what remains with us is homesickness." He took out Xiao Xue's photo from his suitcase again and put it into the inter-layer of his wallet.

Day after day, as he was absorbed in hectic life, the happy experience gradually became memory in the deepest corner of his heart.

Chapter 21 – The Private Detective

Lu Ting fell in love with Xia Zhe. As with many young girls in first love, she desired to use her power or even her life to help the person she loved. Sometimes she imagined herself to be a chivalrous woman who rode on a red horse and braved the bullet storm to save Xia Zhe from the execution ground, and to be severely injured and finally die in Xia Zhe's arms on a slope covered by blooming flowers. Whenever she thought about this scene, her heart throbbed, her cheeks warmed up, and she felt unparalleled happiness. But when she was together with Xia Zhe, she was a bit disappointed, because he was slow to respond to her hints, and did not take them seriously, as if she was yet a little girl who hadn't grown up.

Lu Ting liked reading detective novels. Among the works of Arthur Conan Doyle and Agatha Christie, she preferred the latter. She thought Holmes was too old-fashioned, but Poirot was humorous, calm, and lovely. Therefore, she was very familiar with the figures and plots of *Death On The Nile* and *Murder on the Orient Express*. Now she wanted to become a private detective and prove the innocence of her loved one, and then find out the bad guy hiding behind the scenes.

With this plan, Lu Ting went back to her father. She hoped her father could help Xia Zhe, and she decided to know about Hongyuan Securities through her father, especially about Liang and the female clerk. However, Lu Boping went out early and returned home late, and Lu Ting often worked night shift in the hospital. They didn't have much time to meet each other. Tonight, they finally had the chance to have a meal together at home, but Lu Boping did not want to talk about things in the company. After dinner, Lu Boping said he was tired, and he went to his room to take rest. Lu Ting cleaned the utensils and was watching TV in the living room.

The doorbell rang. Lu Ting opened the apartment door and saw a slim, fashionable woman standing outside the security door. The woman was surprised for a moment, but soon said with a smile, "Are you Ting? You have grown up. What a beautiful girl!"

Lu Ting felt she saw the woman before, but could not remember where she did. So she asked in embarrassment, "Who are you?"

"I'm Fang Qiong. I work in your father's company. Is Mr. Lu at home?"

Lu Ting opened the security door and let Fang Qiong wait in the living room. Then she opened Lu Boping's room door and said, "Daddy, someone is coming for you."

Lu Boping went out of the room while rubbing his sleepy eyes. He saw Fang Qiong and asked in surprise, "Why do you come? What's the matter?"

Lu Ting noticed her father's unnatural countenance, so she came into her room and closed her door, but she put her ear close to the door gap to listen attentively. But the TV was on in the living room, so she could not hear their conversation. After more than 10 minutes, she heard the closing of the security door. Only then did she go out, sit on the couch, and continue to watch TV as if nothing happened.

Lu Boping stood by his daughter's side, commented on the TV program, and then said, "Ting, next time when someone comes, you don't need to hide in your room."

"We have an agreement."

"She is the clerk of my company. She wants to change her job position. I told her to discuss work in the company, not at my home. I worked the whole day and was already very tired. Now even my nighttime rest was disturbed. It's annoying." said Lu Boping. And he went back to his room to sleep again.

Lu Ting felt her father's words were a clumsy denial resulting in self-exposure. By a detective's intuition, she was firmly convinced Fang Qiong was her father's mistress. Where did she see Fang Qiong? Her vision moved from the TV screen to the ceiling. She finally recalled it – it was an evening three or four years ago when her father took her to a dancing party. Her father learned dancing in Shenzhen. After returning to Beijing, her father often took her mother to the ballroom, but her mother was conservative and not willing to learn dancing. Later her father found a dancing partner. It was said that they won a prize in a competition. On that evening, she saw her father's dancing partner. She felt the woman was beautiful and had graceful dancing movements, but she did not like her demeanor. Especially, she disliked the woman's smile to her father. She did not know why, but she just disliked her. Later, she heard from her mother that the home-wrecker was exactly the dancing partner. So she kept the woman's demeanor in her heart as a hated object.

Was Fang Qiong the woman? Lu Ting felt she looked like her but she was not sure. She remembered her father said the woman was a movie actor, but how did she become the security company's clerk? She recalled the words of the great detective Poirot: "A detective should connect things in his mind that seemed to be unrelated to each other." So, was this woman the clerk who set a trap for Xia Zhe? After thinking for a while, Lu Ting decided to ask her mother for information.

On the morning of the next day, Lu Ting came to the hospital. After the shift change and ward round, she went into the internal medicine clinic. Zhang Xiaolan was seeing a patient. After the patient went out, Lu Ting asked the next one to wait outside. She closed the door, went to Zhang Xiaolan, and said, "Mom, I want to ask you something."

"What is it? It seems so mysterious."

"Do you remember the name of my father's dancing partner, the mistress who destroyed our family?"

Zhang said unhappily, "Why do you mention your father again? Before you moved to his house, didn't you promise to not mention anything about him?"

"Mom, this is not my father's issue. It's mine. I want to know the woman's name."

"I can't remember."

"Mom, how can you forget that? I don't believe. I know you are just reluctant to mention past events, but this is important to me. Please!"

"Her name seemed to be...Fang Qiong." Zhang pronounced the name reluctantly.

"It is her, indeed!" Lu Ting widely opened her eyes.

"What happened?" Zhang asked.

"She met my father again last night, and covertly, as if she was afraid to let me know it."

"I can never understand why your father didn't marry her."

"Maybe my father was tired of her later. I cannot stand her witch-like demeanor. I think my father is not as bad as you think. He cares for people's feelings. Mom, don't you want to be reconciled with him?"

"Go to hell, wicked girl. Don't talk nonsense."

"Bye Bye, mom." Lu Ting ran out with light steps.

After returning to the ward, she first wrote on a slip, then came into Xia Zhe's ward and put the slip into his hand in an unheeded manner. She felt she was like a private detective, indeed.

Xia Zhe was lying on the bed and hearing his wardmates chatting. When Lu Ting placed the slip mysteriously into his hand, he was very puzzled. When Lu Ting left, he opened the slip and saw the line: "Invite me to dinner tonight. I have important information to let you know. Destroy this slip after reading." Xia Zhe almost laughed. He felt Lu Ting was indeed a cute girl.

At five in the afternoon, Xia Zhe took off the patient clothes and put on clothes of his own. He went to the small garden outside the hospital – their appointed place. Lu Ting ran out of the door. When they met, Xia Zhe asked mysteriously in a low voice, "The secret signal for meeting?"

"What?" Lu Tind did not understand it in the beginning, and when she realized it, she burst with laughter.

Xia Zhe said gravely, "Be serious, don't let the enemy notice us."

Lu Ting laughed even more, and when she finally stopped, Xia Zhe said, "I'm doing so according to your instructions."

"Up yours!" Lu Ting pushed Xia Zhe and wiped tears of laughter from her eyes with her hand back.

"Miss Lu, choose the place." Xia Zhe said in a humorous way.

"Choose what place?" Lu Ting asked in confusion.

"Don't you want me to treat you? Why not choose the place now?"

"I don't. I really have important information to tell you, but I should have a big meal at your cost"

"If you want it, I'm willing to provide. Haha."

"Then let's have barbecue."

They went along the road towards the city moat. After entering the restaurant, they took seat in a quiet location and ordered the dishes. The waitress served meat, vegetables, spices, and beer, and turned on the electric grill. Soon they smelled the flavor of roasted meat.

"Zhe, you don't want to hear my important information?"

"Are you amusing me?"

"Who are amusing you? I want to ask what's the name of the female clerk you mentioned?"

"Which female clerk?" Xia Zhe did not want to talk about Fang Qiong, so he pretended not to know anything.

"Of course the one who caused your bad luck."

"Why are you asking about her?"

"Just tell me first if she is Fang Qiong?"

"Yes. What's the matter?"

"Let me tell you," Lu Ting looked around and lowered her voice, "she was the witch who destroyed my father and mother's relationship."

"Nonsense."

"I'm definitely not lying."

"How did you know?"

"She came to my home last night. In the beginning I did not recognize her, but later I recalled I saw her several years ago. At that time she always danced with my father."

"Fang Qiong liked dancing, but I did not see she had any special relationship with your father. Did you have a lapse of memory?"

"Absolute not. I asked my mother this morning. She told me the home-wrecker was Fang Qiong."

"Fang Qiong is your father's mistress? If so, their relationship is super secret, because no one knows this in the company, and even Liang does not know. Otherwise he would not dare to pursue Fang Qiong. But why do they do this? This is strange."

"I think my father kicked her off, but she still went after my father, so she gave up her career as a movie actress and worked here as a clerk. I hate witches like this."

"Fang Qiong is indeed a witch. I just felt strange about the fact that she gave up movie acting and worked as a clerk. But your father is the manager, if he had not agreed, she would not have been hired. This is complex, anyway."

"It's not so complex. I have analyzed the case. She was the culprit in your incident. Just think, my father kicked her off, wouldn't she hate my father? But she could not do anything to him, so she decided to play a trick on you, because you were the one my father specially cared for. Is my analysis reasonable? I almost become the great detective Poirot." Lu Ting said with complacence.

Xia Zhe appeared to have not heard Lu Ting's words. He murmured, "Fang Qiong is your father's mistress. She is your father's mistress. She..."

"What are you murmuring? Are you obsessed?" Lu Ting pushed Xia Zhe.

Xia Zhe did not answer. He drank up a whole glass of beer.

After dinner, Lu Ting noticed Xia Zhe was in a bad mood, so she proposed to take a walk. They strolled to the Andingmen Overpass on 2nd Ring Road.

The gentle breeze of spring night touched their body, which was a bit heated by drinking, and gave a pleasant feeling to Lu Ting. Xia Zhe had unknown resentment in his heart, but now it seemed to have disappeared entirely. The stood side by side at the stone railings and overlooked to the west.

There was dim red light at the rim of the night curtain, presumably because of the numerous lights in the city. The scattered window lights at the roadside brought their vision to their present location, but the traffic flow in red and white color – one line made up of red taillights, and the other of white headlights – brought their vision to the colorful and dazzling distance again. Road surface underneath the bridge was gleaming. All kinds of vehicles passed by at fast speed, and the high and low roaring sounds added fervor to the tranquility of the night sky.

Lu Ting raised her head and searched in the dark blue sky. Suddenly, she saw an indistinct red star – it was the red light on the TV tower. She shook her head and said in the way of reciting poetry, "Purpose of life is like the red star. Sometimes you feel it is as far as the horizon, and sometimes it appears in front of your eyes."

Xia Zhe finally smiled, "I think you should be a poet instead of a nurse."

Lu Ting glanced at Xia Zhe and asked him seriously, "Zhe, if you have to choose between two girls: one is a nurse and the other is a poet, which one will you choose?"

"Why should I choose?"

"Don't pretend to not know anything."

"I never thought about this."

"You can think about it now."

"I probably will choose a nurse, because poets are more or less insane, especially female poets. But I would hope my girl is poetic. It's better that she is a nurse in the day, and a poet at night."

"Then I will be an amateur poet." After saying this, Lu Ting looked at Xia Zhe affectionately.

Xia Zhe said hastily, "Ting, it was a casual comment."

"A casual comment comes from the heart." Lu Ting shifted her vision to the sky and changed the topic, "Zhe, what is your sign?"

"I really don't know."

"What are the month and date of your birth?"

"February 16."

"Then you are an Aquarius. Great!"

"Why?"

"Because I'm a Gemini. The book says Aquarius was transformed from a very handsome Troy prince in ancient Greece, and that people having the Aquarius sign are enthusiastic, brave, and creative, but less hardworking and less diligent. Does this matches you?"

"Nearly. How about Gemini?"

"They are smart, loyal, honest, fashionable and have a lot of fantasies. They desire a colorful life but are a bit nervous. The famous American movie actress Marilyn Monroe is a Gemini. Zhe, do you think I have the characteristics of a Gemini?"

"You have a lot of them, but why are the two signs special?"

"Because an Aquarius and a Gemini make a perfect couple. The experts said so."

"Really? What is your month and date of birth?"

"A wonderful day – June 6."

"It means everything goes smoothly. You will turn 17 in a month, right?"

"No, I'm 18 already."

"Really? You are an adult now. So I should give you a nice gift."

"What do you want to give me?"

"What do you want?"

Lu Ting thought carefully and said solemnly, "You can give me a kiss. Now! I heard when people of two signs kiss under the clear night sky like this, they can pass their hearts' information to their respective guardian planets. Do you know? Your guardian plant is Uranus, and mine is Mercury. In this way, the guardian plants will guard our happiness in life. Zhe, do you want to give me such happiness?"

"Ting, you don't know much about me..." Xia Zhe liked Lu Ting but he had never thought about this carefully.

"Why don't I know you?" Lu Ting said with a slightly quivering voice, "I have been adoring you since I was small."

"But I face a trial, and I might be sentenced."

"No, I can save you, and I'm the great detective Poirot."

Xia Zhe remained quiet. He turned around and scrutinized Lu Ting with the help of the bright light on the overpass. He suddenly discovered the silly little girl had grown into a slim and graceful woman. So he held Lu Ting's hands. They looked into each other's eyes, and then put their lips together.

The passers-by glanced at them with all kinds of looks. Xia Zhe realized this and pushed Lu Ting away gently, and said, "Let's not perform for their entertainment. Let's go!"

Lu Ting turned around and saw a middle-aged man standing still and watching them from nearby, so she cursed softly, "Creep!"

Then they held hands and went to the moat under the bridge.

On the morning of the next day, Lu Ting came to the hospital ahead of time and asked Xia Zhe, who just got up, to go to the corner of the corridor out of the ward. After intimate greetings, Lu Ting said, "I thought of another good idea last night."

"What good idea?"

"In order to find out Fang Qiong and my father's relationship, I want to eavesdrop on my father's telephone."

"What's the use of it?"

"I feel that Fang Qiong and my father are still connected. I figure she will not come to my home, and she does not want to talk with my father in the company. If she wants to contact him, she has to call. If we can record their conversation, it will be easy to investigate. Is my analysis reasonable?"

"I think you are already a great detective. But how do you plan to do this?"

"This is what I want to ask you. I remember when you took me out to play when we were small, you often asked me to play the scoundrel, and you played the detective. You tried to catch me, and you always made it. At that time I thought you were smart and could often come up with miraculous ideas. Can't you think about it? We both can be detectives this time."

"This is too professional and I haven't studied police surveillance before, so I cannot think of a method. By the way, I remember a person. She must have a method."

"Who?"

"Her name is Song Jia. She is the assistant of Mr. Hong, the lawyer. Anyway, she is competent.. I heard she was in the police before. Besides, she is reliable in this matter."

"Are you sure?"

"No problem! I can contact her. If it's OK, I will tell you, but you have to find a time when your father is not at home. When will your father be out?"

"He is not at home today. Last night he said he would be on a meeting today and would go back home very late."

"Can you ask for leave today?"

"No problem. I can switch shifts with my colleague and work at night."

After breakfast, Xia Zhe called Song Jia and met her. Xia Zhe told her Lu Ting's idea, and Song Jia found it worthwhile to give it a try, so she told Xia Zhe the exact technique she learned in the police academy.

In the morning, Xia Zhe bought the necessary tools. And at noon, Xia Zhe and Lu Ting went home together. They brought a wire out from the telephone line under the carpet and led the wire into Lu Ting's room. The wire was connected to a recording device. They spent the whole afternoon tossing and turning, and finally made the "tapped phone" work. They were especially happy, and discussed the next move.

Xia Zhe was grateful to Lu Ting in his heart. He decided to disclose his relationship with Lu Ting to his parents, so he called his mother and said he would have dinner at home.

Chapter 22 – The Male Whore in Disguise

Bai Mei was very glad to hear his son would have dinner at home. She went out to purchase food and made a call to Xia Dahu. She asked him to get off work early and have dinner at home. Then she got busy in the kitchen for quite a while. When the father and son entered home, a fancy dinner was already prepared on the table.

While eating, Bai Mei was quite excited. She kept asking Zhe to eat dishes and Dahu to drink, but Dahu was not in a good mood.

Upon seeing this, Xia Zhe asked about the wood business, "Dad, how about the wood? Are the goods delivered?"

Xia became irritated as soon as the wood business was mentioned, "Impossible! I was tricked. I worked hard for so many years and built up this business. I wanted to leave it to you, but it was destroyed by the fake foreigner. They are wicked traitors. They grew up in China but now they are harming Chinese people. What kind of persons are they?"

"How did they trick you?"

"Mr. Hong called me yesterday and asked me to sell the wood as soon as possible. I said he was joking. The wood was manufactured according to the dimensions specified by the Hongya Company. Who else would want it? The garbage collectors? Mr. Hong said he thought Hongya Company did not want the wood at all when they signed the contract with me, so they set a water content standard that we were not able to achieve. I pondered on his words and found they made sense. Isn't this a tricky business?"

"Why don't you take them to court? I read a lot of law books in the detention center. I think they at least violated the principle of fair trade and honesty if their behavior is not called a scam. It is a malicious deal."

"The problem is that I have no proof. My copy of contract was stolen, and I cannot provide evidence to anyone."

"The contract was stolen? When was it?"

"Last week. Someone pried open my safes. Nothing was stolen except the contract."

"Did you call the police?"

"Yes, I called. But there is no clue. The police set up the case but I guess they have not investigated. There is no way to investigate."

"Who do you think did this?"

"It must be Sullivan. Who else want the contract, anyway? It's useless to other people."

"Who is Sullivan?"

"The chairman of the board of Hongya Company, a woman named Sheila Sullivan, a fake foreigner."

"A woman can pry a safe?"

"Of course she didn't do it by herself, but she could ask someone else to do it. She has a lot of money. Wasn't it easy for her to hire a thief? I told this to the police, but they said they couldn't act on suspicion, and they needed proof. But I think they were just afraid of the foreign businesswoman. If she was a Chinese without any background, they would have caught her on zero proof and forced her to confess. And I made a mistake, too. If I had followed Mr. Hong's advice to make several copies of the contract, I would not have gotten into the trouble. But now it's too late to regret. It's useless."

"Do you think the contract is still in the woman's hand?"

"Maybe it is, unless she destroyed it. But she has to keep one copy anyway."

"Maybe we can hire someone to steal it back."

"Ridiculous! Do you think it's easy to find a thief? Don't make trouble. Let me think of a solution." Xia Dahu took a gulp of wine and waved his hand, "Well, don't bother. It's not easy for you to go home. Let's discuss your life instead of talking about my trouble."

In fact, Xia Zhe also had his own business to talk about, so he used this opportunity to mention Lu Ting, "Lu Ting helped a lot with my recognizance on bail. If she had not been in the hospital, many things would have been hard to deal with."

Bai Mei did not find the chance to speak, and at this moment, she said, "Ting is a good girl. She is kind and honest. Besides, you grew up together like brother and sister. You have difficulty now, of course she should help you."

"Dad, how do you think about Ting?" Xia Zhe looked at Xia Dahu and asked.

"The little girl seems to be a bit silly." Xia Dahu raised his wine glass.

"She is not a little girl anymore. She is a woman now, and pretty." Bai Mei said in haste.

"What's the use of being pretty. Lu Boping looks good, too, but he is silly." Xia Dahu took a gulp of wine.

"OK, shall we not mention Lu Boping?" Bai Mei asked her son, "Zhe, you just said you have something to talk about. What is it?"

"My own business." Xia Zhe paused for a moment, as if he was picking the right words, "I need some money."

"Son, why do you make it so serious? I thought it is something big. If you want money, you can just take it. We are a bit short of money, but it's enough for you to spend. How much do you need?" Bai Mei said.

"Two thousand."

"Why do you want so much?" Bai Mei said, and glanced at Dahu.

"Ting's birthday is coming, and I want to give her a nice gift."

"She helped you a lot, so it's good to give her a gift." Bai Mei turned to Dahu and said, "Do you think so?"

"Yes," Dahu nodded, "but a birthday gift does not cost so much money."

Xia Zhe said, "If it's just a birthday, 200-300 would be fine, but this time I want to send her a fancy gift, because we are in a relationship."

Hearing Xia Zhe's words, both Xia Dahu and Bai Mei were astonished.

Xia Zhe saw his parents did not speak, so he added, "Actually this is our own business. We don't need to tell you, but I think our parents were familiar with each other, so we don't want to keep it secret from you."

Bai Mei looked at Dahu and saw he was unwilling to show his opinion, so she said, "Zhe, this might not be appropriate."

"Mom, why isn't this appropriate?"

"You are awaiting trial. What if you are sentenced? You should consider Ting's future."

"She proposed the relationship and she is willing to accept my situation. When I was popular, a lot of girls were pursuing me, but after the incident took place, they were all gone. Ting is different from them, because she wants to develop a relationship with me when I'm in difficulty. This is genuine. Of course I will treat her well so that she won't feel she sacrificed for the wrong person."

"Despite this, you can't be lovers because you don't match each other." Bai Mei turned to Xia Dahu, as if she was pleading, "Ah, why don't you speak?"

Xia Dahu leaned back and said calmly, "What do you want me to say? Our son is seeking a partner, and she is a good girl. What a good thing! What are you worried about? Zhe, I think it's not easy for Ting to show her love to you at this moment. I support you on this matter. You are fortunate to have such stupid good luck." After saying this, Xia Dahu took out a stack of cash from his room and put it on the table.

Xia Zhe was touched and said, "Dad, thank you!"

"No!" Bai Mei was still against this. "You don't match each other!"

"Mom, what's wrong with you today?"

"Your mother drank too much today and talked nonsense. Is it right, madam?"

"I still don't think this is appropriate." Bai Mei said.

"Why do you think so? You cannot just object without giving a reason. Why isn't this appropriate?"

"You should at least ask for the opinion of Ting's parents."

"What? You mean my son is not good enough for Lu's daughter?"

Bai Mei was stumped by his words and unable to find anything to say.

Xia Zhe looked at his father's weary look and a feeling of gratitude arose in his heart. After thinking for a while, he asked, "Dad, what's the name of the American woman you mentioned?"

"Sheila Sullivan. The bitch! I really want to catch her and cut her to pieces."

"Where does she live?"

"She lives in Shangri-La Hotel. Ah, why do you ask this?"

"Let me handle this, and you can leave it alone. Dad, let's drink a toast." Xia Zhe filled his glass and his father's glass with wine, and drank up the wine in his glass.

Xia Dahu drank his wine as well. He looked at Xia Zhe's red eyes, and said, "Zhe, what do you want to do? You can't do wrong things. I was speaking angrily just now. We fell, but we can pick ourselves up. I'm trying to figure out a way to sell the wood. And after I recover a bit, I will settle the account with the bitch. You are on bail, so you can't go out and make trouble."

"You may rest assured, dad." Xia Zhe stood up and said to Bai Mei, "Mom, I'll go now."

Bai Mei sat on the couch and was absorbed in her thoughts, as if she did not hear the conversation between the father and the son.

Xia Zhe went out from his home, and the soothing evening breeze calmed him down. Just now, under the influence of alcohol, he had an impulse to meet the woman, but he did not think about the method or the result. At this moment, he thought of his life in the detention center and the love that just started. He hesitated. But he was a person who acted upon what he thought, and he always felt like doing something for his father. He did not have the chance, but now his father was tricked, so he could not stand by as an outsider. But how to do this? He was not a reckless person; surely he could not act whimsically. He needed to exert his wit. He thought for a while and finally came up with a good idea – do the detective work till the end. So he took a taxi to Shangri-La Hotel.

Xia Zhe went into the hall of the hotel. After walking around, he came to the service counter. He said to the female clerk, "Miss, I'm visiting an American guest named Sheila Sullivan. Can you check her room number?"

"Wait a moment." The female clerk tapped the computer keyboard skillfully with her fingers, and then said, "Sheila Sullivan's room number is 1016."

"Thank you."

Xia Zhe left the service counter and found the telephone booth. He hesitated for quite a while before he dialed Room 1016. After a few beeps, he heard a woman's voice from the phone: "Hello!"

"Hello, is that Mrs. Sullivan?"

"Yes, I am. Who are you?"

"I'm the 'happy bachelor'. And girls call me this."

"What do you want me for?"

Xia Zhe tried his best to speak politely with male charm, "You have traveled to China alone, so you must feel lonely. I can accompany you in your lonely times, bring you happy moments, and leave a fantastic and romantic memory in your China tour."

"You words are pleasant to hear, but I'm traveling with a partner."

Xia Zhe heard a man cough in the phone. He paused for a moment, and said, "Sorry, I did not know you are traveling with your husband. Please forgive me. So..."

"Hahah, don't run away. No one is hunting you. Let me tell you, my partner is a female and she does not live in my room. But why do you approach me? Did you see me before?"

"Ah, I don't have such honor. I found you at the service counter, because your room number is exactly the same as my birth date – October 16. I believe in luck."

"This is your good luck. I think you charge money, right?"

"Yes, it is a paid service."

"How much do you charge?"

"100 dollars a time. Of course, I can make it a bit less."

"You are not mean, but I will pay according to your service quality."

"I will guarantee the quality and duration."

"But I'm not lonely tonight. Don't be disappointed, 'happy bachelor', you can wait for me at 4 p.m. tomorrow in the hall. Do you know me?"

"Sorry!"

"You can hold a rose in your right hand, a purple red one. I will cover the cost of the flower."

"Good. Let's meet at four tomorrow afternoon in the hall. I wish you a sweet dream tonight."

"I hope your appearance is as likable as your voice. Bye Bye."

After hanging up, Xia Zhe had a mood that was hard to describe in words, but he was satisfied with his preparation and performance. He decided to continue to play the role. As to how to achieve his purpose, he could only go and see, and act according to circumstances. He thought of Lu Ting and felt he was cheating her, but on a second thought, he was sure Lu Ting would forgive him. It was not because of his disloyalty to love or his lusty desire. Instead, he was spying on the enemy for his father. He felt he was a double-faced detective. It's exciting. Maybe Lu Ting would admire him more.

In order to get familiar with the environment of the hotel, Xia Zhe decided to explore it first. He came to the elevator at the entrance of the western-style restaurant, and rose to the 10th floor. The corridor of this floor was I-shaped, and the elevator was the vertical line. The corridors on both sides were paved with earthy yellow carpets with patterns. No one was there at this moment, and the place was very quiet in the soft light. He looked at the room number signs on both sides. The northern corridor has number 1 to 15, and the southern one has 16-30. The went along the southern corridor to the east end and arrived in front of Room 1016. He listened attentively outside the door, and heard the voices of two people. He could not get the content of their conversation, but he knew it was a man and a woman. And he remembered the cough of a man he heard in the phone. He really wanted to know what kind of man was in Mrs. Sullivan's room in such late hours. Suddenly, the conversation voice became louder, as if both were walking towards the door. He swiftly turned around and went to the elevator.

Xia Zhe stood behind the corner of the elevator area, stuck out his head and watched. The door opening sound was heard, and a man with a crutch went out of Room 1016. He was Lu Boping! Xia Zhe hastily withdrew to the elevator area. After thinking for a while, he took out the sunglasses and put on them. He then turned into the northern corridor. He hid behind the wall corner and heard the steps of Lu Boping approaching, then he heard the elevator moving. He waited until he heard the elevator door opened and closed. He walked out from the wall corner, and looked at the display above the elevator door. The floor number in red had decreased from 10 to 1, and halted. He looked at it in surprise and thought why Lu Boping came here and what was his relationship with Sullivan. Suddenly, a strange thought arose in his heart which consisted of several persons: father, Sullivan, Lu Boping, Fang Qiong, and Liang Gao. It seemed there was some mysterious relationship between them. What was it? The could not tell, but indistinctly felt the threat of the relationship. Thus, he recalled the weird language on the letter – "As man sows, so he shall reap. Let the father's debt be paid by the son and justice be fulfilled. Either he or you are facing disasters and no regret will help." He had a sudden feeling of chill in his back.

A young woman came to the elevator, so Xia Zhe took the elevator with her down to the 1st floor. He stood at the entrance of the elevator area and looked at the hall. When he made sure Lu Boping was not there, he went towards the western entrance along the corridor beside an artwork shop.

Suddenly, a woman blocked his way. He lifted his head and saw Song Jia. He asked in surprise, "Song, why are you here?"

"I'm about to ask you the same question." Song Jia laughed.

"Ah...I'm looking for someone, but happened to see you here. What a small world!" Xia Zhe laughed and thought why everyone came to Shangri-La Hotel.

"Who are you looking for? Do you need my help? I have an acquaintance here." Song Jia lowered her voice.

"No, thank you. This person has nothing to do with my case. It's a private matter. Are you looking for someone here, too?"

"I'm visiting a friend, so it's a private matter, too." Song Jia smiled.

"Oh, I see. So I won't waste your precious time now. Bye Bye."

Xia Zhe turned around and was about to leave, but Song Jia stopped him, "Xia Zhe, how is the thing going?"

Xia Zhe knew Song Jia was referring to telephone tapping, so he said, "It's done. We tried and it worked well. Thank you for your guidance."

"You are welcome. If any result is achieved, don't forget to tell me."

Song Jia went towards the hall, and Xia Zhe took a bus back to the hospital. He decided to proceed with his plan until his purpose was achieved. And he wanted to control his own destiny.

On the afternoon of the next day, Xia Zhe called Lu Ting, who was resting at home, and lied to her that he would go home to visit his mother tonight. Then he went to Shangri-La Hotel. He put on a straight cream yellow suit, blew his hair, and made himself look very energetic. He inserted the small rose he bought on the way into his small suit pocket, and then sat on the couch. He already prepared an action plan: to gain the favor and confidence of Mrs. Sullivan by cheating, seize a chance to take the contract away, and preferably find out the relationship between the woman and Lu Boping. He repeated the lines he prepared in the heart, and watched women who were sitting, standing, and walking in the hall.

At 4 o'clock, Xia Zhe stood up, held the rose in his right hand, and slowly went towards the cafe in the hall. But he did not enter the cafe; instead, he went around in a circle and returned to the hall entrance. He greeted the attendants at the doorway casually, then went into the hall and stood in an obvious location. Some customers looked at him in a strange way, making him feel embarrassed. He felt he was a model in public vision. Suddenly he started to doubt whether he was cheated. He looked at his watch. It was 4:15 already, so he walked to the telephone booth.

At this moment, a woman in fancy clothes stood up from the couch in the hall. She came to Xia Zhe and asked with a smile, "Sir, was your rose bought just now?"

"Yes!" Xia Zhe observed this charming woman and asked carefully, "Are you Mrs. Sullivan?"

"Yes, but you can call me Sheila. So you are the 'happy bachelor'?"

"Yes!" Xia Zhe handed her the rose.

"Your appearance did not let me down."

"And I didn't expect that you are so young and beautiful."

"I told you that this is your good luck. What's your name?"

"You can call me any name."

"You are quite honest, but I know the name you told me is false. I can't always call you 'happy bachelor'. Let me call you...Jon." Sheila did not know why she thought of Hong Jun's English name all of a sudden.

"Jon? So I have become a foreigner, too. This name is uncommon."

"Let's go, Jon. The weather is so good. We can go for a stroll outside." Sheila stretched out her left arm, and Xia Zhe held it with his right hand.

They went out of the glass door on the north from one side of the cafe, and came to the back garden. In the garden, there was sunshine, green grass, bridges, water, corridors, and pavilions. They passed through a white arch bridge and went slowly in the corridor shadowed by the trees.

"Why did you choose this profession?" Sheila asked.

Xia Zhe said with confidence, "I was not able to find a suitable job since I graduated from high school. Recently, a friend introduced this means of livelihood to me. He said I have good conditions for doing this job."

"How long have you been doing this?"

"You are my first customer!"

"Do you say so to every customer?"

"I'm telling you the truth."

"I don't think you are a veteran, either. Shall I pay you double the cost for your first time? Don't be embarrassed. I think the world should be like this — woman are the dominators of society and men are women's play tools."

They came to a rabbit hutch fenced with wire beside the river. Sheila happily bent over the wire and teased a big white rabbit with grass blades. She turned around and said, "Jon, see it. They are so lovely. I like white rabbits since I was small."

Xia Zhe stood behind Sheila. He really wanted to throw the woman into the rabbit hutch, but he knew he could not do this. So he said, "I can see that you are very kind."

"Really?" Sheila stood straight and looked at Xia Zhe with interest, "How do you know that?"

"Before meeting you, I guessed you were an arrogant and strong woman, but later I saw your kindly looks, especially your eyes. Many people say, 'The eyes are the windows of the heart.' I think you have a pair of understanding eyes. Your look makes people feel indescribable warmth, like sunshine in winter."

"You are speaking pleasantly."

"It's real. I think your look is like that of the Bodhisattva of Compassion."

"Unfortunately I don't believe in Buddhism."

"Then it's like that of Virgin Mary."

"I'm half in doubt about Christianity, but I like your flattery."

"I'm speaking the truth. And your attitude towards the white rabbits confirmed my feelings. I think an animal lover is a kind person."

"Not necessarily. I know some Americans. They love animals because they hate humans, and they cannot eliminate the hate."

"I trust my feelings. You are a woman who does not want to hurt others."

"Not for sure, either. When a kind woman is hurt by others, she will take revenge." said Sheila with a contemptuous smile, "Why don't you speak, Jon? You are afraid? Haha, if you don't hurt me, I will surely not hurt you. By the way, you just said you thought I was an arrogant and strong woman. We didn't know each other, but how did you think that way?"

"Hmm...I don't know. Maybe I thought Chinese-Americans with wealth and high social position, just like you, were all arrogant and strong."

"Jon, don't be nervous. I know anyone is nervous when he is doing something new. You spoke pleasantly, but it was a bit like reciting lines. You didn't sleep well last night, do you? Let me tell you, you must be relaxed; you don't need to flatter me. Now that you want to give me a happy and romantic time, you should treat me as your lover. By the way, do you have a lover?"

"I had one before."

"It doesn't matter. I don't mind if you have a lover or not, because we are acting in a play. If you want to act nicely, you have to put yourself into the play. Just imagine I am your lover, will you say the false and flattering words to a girl you truly love? You see, I'm both an actress and a director, because I truly hope we can act nicely in the play. Let's go, it's time for dinner. I can't make you work with an empty stomach. To let you relax, I can ask them to deliver the meals to the room. Jon, do you like Chinese food or western food?"

"I want to have a taste of western food." Xia Zhe stood straight.

"What wine do you want?" Sheila nodded satisfactorily.

"Brandy."

Sheila went to the telephone booth beside the elevator and called the restaurant, then she took the elevator together with Xia Zhe to the 10th floor. Xia Zhe went into Room 1016 as if he was facing death unflinchingly.

Chapter 23 – The Nightmare at a Rainy Night

At night, Lu Ting sat in the nurse duty room in the middle of the ward corridor alone. All patients were sleeping and the corridor was very quiet. She was bored, so she picked up a magazine and turned two pages, but she was unable to read anything. She looked at her watch. It was nearly 11 o'clock now. She told herself Xia Zhe would not come back. She was a bit frustrated, thinking: "You know I'm working night shift alone, but you don't stay with me. You went home last night, and did it again today. Even if your mother was ill, you still should not stay overnight at home. You were too submissive to your parents." She sighed and lied on her bed.

At the time of shift change on the next morning, Xia Zhe was still not back. Lu Ting was angry and went home to sleep.

At noon, she got up from bed, ate the meal, and sat in the living room to watch TV. But she turned down the TV volume so that she could hear the phone ring. Xia Zhe called her yesterday afternoon, and he might call her today. She thought.

However, things did not work as she expected.

As with all young girls passionately in love, Lu Ting hoped the lover could stay by her side at all times, and she was easy to get angry when her wish was not fulfilled, but she was also easy to forgive him when they meet. She was thinking how to treat Xia Zhe when she met him, but she could not figure out a satisfactory solution.

In the afternoon, Lu Ting came to the hospital early to take over shift. She came to No.4 ward directly after she arrived, but Xia Zhe was not there. She asked other patients where the No.3 bed patient was, and they said he had not been back. She lost her composure, walked two rounds in the corridor, then came into the duty room and called Xia Zhe's home.

Bai Mei picked up the phone. She said Xia Zhe was not at home last night.

Lu Ting felt Bai Mei's tone of speech was not as warm as before. With doubt, she put down the phone and thought: is it possible that Xia Zhe's parents objected to their relationship? But Xia Zhe did not say so in the phone yesterday afternoon. What made her most angry was that Xia Zhe lied to her – he was not at home last night but had said to her he would go home. But on a second thought, she was afraid Bai Mei lied to her by saying Xia Zhe was not at home when he was. She thought of the stories of arranged marriage in movies.

After thinking over, Lu Ting decided to check it once more. She asked a male patient to pretend to be Xia Zhe's friend and call his home.

Again, it was Bai Mei who received the call, and she gave the same answer.

Lu Ting was indeed angry. She told herself not to bother with Xia Zhe anymore.

It started to rain after dinner, and thunders came intermittently over the roof. Lu Ting sat alone before the desk in the nurse duty room. As time passed, her grudge against Xia Zhe decreased, and an uneasy feeling became stronger and stronger. She thought, where he would go? If he went out to borrow money from friends, he would have told her. And social security was not good at present...An ominous feeling arose in her heart.

She went out of the duty room, came to the staircase, and expected to hear familiar footsteps from downstairs.

The night grew late. The rain got heavier and the wind appeared.

Lu Ting toured every ward. All patents were sleeping and the ward area was very quiet. The sounds of the wind and rain were almost blocked outside. The lights in the wards were all turned off, and only the wall light in the corridor, which was distant from her, were giving soft and dull light. Her soft-soled shoes got wet when she passed the bathroom. They produced squeaks while she was walking, which made her feel as though someone was following her.

Suddenly, a partially closed window at the end of the corridor was blown open by the wind, making a sudden loud noise, and the sounds of wind and rain, which was blocked outside, came in altogether. She was so scared that all her skin hair stood straight. She summoned up her courage to go there and close the window, and then she went quickly back to the nurse duty room.

Lu Ting sat beside the desk. Her heart was beating fast. She used to work night shifts and was never scared. But today, she didn't know why fear gripped her heart and body. She kept looking back with wide-open eyes at the white wall behind her, as if some unforeseen danger was creeping towards her from the wall. Suddenly, she subconsciously felt a black shadow was moving outside the window. She turned her head and saw it was the white light of lightning which cast the swaying tree shadow on the curtain. She laughed at her timidity in her heart, so she decided to not look at anything. She bent over the desk and closed her eyes.

She hadn't slept well for two days, and the fear had tortured her till exhaustion. It was very quiet in the room, and the small alarm clock on the desk was ticking. Dream words of the patients came occasionally through the corridor.

……………………………….

Suddenly, heavy steps came from the corridor. Lu Ting got very nervous and scared. She tried to stand up, but her legs were too flaccid to use any strength. She wanted to call out to the doctor sleeping next door, but she could not make a sound, as if her throat was blocked by a cotton. The steps drew near her room and finally stopped outside the door.

Lu Ting stared nervously at the cream yellow door.

The door moved twice and opened soundlessly, but no one was there, and it closed again soundlessly.

Lu Ting rubbed her eyes with confusion. And when her eyes were opened again, she saw a man with blood all over his face. She looked carefully and found he was Xia Zhe.

She exclaimed and ran towards him...

Lu Ting rubbed her knee, which was hurt by the desk edge, and kept thinking about the nightmare she had just now. She stood up swiftly and went to No.4 ward, and saw No.3 bed was still empty.

Lu Ting spent the night in anxiety and fear.

The shift changed, but Lu Ting did not leave immediately. She waited until 8 o'clock but Xia Zhe was still not back. Then she went home with fatigue.

After entering, she saw no one was at home, so she first called Bai Mei first and knew Xia Zhe was not at home. Bai Mei asked her what happened, and she said he was not back in the hospital. Since Xia Zhe often stayed nights outside, Bai Mei was not too worried. She said Xia Zhe was busy with his case and told her not to meet him too often.

After hanging up, Lu Ting was very frustrated. She wanted to have a nice sleep, but was not able to. Xia Zhe's appearance in her nightmare kept coming to her mind.

She suddenly recalled the "tapped phone", and thought maybe Xia Zhe called her home, so she took out the tape and played it in the tape recorder. There was no Xia Zhe's phone call, but in the recordings of different lengths, two dialogues attracted her attention. They were the conversations between her father and two women, who did not mention their names but whose voice sounded familiar. She thought for a while and considered it was necessary to talk to Mr. Hong and Song Jia. She would ask them to hear the recordings and to help find Xia Zhe.

Lu Ting took out the tape with recordings and put in an empty one. Then she went to Friendship Hotel by bicycle. Xia Zhe mentioned Mr. Hong was working in Friendship Hotel. By asking around, she finally found Hong Jun Law Firm in the business building at the northeast corner of the hotel.

Hong Jun was not there, but Lu Ting met Song Jia. She told Song Jia her name. Song Jia warmly received her and asked her what was the matter. She took out the recording tape and asked Song Jia to hear the two dialogues. Song Jia also felt both dialogues might be related to the case, so she copied them. Then they talked about Xia Zhe. In response to Song Jia's inquiry, Lu Ting admitted her romantic relationship with Xia Zhe, and mentioned the incident she was most worried about – Xia Zhe was missing.

Song Jia heard Lu Ting's words and pondered for while. Then she said, "I saw Xia Zhe in Shangri-La Hotel three days ago. He said he was looking for someone there. Do you know whom he was possibly looking for?"

Lu Ting said, "I only know he planned to borrow money from some friends, but he has a lot of friends, so I'm not sure."

"He is on bail now. If he runs away, things will get more complex. Ting, from your judgment, do you think he will run away?"

"Absolutely not! He trusts you and Mr. Hong the most, and he is confident with the lawsuit. So I think it's not possible for him to run. I'm worried something bad might happen to him. If he has got a large sum of money...Song, I dare not think further." Lu Ting said with tears in her eyes.

"Don't make blind conjectures. Let me analyze for you." Song Jia paced with hands behind her back, and imitated Hong Jun's tone, "First, Xia Zhe did not tell you his plan before he left, but given your relationship, if he will take some important actions, he will surely not keep it secret from you. So it's likely that he suddenly decided to do something that was not in his plan. Second, he did not see you since he had dinner with his parents, but he called you once, and lied to you on the phone. Therefore, he was probably doing something related to his family and not related to yours in the past two days, and he probably did not want you to know what he was doing. So what was the most probable thing that a man in love would prefer to lie instead of telling the lover? It was looking for another woman. Third, his father was doing some big business with a Chinese-American woman, and the woman lived in Shangri-La Hotel. Therefore, it was very likely that he came to Shangri-La Hotel to find the woman. This is my rational conclusion."

"Song, your analysis makes sense, but where is Xia Zhe now? He can't live with the woman, right?" Lu Ting frowned.

"Oh, yes! This is a problem. He certainly cannot live there, but where is he living? I reasoned for a while but came back to the starting point." Song Jia made a fist with her right hand and moved it in two circles as Hong Jun did, and then suddenly tapped on her head and said, "By the way, let me make a call."

Song Jia dialed the number of the telephone exchange of Shangri-La Hotel, and then reached Mrs. Sullivan's room. Chen Jingyi received the call. Song Jia said with her less fluent English, "Hello, may I speak to Mrs. Sullivan?"

"Mrs. Sullivan is not in. May I pass on the message for you? I'm her secretary."

"I am a journalist of *China Daily* and want to interview her. When will she be available?"

"I think she will be available tomorrow. How can we contact you?"

"I will call you tomorrow morning. Thank you! Bye!" Song Jia put down the phone and stuck her tongue out towards Lu Ting. Fortunately Lu Ting did not understand what she said.

"Song, what did you say?"

"I guess Xia Zhe is tracking the woman. You know, one cannot make phone calls when he is tracking someone. Maybe this is the reason he lost contact with you." Song Jia put her hands behind her back again and said with contracted brows, "If my reasoning is correct, Xia Zhe should be back to the hospital tonight."

"Song, I think you are extraordinary. You learned it from Mr. Hong?" Lu Ting said with admiration.

"We learn from each other. Everyone has his own advantages and disadvantages. We are all the same." Song Jia had a feeling that she became the king when the real one was absent.

"Song, I heard from Xia Zhe that you and Mr. Hong are a perfect pair. Mom-and-pop stores are so popular nowadays. Maybe you can change the law firm into a mom-and-pop firm." Lu Ting said in earnest.

"Hi, unfortunately I don't have a good birth. We all have our own destinies. We can't expect to obtain something that does not belong to us."

"I think you have a good destiny. You work in such an upscale office, and it's like your home."

"No way! I'm a servant with keys, but I don't own the place. I was born a servant. It's not possible for me to be a lady." After saying this, Song Jia noticed she said something wrong, so she stuck out her tone and added, "I mean I'm destined to be a secretary, and not a lawyer."

But Lu Ting was laughing incessantly.

"What are you laughing at?" Song Jia pretended to be angry, and said, "Go back to the hospital and see if he has returned."

When Lu Ting walked out of Friendship Hotel, she was enormously relieved.

Chapter 24 – The Telephone Tapping

Hong Jun came to the Physical Evidence Authentication Center of Renmin University of China. He found his previous teacher and asked him to compare the handwriting on Xia Zhe's handwriting sample with Xia Zhe's signature on the copy of the authorization sheet. And he decided to submit an authentication application to the court if the teacher considered the signature to be forged. Then he came to the Residence Registry Section of the Public Security Bureau of Xicheng District. After taking some effort, he finally obtained the information he wanted. He was relieved because now he had a basic understanding of the case, but some details should be verified.

Hong Jun visited Lu Boping again at Hongyuan Securities. But he had a different intention from his last visit. Last time he was seeking Lu's support for his investigation, but now he considered Lu as his object of investigation.

Upon meeting, Lu shook hands with Hong Jun warmly as before. He offered a seat and asked, "Is everything going well? I have a lot of work, so I did not ask. Do you need some more help?"

"It goes very smoothly. Thank you for your help, Mr. Lu."

"It's nice to hear. How about Xia Zhe's case?"

"It depends on the verdict of the judge, but I'm confident with the defense. I want to have a look at the form he filled out at account opening and the sheet he made at the time of closing. Is it OK?"

"Of course. We are obliged to assist in the lawyer's investigation. These files are kept by the deputy manager Liang. Wait for a moment." Lu picked up the phone and asked the secretary to bring Liang Gao here.

While waiting for the secretary's response, Hong Jun stood up and went to the writing desk. He appreciated the exquisite electronic calender with great interest. Lu saw it and laughed, "This calendar is a gift from a Hong Kong friend. If you like it, you can take it away."

"How can I do this? I can't take things people love. Besides, the thing I'm most interested in is your crutch. It's uncommon and practical. I want to have someone make the same for me, so that I can use it for physical defense and safekeeping of important files. It's safer than the safes, right?" said Hong Jun. He picked up the crutch beside the writing desk and started appreciating it.

"I totally agree. Safes are actually not safe at all. They can only guard against amateur thieves. I have a comrade-in-arms who works in the police station. If you have listened to his explanation of how professional thieves pry open safes, you won't put precious items in the safe anymore. I can tell you, this is similar to battles. Obvious forts are easy to capture, but hidden blockhouses are hard to conquer. You should put things at invisible locations. To tell you the truth, when I'm on a trip, my safe only keeps some daily use items. The important files and cash are put in the crutch. However, it is empty at ordinary times."

"Can I open it and have a look?"

"Of course."

Hong Jun screwed off both ends of the crutch, and closely looked at the long tube in the middle. He spoke some words of praise, and put them together again.

At this moment, the secretary came in and said, "Mr. Lu, Liang has a female guest who seems to be a Hong Kong businesswoman, can you ask Mr. Hong to wait for a while?"

"I asked Liang Gao not to deal with the messy Hong Kong business people, but he did not follow my instruction. Mr. Hong, let's go and have a look." Lu started going out.

"Maybe it's inappropriate for me to go." Hong Jun said.

"Didn't you hear it is a female guest? If we don't go there, they will chat until the off-work time."

Hong Jun followed Lu Boping to Liang's office. Lu knocked on the door with his crutch, and pushed it open and went inside before they could answer.

When Liang saw it was Lu Boping and Hong Jun, he stood up unnaturally and said, "Mr. Lu and Mr. Hong, let me introduce to you: this is Miss Chen Jingyi from America. She is interested in Chinese stock market. Miss Chen, this is our manager Lu."

Lu shook hands with Chen.

Then Liang said, "Miss Chen, this is Mr. Hong. He is an overseas PhD who studied in America."

Chen nodded at Hong Jun and said, "We know each other."

Hong Jun nodded with a smile.

"Really?" Liang said, "so the world is too small."

Lu said to Chen, "Miss Chen, sorry for interrupting your conversation." Then he said to Liang, "Mr. Hong wants to look at some materials in connection with Xia Zhe's case. Please make necessary arrangement and let him have a look. He can make copies, and we should support him."

"Yes!" Liang answered. Then he asked Miss Chen to wait for a while, and led Hong Jun away. And Lu went back into his office, too.

Liang led Hong Jun into an office, said something to a Miss, and went out quickly.

The Miss took out some forms and sheets according to Hong Jun's requirements. Hong Jun looked at them and found a few worth research, so he asked the Miss to make a copy.

Hong Jun left Hongyuan Securities with a satisfactory smile, but some question appeared in his mind – why did Chen Jingyi come here? Why did he happen to see her? Is it really because the world is too small? I thought of an American proverb: if something is too good to be true, then it is not true.

When Hong Jun was back to the law firm, it got dark already, but Song Jia was still waiting for him.

Upon meeting him, Song Jia said mysteriously, "I have found the caller ID and identified its location."

"The call asking for my leg?"

"Yes!"

"How did you find it?"

"This is called 'Fancy finding by sheer luck what one has searched for far and wide.'"

"Don't keep me guessing."

"I found the number on the phone bill record at the telephone office, and noticed someone used this phone to call our firm before that."

"So he called twice, and the first call was not received."

"The first one was received. I received it."

"Why didn't you tell me?"

"Because it was not him who called."

"Who is it?"

"Guess it." Song Jua put her hands behind her back and looked at Hong Jun with a faked serious countenance, "Let me test you today. Actually this is a very simple IQ test."

Hong Jun looked at Song Jia's face with interest, thought for a while, and said, "It's me, isn't it?"

"How did you guess it?" Song Jia was a bit disappointed.

"Your facial expression told me." Hong Jun's thought quickly returned to the phone call, "therefore, the person called me from the telephone booth beside Hongyuan Securities. Good news!"

"Why?"

"Because the real intention of the call was neither my leg nor money. It is intimidation. The people of Hongyuan Securities called to intimidate me. This is the logical explanation."

"So you ended up as the smart one. Why?" Song Jia murmured.

"Because I'm smarter than you, indeed."

"You are annoying."

"You look good when you curl your mouth."

"Go to hell."

"Let's get to work. Did you buy the cellphones?"

"I bought them." Song Jia took out two cellphones and put them on the table. Then she took out a cassette and said, "Mr. Hong, you can listen to this. We have an accidental discovery." She put the cassette into the recorder and pressed the "Play" button. A phone conversation came out from the recorder.

…………………………..

"Hello?" This was a man's voice.

"Hello! Boping, it's me." This was a woman's voice.

"Oh, honey, what's the matter?"

"How was the thing going?"

"It's almost done. You can't be too anxious in this matter."

"But I'm worried. You know, Hong is hard to deal with. I'm worried not only this thing will fail, our other things will also…"

"Watch your words."

"I know, but I'm afraid."

"What are you afraid of? Even if the sky collapses, the taller people can support it on their heads. As long as you are patient, we can pass through this difficulty. OK, darkness will end and the dawn will come. Just wait for my good news."

…………………………..

When the cassette was running blankly, Song Jia said, "Is this dialogue interesting? But the following one is even more so."

…………………………..

"Hello?" It was the voice of the same man.

"Hello, Boping! Is that Lu Boping?" This was the voice of another woman. She spoke in a haste and low voice.

"This is Lu Boping. Who is that?"

"You can't even recognize my voice?"

"OK, now I know who you are. How are you? Why are you calling me? Do you have anything urgent to deal with?"

"Of course something urgent came up. Very urgent!"

"Please tell me."

"I can't tell you on the phone."

"It's so late now. It's inconvenient."

"Tomorrow morning. We can appoint a place."

"I can't meet you tomorrow morning. I have an important meeting and I have to go."

"Then at noon."

"How about 1:30 p.m.? Where do you think is convenient for you?"

"Suit yourself."

"We can meet at the back gate of Beihai. I'll have a meeting there."

"OK."

"Don't meet at the park entrance. Turn right after entering and see me at the 3rd bench beside the lake."

"OK."

....

Hong Jun looked at Song Jia, frowned and asked, "Where did you get this?"

"From the telephone in Lu Boping's home, of course." Song Jia said with satisfaction.

"It's illegal to tap phones. Who asked you to do this?"

"I didn't do it. I just told them how to do it."

"Who did this?"

"Lu Ting. Who cares when the daughter wants to tap her father's phone at home? I just provided some free technical consultation for her."

"Did Xia Zhe know it?"

"He is the accomplice. But he hasn't heard the recording, because he was missing." Next, Song Jia narrated Lu Ting's visit in the afternoon and her analysis, and said with satisfaction at last, "How is it? Did I do a good job, Mr. Hong?"

"You want a bonus again?" Hong Jun teased her.

"You only know the bonuses. Don't you have any other means of rewarding me?" Song Jia murmured.

Hong Jun heard her words and laughed, "Are you complaining? OK, I can treat you to a seafood dinner at Friendship Palace. We can play bowling after dinner at my cost. Is it OK?"

Song Jia liked playing bowling, so she jumped happily like a child.

After dinner, Hong Jun and Song Jia came to the bowling alley. They rented a lane, put on special leather shoes, and started playing. Hong Jun was not skillful in bowling, but he could play steadily and accurately. He was eager to perform before Song Jia was ready, so he won a game first. From the second game, Song Jia kept playing "all down" by a good hook, and eventually won two games consecutively with a much higher score. Both of them played happily until they left the Friendship Palace at 10 o'clock.

Hong Jun drove Song Jia home. On the way, Song Jia wanted to show that she was well-informed of current events, so she talked lightly about what she heard at the police station two days ago: "Mr. Hong, the No.2 case in Beijing was finally cracked. It's not easy."

"What No.2 case?" Hong Jun was interested.

"It was a case of burglary targeted at large yards and houses in which senior officers and celebrities live. A total of 15 cases took place last year in the eastern and western parts of the city. It's said the stolen properties are worth more than 1 million yuan."

"Is it the 'cat burglar' case?"

"Yes, the lad had real skills. He was chased by the investigators to the dead end of an alley, but he scaled the wall and escaped. It's said that he was good at high jump in the middle school, and later learned martial arts."

"It seems this case has only limited influence on people's sense of safety."

"That's true. Just see what kind of people he was stealing from. Someone said this was the '2nd land reform', and others said the police should check how the officers could be so wealthy. At present, all kinds of people exist in the world. I saw two guys quarrel on the street that day, presumably because their bicycles crashed, and many people surrounded and watched them. No one mediated; instead, some people said, 'They don't fight. Boring!' Later a lad said to one of the quarreling guys, 'He crashed into you while riding, you just swore at him? It's too easy for him.' And then he sneaked to the other guy and said, 'He swore at you that way, but you dare not beat him, you are a coward.' At his instigation, they fought and he watched the fun. What kind of people are they?"

"It's indeed abnormal." The red light of the intersection ahead was on. Hong Jun stopped the car, looked at Song Jia, and said, "Aren't you watching the fun at that time?"

"What can I do? Two guys were fighting. And I'm a woman. If I mediated, what would people think of me?"

"Fine, the duty of improving social morality has fallen on the shoulders of men like us." The green light went on, and Hong Jun started the car.

"But don't forget men are backed up by women. Without women's encouragement and support, men can't achieve anything." Song Jia curled her lips.

"So you women like instigating others to do things." Hong Jun was in a good mood, so he was joking with her.

"Up yours! You men are the instigators. I'm instigated by you to run errands. I'm tired but I have to maintain a good attitude." Song Jia complained.

"You are doing so to make money." Hong Jun rejoined.

"Oh, please spare me. If my intention was to make money, I would have gone somewhere else." Song Jia retorted.

"What are you working for?"

"I'm working for nothing."

"You are serving the people wholeheartedly."

"I don't have such kind of high level political awareness."

The car arrived at the downstairs of Song Jia's place. Song Jia got off and said in earnest, "Thank you, Mr. Hong, I'm very happy tonight. You don't need to give me bonuses anymore. As an alternative, you can play bowling with me every month. Good night!"

Chapter 25 – The Full Sexual Service

Sheila's suite consisted of two parts: inside was a bedroom with a bathroom, and outside was a multipurpose living room. Upon entrance, one could see a large wardrobe on the left and a square space separated by the lattice shelf. A glass tea table and four soft chairs were placed in the square space. On the inner side of the large wardrobe was the door to the bedroom, and a set of sofas were placed between the door and the French window. Opposite the sofas was a TV set, and between the TV set and the window were a writing desk and a chair. There was another door between the TV set and the lattice shelf, which was closed. A large bed was inside the bedroom, and two armchairs were beside the bay window. A TV cabinet and a luggage desk were opposite the bed. And there was a door to the bathroom. The carpets, curtains, sofas, and bedspreads of the entire suite were in the color of orange yellow, which appeared splendid under the golden ceiling lamp.

After entrance, Sheila sat on the couch in the living room and looked at Xia Zhe with interest in the way of watching a pet.

Xia Zhe walked around in the living room and praised it with an amazed expression. He went to the large French window, looked at the scenery outside and said excitedly: "This is 3rd Ring Road, and that is Yuyuantan Park." Then he turned around and went to the writing desk. He looked at the files piled on the desk while pointing his finger to the closed door, and asked Sheila what was the use of the door. Sheila laughed and said it was for escaping. She said, "If you want to flee from battle at night, you can run out through the door." Xia Zhe said in earnest, "I won't flee from battle." He took off his coat, opened the wardrobe door, and hung his coat on the hanger. He found there was a small fridge and a small safe within the wardrobe, and a black code case was placed on the safe. He said it was his first time to see such a safe and he was very interested. He looked at it carefully and asked Sheila why there wasn't a key. Sheila said it was a coded lock which required the customer to set a password, and the customer only needed to memorize the password after locking the safe. Xia Zhe praised it, then he came to the bedroom door and asked Sheila if he could get inside and have a look. Sheila said, "Of course you can. You need to get familiar with your work environment." Xia Zhe took a turn in the bedroom and bathroom and saw the red suitcase on the luggage desk was half closed, so he pretended to look at the TV cabinet while glancing at the suitcase. He saw the number of the coded lock was left at 516.

At this moment, the doorbell rang, and a hotel worker went inside while pushing a double-layer dining trolley. He put food on the tea table as directed by Sheila and exited.

Sheila stood up, walked to the table, and offered Xia Zhe a glass of Brandy. Then she got a glass of red wine for herself. She raised the glass and said to Xia Zhe, "Come on, Jon, let's drink a toast and celebrate our chance meeting and love at first sight."

Xia Zhe walked to her, picked up his glass and clinked it with Sheila's, then drank up the wine. But he said bitterly right away, "It tastes bad. It's even not as good as Erguotou."

Sheila said with a smile, "If you are not accustomed to drinking Brandy, you can drink some red wine. This is French wine with good taste."

Xia Zhe prepared a glass of red wine and filled Sheila's glass as well. Then he raised the glass and said, "Maybe we can drink 'cross-cupped wine'".

"You can't wait to do it? The bridegroom is always so impatient when he gets in the bedroom." Sheila squinted at Xia Zhe, "But we can't get in bed immediately after drinking the cross-cupped wine. You have a lot of things to do before your work."

After drinking the cross-cupped wine, Xia Zhe ate milky grilled fish and drunken snails with a great appetite, but Sheila only ate some green vegetable. So Xia Zhe asked, "Sheila, are you bored with daily consumption of delicacies?"

Sheila smiled and said, "Yes, people are bored with whatever they have taken too much of."

"So you are living a happy life."

"Happy? Do you think eating delicacies every day is happy? If so, happiness would be way too simple. I can tell you, Jon, happiness is a personal feeling. It does not have a universal standard. The happiest thing for you may not be happy for others. And your happiest experience today may not appear happy to you tomorrow. Take me for example, I had considered having a big meal in a restaurant as the greatest happiness in life, but when I had the capacity to eat in the best restaurant every day, I was unable to connect the delicacies with happiness."

"So you once were a poor person."

"Yes, a total proletarian. Once I only had 5 pennies with me."

"How did you get rich?"

"You want to learn it? Let me tell you, luck is as important as personal effort."

"When I can have such good luck?"

"I think you have good luck now."

"This is my worst time."

"Why?"

"I have no work, no money."

"But you have met me. It's your time of good luck. If you can make me satisfied, I can help you."

"Can you give me a job?"

"There are plenty of jobs, but what can you do?"

"I have a variety of interests, such as stocks..."

"You trade stocks, too?"

"Ah, no. I don't have enough money to trade stocks, but I'm interested in it. I heard it's easy to make money by trading stocks. If you can lend me some money, I'm sure I can win." Xia Zhe suddenly had a new idea – even if the original purpose could not be achieved, he could still gain her trust by cheating and let her invest for him. This is "killing two birds with one arrow."

"Jon, I understand your feelings. When you are poor, you are anxious to become a millionaire overnight. But stock trading is highly risky. Besides, it's too early to discuss this. It's better that you do your work at hand."

Xia Zhe also realized that he had made an unreasonable request, so he said hastily, "Actually the thing that most interests me now is not the stocks or such."

"What is it?" Sheila lifted her eyebrows.

"It's what I should do now."

"Great! This is appropriate for your position. OK, you can take a hot water shower, and then," Sheila took out a bottle of perfume from her room, handed it to Xia Zhe and said, "spray this on your body. It will make you more charming."

Xia Zhe went into the bathroom.

Sheila called the hotel staff to take away the utensils, then she put on a light pink silk nightgown. The nightgown only consisted of two parts at the front and back, and there was only hollow embroidery at several parts. A few silk belts were tied on both sides of the waist, which perfectly delineated the female figure. Sheila added some perfume to her body, turned on the luminous light, half-leaned on the head of the bed, and waited. But she did not see Xia Zhe come out after quite a while. She felt strange so she walked into the bathroom.

Xia Zhe had already finished a shower. He was wearing a yellow silk nightgown and sitting on the toilet. Sheila asked him what was the matter, and he said he was not feeling well in the stomach, presumably because the food was too cold. Sheila looked at him carefully and joked, "Dear bridegroom, you are too nervous. Xia Zhe nodded and admitted that, because it was indeed his first time. Sheila said, "It's fine. You can relax, and I will wait for you on the bed."

After struggling for a while in the heart, Xia Zhe finally made up his mind. After standing up and plucking up his courage, he exited the bathroom and walked towards the bed.

……………………………

Xia Zhe lay naked in the quilt. He was very tired but could not go to sleep. His mood at the moment was very complex. He did it with hatred, and he even imagined he was raping the woman, but the intimate physical contact gave him the illusion of love. Because of this, he was ashamed and distressed, although he kept telling himself this was simply a means to finish his special task.

Sheila gave out even snores. Xia Zhe quietly got up, put on his nightgown, and sneaked to the living room. He closed the bedroom door, came to the writing desk, opened the desk lamp, and skimmed the documents. Most of these files were written in English, and he did not find the wood purchase contract. He was a bit disappointed. On a second thought, he came to the wardrobe. His opened the wardrobe door very gently, yet the door still produced squeaks. He pushed open the bedroom door and saw Sheila was still sleeping. Then he pulled the door of the small safe; he was happy it was unlocked, but when he opened it, he saw it was empty. He looked at the code case; it was locked. He tried to turn the coded lock but he could not open it. At this moment, he heard voices behind the closed door, so he went to it and put his ears on it. It seemed someone was talking behind the door. He hesitated again and again, but he finally turned the key on the door out of curiosity. It was opened, but there was another door inside, and the voices came from behind the door. He gently turned the handle, but could not open the door. Suddenly, someone patted him on the back and caused him to start. He looked back and it was Sheila.

Sheila was in a nightgown. She stared at him with her sleepy eyes and asked, "What are you doing?"

Xia Zhe said with trembling voice, "I got up to go to the toilet, and I heard voices behind the door, so I had a look. You terrified me."

"Really? I thought you are escaping."

"Is it another room on the other side?"

"That's someone else's room. It's midnight. Don't scare them. Go back to sleep."

Xia Zhe followed Sheila back to the bedroom and crept into the quilt.

On the morning, Sheila was in high spirits. She felt as though she was many years younger. After breakfast, she said to Xia Zhe, "I want to travel in Shidu, and you can accompany me. This is called 'full sexual service' – eating, sleeping, and playing."

"Why should we go to Shidu?" Xia Zhe thought about the contract and asked casually.

"To visit an old friend." Sheila said with a dignified countenance. Then she took out the code case from the wardrobe, put it on the bed and opened it. She took out some documents from the code case and put them into her suitcase. At a glance, Xia Zhe saw the word "Contract" at the head of a document. He got nervous. Sheila took out some clothes from the suitcase and put them into the code case. Then she locked both boxes and carried her code case out of the bedroom. She called the front desk staff and asked them to hire a taxi, then said to Xia Zhe, "Let's go."

"Wait for a while, I'll go to the bathroom." Xia Zhe went into the bathroom.

Xia Zhe helped Sheila to carry the code case and took the elevator down to the 1st floor. The taxi was already waiting outside. Xia Zhe put the code case in the trunk. When he was about to get on the taxi, he suddenly shouted, "Ah, my watch! I must have lost it beside the wash basin while washing hands. Sorry for that, I'll go get it."

"Why are you so forgetful. Go quickly. Here's the key." Sheila frowned but she had no other way.

Xia Zhe took the elevator to the 10th floor and ran to Room 1016. He opened the door and closed it after entrance. He went into the bathroom and took the watch which he had left there purposely; then he came to the luggage desk and swiftly turned the coded lock of the suitcase to number

"516"; then he pressed the block pins, and they opened as expected. He was excited, but when he was about to unzip the suitcase, he heard the sound of someone opening a door with a key. He stretched out his head and saw the mysterious door moved and opened, and a young woman walked out.

They surprised each other upon meeting. The woman asked, "Who are you?"

Xia Zhe said, "I think I should ask you this question."

"I'm Mrs. Sullivan's secretary. I live in the next door. What do you do?"

"I'm her friend. Today I'm going to accompany her to travel to Shidu. I came back to get my watch." Xia Zhe said while taking out his watch from the pocket and showing it. He did not intend to stay longer, so he said "Lock the door," and went out quickly. When he went downstairs by elevator, he was a bit afraid and regretful.

Xia Zhe and Sheila got on the taxi and left Shangri-La Hotel. They headed west all the way and arrived in Shidu near noon. After getting off at the parking lot, Sheila went to the ferry along the trail at the mountain side. She stopped and went again and again silently on the way, and occasionally picked white flowers from the grass at the roadside. Xia Zhe followed her and asked her why she was picking white flowers, but she did not answer.

When they came to the bridge, Sheila squatted beside the water. She tore down the little white flowers one by one and threw them into the clear water. Her lips were trembling slightly and tears rolled down from her eyes. After quite a while, she stood up and wiped her tears with a tissue, and then took out a powder box and fixed her makeup.

Xia Zhe looked at her quietly. He seemed to have seen another side of the woman.

Sheila finally shifted her vision to Xia Zhe and said, "OK, let's go."

Xia Zhe asked in a low voice, "Your friend died here?"

Sheila nodded, "Yes, many years ago."

"How did he die?"

"He died for me."

"Drowned?"

"No, he was stabbed to death. I'm visiting him today and now I fulfilled my wish. OK, let's not mention him now. The painful thing has passed, and it's time for us to play happily. Jon, I like this place most in Beijing. It has beautiful mountains and clear waters. It's awesome. Have you been here?"

"No, I just heard of it."

"OK, let me be a free tour guide for you."

Sheila and Xia Zhe climbed up the mountain slope on the north along a small path and saw the Grand Buddha. Then they came back to the river and took a ride on an amphibious tank. Sheila was very happy and laughed from time to time.

Weather changed very fast in the mountains. It was all clear in the morning, but dark clouds converged in the afternoon. They went back along the river. On the way, Sheila noticed Xia Zhe was a bit listless, so she ridiculed him, "Jon, you are thinking about money again? You made 200 dollars last night, and today I can pay you another 300. It's enough for you to spend for half a year. Our ancestors said men's happiest moments are no other than the wedding night and the time of promotion. Of course, modern people are a little different. They want promotion, money, and a mistress. You are doing good now. You slept with a woman and made money. What are you unpleasant with?"

"I'm not unpleasant. I'm just a bit tired."

"You were worn out last night. Someone said sexual impulse could transform a gentleman into a rough barbarian. I experienced it last night, but I liked it." Sheila said with a smile, "Oops, my bridegroom, you should have got up late after the 'wedding night', but you had to rise early and travel so far. It's hard for you. OK, let's live here today and have a good rest."

They spent the night in Shidu Hotel.

After breakfast of the next day, they went down the river by car and came to Liudu. They got off and went to the picturesque Gushan Village along the earthen road at the mountain side.

The sun rose from the east, and the mountains and waters under the blue sky were beautiful and comforting. They took a ride on a motorboat and started entering the village and mountains. Many local farmers were pulling their horses outside the village gate. They were trying the best to solicit business from tourists.

Sheila had never ridden a horse, and she could not resist the horse owner's persuasion and Xia Zhe's instigation, so she finally sat on the horse, but she insisted Xia Zhe escort her on her side. After entering the village gate, they went upwards along the valley. Sheila was nervous in the beginning, but after going for a while, she felt the horse was submissive and knew the way, so she relaxed herself and relieved the horse owner of the duty of pulling the rein.

The mountain road wriggled up along a creek. The upper you reached, the narrower the road became, and sometimes you had to wade through the water. The horse was well trained. It was able to walk steadily on stones in water and narrow stone steps. When they came to a steep cross wall, the horse could not continue forward. So Sheila got off the horse and went with Xia Zhe on foot.

The scenery was extraordinary. Green forest was on both sides, clear water was under the feet, and bizarre rocks were seen over the head. The passed through the "one-line-sky" valley, which was worthy of the name, and watched the thrilling "roller rider" performance. If not for the drizzle, Sheila really wanted to play until the night.

The went back under the cross wall and found the horse owner. Sheila rode the horse and pulled the rein in an experienced manner, and shouted randomly as the horse owner did. Xia Zhe had to hide and follow beside her from time to time, which made her laugh heartily. Suddenly, a horse behind push the buttocks of Sheila's horse with its head. Sheila's horse rushed forward all of a sudden, and caused her to shake and fall. Fortunately, Xia

Zhe took action swiftly. He jumped to her and supported her, but he fell onto the stone.

Sheila picked up herself and hurried to prop Xia Zhe. Xia Zhe's right leg hurt badly and could not stand up. The horse owner was terrified. He swore at his horse and said he would return Sheila's money.

Sheila lifted Xia Zhe's trousers and saw a large swollen part below the right knee, and it was bleeding. There was blood on Xia Zhe's hand as well. In an experienced manner, she asked Xia Zhe to try to move his right leg, and she was sure the bone was not broken, so she said to the horse owner, "Rest assured you don't need to pay for this or return the money. Just send him down the mountain."

The horse owner nodded and hurried to carry Xia Zhe on his back, but Xia Zhe declined. At this moment his pain was relieved a bit, so he stood up with Sheila's help. After discussion, Xia Zhe agreed to go down the mountain by riding the horse. So Xia Zhe got on the horse with the help of the owner and two other tourists. The horse owner pulled the horse in front and Sheila protected Xia Zhe at his side. In this way, they went down the mountain.

After exiting the village, Sheila asked Xia Zhe to rest on a large stone, and she hailed a taxi. On the way to the urban area, Sheila put Xia Zhe's right leg on her own. She looked like a sister who cared for her younger brother.

When they arrived in Shangri-La Hotel, Sheila insisted that Xia Zhe stay in her room first and they send for a doctor to bind up the wound. When the doctor left, Xia Zhe insisted on going home and did not let Sheila see him off.

Sheila put 1,000 dollars in an envelop and gave it to Xia Zhe. Then she asked in earnest, "When will you come again?"

Xia Zhe said, "It depends on when you need, but I hope you can give me other kinds of opportunities."

"You don't want to work in this profession anymore?"

"I hope it is a part-time job."

"What else do you want to do?"

"Maybe I can be your assistant or your agent in China, if you trust me."

Sheila laughed, "So you are ambitious, but I like ambitious men. OK, you can visit me at 10 tomorrow morning and tell me what you think. You can't expect too much, either."

Xia Zhe limped off the place. Now he had a definite target: he would make use of this opportunity to get a large sum of fund from Sheila. And he was confident in this matter.

Chapter 26 – The White Lie

Since Lu Ting said goodbye to Song Jia, she left Friendship Hotel and went back to the Peace Hospital. She directly came to No.4 ward. Upon entrance, she saw Xia Zhe lying on No.3 bed. In an instant, the forgotten anger came back to her heart. Xia Zhe saw Lu Ting, so he sat up and greeted her, but Lu Ting turned around and went out.

Xia Zhe sighed, lied on the bed resignedly, and closed his eyes. He was a bit distracted. When he left Shangri-La Hotel, he felt he did a good job and was considering how to continue his action to the end. But when he returned to the hospital, another feeling prevailed. He wanted to see Lu Ting, but he dare not face her clear and bright eyes. A sensation of shame tortured him in the heart, and he felt sorry for Lu Ting.

Lu Ting went back to the duty room and said to herself: "Ignore him! Ignore him!"

After shift change, she went the rounds of the wards. While passing by Xia Zhe's bed, Xia Zhe called her name, but she pretended to have not heard it and walked away.

In the evening, Lu Ting sat in the duty room alone. Suddenly someone knocked on the door, and she guessed it was Xia Zhe, so she deliberately sat with her back facing the door, and said aloud, "Come on in!"

It was Xia Zhe, indeed. After coming inside, he went over to her and put his hands gently on her shoulder, and said, "Ting, are you still angry with me?"

Lu Ting moved his hands off her shoulder and said angrily, "How can I get angry with you? I'm angry with myself."

"Ting, I know you must be worried these two days. Actually I wanted to call you but I did not have the chance. Ting, don't be angry with me, OK?"

Lu Ting suddenly turned around and asked, "Please tell me first what did you do these two days. Don't tell me you were visiting your mother."

"Of course I was begging people to lend me money. What else can I do?"

"Nonsense! Who did you borrow from in Shangri-La Hotel?"

"I...one of my brothers got rich and he lived in Shangri-La. So I met him there."

"Brother? I guess it was a sister."

"You...who told you?" Xia Zhe was surprised and said slowly, "I have done this already, and you won't believe me anymore. Maybe I should not have done this, but I don't mean to cheat you. One day you will understand." Xia Zhe said with sentiment. Having said this, he turned around and limped towards the door.

Lu Ting was surprised and caught up with him, "What's wrong with your leg?"

"Nothing, I was injured by collision." Xia Zhe held the door handle with his right hand, turned around his head and said.

"Don't move, let me have a look." Lu Ting grasped Xia Zhe's arm, propped him, and dragged him to the chair. She had him sit on the chair, and then she crouched, lifted his trousers, and saw that his right knee was wrapped in gauze and blood was seeping out. Lu Ting raised her head and saw Xia Zhe's hand was bleeding as well. She opened her eyes widely and looked at his face, and asked, "How did you get these?"

Xia Zhe smiled slightly and said, "I accidentally fell onto the curb when I got off the taxi. It doesn't matter. I'll be fine very soon."

"This wound was not made by falling onto the curb. You are cheating me."

Xia Zhe remained silent for a while, then he stood up slowly and said, "You'd better not ask me anymore. There is a lot of confusion in my mind. Please forgive me. I don't know what I did in the two days, either. You'd better forget me. I can't give you happiness, I only make you suffer."

Lu Ting was stupefied by Xia Zhe's words, but she soon came to her sense. She said, "No, you can't leave me. I won't ask you anymore. I love you no matter what you did or what happened to you. I love you forever." She placed herself in Xia Zhe's arms and wept, as if all frustration, distress, anxiety, and fear had flowed out of her body, and only love remained – the love more precious than life.

Xia Zhe lifted his head. Tears rolled down his cheeks and fell onto Lu Ting's hair. He was moved by Lu Ting's pure love. He really wanted to tell her everything, repent, and ask her forgiveness. Even if he had a just cause, would she forgive him? Xia Zhe felt he betrayed his conscience, because he did something mean.

Xia Zhe and Lu Ting stood face to face silently. Both of them wanted to get rid of the embarrassment, but had no idea how to do it. For the first time they felt they did not have an appropriate topic.

Lu Ting broke the silence, "Zhe, do you have a recorder?"

"I have a small one. What's the matter?"

"I almost forgot our action worked."

"What action?"

"Eavesdropping."

"Oh, really? Where's the cassette? Let me listen."

"I have brought the cassette with me. Go get the recorder."

Xia Zhe took out his small recorder from his ward. Lu Ting put the cassette in it and played the phone recording. Then she looked at Xia Zhe and said, "The second woman was like your mother, but I could not figure out the first one. Was she Fang?"

"The second one was my mom. No doubt. The first one was like Fang Qiong, but it was also not like her. She did not speak in that way normally. Let's listen again."

Lu Ting played the tape once again, but Xia Zhe was still not sure whether the first female caller was Fang Qiong due to the noise. But he was most interested in the second call. He said, "My mother called your father at midnight. What urgent business did she have? And they planned to meet each other in the park."

Lu Ting said, "I also feel this is strange. It's just like they were dating."

"Don't guess. Their speech tones showed that there was some urgent business. Was it in connection with your mother?"

"Absolutely not. Maybe it had something to do with your father?"

"If it had been in connection with my father, my mother would not have spoken with your father. When did they call?"

"Maybe the night three days ago."

"The night three days ago?" Xia Zhe pondered for a moment and said slowly, "Was it in connection with us?"

"Why?"

"On that day, I told them about our relationship at dinner, and my mother reacted strangely."

"What did she say?"

"Nothing."

"She felt I was not good enough for you?"

"No, she just said..."

"What did she say?"

"She just said she was afraid your parents would not agree."

"Really? But when I called her these days, her attitude was very different from before. She was cold to me."

"Why did you call her?"

"To find you. Didn't you say you were home?"

Xia Zhe became speechless.

Lu Ting did not notice Xia Zhe's facial expression. She frowned and said, "But there was no reason for her to call my father so quickly and make things so mysterious."

"I think there was nothing serious. My mother, you know, makes a mountain out of a molehill when anything happens."

"I hope so, but I have a premonition these two days."

"What premonition?"

"I feel our relationship will probably not go smoothly. I don't know why, but I have such a feeling."

"Good things take place after setbacks."

"I'm just afraid good things might turn into bad things after all the setbacks." Lu Ting sighed.

Xia Zhe saw Lu Ting's sad expression. He held her to his chest and said affectionately, "Ting, I'm sorry I made you suffer. I will repay for your love in future. Trust me!"

"I don't want you to repay me. As long as you truly love me, I'm not afraid of frustrations or sadness. I'm willing to take them, because I love you. My life and everything is yours."

"I love you, too. I was in love with other women before, but only by being in a relationship with you have I understood real love. Perhaps I cannot tell you at this moment some things I did, but please trust me I'm loving you sincerely, and you are my only lover. Ting, do you trust me?"

"Zhe, I trust you!" Lu Ting's eyes brimmed with tears again, but she could not describe what she was feeling at the moment – happiness, joy, grief, or pain?

The night grew late.

Chapter 27 – The Investment Trap

At 10 a.m. the next day, Xia Zhe came again to Shangri-La Hotel. He first made a call downstairs and then came into Room 1016. After entrance, he held Sheila's hands as prepared, looked at her affectionately and said, "Do you know I did not sleep well last night because I was missing you."

"Really?" Sheila said indifferently, and gently but resolutely pulled back her hands. She turned around and walked into the living room, sat in her armchair, and spoke to Xia Zhe in an official tone, "Sit down, sir."

Xia Zhe was surprised. He sat down slowly, but his eyes were fixed on Sheila's face. He asked in confusion, "What's going on? Are you angry with me? Am I late?"

Sheila smiled and said, "Don't expect too much. I just want to remind you not to forget your position. You are not the 'happy bachelor' today. You are visiting me to get another kind of job. People need to always remember their roles in life, and one person might have multiple roles. This is like acting. When you try to play a new role, you must forget your previous one. In this way, you can avoid chaos and unnecessary trouble. This morning I'm not the woman who seeks pleasure with you. I'm the chairman of the board of Hongya Company. I must talk with you from the standpoint of the company."

"I understand." Xia Zhe straightened his back.

"Sir, since you want to work for us, you should let me know your real name."

"Oh, I'm She Guo." Xia Zhe was prepared for this, and "She" was derived from "Zhe".

"What's your name? 'Zhe Guo'? It's interesting."

"It's not 'Zhe Guo', my name is 'She Guo' – the word 'She' is the same as the one in 'She Taijun' (a famous heroine), and 'Guo' is the same as the one in 'Guo Jia' (means the country)."

"Ah, the phonetics of Chinese language is really complex, and this is the most difficult aspect for foreigners who are studying Chinese. OK, Mr. She, let's return to the subject. Tell me your thoughts." Sheila leaned her head on the back of the armchair.

Xia Zhe took out a packet of cigarettes from his pocket, and asked, "Can I smoke?"

"Sorry, this is the business zone."

Xia Zhe put the cigarettes back into his pocket and said confidently, "Mrs. Sullivan, I have studied the stock market a lot in these two years. There is no doubt that Chinese stock market is not mature yet, and it is at a preliminary stage of development. Since it is immature, the regulations are not yet fully developed. And this is where we can make great achievements. Heroes rise up in chaotic times. Once Chinese stock market is fully regulated, people have to obey the game rules, and the profit would become very small. I think this is the best time to invest in Chinese stock market. If we succeed, we'll get a return that is 10 times or 100 times of the cost within half a year to a year. But high income depends on a large capital, and only in this way can we control or even manipulate the market."

"Mr. She, do you have a specific standard for 'large capital'?" Sheila asked with interest.

"At least 1 million."

"RMB?"

"Yes, RMB."

"This is not much money, but how can I believe you are a suitable person for doing this type of job? You are just an armchair strategist."

"In fact, I often study the stock market in these two years, and sometimes I trade for my friends. Unfortunately I don't have the capital, otherwise I would have become a millionaire. I'm not boasting. If you give me 1 million, I'm sure I can double the amount in a year." Xia Zhe stood up with excitement.

"Sit down, Mr. She, don't be excited as soon as you think about money. It seems money is more attractive to you than women."

Xia Zhe sat on the sofa again, and smiled with embarrassment. He said, "They are different."

"Of course they are different. Women are the controllers of society, and money is their tool to dominate. Mr. She, I can see that you are fascinated by the stock market. OK, let me think how I can help you. I have a friend who is the manager of a security company in Beijing. I can introduce you to him and see if he can give you any opportunity."

"Certainly it's good if you have the relationship..." Xia Zhe hesitated a bit because he thought of Lu Boping. On one hand, he wanted to find out the relationship between Sheila and Lu Boping; on the other, he was afraid Lu Boping would destroy his camouflage."

"Ah, by the way, I have a person here who has the same interest. Do you want to know her?" Sheila stood up.

"Who?" Xia Zhe was a bit nervous, but he tried to maintain his smile.

"Don't be nervous, you have met already. A peer may not be an opponent. You can help each other or compete with each other." Sheila went to the writing desk, picked up the phone, dialed a number and said a few English sentences. After a few minutes, Chen Jingyi walked inside from the door beside the TV.

Xia Zhe saw that it was the woman who messed up his plan on the morning two days ago. He stood up quickly and shook hands with Chen. Chen sat on the sofa beside her.

Sheila said to Chen, "Mr. She knows a lot about Chinese stock market and advised me to invest in it. You are also interested in Chinese stock market. So I want to hear your opinions."

Chen said to Sheila, "Madam, my knowledge of Chinese stock market is very limited, but I'd like to hear the valuable opinions of Mr. She." Then she turned to Xia Zhe and said, "Mr. She, you have become a stock expert at such a young age. You are a promising young man. How long have you been trading stocks?"

"Miss Chen, I'm far from an expert. I just help my friends and learn by myself."

"There are a lot of security companies in Beijing. Which one do you go to most often?"

"Hongyuan..." Xia Zhe said the word thoughtlessly, but then regretted.

"Hongyuan Securities? What a coincidence. I'm very familiar with their managers Lu and Liang. Do you know them?"

"Ah, I don't know. I often go there with my friends, but I'm not familiar with the brokers." Xia Zhe swallowed and said, "I just told Mrs. Sullivan. I did not trade much, but I understand a lot about Chinese stock market and I have reliable information sources. Maybe you also know that Beijing stock market is not fully developed yet and it has a similar pattern to Shanghai. Not to speak of the rest, Shanghai has millions of stock investors, but Beijing has only 0.2 to 0.3 million. One should have a good understanding of the trend of Shanghai stock market if he trades stocks in Beijing. I think I have advantages in this matter."

"Mr. She, do you have friends in China Securities Regulatory Commission?"

"Sorry, this is my business secret."

An elusive smile appeared on Chen's face. She asked again, "What do you think is the most important thing in stock trading in China?"

"It's the capital. As long as you have a large capital to back up your trade, the market will work according to your command."

"Do you mean manipulating the stock market? I'm afraid it's not easy. Suppose you have enough fund, will the mainland government turn on the green light for you? The '2.23' incident in Shanghai, which took place recently, is a good example, isn't it?"

"Do you mean the '327' treasury bond futures trade incident in Shanghai Stock Exchange? It was futures trading and was different from stock trading."

"But it showed the mainland government's decision to reorganize the securities trade market and prevent the few from manipulating the it."

"In China, things depend on the human. It's all about how people do. Different people do things in different ways. And you may not know the secret in it."

"Not necessarily. I think outsiders know more about China mainland than insiders. Although you live in China mainland, I see thing more clearly than you."

"I'm only talking about the stock market."

"It's the same. I think the mainland's stock market is far from regulated. It is very risky and therefore not suitable for large investment."

"High risks yield high profits. Nothing ventured, nothing gained."

"But there are a world of difficulties in investing overseas capital in mainland stock market."

"That's the question of operation. If Mrs. Sullivan believes me and entrusts the matter to me, I can solve all these difficulties."

Sheila listened to their conversation calmly, and when the discussion became heated, she straightened up and said, "Well, you two made a simple issue more and more complex. Let's do it this way, Mr. She, you can go back and write a feasibility report. Write your plan and reasons in detail, and hand the report to me as soon as possible. I will go back to America in a few days. Then I'll ask the board to discuss your proposal. I can tell you, there is great hope." Then she turned around and asked, "Jingyi, what's the time of entertaining at noon?"

Chen said, "Eleven thirty."

Xia Zhe knew Sheila wanted him to leave, so he stood up and said, "Mrs. Sullivan, I have to go now. I will give you the feasibility report as soon as possible."

"OK, Mr. She." Sheila stood up and said again, "By the way, can you leave your telephone number for easier contact?"

"Sorry, I don't have a phone in my place. Can I call you?"

"Yes, you can. Normally I'm here after 10 at night."

Chen Jingyi sent Xia Zhe out. When she went back into the room, she said to Sheila, "I think this guy must be obsessed with money. Madam, do you really want to see his feasibility report?"

Sheila did not answer Chen's question directly. She said with a smile, "This lad is cute, isn't he?"

Chen looked at Sheila for a moment and did not speak.

Sheila went into the bathroom. She asked while making up herself, "Jingyi, did the journalist of *China Daily* whom you mentioned yesterday call us again?"

"No! I just called *China Daily*, but the woman did not leave her name, so they cannot check it."

"Hey, you can't take a journalist's words seriously; besides, we'd better keep a distance from the journalists."

"But she called in and said she wanted to interview you, and she seemed to be in a hurry. I think this was strange."

Sheila did not speak. She gazed at herself blankly in the mirror.

Chapter 28 – The Family Privacy

On that evening, when Xia Zhe left, Bai Mei was not in the mood to clean the utensils. She sat on the couch and was anxious and unhappy.

Xia Dahu seemed to be very relaxed. He paced in the living room and even started singing Li Yuhe's tune in the revolutionary model drama *The Story of the Red Lamp* – "Today we drink the celebration wine heartily, and we won't go back before we realize our dreams. There is a long way to go, and we are willing to sacrifice our life to create the history."

Bai Mei could not stand it anymore, she frowned and said, "Stop singing. Don't you find yourself annoying?"

"Why am I annoying? My son is in a relationship. This is a happy event."

"A happy event? I think it is..."

"What is it? Tell me."

"I..." Bai Mei was about to say something, but she held it back.

"I know someone will be annoyed, but it's not me."

"Who is it?"

"Do I need to say? You know it for sure."

"Dahu, don't always talk with me in such an attitude and find fault with me. What did I do? I have performed my duties in the family over the 20 years. In those days you returned to the city, leaving me and my child alone in the farm. Do you know how I lived through it? I suffered a lot, do you know? After coming to Beijing, you worked as a furniture maker outside, and I took care of children and your parents. Later, I did carpenter work and went about soliciting business deals together with you. Don't always think the business was built up by yourself. I did no less than you."

"You said this numerous times. It's boring. I know you lived a tough life those years, especially in taking care of my father. I know this. That's why I asked you to take rest and enjoy yourself at home. But I've been working so hard for the family that my hair is all gone. Is it easy for me?"

"I did not say you don't care for the family. I mean your attitude. When you are happy, you speak something pleasant; and when you are unhappy, you don't give a damn. Looked at your expression. It's so grave, as if I owe you a lot."

"I didn't say you owe me. Even if you owe me, I have no intention to ask for repayment."

"You saved my life at that time, and I rewarded you already. If you considered it as a repayment, I have repaid you in full over the years."

"I didn't say I need you to repay me."

"Then why do you treat me so indifferently?"

"What do you want me to do?"

"What to do? You are clear about it. Take sex for example, I'm enthusiastic but you are indifferent. What a huge difference!"

"Don't always talk about the nonsense."

Bai Mei was already unhappy, and when she heard these words, she was even more upset. She could not hold back her complaint anymore, "What is nonsense? Sex is necessary. Why is it nonsense? Just think, how active you were in those years. You could do it several times one night. But now the frequency is less than once per week, and you do it as homework. My grandma said the most important thing in marriage is sexual happiness. And to enjoy sexual happiness, people must have sexual interest. Your tiny sexual interest cannot possibly create sexual happiness. And without sexual happiness, isn't marriage a dull affair?"

Xia Dahu did not want to quarrel. He said, "As I told you before, men and women are different. It's said that women are like sheep in their 20s, wolves in their 30s, tigers in their 40s, and pigs in their 50s. By careful analysis, you will understand this saying makes sense. A woman in her 20s is shy and half-consenting, and as meek as a sheep. In her 30s, she becomes a wolf which bites you. And in her 40s, she is sexually more active, like a tiger, which bites and eats people. But after 50 years old, the woman becomes a fat pig with a lot of redundant flesh. She will be lazy and not interested in sex anymore. You are like a wolf or tiger in your age, so you always wants to make love with me, and in a fierce way. How can I stand it?"

"Don't brag about your theory. I know men are not interested in their own wives but interested in all other people's. Don't you often say, 'My child is the best but my wife is the worst' when you are drinking together?"

"You wronged me, indeed. Just ask yourself if I had an affair in all these years. You know, all the company owners in my circle have their mistresses, but do I have one? Last time you told me, those wives said they have big houses and money, but live like widows. To be honest, I have a lot of chances, but I never slept with any other woman. I only have you in my life, and I have never gone against my conscience."

"I believe you in this matter, but when you watch TV and see the female singers and actresses, you stare at them, as if you are eager to get inside the TV set."

"What's wrong with the thoughts? I didn't do anything."

"Even if you wanted to do it, would they allow you? I have some words that I have kept in my heart for many years and do not want to say."

"It's OK. You can say it now."

"Fine. I want to say this. When you made love with me, you put a wall calendar on my face and said you were seeking the feeling of obscurity. Do you think I didn't know what was going on in your mind? The photos of Liu Xiaoqing and Mao Amin were on the calendar. If I hadn't tolerated you, I would have kicked you off the bed."

"I had no other way. You wanted to do it but I was not able to, so I had to think of a way to increase stimulation."

"Other people's photos can stimulate you, but a living person like myself cannot?"

"That's different."

"Different? It's because I'm your wife, right?"

"It's not that simple. There is something I don't want to say."

"Just say it. I allow you to tell me everything."

"You know I'm fully functional, but whenever I have sex with you, I can't achieve a hard-on. Why? Because I'm not comfortable in the heart."

"What made you uncomfortable?"

"The things you did."

"What did I do? You know everything that happened before we were in love, and you are willing to accept it."

"I can accept these things. I have always considered our marriage as a second marriage. It's fine. I mean what you did afterwards."

"What did I do then?"

"You really want me to say it?" Xia spoke with a threatening tone.

"Just say it." Bai Mei softened her voice.

"I think this is called 'Fire cannot be wrapped up in paper'. Let me ask you, why don't you consent to Zhe and Ting's romantic relationship? Dare you tell your reason? You dare not. OK, let me say, it's because they are brother and sister."

"You..."

"Me? You think I'm a fool? My son does not look like me. You think I didn't notice this? Both you and I suffered over these years. I was working hard to raise someone else's son. What did I get?"

The room suddenly became silent.

As the saying goes, "One day of marriage is worth a hundred days of friendship." They stayed together for more than 20 years through thick and thin. After quarreling and saying words of anger, they felt gratified but also regretted, especially Bai Mei. However, the secret which she was burdened with for many years was now uncovered. She felt relieved as a result. She hesitated again and again, and finally asked, "You knew this earlier, right?"

Xia Dahu nodded.

"Then why didn't you say this?"

Xia gave a deep sigh and said, "I don't want to ruin our family."

Having heard Xia's words, Bai Mei had a strange feeling in her heart. She really wanted to cry loudly and wash everything with tears, but she was not able to.

Xia Dahu also had conflicts in his heart. When Xia Zhe was over 10 years old, Xia Dahu felt more and more strongly that his son did not look like him. At that moment, he was struggling hard in life, and the doubt haunted him from time to time. Later when he got rich, he had a burning desire to find out the truth. Therefore, he did the DNA test. When he knew that Xia Zhe was not his blood son, he felt humiliated and extremely angry, and he really wanted to beat up the mother and son, and then kick them out of his home. But when he went back home and saw his wife, who shared his happiness and sorrow for more than 10 years, and his son, who was raised by him with great effort, his heart was softened. He did not want to destroy the family. Meanwhile, he thought about his fame and career. After balancing advantages and disadvantages over and over, he decided to accept this fact silently and not to make further inquires. Let the past be the past. So he hid the DNA test report in the safe in his office. If it was a difficult decision, then practicing it afterwards was even more difficult. He could remain silent, but he couldn't refrain from thinking. He really wanted to know how everything happened, and he guessed all kinds of situations. He often felt distressed and had weird thoughts. When Xia Zhe was accused of being guilty in Lu Boping's security company, and when Xia Zhe was in love with Lu Ting, he took pleasure in their misfortune. Although he knew he was mean in this matter, he couldn't help wanting to add fuel to the fire. His trial in the business field over these years enabled him to not reproach himself for immorality. He could be treat his rivals heartlessly to make money, but he was not able to do the same to family members.

Bai Mei looked at Xia Dahu, as if she was waiting for the verdict of the judge.

Xia Dahu looked through the window and asked calmly, "Do you plan to tell Lu Boping?"

Bai Mei lowered her head but lifted it up quickly. She said, "Originally I didn't want to tell anyone, but now I'm utterly confused. I don't know whether I should tell him. My main concern is whether this will hurt Zhe."

"Zhe will know it sooner or later, but I think you should tell Lu Boping. He must know this. Telling him is the way to act responsibly for the children."

At the noon of the next day, Bai Mei came to Beihai Park. Since it was a weekday, there weren't many tourists in the park. Bai Mei walked west along the lakeside. She found the third bench and sat on it.

The gentle spring breeze were swaying the tender willow branches, and bright sunshine soundlessly fell onto the tranquil lake. Seeing the lake water before her, she had an indescribable feeling in her heart. She thought people can't refuse to believe in destiny, because many things are destined to happen. The beginning determines the end. No one can change destiny, and everyone has to surrender to it. She took off her sunglasses and wiped tears off her eyes with a handkerchief. It has been many years since the incident, but she still felt sad and painful whenever she recalled it.

"Bai Mei!" A soft voice was heard. She turned her head and saw Lu Boping standing behind her. He was wearing a hat and holding a metal crutch.

Lu Boping went around the bench and sat next to Bai Mei. Although he lost interest in his ex-lover a long time ago, he has the habit of pleasing women. "This place is idyllic. I feel as if I have returned to 20 years ago. I remember our first date was near the reservoir..."

"Boping, I asked you out not to talk these."

"Oh, yeah, you have some urgent business. What is it?"

"Do you know Zhe and Ting are in love?"

"Ting told me. Are you proposing a marriage?"

"Marriage? They can't marry at all."

"Oh, I didn't expect you object to their marriage. Don't you want them to finish what was not finished by ourselves?"

"Don't talk nonsense. Let me ask you, do you feel Zhe looks like you?"

"What do you mean?"

"Zhe is your son."

"You..." Lu Boping looked at Bai Mei in astonishment and involuntarily moved his body backwards. He had also felt that Xia Zhe did not look like Xia Dahu, but he had thought it was because the son was more like the mother. He did not even think of himself in this matter, because he had left past events behind. He swallowed, frowned and said, "Zhe should be 21 years old this year, right? What is his date of birth?"

"February 16, 1974. You should know this."

"How could I remember this?" Lu Boping calculated in his mind, and thought it was not good for him to deny this. "But why do you tell me this now?"

"Why? Because I want to let you know Zhe and Ting can't be lovers, because they are brother and sister."

"Ah, this is a problem. I think it will be troublesome."

"It was not my intention to disclose this." Bai Mei sighed. "This is my fault. I planned to take the secret to the grave, but now they are in love. So I have to say it. What do you plan to deal with this?"

Lu Boping stared at Bai Mei's eyes, pondered for a moment, and asked, "Does Dahu know this?"

"I figure he does not know." Bai Mei told a lie.

"OK, please don't tell this to anyone. Let me take care of this matter." Lu Boping leaned back, squinted, and talked to himself, "Zhe is my son! So many things happened but I did not know he is my son! I didn't even recognize my family. What should I do now?"

"What are you saying? What's your plan? You can't just tell Zhe directly. If necessary, I can tell him." Bai Mei looked at Lu Boping uneasily.

"You may rest assured that I have ways to solve this." Lu Boping sat up and gazed at the white pagoda opposite.

Chapter 29 – The Premarital Pregnancy

In the autumn of 1969, a train departed from Beijing Railway Station in cheerful sounds of gongs and drums. Young men on the train waved goodbye to their relatives on the platform, and then soon started light-hearted talks. Some people even took the lead to to sing revolutionary songs. The passion of youth was burning in their body, because they were acting in response to the great leader Chairman Mao's call – to make great achievements in the wide, open rural areas.

Xia Dahu and Lu Boping grew up in the same yard, and went to school and the countryside together. At this moment, they sat beside the train window face to face, looked at the ever-changing scenery outside, and talked about their lives in future and their dreams. Whenever the train passed by the cities and towns, or a group of children ran with the train along the subgrade and shouted joyfully, the sense of pride and mission would arise in their heart. But as the rumble of wheels continued, their senses became duller and duller, and only those specially prepared singing and dancing performances on the train platforms of big cities could arouse their temporary excitement. After the train passed Harbin, towns and villages on both sides of the railway were fewer and fewer, and the noise in the carriages were reduced. It seemed everyone was thinking about their forthcoming arrival in destination.

At the midnight of the next day, they finally got off the train. In the dim train station, they carried their luggage and ran to different trucks. Xia and Lu were assigned to the same truck. The truck went for more than one hour on the bumpy earthen road and finally stopped beside several low houses. An old commander in his 50s greeted them. He carried a lantern and led them into a low earthen house. He asked them to spend the night here and said the living quarters would be provided on the next day.

It was the warehouse of the dining hall. In the room, there was a large heatable brick bed covered by a straw mat. A row of large tanks were placed on the floor. The tanks were giving out a smell of brined vegetables. A dozen of students were sitting on the brick bed with clothes, and male and female students sat separately from each other. They were worn out by two days' trip, but none of them were sleepy. And they remained quiet. The flame of the oil lamp swayed feebly and eventually went out. Girls' weeping was heard in the darkness.

After breakfast, the old commander provided living quarters for the new educated youths. It was a row of black brick houses. Men's dormitory was on the left and women's was on the right. In every room, there were two large heatable brick beds located on the north and south, respectively. The educated youths who came earlier already stayed here, including those from Beijing, Tianjin, and Harbin. The experienced youths warmly helped newcomers to place their luggage. More than 10 people slept on one brick bed, and one person's space was 1m wide and included the wall hanger board on the corresponding position. The commanding explicitly told them to keep their quilt folded neatly during the daytime, because they were now the "soldiers" of the Heilongjiang Construction and Production Regiment. They placed their luggage orderly and put handbags and sundries on the hanger board, and then went out impatiently.

The place was like a village under the Lesser Khingan Mountains, which used to be called a farm, but now it was named a company. The dormitory of the educated youths was located on the southeast corner of the field area and faced the road to the county. On the northwest was the family area of the old workers, and on the south was the field yard, machine work company and livestock farming company. The field area was surrounded by a boundless field, and the remote rolling hills can be seen. They felt it was indeed a wide and open area, and expected to make great achievements.

However, the Great Northern Wilderness has not only the green spring and golden autumn, but also red summer and white winter. Life cannot be chosen. Hard labor day after day and the simple meals made the young people realize the difficulty of life. But they were enriched in the heart, because they believed they were making contributions for the realization of communism.

Xia and Lu once looked at the stars in the sky, and seriously discussed the communist ideal. They looked forward to such a society in which all people can make use of their talents, get what they need, and be treated equally, and they believe the ideal society is not remote from them, maybe only several decades ahead. However, they had different opinions on how to realize the ideal. Xia thought a high degree of material abundance must be achieved first; for example, no matter how much pork you want to eat, you can get it. But Lu's understanding was that people's political awareness must be improved, so that everyone can be selfless. They had a heated debate, but could not convince each other.

Sometimes, they secretly talked about topics of "vulgar interests", such as nocturnal emissions, which locals called "horse running". Boping said he had a nocturnal emission again when he dreamed that he pulled a young woman's hand while working. Dahu said he had one, too, and it was also because of a dream, in which he kissed a young woman. Boping said it was dangerous, because when a man and a woman kissed, the woman would get pregnant and give birth to a baby. Dahu said, "Come on. Kissing does not cause pregnancy. Only after a man and a woman do that thing – peeing in the woman's genital – will the woman get pregnant." Boping said, "If you are right, did our great leader Chairman Mao do this kind of thing?" Dahu was rendered speechless, because a great leader surely will not do such a thing of "vulgar interest".

In those days, young men and women seemed to be separated by an invisible wall. They did not work together, eat together or enjoy life together. When they had to talk with each other, they kept a distance over 2 meters. And only when the company held meetings did the men and women have chances of face to face communication.

The company meetings were generally held in the large dormitory of the female educated youths. The women sat on the heatable brick bed on the south, and men sat on the one on the north. The singing session preceded the the meeting – the men sang a song, and women sang a song, and sometimes the men and women sang a song together. Although tired from a day's labor, many people liked such activities. After the meeting, the men might talk about the women, but mostly with mocking or derogatory language. If a young man uttered something good about a young woman out of carelessness, he would attract a burst of laughter. But later, the chances of communicating with young females came upon Xia and Lu.

In order to participate in the art performance of the regiment, the company leaders organized the youths to rehearse revolutionary model drama *The Story of the Red Lamp*. Xia was tall and had a loud voice, so he acted the hero Li Yuhe. Lu was white and talkative, so he acted the traitor Wang Lianju. But in this drama, the most remarkable figure was the revolutionary successor Li Tiemei.

The role of Li Tiemei was played by Bai Mei, who was an educated youth from Harbin. It was said she had the blood of Russians. She was tall and had white skin, big eyes, high nose, and thin lips. She also had a cheerful character and liked laughing. Her pretty teeth were revealed whenever she laughed. She learned dancing in childhood and had a beautiful voice. Therefore, as soon as she came onto the stage, all of the audience applauded her. In the singing sessions of company meetings, she was definitely a leader, and sometimes she would sing a solo. In a word, she was an extraordinary young woman in the company.

Xia Dahu and Bai Mei played the roles of the father and the daughter, respectively, while rehearsing *The Story of the Red Lamp*, so they often practiced together. Xia was not good at talking with girls, and he was always a bit nervous when they practiced together, so Bai Mei often laughed at him and called him "a conservative lad", but he was not averse to this.

Although Lu played a loathsome traitor in the drama, and had an ugly nickname "Lu Buping (uneven road)", he was cheerful and liked talking and laughing. As a result, he was popular among the educated youths and a lot of young women had a good impression of him.

Of course, cultural activities in spare time were only decorations on the lives of the educated youths, and their most vigorous times were dedicated to hard labor on the black soil. In spring, they braved the windy and dusty weather to sow the seeds; in summer, they cut grass in intense heat; in autumn, they harvested in muddy water; and in winter, they dug for stools in lands covered by ice and snow...

Year after year, the educated youths seemed to be used to a mundane life of hardship.

Meanwhile, the ideal of communism became farther and farther from them.

One day after dinner, Lu asked Xia to go out of the room and said he wanted to show him something. They came to a place on the south of the field yard where nobody was around. Boping took out a letter and handed it to Dahu. It read: "Dear Boping..."

Dahu folded the letter in a hurry and gave it back to Boping, and said, "I can't see this."

Boping said disapprovingly, "There is nothing to be afraid of. We are good pals, just see it."

Dahu finally returned the love letter to Boping and asked, "Who wrote it?"

"Bai Mei!"

"It's her?"

Boping noticed Dahu's strange voice and asked hastily, "Why? You think she is not good enough?"

"She is good. Capable and pretty. Just two years older than you, a little unsuitable."

"It doesn't matter. An older woman can look after people nicely. By the way, she is at the same age as you, and you two are a match."

"Nonsense. She is writing to you." Actually Dahu liked Bai Mei, too.

"But I don't want to consider love at this moment."

"What are you going to do?"

"She asked me to meet her in the groves beside the reservoir. It's not good to reject the appointment; besides, I want to return the letter to her. But how can I go there alone? Can you go with me?"

"Are you kidding? She's dating you. What can I do there?" Dahu was a bit envious.

"Dahu, I think you should help me in this matter. Just think, if I meet her alone and someone else sees us, I will not be able to prove my innocence. If the commander knows it, he would chastise me."

Dahu found it difficult to decline, so he said, "It's fine that I go, but I won't speak. It's you who should tell her what you think."

"Of course."

"But you'd better be mild and indirect. Don't hurt her."

"I have thought over already."

They went towards the reservoir side by side.

The reservoir was located on the southwest of the company and was formed as a result of the dam construction. The dam made use of the terrain of the ditch to retain water. The size of the reservoir was not large, but water was deep. On the southeast of the reservoir was the dam, on the southwest were the woods, and the terrain on the northeast was mild. A pinus massoniana forest was cultivated on the northeast. Boping and Dahu came to the pine forest and saw Bai Mei waiting there. Boping walked to her, but Dahu stopped, turned around and looked in the direction of the company. However, he was listening to their conversation.

Boping said, "You came here so early."

"Yes, but why don't you come alone?" Bai Mei whispered.

"Dahu is my good friend. We tell each other everything, so I asked him to come."

"I know, but some words should...Can we go over there?"

"You can say it here."

"How can I say it here?"

"OK, let me say. I read your letter."

"What's your idea? Do you accept it?"

"I think we are young, so we should think more about work and study. We can talk about your proposal later."

"You don't like it?"

"I don't mean it. I mean, if other people know this, we will be in a disadvantageous position."

"So you are just afraid of letting people know it?"

"This is not the only reason."

"What else?"

"I'm not sure."

"How do you think of me?"

"You are good, but..."

"Not good enough for you?"

"I don't mean it. I think we are young, and it's way to early to consider love."

"Then we can take it slowly. A relationship is not established in a couple of days. Boping, I think you are a good man, and I want to go together with you. I know people in the company will gossip about us, but I'm not afraid of it. They can say whatever they want, and I'm not going together with them, anyway."

"But...I think we had better consider this later. Really, I don't mean anything else. This is your letter, please keep it to yourself. I have to go now. Dahu is waiting for me."

"Boping..."

Boping came close to Dahu, pushed him, and they both went to the company quickly.

The weather was rainy in the autumn that year. The tractor was not able to work in the land, so the wheat had to be harvested manually. The lads swung the cutting knives for the whole day, and slept like dead pigs when lights went out at night.

One morning, when everyone was woken up by the commander's whistle, they discovered in surprise another head in Lu's quilt, a long-hair one. Lu was awake, too. When he saw Bai Mei was lying beside him, he was really scared. At this moment, the young men were stunned. Bai Mei did not care. She put on her shoes and walked out calmly. Of course, she had clothes on her.

After Bai Mei got out, the young men burst into laughter and shouts. Some said, "Why didn't Bai Mei crawl into my quit by mistake at midnight?" Some said, "Li Tiemei fell in love with Wang Lianju, but she was on the wrong side." And some asked Lu to confess what he did at night.

Lu faltered and was speechless.

At this moment, laughter and small talks came out from the female dormitory, too.

This incident added a romantic tinge to the dull lives of the young people, and people now had the chance to discuss the topic which they dare think but dare not talk about. However, people felt strange about the fact that the company leaders turned a blind eye to this incident.

After wheat harvest, the company decided to rest for one day. In the morning, the old commander called the young people together to hold a meeting. They sat next to each other on the brick beds on the south and north side. The old commander stood in the middle and spoke loudly:

"Dear comrades, I want to talk about two things. One, everyone should protect the items of the company, because these are national property. While we were harvesting wheat, I saw someone play with the combine harvester. If you don't know how to use it, please don't play with it. If you break it, who will fix it? And there were some people who did not take good care of the horses. Don't ride the carriage horses for fun. Do you understand? Now we are members of the Construction and Production Regiment. It's the same as the military. Absolutely you can't play with the property of the army, such as the horses, cars, sheep, and pigs. Ah, this is the first thing. Two, well, I have to talk more about this second point. A few days ago a young woman went into the male dormitory at midnight. It happened indeed, right? Isn't it absurd? It's said she went into the wrong door after going to the toilet at midnight. I don't believe it. There was a living person in the quilt, and you didn't notice it? This was not a small incident. It was the reflection of the thinking pattern of capitalism. Such thinking pattern drives young people to pursue vulgar interests of the capitalist class. Do you know? Vulgar interests. And our company is fighting against these interests. This is called... 'The tree wants to move, but the wind does not come'!"

Everyone laughed. A young man said, "The saying should be: 'The tree desires stillness but the wind does not cease.'"

"What are you laughing at? I'm uneducated, but I was referring to the same thing. As Chairman Mao taught us, don't ever forget the fight against exploitative classes. Do you understand? Boys and girls can get married when they have grown up. I don't object to it, but you can't fall in love like this. Now we are members of the Construction and Production Regiment, and half soldiers. Do you understand? Therefore...I have no more to say. Bai Mei and Lu Boping, please come to the company office. Chairman Mao told us to fight against the capitalism and criticize the revisionism. Dismiss!"

After the meeting, young men went back into their dormitory. Some made use of the time of rest to write a family letter, some go to the water house to do the laundry, but most people were sitting on the brick bed and playing a card game named "Qiaosanjia". Xia liked playing cards, and surely he joined the game. But he was thinking about Lu Boping, who was called by the commander to the office. So he was a bit absent-minded. At this moment, the audience behind him couldn't help but shouted, "Duicha, Go Duicha, then move and go Dagong! Hey, what a dead bear!"

Xia had to give his seat to others and went outside to take a look.

Near lunch time, Lu Boping and Bai Mei went back from the company office one after another. After entering the room, Lu Boping lied on the bed, closed his eyes and remained quiet. When the lunch started, Dahu asked Boping to buy the meal, but Boping shook his head and said he did not want to eat. Dahu bought two person's meals and asked Lu Boping to share. Boping initially did not want to eat, but then he could not resist the temptation of meat in fried cabbage and the deep fried potato chips, so he finally sat up.

After lunch, young men crept into their quilts to make up for their lack of sleep in working days. Dahu went into sleep, too. Boping lied on his luggage and was absorbed in his thought.

Dahu woke up and saw Boping was not by his side, so he put on his clothes and went out. He walked around and finally found Boping underneath a tree on the south of the field yard.

Dahu went to him and asked, "Why did you get here alone."

Boping smiled with embarrassment, "Hi, I'm terribly bored, so I'm strolling."

"The commander chastised you?"

"Nothing. I just felt sorry for Bai Mei. She did this because of my rejection, right? In fact, I never expected she is so steadfast in her love pursuit. In the morning, when we were in the office, she said it was her own decision. She said she had unrequited love for me and I did not know anything. And she stated her willingness to accept all punishment alone. She also said she really wanted to marry me. In the beginning, the commander asked us to make a self-criticism in a meeting, but Bai Mei persuaded him into letting her write a self-criticism article and taking no further proceedings. That's why I felt sorry for her."

"What do you plan to do now?"

"I want to ask her out to have a talk."

"Don't get caught by the commander."

"I know."

"To tell you the truth, I think Bai Mei is good."

"Then you should help me." Boping took out a folded piece of paper. "Find an opportunity to hand her this at dinner. It's inappropriate for me to meet her now, because people will see it."

"No problem!" Dahu received the paper slip.

At dinner, Dahu handed the slip to Bai Mei. When he said, "Boping gave you this", he saw Bai Mei's eyes were shining. He smiled bitterly and left.

On that night, Boping came back to his dormitory very late.

Since then, Boping often went out after dinner, and his relationship with Bai Mei became an open secret in the company. In those days, romantic relationship is forbidden, and naturally, the brave couple's behavior became the common conversational topic of the educated youths. Although they talked about Lu Boping and Bai Mei in mocking language, they secretly envied and admired the couple in their hearts.

Indeed, Bai Mei took care of Boping like an elder sister. She knit sweaters and wash clothes for him, and sometimes brought him with goodies. Young men said she was Boping's stone woman, namely a girlfriend whose love is as stable as a stone.

Dahu found that Boping did not talk much like before, but he benefited as well, because when Bai Mei did the laundry for Boping, she might also wash two or three pieces of his clothing together with Boping's. And whenever Bai Mei brought goodies to Boping, Boping would share with him.

The lads were accustomed to Boping's late return at night, but sometimes they made fun of him.

One midnight, Boping went into the room in darkness. He found there was a person in his quilt. He dare not let people know this, so he had to find an empty place at the head of the brick bed to sleep. On the morning of the next day, he found the "person" in his quilt was just a pillow and clothes made into a human shape. However, Boping was not angry with the mischief, because he knew his comrades did not have ill intentions.

In the spring festival of 1972, Xia Dahu and Lu Boping returned to Beijing to visit their family. They noticed a lot of change in Beijing over the two years. Particularly, a subway was constructed in front of the Beijing Railway Station, and they took some effort to find the trolley bus station where they could get on the bus and go home. When they went into their familiar small yard with bags on their backs, their family were filled with joy.

It was a lively new year.

In the one month's home leave, they almost went out every day to meet previous schoolmates and young comrades.

The holiday passed quickly. When they were about to buy the train tickets to the northeast, Boping suddenly told Dahu that he would not go back, because his father had found a way to send him into the army. His father worked in a government department and had access to the authorities who could make such an arrangement. In those days, all young people wanted to have the privileges of a soldier, but it was definitely not easy to get into the military by using the relationships. Dahu was a bit envious, but he was also happy for Boping.

On the day when Dahu returned to the northeast, Boping saw him off at the train station. None of them felt good, but they tried to exchange positive words. At the time of parting, Boping asked Dahu to bring a letter to Bai Mei.

After returning to the company, Dahu told Bai Mei the good news that Boping joined the army, and gave the letter to her. Dahu thought she would be happy, but she remained silent for quite a while and ran away with the letter.

In the beginning, she could receive letters from Boping, but gradually no news was heard from him. Dahu didn't mind this, but Bai Mei was anxious. Whenever she met Dahu, she would ask him whether there was any letter form Boping. When she knew there wasn't, redness appeared in her eyes. Dahu had to console her, saying that the army had strict discipline and a tight training schedule. Initially she would listen to the consolation, but later she listened and asked no more.

At a night half a year later, Dahu saw Bai Mei walking towards the reservoir when he was going to the water house to fetch water. Dahu called her name, but she did not turn around. After going back into the room, Dahu had an increasingly strong feeling that something was wrong, so he hurried to the reservoir.

It was a full moon night. Dahu saw from a distance that Bai Mei was standing beside the water. He did not want to alarm her, so he hid in the pine forest and went around to a place near her. He could not see her face, but he indistinctly heard her crying. When he was hesitating if he should go out and comfort her, he saw her slowly walking into the water. He rushed to her and held her arm. At this moment, water had covered her knees, and she was struggling to throw herself into the water. Dahu had no time to think. He carried her in his arms and went back to the shore.

Bai Mei used her fists to hit Dahu, but then she rested herself on his chest and cried loudly. Dahu could not push her away, so he had to comfort her. She finally stopped crying and noticed she was in Dahu's arms. She felt embarrassed, so she stood up next to him.

Dahu asked her what happened. She said she received a letter from Lu Boping in which Lu said he wanted to break up with her. She could not accept this and decided to take her own life. Dahu persuaded her for a long time until eventually she agreed not to give up her life. Then he sent her back to the dormitory.

On that night, Dahu wrote to Lu Boping to question him about the ruthless abandonment, and tell him how much Bai Mei loved him and was even willing to die for him. Dahu said in the letter that if a girl loved him so deeply, he would not leave her at any rate.

Dahu was touched by Bai Mei indeed. He thought Bai Mei was like those characters in the novels. She was so noble and beautiful.

Dahu received Lu's reply in which Lu said in order to join the Communist Party and rise through the ranks, he had to sacrifice love life. Besides, he lived far from Bai Mei and it was unrealistic to maintain a relationship. Both of them would suffer from this. He said if they had to break up, they should do it early. At last, he said he did not expect Dahu to take his position.

At the moment, Dahu did not take the final sentence seriously. He did not take advantage of people's vulnerabilities. He often consoled Bai Mei, but mostly due to sympathy. However, he did not expect that as they spent more time together, his sympathy for her gradually turned into love, and they were progressing fast.

In the spring of 1973, Xia Dahu went back after logging in Great Khingan Mountains and met Bai Mei. Months of separation intensified their love. At night, they stood under the tree at the back of the field yard and confided how they missed each other. When Dahu wasn't able to express himself in words, he would embrace Bai Mei and kiss her. Then, Bai Mei said she was not feeling well, and Dahu asked her why. Bai Mei tried to avoid the question, but then she said she should have got her period, but it didn't come, so she was not feeling well in her stomach.

Dahu lacked sexual knowledge, and he only knew about sex from vulgar language that was used to curse people. He asked Bai Mei what was the period. Bai Mei told him liberally. She asked him to massage her belly and said it would make her feel better. In the beginning, Dahu massaged her on her clothes, but later he put his hand under her clothes, and even reached up and fondled her breasts.

Bai Mei let him touch her freely; suddenly, she asked, "Do you dare to reach downwards?"

"I dare to if you allow me."

"Please touch it."

Dahu's fingers moved downwards on her belly and felt the dense hair. He was startled and pulled back his hand.

Bai Mei asked in surprise, "What happened?"

Dahu said in embarrassment, "Why do you have so much hair down there?"

"What's wrong with the hair?"

"Men have hair at the place, but I thought women don't have."

"Who said it?"

"The tractor driver Zhao said."

"How did he say?"

"He asked us to guess a riddle – "One end has hair, and the other is bare. When put into the mouth, white fluid appears." We thought it was about sex, but he said it was a toothbrush. But later he told us it was a sexual riddle with a non-sexual meaning. So I thought the female genital should be without hair."

"Did you ever see it?"

"No, who would let me see, anyway?"

"I can let you see it later. Let me tell you, this is called pubic hair. Every adult woman has it. You don't know this, and you are conservative. I should be your teacher and teach you physiology."

Soon afterwards, the company leaders allowed the young people who did logging work to take home leave. Since Bai Mei stayed on duty in the company in winter, she was granted the leave, too. Both of them were very happy. They decided to go home together, first to Harbin, and then to Beijing.

Bei Mei's grandmother was a Russian. She wandered with her parents to Harbin during the Russian Civil War, and married a Chinese after she grew up. Bai Mei's parents were military officers in the Liberation Army, and they settled in Beijing after moving south with the military. When Bai Mei was 5 years old, her grandfather passed away, and her parents sent her to Harbin. She grew up with her grandmother in Harbin, and later came to the Great Northern Wilderness. She had a younger brother and a younger sister who grew up with her parents in Beijing.

Bai Mei's grandmother worked as a senior translator and spoke fluent Chinese and Russian. She was retired but still doing some written translation. She was cheerful, talkative, and liked laughing. And she had two hobbies: ballroom dancing and drinking liquor. When she saw the two bottles of Vodka bought by Dahu, she was excited and had a good impression of him. After dinner, she taught Dahu the ballroom dance and sang the Russian song *Moscow Nights* with him.

Her grandmother's house had two bedrooms, one for herself, and one for Bai Mei, and there was a large kitchen. After washing, Dahu asked Bai Mei softly, "Where shall I sleep tonight?"

Bai Mei smiled and asked, "Where do you want to sleep?"

"I want to sleep in your room."

"How about myself?"

"You sleep with your grandma."

"No, my grandma had poor sleep and was afraid of noise."

"It seems I have to sleep in the kitchen."

"I won't let you suffer. You can sleep in my room"

"But you won't sleep in the kitchen, will you?"

"I won't. I'm back home. Of course I will sleep in my room."

"So...Will your grandma agree?"

"It's her proposal actually. She is very open-minded. But there is a condition for sleeping in my room."

"Whatever it is, it's OK for me."

"Just sleep, don't touch me."

"I will absolutely obey the rules."

Dahu was very excited. He said good night to Bai Mei's grandmother, and she wittily winked at him.

Dahu and Bai Mei closed the door and embraced each other impatiently. After a passionate kiss, Dahu said, "Didn't you say you wanted to be my teacher and teach me physiology?"

"I can teach you, but you should be a good student. You can see me, but not touch me, OK?"

"OK, I agree."

Bai Mei stripped herself naked.

....

Bai Mei wept. Dahu held her and kept saying comforting words.

Bai Mei finally stopped crying. She said, "I don't blame you. I'm willing to give myself to you. I'm sad because I truly wish I had fallen in love with you in the beginning. It would be much better if I had not been in love with him. Can you forgive me for my past?"

Dahu said sincerely, "I don't care whom you loved. As long as you love me wholeheartedly in future, I will love you for the rest of my life."

"Dahu, you are so nice." Bai Mei gave him a kiss.

Dahu suddenly recalled a question, "We did this. Will you get pregnant?"

"Rest assured I won't. My grandma told me if I am right about the date of my period, everything will be fine. This is called the rhythm method."

"Your grandma is really a good person."

Xia Dahu and Bai Mei lived for three days in Harbin before they took the train to Beijing. Bai Mei lived in her parents' home, but she was not close to her parents and siblings. So she came to Dahu's home almost every day. Dahu's parents were initially not happy that their son had a girlfriend from Harbin, but when they saw Bai Mei, they felt she had a good character and family origin, so they agreed with the relationship.

Soon after Dahu and Bai Mei went back to Beijing, Lu Boping was also on an official trip to Beijing. When they met in the small yard, all three were a bit embarrassed, especially Bai Mei. She found that Lu Boping was more handsome in his military uniform, and she could discern the sadness and resentment in Lu Boping's eyes. She was a bit upset.

In the afternoon, Dahu went shopping, and everyone in the yard went to work. Bai Mei sat alone beside the bed in the back room and read books. Suddenly, she heard a knock on the door. She went to the outer room and saw Lu Boping through the door window. She hesitated before she opened the door. "Dahu is not at home, do you have something to talk with him?" She said while standing in the doorway.

"No, I want to talk with you. Can I come in?"

"What do we have to talk?" Bai Mei said so, but her body made way for him.

Lu Boping went into the outer room and sat on the wooden chair beside the square table, "I think we have some misunderstanding."

"What misunderstanding?"

"Maybe I should not say it. It has passed and the relationship between you and Dahu progressed to this stage. What can I say?"

"I want to listen to your explanation."

"Even if I tell you, you won't believe it. But if I don't say it, it will remain a burden in my heart. Whenever I see you and Dahu are together, I feel terrible."

"Why do you feel that way?"

"Because I always love you. Don't you remember the oath we took in the groves beside the reservoir? 'The seas will dry up and the rocks will decay, but our love will remain unchanged.'"

"You changed first. When I read your letter, I wanted to die."

"I was testing you. I thought you could pass the test. And I thought it would make our love more romantic, but I didn't expect we really separated. You forgot our oath."

Having heard Lu's words, Bai Mei was gripped by a feeling of dizziness. She was falling backwards, and Lu held her close to his chest.

Bai Mei came to her senses, and tears rolled down from her eyes. She pushed Lu away and said, "No, you are lying to me." She went into the back room, lied prone on the bed and cried bitterly.

Lu followed her into the room and stood by her side. "I did not cheat you. I'm telling the truth. I have been thinking true love can go through all tests, and only the love which has passed tests is the true love. I thought I have got true love..." he said.

Bai Mei's cry trailed off and changed into intermittent sobs. She raised her head and said, "But why...didn't you...write to me and tell me this?"

"I had too much faith in our love. I thought love is sacred, but now I understand there isn't sacred love in the world. Solemn pledges are simply deceptive nonsense."

"You can't speak ill of me in this way. You don't have the right to criticize me. This is not my fault."

The room quieted down. Lu was looking blankly at Bai Mei, who was sitting at the bedside, and felt a sudden impulse. He sat beside her, held her hand, and implored, "Dear Mei, I love you sincerely. Won't you give me another chance? I wont' do the stupid thing anymore."

With trembling lips, Bai Mei said shortly "It's too late."

"Why?" Lu stood up in an instant, and said, "He took possession of you already?"

Bai Mei nodded unwillingly.

"You..." Lu raised his right hand. It paused for a moment but fell onto his own face.

Bai Mei stood up hurriedly and held Lu's arms with her hands. She cried, "Boping, you can beat me if it makes you feel better."

Lu suddenly calmed down and looked at Bai Mei's eyes, "Then you should let me enjoy your body once more."

"No, don't." Bai Mei stepped back to her bedside.

"Why not? You were mine, but he took possession of you. I'm snatching you back."

Lu's expression showed his burning desire. Bai Mei looked at him, fell onto the bed powerlessly, and closed her eyes.

……………………………..

On the next day, Lu went back to the army.

After returning to the farm, Bai Mei was very considerate and submissive to Dahu, but soon she brought bad news to him – she was pregnant. They were afraid and anxious to remove the trouble, but all efforts failed. They made inquires and knew that the county hospital managed induced abortion very strictly.

Bai Mei wrote to her grandma for help, but her grandma objected to abortion. She hoped they could get married and have a baby.

Dahu decided to marry Bai Mei. He wrote to his parents but did not explain the real cause. His parents were totally opposed to his marrying in the northeast. Bai Mei informed his parents, too, but her parents did not approve the marriage, either. However, Bai Mei's belly size was increasing. They can't delay anymore.

Dahu and Bai Mei talked with the old commander. They said plainly that they would get married. The commander was understanding, and he had figured out the real cause of the proposed marriage. So he agreed to write a reference letter for marriage registration based on their nominal ages, and made up a noble cause – "To stay at the borderland and work for revolution."

After registration, the commander allocated them an adobe house beside the field yard for them to live. At this moment, Dahu was already a carpenter, so he made a pair of wooden boxes and a brick bed table by himself. And these were all the furniture they had.

In the autumn of 1973, Xia Dahu and Bai Mei formally got married. They did not hold the celebration, but prepared some wedding candies. However, the educated youths put money together and bought them towels and wash basins as the wedding gifts. After all, they were the first marriage couple among the educated youths.

Life after marriage was cozy and pleasant. The material conditions were hard for them, but they could legally eat and live together. And they were hard workers. With combined effort, they lived a happy life.

At the end of the year, they went back to Harbin to celebrate the new year with the grandmother. She was very happy and presented each of them with a watch, and gave them 200 yuan – it was quite a lot of money in those days.

The new year was probably the happiest time in their life.

After the birth of the child, their life changed a lot. Since the parents of both families were opposed to the marriage, they could only depend on themselves. Therefore, life became simple, repetitive labor. It only consisted eating, sleeping, and working for food. Everything was necessary, and everything was tedious. But they neither complained nor regretted.

Bai Mei was sad sometimes, because seemed to have become an old lady in the eyes of other educated youths.

When the child was 2 years old, Dahu and Bai Mei went to Beijing with the child to celebrate the Spring Festival. They visited their parents. The marriage was a fixed matter, so their parents had to accept it.

In the year when the child was at the age of 4, the educated youths went back into the city one after another. Dahu and Bai Mei also wanted to go back to Beijing, but Bai Mei's registered permanent residence was in Harbin and she had a child, so it was hard to go through the legal procedure. At this time, Dahu's father was sick in bed, and the department he worked in arranged the legal procedure for Dahu's return to Beijing. Dahu did not want to leave Bai Mei and their son in the Great Northern Wilderness, so he hesitated. But Bai Mei insisted on Dahu's leaving first. She said it was for their son's future.

In the spring of 1978, Dahu returned to Beijing and found a job in a small factory run by the subdistrict office.

Bai Mei stayed on the farm with children. By then, "Staying at the borderland and working for revolution" had become an unwelcome slogan. And the educated youths like Bai Mei who stayed there became unwelcome individuals. Later, Bai Mei's parents made use of their social relationships to transfer Bai Mei to Sanhe County, Hebei Province, which was near Beijing. And she worked as a saleswoman in a supply and marketing cooperative. But their place of residence was not transferred to Beijing until the child was about to go to primary school.

Life after the reunion was not easy. The three of them and Dahu's parents were accommodated tightly in two and a half bungalows – the additional half of a room was built by Dahu himself, and Dahu's father was sick in bed all day. Bai Mei did not have a job, so she helped her mother-in-law with housework and served her father-in-law. The small factory for which Dahu worked was not profitable and could only give a salary that barely covered the basic living costs.

In order to support the family, Dahu started walking about the streets and making furniture for people. He was clever, skillful, and sincere, so more and more people asked him to make furniture. Bai Mei often assisted him after finishing the housework. They finally had a steady income.

In the year when the child went to junior high school, Dahu's father passed away. Thus, a burden was removed from the family.

Doing business became a popular activity in those days. Dahu and Bai Mei used their savings to travel around and resell goods. They resold a lot of things, including clothes, socks, electronic watches, sunglasses, and smuggled goods. One winter, he seized an opportunity and gave up days of sleep to bring a carload of watermelons from Hainan to Beijing. They made a lot of money from this business. Although sometimes they were cheated and lost money, their diligence and shrewdness enabled them to become one of the earliest rich people in China.

In the year when the child went to senior high school, Dahu discovered the market potential of interior decoration and set up Meihu Decoration Company. After years of operation, Meihu grew into a large company. Bai Mei did not need to work anymore. She became a housewife in her comfortable home. They were a happy and successful couple in other people's eyes.

Chapter 30 – The Accidental Suicide

From Xia Zhe's words, Lu Ting indistinctly felt he did something inappropriate. But what was it? She could not figure out. The more difficult it was to reason, the more she guessed. And her guesswork further increased her vexation. She had conflicts in her heart. When she saw Xia Zhe, she wanted to forgive whatever he did, but when he was not around, she felt inexplicable resentment against him. She had a vague premonition in her heart that their love would end up as a tragedy. So she thought of Xia Zhe's words to ask her to be an amateur poet, and wrote a small poem after contemplation:

Love approaches together with the miracle,

But it leaves vexation behind.

Love leaves together with vexation,

But the miracle remains.

When vexation becomes superficial,

Love laughs at it loudly.

Only when the miracle turns profound,

Does love sleep quietly.

After night shift was over, Lu Ting went back home. Lu Boping went to work already, and Lu Ting stayed alone in the spacious room, feeling empty at heart. She even lost the interest to be a private detective and the desire to sleep. She lied down for a while but was not sleepy, so she sat up. In order to spend time, she tidied up the room, washed clothes, and then went out to buy vegetables. The whole morning was eventually whiled away.

In the afternoon, she called Song Jia. She thought Song Jia was a trustworthy person whom she can confide in. "Xia Zhe came back yesterday afternoon," she said.

"Really?" Song Jia was happy that her prediction came true, "Where did he go in these days?"

"He didn't say, and I didn't ask. But he had a wound in his leg."

"What wound? Was it serious?"

"It was wrapped up with gauze. The bones were not harmed, but it still hurt."

"He hurt or you hurt?" Song Jia laughed.

"I'm not feeling well, but you are teasing me. You are so bad." Lu Ting cried.

"Oh, sorry, I didn't mean it. Did he tell you how he got the wound?"

"He said he fell when he got off a taxi, but I thought it was not the case. He didn't want to say, so I didn't ask further. I'm confused now and I don't know what to do."

"Since he didn't want to say, you'd better not ask. Maybe he will tell you after some time."

"I really want to disregard him because I'm angry."

"But you don't have the heart to do that, right? Don't be silly. It's not the time to get angry. You should treat him the same way you did before, or even give more care to him. What he most needs now is your understanding and care."

After hanging up, Lu Ting felt better.

At night, Lu Boping came back. The father and daughter had dinner together, but Lu Ting spoke few words, because she was thinking about Xia Zhe.

Lu Boping understood her daughter's anxiety. He asked, "Did you quarrel with Zhe?"

"No, we are fine." Lu Ting did not want to tell the incident to her father.

"You are not able to hide things from me. OK, you can ask Zhe to have dinner with us tomorrow, and I want to talk with him."

Lu Ting knew Xia Zhe wanted to see her father, so she agreed.

On the morning of the next day, Lu Ting came to the ward. Other patents had gone out for a stroll, and only Xia Zhe was resting on the bed. With a smile, she said to him, "I have good news for you."

"What good news?"

"Guess it."

"I'm not able to guess it."

"Let me tell you, my father said last night that he wanted you to visit our home tonight."

"For what?"

"For something good. He will treat you to dinner."

"Treat me to dinner? Why?"

"Does my father need a reason to treat you to dinner?"

"I don't mean it. I just wonder if he had anything to talk with me."

"He didn't say that, but I knew from his words that he was serious. Maybe he will talk about our relationship."

"Did he agree?"

"Last time I talked to him, but he neither agreed nor objected. This time he seemed to be very happy."

"Shall I go or not?" Xia Zhe always felt sorry for Lu Ting and did not want to meet her family because of his inappropriate contact with Sheila.

"My father treated you to dinner, how dare you reject his invitation?" Lu Ting complained.

"I dare not. So when shall we go?"

"We can go home together when I'm off work."

"OK, I will wait for you."

Some voices came through the corridor, and Lu Ting went out.

At dusk, Lu Ting and Xia Zhe went home together, and Lu Boping was waiting for them. He sat on the couch in the living room and observed Xia Zhe as if he was identifying him.

Xia Zhe was nervous under his vision, so he initiated the conversation, "Uncle, do you have something to talk with me?"

"Nothing serious. I heard you came out and wanted to see you. You suffered in the detention center these days, right?"

"I'm fine." Xia Zhe was relieved.

"What do you plan to do now?"

"I don't know. It depends on what judgment the court will enter."

"I've been thinking about your case these days. The most important thing required to help you is money. I thought your father could fix things for you, but I didn't expect he was blind indeed, as his name suggests. If I were him, I would sell everything to save the child. Well, we can't wait for him. Let me figure out a way. In fact, the incident took place in my company, and I'm liable for this."

"Uncle, it had nothing to do with you. I was too careless at that time."

"Just let it pass. I will ask a friend to wipe out the debt for you. Please consider it as a loan. There is no interest, of course. You can repay him the money when you have the capacity to do so."

"If it is possible, I will be truly grateful for your help." Xia Zhe was a little excited.

Lu Ting was happy, too. She said, "You are really a good father, thank you!"

"You are welcome. Now let's have the meal. The food was prepared by myself."

"It's great!" Lu Ting ran into the kitchen.

Lu Boping was in a good mood. He served the dishes and opened a bottle of French red wine. All three people sat beside the table, ate, and chatted happily.

When half bottle of wine was consumed, Lu Boping said with a parental tone, "Let me tell you, I experienced a lot in my life and had some realizations. The most important thing in life is to spot the working direction at critical moments and hold on. When you hold on, you can move up the ladder and seize opportunities. Most of my old schoolmates were not successful, but Xia Dahu was better off. In fact, we all have similar cleverness and capacity. The difference is that they did not hold on at the critical moment, but I did. As a result, they failed..."

"Dad, you won't talk about the Sino-Vietnamese War again, right? I heard it many times when I was small." Lu Ting interposed.

"Today I will talk about you two instead of myself. You are young at this moment. Zhe is 21 years old now, right? It's the most critical moment in your life, and you have to discern the right direction and work hard. We were meant to go to school when we were young, but we didn't. Fortunately, most of the people in our generation had wasted time and did not go to college. So it was not a big deal for us. But you are in a different environment. You must go to college. Therefore, I have set a goal for you two – go to college. Ting, you should not be satisfied with being a nurse. You need to take the examination, and go to the medical college in two years. How do you think?"

"I have been studying the courses."

"Zhe, you are interested in the stock market. It's fine, but you should also go to university and study it systematically. When your case is solved, I will contact my friends in Hong Kong to help you enroll in the University of Hong Kong to study finance. You may also study in Hong Kong Stock Exchange. If you want to be a top talent in the field of stocks, you have to go to Hong Kong."

"I heard the tuition in Hong Kong is very expensive, and they teach in English. But my English is poor."

"Don't worry about the tuition. I can cover it for you. But you have to depend on yourself to study English. You are the key. If you hold on, you will succeed."

Xia Zhe had nothing to say for the moment. He didn't understand why Lu cared for him so much all of a sudden. Maybe Lu already acknowledged him as the son-in-law? But he was touched indeed and was very grateful, so he kept raising his glass and drinking toasts with Lu.

Lu was happy, too. When one bottle was drank up, he opened another. Therefore, Xia Zhe's eyes were getting red and he became more talkative.

The doorbell rang. Lu Ting opened the door, but she was disappointed to see it was Fang Qiong.

After entrance, Fang Qiong said arrogantly, "Today, when Mr. Lu called his daughter, I was at his side. When I heard our VIP investor Xia was visiting the father-in-law, I decided to come here to celebrate, because Xia had an uncommon relationship with me, right?"

"Aren't you tired?" Xia Zhe frowned and said with a sulky expression.

"Hey, you are pretending to be serious! You forgot the sweet words you said when you were pursuing me?"

"You..." Xia Zhe flushed and stood up suddenly, but Lu Ting pulled him and had him sit down.

Lu Ting said, "Zhe, just ignore her."

"Ting, watch your words. If I tell you what he did, I'm afraid you'll cry."

"Fang, since you have come, you'd better chat with us. Don't speak unpleasant words." Lu Boping looked at Fang's red face and asked, "You drank again, right?"

"Mr. Lu, don't try to be the mediator. Let me tell you, I'm not someone to be messed with. Don't think you can fool me!" Fang Qiong took out a gun from her little briefcase suddenly and pointed to Xia Zhe, "Xia, if you don't get on your knees and beg for mercy today, I will let you die in this room."

Fang Qiong's move startled everyone in the room. They stood up and stepped back. Lu Boping said, "Fang, if you have something to say, you can say it peacefully. A gun is too dangerous."

"Mr. Lu, don't interfere. When I finish Xia, I will settle accounts with you then."

At this moment, Lu Ting rushed to Fang and grasped Fang's right hand, which was holding the gun, and they wrestled with each other. Xia Zhe and Lu Boping were separated from them by a table. They wanted to help but were afraid of the gun moving about with Fang Qiong's hand.

Finally, the gun dropped to the ground.

Xia Zhe moved aside the chair and picked up the gun quickly. His eyes were red due to the effect of alcohol. He stared at Fang Qiong and pointed the gun to her across the table, and said, "Ting, stay away, I think this woman is seeking death."

Lu Ting dodged out of the way in a hurry.

Fang Qiong looked at the gun in Xia Zhe's hand. She moved back to the wall and said, "Don't fire! Don't..."

Lu Boping also shouted, "Zhe, you can't fire!"

But before Lu Boping could finish this sentence, he heard a bang, and Fang Qiong's body shook violently. She covered her left chest with hands, and red blood came out through her fingers. Her face twitched painfully, and her body slowly slid down to the floor along the wall.

Lu Ting screamed and rushed to Xia Zhe.

Xia Zhe stood there in surprise, and the gun fell onto the floor.

Lu Boping ran to Fang Qiong and held her. He shouted, "Fang Qiong! Fang Qiong!" Then he looked back and shouted to Xia Zhe and Lu Ting, "Run! What are you waiting for? Leave this place and flee as far as possible, dear kids!"

Having heard her father's words, Lu Ting held Xia Zhe's hand and ran out in a hurry.

When they were out, they saw no one was in the corridor, so they ran downstairs softly and went towards the street along a narrow lane. After a while, Xia Zhe calmed down, slowed down his steps and finally stopped.

Lu Ting urged him, "Go quickly."

"Where can we go?"

"I don't care. First leave Beijing and then think of a way. As long as I can stay together with you, I don't care where I am."

"How about your father?"

"Him?"

"I can't go! I did it, so I can't let your father take punishment for me." Xia Zhe turned around and started walking back.

"Wait a moment." Lu Ting was contradictory in her mind, but after thinking twice, she had no choice but to go back with Xia Zhe.

Lu Boping was surprised when she saw Xia Zhe and Lu Ting coming back. He said anxiously, "Why do you come back? I told you to run away."

"Xia Zhe didn't want to implicate you in this." Lu Ting said.

"I won't be implicated. I will say you did it, but you ran away. Let them go and catch you. China is so big and there is a large floating population. Where can they find you? After one or two years, when the incident is forgotten, you can come back."

Xia Zhe said, "Uncle, if I run away, they will suspect you. Besides, I can't let Ting escape with me."

"What can we do?" Lu Boping looked at the body beside the wall, walked around twice, and said, "There is only one way out. We can just say when Fang Qiong came in, she threatened with her own death to ask Zhe to marry her. But Zhe did not agree, so she shot herself. When she took out the gun, we didn't expect she would truly commit suicide." Having said this, Lu Boping kicked the gun to Fang Qiong's right hand.

Lu Ting and Xia Zhe thought there wasn't a better solution, so they agreed.

Lu Boping called the police. While waiting for them, Lu Boping made up the story again so that all three would give the same depositions.

The police came. They examined the body, surveyed the site, took photos and took notes, and then asked Lu Boping and two others about the proceedings. Activities continued past midnight, and eventually they took Fang Qiong's body away in the police vehicle.

After the police was gone, Lu Boping and two others sat on the couch in the living room. They did not speak for quite a long time.

Xia Zhe was very anxious and utterly confused. He looked pale and his lips trembled. He thought the things that happened to him these days were really inconceivable. It seemed some mystic power was working against him and tossing all kinds of misfortune towards him. As the paper slip read, he was facing a disaster. He wanted to break the embarrassing silence, but he could not find the appropriate words.

Lu Ting was calm, but she did not want to talk, either, because she was thinking about strategies. Although the police did not say anything after hearing their statement, Lu Ting felt the police did not totally believe the idea that Fang Qiong committed suicide. What if the police did not believe them? After pondering over and over, she thought the only way out was to take on the guilt for him. She was willing to go to prison for her lover. But Xia Zhe would definitely not agree. In what way could she bear responsibility for his guilt? Voluntary surrender? No, if the police was not investigating further, the sacrifice would be made in vain. Maybe it was better to wait.

Lu Boping did not want to talk, either, because he had secrets. He had been confident that he could overcome all difficulties, but when he saw the two youngsters who carried his genes, he felt there was something that he was not able to achieve. He did not believe in destiny, but at this moment, the word occurred to him with resilience. He looked at Xia Zhe blankly.

Xia Zhe was a bit nervous under Lu's vision, and he finally lost his composure and asked softly, "Uncle, what's wrong? You have something to tell me?"

"Ah, nothing." Lu Boping was a little nervous. He said, "I think this is not finished yet. We can't always look like this, especially Zhe. Fang Qiong's death was a suicide and had nothing to do with us. She was trying to provoke conflicts between us and frame Zhe. She deserved it. The police will investigate for sure, and they may monitor us. We should behave in a way we normally do, and not let others perceive the truth. I believe that as long as we are united, we will go through the hardship."

Lu Boping stood up, went to the window, and drew the curtain aside.

Dawn already appeared in the east.

Chapter 31 – The Kin Concealment

After going back to the hospital, Xia Zhe lied on his bed restlessly and pretended to be sleeping. He had been an assertive and brave person among his contemporaries, but the sudden accident threw him into confusion. Thinking that he should have become a murderer, he was scared and regretful. He went over the proceedings carefully and regretted that he took the gun and pointed it to Fang Qiong, because Fang Qiong was not a threat at the time. He regretted drinking too much, because if he hadn't, he would not have been so impulsive. And he regretted going to Lu Boping's home to have dinner, because the incident would not have taken place if he hadn't been there. He also regretted his making friends with Fang Qiong, because he had discovered earlier that the mysterious woman was not treating him with sincerity. In a word, he had a lot of regrets, but it was too late. Therefore, he thought of the mysterious paper slip. It seemed the words on it were turning into reality – "As man sows, so he shall reap. Let the father's debt be paid by the son and justice be fulfilled. Either he or you are facing disasters and no regret will help." What was the debt? Was there any unresolved resentment between his father and Lu Boping?

Xia Zhe had a grudge against Lu Boping. He thought Lu should not have let Fang Qiong know he was eating there. Suddenly, a question flashed in his mind – how did Fang Qiong know it? She said she heard Lu Boping calling. But Lu Ting said Lu Boping informed her of the invitation at home the previous night, and it was a fixed matter. It was not possible to call again the next day. If Fang Qiong lied, then how did she know it? Only Lu Ting and Lu Boping should know this. Was it Lu Boping who told Fang Qiong? Why did he tell Fang Qiong? Was it Lu Boping who asked Fang Qiong to come to his home? But why did he do this?

Xia Zhe was lost in his reasoning when someone called his name. It was Bai Mei. So he stood up and asked, "Mom, why do you come?"

Bai Mei was anxious. Having no time to greet other patients, she took Xia Zhe out of the room. They went to the patient activity room at the corner of the corridor. There was no one in the room, and they sat face to face on the chairs.

Bai Mei looked to the outside and asked in a low voice, "What happened?"

"What are you talking about?" Xia Zhe had no idea how to tell his mother about this incident.

"You shot the woman dead?"

"How did you know it?"

"Your uncle Lu told me."

"How did he say?"

"He said when you were eating, the woman came and brought a gun. Later you took away her gun, but suddenly the gun discharged accidentally and the woman was shot dead. Was it correct?"

"Why did he tell you all the details?"

"He was afraid you could not take the stress and asked me to visit you. He was worried you might do something stupid."

"Why did he care for me all of a sudden?"

"In fact, he cared for you always."

"By the way, did you call him a few days ago and asked him to meet you at the back gate of Beihai?"

"How did you know it?"

"Ting told me."

"He was so ridiculous! He told his daughter everything!"

"What did you say in the meeting?"

"Nothing serious. We just talked about the comrade gathering."

"Why did you need to meet at the back gate of Beihai? Are you hiding something from me?"

"Zhe, you know, I do everything for your benefit."

"I know. But I feel that you met uncle Lu because of Ting and me."

"Don't guess."

"I'm not guessing. Besides, the incident was strange. I went to uncle Lu's home to have dinner, but Fang came at that time. It appeared that the whole thing was arranged by him. Mom, do you think uncle Lu tried to harm me?"

"It was impossible. He was a bit selfish, but I can guarantee that he was trying to help you."

"Trying to help me? He asked Fang to help me?"

"He was doing so with good intention, but he did not expect things took the wrong turn."

"What good intention? So he asked Fang Qiong to come. Mom, how did he know this? I'm utterly confused. You should tell me the truth, otherwise I will die for sure."

"Is it so serious? Didn't the police believe the woman committed suicide?"

"Too easy! Do you think the police are easily fooled? Impossible!"

"But your uncle Lu did not expect the gun would discharge accidentally."

"So you have known it already. Why did uncle Lu asked Fang Qiong to come? What was he doing? You must know it. Mom, you can't hide things from me."

"I..." Bai Mei's eyes turned red, and she said, "It was all my fault."

"Mom, what do you mean?" Xia Zhe was confused.

"I asked Lu to think of a way to prevent you from building a relationship with Ting."

"Why?"

"Hmm..."

"Mom, if you know something, you'd better tell me. Actually the other night I felt you did not consent to my relationship with Ting. I felt strange. Was it because..."

"Let me tell you the truth. Ting is your younger sister. You can't fall in love with her."

"What? Do you mean Lu Boping is my father?" Xia Zhe said with wide-open eyes.

Tears finally rolled out from Bai Mei's eyes. She looked at Xia Zhe and felt piercing pain in the heart. However, she was speechless and could not cry loudly. She could only swallow the bitterness she created for herself. She remembered that in a classmate reunion party, a girl friend said: "We did not understand love when we were in love, but when we finally understood love, we could not love anymore." At that time, a lot of classmates sighed with emotion when they heard this sentence, and they all agreed to drink heartily for it. Bai Mei gave a sigh, wiped her tears, and said slowly, "It's a long story. When we were in the northeast, Lu was my partner, but later he joined the army and we broke up. That's why I was in love with your father. Lu is your blood father indeed, but he did not know it. I didn't tell him until I heard you are in love with Ting. I asked him to think of a way to separate you, but I did not expect such a thing happened. So it's destiny."

Initially, Xia Zhe could not accept the fact that Lu Boping was his father, but when he heard his mother's words and saw the tears on her face, he had to believe it. He did not hold any grudges against his mother. He had grown up already and could understand his parents' behaviors. He talked to himself, "I just wondered why he looked at me in a strange manner and tried his best to help me. It was because he was my father."

"He was trying to atone for his misdeeds. It has been 20 years now, and he felt sorry for you."

"Does my father know this?"

"He knew it very early, but he did not speak. He did this for you and our family. He is a good person."

"I know. But what should Ting and I do?"

"You are brother and sister. Absolutely you can't marry each other."

"But how to tell her? Is she able to bear this?"

"I think you should tell her later. You can comfort her. This is the fact, and no one can change it."

"Let me try." Xia Zhe left his mother and went to his ward with a heavy heart.

After dinner, Xia Zhe asked Lu Ting to go for a stroll in the small garden next to the hospital. He wanted to tell her the truth, but held back the words several times.

Lu Ting thought Xia Zhe's worries and regrets were due to Fang Qiong's death, so she consoled him, "Don't be upset about the incident anymore. The woman is a bitch. She broke the relationship between my father and mother, and now she was trying to break ours. I think she was seeking death herself."

"But I did not want to shoot her. I never held a gun before. I didn't know why the gun discharged accidentally."

"I know it was an accident, but she asked for it. If she had not come to our home with a gun, and if she had not taken out the gun to threat you, she would not have died. So we were not lying when we said she committed suicide. Don't be uneasy."

"I'm worrying not just because of Fang Qiong."

"Who else is there?"

"You, and our father."

"Our father?"

"Oh, I mean your father."

"Why?"

"You had to make up a story because of my mistake. This was inappropriate."

"Why was it inappropriate? Let me tell you, I read an interesting article in the newspaper a few days ago which was entitled 'Kin Concealment'. The general idea was that the saying 'placing righteousness above family loyalty' was not good. Such an act destroyed families and hurt people's feelings.

There was a policy in ancient China: 'Kin concealment is not a crime'. When the parents screened children, or the children screened parents, or the husband and wife screened each other, it was not considered a crime. And this was the correct way. And even foreign countries now have similar policies. So we are doing the right thing."

"But will the police believe our story?"

"What can they do even if they don't believe us? The three of us are the only witnesses. They can't find any other proof."

"Certain things are hard to cover from their vision, even if they don't have proof."

"Don't always be so pessimistic. My father was right to say that you should not always be like this. You should cheer up. Don't worry, as long as we stay together, we are not afraid of anything."

"But you don't know me in full..."

"You are saying that again!" Lu Ting interrupted. "What happened to you today?"

"There is another thing I must tell you."

"What is it?"

"The thing that happened a few days ago. I lied to you. I'm sorry." Xia Zhe wanted to tell her about their brother-sister relationship, but changed the subject suddenly.

"I told you already that I would not ask about it. No matter what you did, I can forgive you, because I love you." Lu Ting said this to Xia Zhe and to herself.

Xia Zhe became silent. He did not have the heart to see Lu Ting suffer, so he made the decision to hide the truth in his heart. An idea occurred to him all of a sudden – he wanted to take Lu Ting to a faraway place. He could give up his dreams and pursuits to live together with her. They might find an isolated place in mountains and forests, and forget the past and everything. He decided to bear all condemnations from other people and his heart. He thought this was his only way to repay Lu Ting. He made the decision and held her close to his chest.

At this moment, a female nurse went to him and said, "No.3, please go back to the ward. Two policemen are looking for you."

"OK, I'll go right now." Xia Zhe answered, and the female nurse went away. Xia Zhe turned around, held Lu Ting's hands and asked eagerly, "Ting, are you willing to flee with me to a place where no one is around? We can stay side by side for the rest of our lives. Are you willing to do that?"

"Now? Why?"

"Because we might not have the chance later."

"You are afraid they will arrest you?"

"I just want to ask you."

"We can't go for now, because you can't vindicate yourself if you go. They will say you committed intentional homicide and fled to escape punishment."

"Yes, I can't prove my innocence if I run." Xia Zhe suddenly held Lu Ting in his arms, kissed her frantically, and then he pushed her away and went back to the hospital.

Two men with police uniforms walked towards him.

Chapter 32 – The End of Investigation

Two criminal police officers, one man and one woman, were responsible for Xia Zhe's case. The man's name was Lan Weiwen, and the woman's name was Lyu Hejie. They did not interrogate Xia Zhe after bringing him back to the detention center. After analyzing the case details, they did not believe the statement that Fang Qiong committed suicide; rather, they thought it was highly probable that Xia Zhe killed her in revenge, but they did not have evidence. At this moment, they received a phone call. Someone claimed he could provide some information in connection with the case. The person was Liang Gao, the deputy manager of Hongyuan Securities. After making an appointment, they met Liang in a private room of a tea house.

Lan Weiwen and Lyu Hejie were in plain clothes and sitting opposite Liang. Lan said with a smile, "Mr. Liang, this place is good, right? You don't want to go to the police station; nor do you want us to go to your company. I can understand. This place is quiet, and I have asked them not to disturb us. You can take easy and tell your story."

Liang grinned and said, "OK, I will make it short. I know you are investigating the case of Fang Qiong. I don't know what happened in Mr. Lu's home the other night, but I can assure you that she would not commit suicide. She is an optimistic person who has dreams and pursuits. Let me tell you, a person like her would definitely not commit suicide."

Officer Lyu asked, "I heard you and Fang Qiong have an intimate relationship. Is it true?"

"Yes, we are getting along very well. As a matter of fact, I like Fang Qiong, but we are just friends. I have my own principles. I have a wife, and I can't have an affair. My relationship with Fang Qiong did not pass the borderline. If you have doubt about this, you can investigate."

Officer Lan said, "We can believe you in this regard, but you said Fang Qiong could not have committed suicide. So it was a homicide. Who do you think is the murderer?"

"Xia Zhe. He hates Fang Qiong. There are two things. First, he has been pursuing Fang Qiong, but she looks down upon him, so he has grudges in the heart. Second, he was charged with fraud, you know. Both transactions were operated by Fang Qiong, so he thought Fang Qiong framed him. He is a revengeful person."

Officer Lan said, "Xia Zhe looks like a gentleman. He could possibly shoot Fang Qiong?"

"He looks gentle but is actually ruthless."

Officer Lyu said, "Mr. Liang, I have another question. Have you heard Fang Qiong had a gun when you associated with her? Or do you think she possibly had a gun?"

"I didn't hear that. She has a mysterious background and a lot of connections, but I don't think she looks like someone who possesses a gun. Let me say something I shouldn't. If you say our manager Lu has a gun, I will believe it. But I tell you this just to help you with your case work."

Officer Lan said, "You may rest assured that we will keep your words confidential. So you suspect Lu Boping, too?"

"I'm not suspecting him. I'm just guessing. Xia Zhe is in a relationship with Mr. Lu's daughter, but he dated Fang Qiong before. If Fang Qiong made trouble for them, Mr. Lu would certainly be unhappy. But I think Mr. Lu was not directly involved in this. I just feel Xia Zhe had the motivation to kill Fang Qiong. As to Mr. Lu, you can assume I said nothing. You are experts. You can analyze it by yourself."

The officers went back to the police station after parting from Liang Gao. Now they had obtained the gun identification result. As confirmed by gun experts, the gun was an old-fashioned Browning M1900 made in Belgium with a caliber of 7.65 mm. It was maintained very well despite its age of nearly a hundred years old, and all parts worked well. There was no record on this gun in relevant gun documents. It's said that many social elites kept this type of guns in their homes before the founding of PRC, but they did not know how the gun was transferred to Fang Qiong. Fortunately, fingerprint experts identified fingerprints on the grip. After comparison, there were fingerprints of both Fang Qiong and Xia Zhe. This served as valuable evidence. However, it only proved Xia Zhe touched this gun, but did not indicate he ever shot with it. Although there was suspicion of collusion in the statements of Lu Boping, Lu Ting and Xia Zhe, the problem was how to expose their trick. Therefore, the key to uncovering the facts of this case was to find flaws in their statements and get their oral confessions.

Lan Weiwen was an experienced investigator who had extensive knowledge in interrogation methods. He knew the modified *Criminal Procedure Law* strengthened legal restrictions on interrogation and strictly prohibited extorting confessions by torture and using other illegal means to obtain evidence. Therefore, interrogation methods must be modified accordingly, and learning from foreign practice was a shortcut. Recently he purchased a translated book *Criminal Interrogation and Confessions* published by The People Press. After reading, he liked it a lot. The author was Professor Inbau of the law school of Northwest University, USA and two successive principals of Reid Joint School in Chicago which specialized in training interrogators. They advocated the civilized and scientific "soft interrogation" method and used examples to illustrate the psychological principles and behavioral analysis methods in interrogation. The "nine-step interrogation" method invented by Mr. Reid was also explained in detail.

Lan Weiwen thought that although the "nine-step interrogation" method did not fit into the situation of China and could not be copied indiscriminately, there were things in it that should be learned from. Especially, the "soft interrogation" method was an entirely new idea for him. From his understanding, the "soft interrogation" method was based on psychological science and behavioral analysis. The psychological characteristics and behavioral patterns of the interrogee were analyzed first, and then certain language and other human actions were used to persuade the suspect into faithful confession. The major difference between "soft interrogation" and the traditional "hard interrogation" was that in "soft interrogation", the interrogators did not force a confession; rather, they used the "soft" method to persuade the suspect, including using traps and presenting evidence so that the suspect would willingly confess. The "soft interrogation" method was "soft" in three aspects: First, the interrogators treated the suspect with a soft attitude; second, the interrogators used soft language while talking about the criminal acts; third, the interrogators gave soft descriptions of the crime consequence. On the basis of careful reading, he wrote a doggerel to summarize the "nine-step interrogation" method:

Present accusations directly, and increase tone weight gradually;

Give disculpation reasons, and discuss realistic topics;

Interrupt innocence denial, and ask questions orderly;

Refute innocence explanations, and provide logic reasoning;

Maintain a sincere attitude, and keep the suspect's attention;

Strengthen eye contact, and overcome negative moods;

Provide choice questions, and solicit unified answers;

Urge guilty confession, and obtain clear details;

Take interrogation notes, and ensure loyalty of contents.

Lan Weiwen decided to use certain principles and techniques of "nine-step interrogation" during investigation of this case. He and Lyu Hejie carefully studied the situation of every respondent and made an inquiry and interrogation plan according to the situations. The decided to start from Lu Boping.

In the manager office of Hongyuan Securities.

Lan Weiwen and Lyu Hejie were sitting on the couch.

Lu Boping sat on the opposite. He looked at the police officers with a calm demeanor and recounted the whole story of Fang Qiong's suicide the other night. He emphasized again and again that he obeyed the principle of "being true to facts" in his speech and actions due to many years of Party education.

Having heard his words, Officer Lan said politely, "Mr. Lu, it's not that we don't believe you, but the suicide version of the story is really hard to believe, right? Our investigation proved that Fang Qiong was in her right mind and was an optimistic person. She did not have any motivation to commit suicide. She was a friend of Xia Zhe, but we heard that she did not really like him, but he was pursuing her. It's totally unreasonable to say that she took her own life for love when Xia Zhe was in love with another woman, right? And you just said she wanted to give a lesson to Xia Zhe after entering the room, but she took out the gun and killed herself. This is unreasonable indeed, right?"

Lu Boping smiled and said, "Officer Lan, what is reason? It is human realization, and different people have different realizations. Your reason might be different from mine, and my reason might be different from Fang Qiong's. For example, she might think her suicide was a lesson to Xia Zhe. And this was her reason."

"Mr. Lu, I agree that people's understandings of reason are different. But in a society, people have some common realizations about reason. For example, generally people don't hurt their relatives, especially the ones they love, right?"

"Not necessarily. Some people hurt their relatives, and some even deliberately do so."

"You are referring to the special cases, but I'm talking about the common people and common situations. Reason applies in common situations."

"Then from your perspective, many things in life are unreasonable. During Sino-Vietnamese War, many things I saw were unreasonable. And in modern society, many things are unreasonable. Take the stock market for example, it goes up sharply today, but may decline drastically tomorrow. Is it reasonable? Therefore, reason is not as important as facts. This is called being true to facts. The Communist Party attaches importance to this principle. No matter what we do, we should be true to facts. I'm a leader, and I follow this principle in my dealings with seniors and subordinates. You are police officers who represent the country and its people, so being true to facts is even more important to you. HIstory has taught us that if we disobey this principle, we will make mistakes."

"Mr. Lu, it's a good lesson. We will adhere to the principle of being true to facts when we handle cases. And this is a basic principle in the *Criminal Procedure Law* of China. Well, I'd like to ask you to write the sentence 'Be true to facts.' after the inquiry record. Is it OK?"

"Of course. I'm true to facts. Where shall I write it?"

"This paper sheet is full; you can write on this one, and note down your name and the date."

Officer Lan took a sheet of blank paper from Officer Lyu and placed it in front of Lu Boping. Lu wrote the sentence carefully and handed the paper to Officer Lyu. Then the two officers parted from him: "Mr. Lu, thank you for your support for our work."

Lu Boping stood at the doorway and watched the officers as they went downstairs.

In the security office of the Peace Hospital.

It was the same two officers in plain clothes, but in this time, Officer Lyu asked, and Officer Lan took notes.

Lu Ting sat on the chair opposite the officers, and narrated the whole story of Fang Qiong's suicide. She had told herself over and over to stay calm and not be afraid, but her voice was still trembling, and she dare not look at the officers' faces. She had been thinking she was not afraid of the police, but when she sat alone in front of them and was questioned, fear gripped her.

"Lu Ting, I have told you already, and now I remind you again: According to the law of China, the witness must state facts faithfully when he was asked by the investigators. Purposely presenting false evidence would cause you to be charged with perjury, do you know?" Officer Lyu's voice was not high, but stern.

"I know." Lu Ting lowered her head.

"How did Fang Qiong die?"

"She killed herself."

"Lu Ting, you are lying."

"I'm telling the truth."

"Lu Ting, raise your head and look at my eyes."

Lu Ting raised her head, glanced at Officer Lyu, but lowered her head again soon.

"Lu Ting, I know you want to help him. But I can tell you, you can't help him by doing this, and you are harming yourself. Do you know perjury is not funny? It will put your in prison. Let me tell you again, fabricating a story will make things more complex."

"I'm not making things up." Lu Ting spoke with a low but resolute voice.

"OK, I won't persuade you anymore. I can tell you, your father Lu Boping has told us the truth. Fang Qiong did not commit suicide, and your father asked you to tell us the truth, too. He wrote this to you." Officer Lyu took out the piece of paper with the words "Be true to facts." written by Lu Boping, and put it in front of Lu Ting.

Lu Ting looked at the paper sheet with wide-open eyes. It was her father's handwriting! Why did he do this? Probably they were powerless to cover the facts anymore. What can she do? She was terribly upset and dizzy. She could not hold on anymore. Her line of defense broke down, and she burst into tears.

"Lu Ting, we'll give you a last chance. As long as you tell the truth now, we won't take legal actions for your collusion in giving false evidence. It's not just your responsibility."

Lu Ting raised her head, looked at Officer Lyu and took a deep breath. Then she said with a low voice, "Xia Zhe shot Fang Qiong because of an accidental discharge."

"Xia Zhe shot her dead? Please tell us the proceedings. Neglect the former events; we only want to hear what happened after Fang Qiong took out the gun."

"Fang Qiong took out the gun and wanted to shoot Xia Zhe. Then I was worried, and I tried to snatch the gun, but it fell on the floor. Xia Zhe picked the gun up and pointed it to Fang Qiong. Then I heard the gunshot, and Fang Qiong died. Xia Zhe did not want to fire. The gun discharged itself."

After making the faithful statement, Lu Ting signed on the inquiry record. Having lost all her wits, she went out of the security office.

In the interrogation room of the police station.

The two police officers sat behind the table.

Xia Zhe sat on the chair opposite them. He put his hands on the knees and his fingers were slightly trembling.

Officer Lan said, "Xia Zhe, don't be nervous. It's not your first time to be interrogated, and you know the policies and rules, right? As long as you are honest, everything will be fine. Now we can have a casual chat. You are 21, right? Where did you celebrate your last birthday? And did you eat a birthday cake?"

Xia Zhe was relaxed a bit. He lifted his head, looked to the right and scratched the back of his head with the left hand. After thinking for a moment, he said, "I celebrated my birthday at home with my father and mother. I ate a birthday cake, the cream one my mother liked most."

"By the way, I heard you are a stock market expert. My wife trades stocks, too. Can you tell me what is the trend in the latter half of this year?"

Xia Zhe looked at Officer Lan. When he saw the officer's sincere attitude, he started thinking seriously. He slightly lowered his head, looked to the left, and knocked on his leg with his right hand fingers. "This issue is complicated. If the government does not issue any major policy, Chinese stock market may remain sluggish for a long time. Certainly, the trend of international stock market may affect the Chinese one; especially, the change of Hong Kong stock market quotations will surely cause great swings in Shanghai and Shenzhen stock markets. I predict there will be a temporary small upward trend in July to August. If you take advantage of the opportunity, you can earn a considerable profit."

"You are a stock market expert indeed. Whenever the topic changes to the stocks, you are enlivened. You are not nervous now, right? OK, let's get to the subject. Tell us the whole story of Fang Qiong's death the other night."

Xia Zhe retold the story made up by Lu Boping once more.

Officer Lan had a look at Officer Lyu's records, then he turned his vision to Xia Zhe and asked, "Please recall what position you stood at when Fang Qiong shot herself."

"Let me think." Xia Zhe's head was slightly lowered and his vision tilted to the left. He knocked on his leg with his right hand fingers and said, "I was standing opposite her at the time. We were separated by the dining table and Lu Ting."

"Do you remember what gun she was holding at the moment?"

"It was my first time to see the real gun and I did not know what model it was."

"Was it heavy?"

"Hmm...it did not seem to be heavy. I didn't touch it, how could I know how heavy it was?" Xia Zhe sweated.

"You didn't touch it even after Fang Qiong died? When young people see a gun for the first time, they are generally curious and want to pick it up and have a look. You didn't?"

"No! I was scared. I was not in the mood to observe it."

"Are you sure?"

"Yes, I am."

"Xia Zhe, don't play tricks on us! You think your fabrication is perfect, but you can't cheat us! You know, our policy is "Leniency to those who confess,severity to those who resist." Your fabrication is considered resist and therefore unfavorable for you. I'm persuading you with good intentions."

"......"

"Xia Zhe, I have every reason to say you made it up. Now I will let you know so that you'll be fully convinced. First, you said Fang Qiong took her own life for love, but why didn't she kill you first? Since it was death for love, why should she allow you to live till now? It's unreasonable, right? Second, do you think my first two questions were asked for fun? I was observing your behavioral patterns. My first question was a retrospective one, and your behavior pattern was raising the head, looking to the right, and scratching the back of your head with your left hand, right? My second question was an analytical one, and your behavior pattern was lowering your head, looking to the left, and knocking on your leg with your right hand fingers, right? Then I asked you where you were standing at when Fang Qiong fired. This was a retrospective question, and if you answered it faithfully, you should have raised your head, looked to the right, and scratched the back of your head with your left hand, but your movement was lowering your head, looking to the left, and knocking on your leg with your right hand fingers. It indicated your thinking activity at the moment was not recalling, but analyzing. Faithful answering requires no analysis, right? You were analyzing. It meant you lied, because you were afraid of revealing the facts without being aware of it, right? You thought your thinking activities were all in your brain and nobody knew it. You were wrong, because your behavior patterns told me how you were thinking. Third, you said you did not touch the gun, but how were your fingerprints left on the grip? Man, you had a swift reaction. I asked you whether the gun was heavy, but you did not fall into my trap. However, your fingerprints on the grip were irrefutable evidence which could not be denied. And one more thing, Lu Ting and Lu Boping admitted Fang Qiong's death was not a suicide. Xia Zhe, you are a smart person. Please confess. Did you kill Fang Qiong deliberately, or accidentally due to an uncontrolled discharge?"

Till now, Xia Zhe's line of defense collapsed. He said dejectedly, "The gun discharged accidentally."

"OK, please tell us the whole story again."

Xia Zhe narrated faithfully the proceedings that took place the other night.

Officer Lan said with a softer tone, "Xia Zhe, you have admitted you shot Fang Qiong. This is good. But if you want lenient treatment, you have to confess all your crimes. What were you thinking when you fired the gun?"

Xia Zhe raised his head and said, "I did not fire indeed, and I don't know how the gun discharged."

"Let me tell you, we did the investigative experiment. The gun has very tight parts and is not easy to discharge accidentally. Your fingers must have touched the trigger, right?"

"Maybe I touched it, but I did not fire indeed."

"I want to ask you one more question. If someone betrayed you, will you take revenge?"

"It depends on what happened."

"For example, if someone cheated you, will you retaliate?"

"Not necessarily."

"Do you hate Fang Qiong?"

"I don't."

"You made friends with her, but she dumped you. You don't hate her? She made you lose a lot of money in the stock market and caused you to be detained. You don't hate her?"

"I..."

"I did not say you wanted her to die, but if she was shot dead, you were OK with that, right?"

"I'm not sure, but I didn't want to kill her."

At last, Xia Zhe signed the interrogation record and put his fingerprint on it.

The police officers were happy to get Xia Zhe's oral confession. They followed up the victory to question Lu Boping. In the face of Lu Ting's testimony and Xia Zhe's confession, Lu Boping revised his statement and admitted Fang Qiong was shot by Xia Zhe, but he insisted that it was an accidental discharge. As to Xia Zhe's relationship with Fang and Fang's social network, Lu said he did not know anything. What truly surprised and impressed the police officers was Lu's attitude after his "be true to facts" fell apart. He was not ashamed at all. Instead, he eloquently talked about the "kin concealment" policy in traditional Chinese culture, and said that it was a noble act for the father to cover his child's crime. He emphasized that "placing righteousness above family loyalty" went against human nature. The two police officers sighed and thought that Lu Boping was really a talented leader. But they did not want to reason with him, because they already obtained sufficient evidence of guilt and could put an end to the investigation.

After reporting the case investigation details to the leaders of the crime investigation division, Officer Lan and Lyu wrote a final report, which included comprehensive case materials and the case cracking process, and then transferred the case to the pre-trial division. After interrogating the suspect and reviewing relevant evidence materials, the pre-trial personnel considered that there was sufficient evidence in this case, including the suspect's oral confession, witness testimonies, site survey record, forensic autopsy report, murder weapon, and fingerprint identification conclusion, and that the details of evidence supported each other. According to Article 93 of *Criminal Procedure Law*, the criminal facts were clear and evidence was irrefutable and sufficient; therefore, investigation was finished. Under approval of responsible leaders, they sorted out the case materials and wrote the *Letter of Proposal for Prosecution*, which stated that Xia Zhe's acts constituted the crime of intentional homicide as specified in Article 132 of the *Criminal Law*, and transferred the case to the procuratorate for review and prosecution.

Chapter 33 – The Disproof from the Defense

Xia Zhe went into the interview room of the detention center and sat beside the table. He looked through the window at Hong Jun, who was talking with the police, and thought about the upcoming trial. From the police's words during interrogation, he felt the police had affirmed that he killed Fang Qiong intentionally. This time probably Mr. Hong could not help him, either. A life for a life. He thought about death sentence. He trembled for a moment and felt the horror of death. He was only 21 and his life just started, or so to speak, hadn't really started yet. I would finish in this way? He was not resigned to it! He did not understand how everything happened. Why did all of these unfortunate events come upon him? He thought of his birth. Maybe it was the arrangement of destiny – he was a living being that should not have arrived in the world. Since his parents brought him to the world by mistake, he would certainly not be welcome. When there was an error, there would be punishment. In the unseen world, destiny worked to maintain justice. He had no right to blame life, and he could only resent his parents who brought him into life. But what was the fault of his parents? They just stepped into life at that time, maybe at the same age as he was now. Wasn't it unfair to put all blame on them? Xia Zhe thought this question had no answer. Maybe life itself had no answer. For any living being, there was neither cause nor result, and only longer or shorter existence remained. Indeed, any life was a continuation of other lives, but why should there be such a continuation? He did not know.

Hong Jun went inside and sat opposite Xia Zhe. After hearing Xia Zhe's narrative, he pondered for a moment and asked, "Did you put your finger on the trigger at the moment?"

Xia Zhe made a movement of holding a gun, "I thought I placed my finger on the trigger. I had never held a real gun. I did not want to pull the trigger, but maybe my finger touched it. I did not know a gun could discharge so easily."

"Do your hands tremble when you are nervous?" Hong Jun looked at Xia Zhe's slightly trembling fingers.

"A little." Xia Zhe also looked at his hand.

"Did your hand shake when you heard the gunshot?"

"I can't remember. It seemed my whole body shook, because I was scared by the gunshot. Then I saw Fang Qiong was bleeding in the chest, and I was extremely frightened."

"How far were you from Fang Qiong?"

"We were separated by a dining table, maybe two meters."

"Did you know Fang Qiong would come?"

"No, absolutely not!"

"I have a question. I hope you can answer me honestly – were you in love with Fang Qiong?"

"I think I did."

"Do you think she loved you?"

"Hmm...I thought she loved me, but later I found that she was acting with me and had never been in love with me."

Hong Jun could understand Xia Zhe's words, because he thought of his relationship with Sheila. He nodded and said, "If your feeling is correct, then her behavior on the other night was very strange. Let us analyze this. Suppose the accidental discharge had not taken place the other night, what would have been the result? Or what result she wanted to achieve by doing this? Obviously it was the breaking up of you and Lu Ting. If she had truly loved you, it would have been easy to understand, because she would have wanted to break your relationship. But, since she did not love you, why should she do this? What was her purpose?"

"I guessed it was Lu Boping who asked her to go."

"Lu Boping? Why?"

"Because Lu Boping did not wish me to be in love with Lu Ting."

"So you mean this was a play directed by Lu Boping, and Fang Qiong was only an actress in it. This is interesting! But didn't you say Lu Boping was good to you? Besides, even if he didn't approve your relationship, was it really necessary to arrange such a play?"

"I think he has his own difficulty that he is reluctant to mention. Anyway, it's a private family matter, and I don't want to say."

"OK. I have another question that I hope you can answer faithfully – do you hate Fang Qiong?"

"I don't hate her. Of course, when I came to know that she did not love me, I felt she cheated me and played with my emotions. Once I was very angry, but it was not hate. I didn't have the intention to kill her. Mr. Hong, I have a question, too. What is indirectly intentional? I heard this phrase from the procurator."

"According to the *Criminal Law*, there are two kinds of intentional offense. One is directly intentional offense, and the other is indirectly intentional offense. It refers to the subjective psychology of the perpetrator. If the perpetrator knew his action would cause harm to the society, and he wanted the harmful result to occur, then his offense was called directly intentional offense. On the other hand, if the perpetrator knew his action would cause harm to the society, although he did not want the occurrence of the harmful result, he did not object to it, either; or in other words, he turned a blind eye to the occurrence of the result, then it was called indirectly intentional offense. Both directly intentional offenses and indirectly intentional offenses are crimes, and the perpetrator had to bear criminal responsibilities."

"I did not want to kill Fang Qiong, but I pointed the gun at her, was it indirectly intentional?"

"It depends on the exact circumstances at that time. It's all about how you were thinking. If you knew she might be shot dead if you pointed the gun at her, and you thought it was fine, this was called turning a blind eye to it, and your behavior should be considered indirectly intentional."

"I did not know the gun would discharge accidentally, and I did not expect she was shot dead. But I seemed to have said she was seeking death or such. Was it indirectly intentional?"

"It's hard for me to answer this question. I have to read all the evidence in the case files before coming to a conclusion."

"I really didn't expect Fang Qiong could be shot dead, so I didn't turn a blind eye to the incident. Mr. Hong, I'm telling you the truth, do you believe me?" said Xia Zhe with slightly red eyes.

Hong Jun sympathized with Xia Zhe, but he could not give any promise at this moment. He gave a sigh and said, "I believe you, but the problem is how to make the judge believe you. I hope we can find favorable evidence."

Hong Jun parted from Xia Zhe and went out of the detention center with a heavy heart. When he accepted Xia Zhe's case, he did not expect things would take such a turn. It was an unexpected event that he was powerless to handle.

After review, the procuratorate decided to combine the murder and the earlier fraud to institute a public prosecution.

Hong Jun read the copy of the indictment of the procuratorate, then he went to the court to carefully read and take note of the case files. Afterwards, he came to the Physical Evidence Authentication Center of Renmin University of China. He asked the teacher who did the handwriting authentication about the authentication result. The teacher said the signature on the authorization sheet was not faked, and its handwriting characteristics were identical with those of Xia Zhe's sample handwriting. It could be confirmed that the signature was Xia Zhe's handwriting. Since it was the teacher's opinion, Hong Jun thought it was unnecessary to ask the court to do the same. He took back the authentication material and asked some questions related to bullet examination, and then he left the university.

Hong Jun came to the detention center again and met the defendant Xia Zhe. He briefly introduced his defense opinions, verified some details about the case, and explained some matters that they should pay attention to during court investigation. At parting, Xia Zhe asked Hong Jun to deliver a letter to Mrs. Sullivan and said it was unrelated to this case.

After coming out of the detention center, Hong Jun came to Meihu Decoration Company and went directly into Xia Dahu's office.

Xia was reading a document. When he saw Hong Jun, he asked in surprise, "Mr. Hong, why do you come here? You have anything to talk with me?"

Hong Jun did not answer. He asked instead, "Mr. Xia, you already knew the incident that took place in Lu Boping's home, right?"

"The murder of the female clerk? I heard it."

"It seems you do not care much about this."

"I have a lot to care about myself. Why should I care for others?"

"But it involves your son. Don't you know Xia Zhe was arrested again?"

"Yes, but he's above 18. He should be responsible for his acts. I can't be executed on behalf of him for his murder crime, anyway."

"I don't mean it. I just want to discuss the defense with you."

"You want money? To tell you the truth, I can't help with this anymore."

"I'm not trying to charge money. Since I accepted his case, I will defend him for no personal benefit."

"I know you are never a money grubber. But how can I help?"

"I want you to give a testimony."

"What is it?"

"To tell the details of the prying of your two safes." Hong Jun pointed to the two safes, one big and one small.

"What does this have to do with Zhe's case?"

"Maybe it has, but I'm not clear about it."

"OK. I wrote a document to the police before, and I kept the manuscript."

"And I need your cooperation in the court session. You are Xia Zhe's father." Hong Jun intentionally paused when he said this.

"Of course!" Xia answered.

"So you understand him the most. To speak your mind, do you think he could ever shoot a person?"

"He is quite an asshole, but not enough to kill a person. He is not someone who does things without considering the result."

"So I hope you can appear as a witness in court."

"What do you wish me to say?"

"I hope you can talk about Xia Zhe's personality and character as shown in daily life and prove to the court that he could not possibly murder a person. This is called 'character evidence', which is persuasive to the judge." Hong Jun looked at Xia's eyes.

"It's OK, but will the judge believe me? I'm Xia Zhe's father."

"The father is generally partial to his son. It's human nature and justified." Hong Jun paused, as if he was observing Xia's expression. "I have another question. It's my guess, but it concerns your privacy, so I don't know if I should talk about it."

"You can tell me. I'd like to listen."

"OK, I'll tell you directly. Please pardon me for any offense."

"Just say it."

"When I met Xia Zhe for the first time, I felt he did not look like you in appearance and demeanor. Besides, Xia Zhe had trembling fingers. As far as I know, the tremor is hereditary, and is passed down by dominant inheritance. The tremor is generally on fingers, but if it's serious, the head and body may tremble as well. Trembling will be aggravated when the patient is nervous or excited. I noticed that neither you nor Bai Mei has the finger tremor, but Lu Boping has it. And Xia Zhe's speech tone and expression were like Lu Boping. Am I right?"

Xia Dahu looked at Hong Jun, but did not answer.

Hong Jun looked at Xia's reactions and continued, "I remember you once mentioned Xia Zhe's birth was an accident. So I guess that Xia Zhe is not your biological son. I hope you are not angry with my words."

Xia's body moved slightly, but he still kept quiet.

"You are a careful observer. It's not possible that you did not find anything in many years' life together. It's easy to understand why you have been keeping quiet. There is a saying, 'Domestic shame should not be made public.' You are a person who has high social status and values the family. In other people's eyes, you have a happy family, so you don't want outsiders to know this truth, and you don't want to break the family. Am I right? You may rest assured that I won't discuss this issue in court defense, but I need an answer, because it will help me solve certain doubts in the case."

Xia finally gave a sigh. He nodded and said, "Other people think I have a happy family, but every family has its own problems."

"Yes, as the English said, every family has a skeleton in the cupboard. I guess you have a document in your safe that can prove Xia Zhe's real birth, and this was why you did not first check the wood purchase contract after the safe was pried. Am I right?"

"I think you have enough wits to write a whodunit, hahaha!" Xia's laughter was not quite natural. Maybe he felt a bit embarrassed, so he changed the subject. "When a man gets married, he is shackled and deprived of freedom. If you have a happy family, you are lucky; if you do not get along with the wife and have divorced her, it's cool; but a lifeless marriage is the most horrible thing of all. You don't have the heart to divorce, and you feel sick when you stay together. This is great suffering. So it's wise of you to not get married."

Hong Jun thought Xia admitted it by default, so he did not ask further. He replied casually, "I have no alternative. I want to get married, but if the other person does not agree, what can I do?"

"You are so modest. You have talents, good looks, and money; all women would agree to marry you. I'm afraid the one who does not agree is yourself."

"I don't even understand myself." Hong Jun did not want to discuss this topic, because he thought of another question, "Mr. Xia, do you know Han Xinyun?"

When Xia heard the name, he was surprised for a moment. Then he said, "Yes, I know her. She was my childhood neighbor and classmate, but I haven't seen her for over 20 years. You know her?"

"Yes, and you saw her recently."

"Really? Where?" Xia widely opened his eyes.

"Right here." Hong Jun smiled.

"Here? You mean..."

"Her current name is Sheila Sullivan."

"Ah..." For quite a while, Xia sat still with half-open mouth. Then he stood up, went to the safe, opened it and took out a plastic bag. He opened the bag carefully and took out a neatly curled dark red waist belt.

Hong Jun recalled he saw the waist belt on the day of burglary and felt strange at the moment.

Xia sat in front of the writing desk again and looked blankly at the belt in his hand. He asked himself, "Is this Mrs. Sullivan really Han Xinyun?" He remembered when he first met Mrs. Sullivan, he felt this American looked like someone, but he did not think of Han Xinyun at that time, because Mrs. Sullivan did not speak Mandarin. And he said to her that he felt familiar with her. Mrs. Sullivan appreciated this sentence of him, but then said she often appeared on TV in China.

Having heard Hong Jun's words, Xia compared the appearances of Mrs. Sullivan and Han Xinyun. They looked similar indeed, but Mrs. Sullivan did not have the obvious black mole on her face.

However, there could be no doubt in Hong Jun's words.

A mixed feeling of helplessness and resentment arose in Xia's heart. He wanted to cry out, but did not know which place he could shout to. He wanted to swear, but did not know whom he could curse. He wanted to wail, but did not know which location his tears could fall on. He thought there were many, many misunderstandings and helpless situations in life. He did not believe in destiny, but could not run away from its game. He was exhausted in heart and soul, and his vision blurred...

Chapter 34 – The Blood Red Belt

There was a saying among locals in old Beijing – "The powerful are in the east, the wealthy are in the west, and the slums are in Xuanwu and Chongwen". Therefore, there were many grand courtyards in the eastern part of the city, and many small quadrangle courtyards in the western part; and in the south were many warrens.

There was a small quadrangle courtyard in an alley on the north of Xisi. The yard was small but very tidy. The three-room north house was complete with two side rooms. Each of the east and west wings has two rooms. All the houses were built with the same black bricks and grey tiles. A grape tree was planted in front of the north house, and on each side of the grape trellis was one clove tree as tall as one man. Two jujube trees were growing at the foot of the south wall. One produced round sour jujubes, and the other long sweet jujubes. Therefore, the residents in his small yard could smell the fragrance of cloves and eat purple grapes and red jujubes every year.

Three families lived in this yard: the north house was owned by the man Han Wenbo, a senior engineer; the east house by the man Xia Yongxiang, a timber mill worker; and the west house by the man Lu Xirui, a section chief in the government. Accidentally, each family has one child, which was at similar ages. The girl in the north house was Han Xinyun, the youngest. The boy in the west house was Lu Boping, who was one year older than Han Xinyun. And the boy in the east house was Xia Dahu, who was two years older than Lu Boping. The three children used to play hide and seek, guessed shadow riddles, folded paper dogs and swallows, and sat in the yard counting stars together.

Dahu fell ill in childhood, so he was two years late for school. Xinyun was smart and went to school one year earlier. Therefore, the three kids were put in the same class and all of them were good students. Dahu was the class monitor, Boping was the recreation and sport secretary, and Xinyun was the study secretary. After a class committee meeting in Grade 4, the class teacher Tang asked them to discuss their dreams.

Dahu said, "I want to be a soldier after I grow up, and protect our great nation with guns, and I will liberate Taiwan and all the laboring people, which account for two thirds of the world population."

Boping said, "I want to be an athlete, a ping-pong player, and win honor for the country like Rong Guotuan."

Xinyun said, "I want to be poet after I grow up, and use my pen to glorify our country, the people, and our happy life."

After the meeting, Xinyun wrote a poem. When Dahu read the poem, he copied it on the school's blackboard newspaper:

Dreams are like beautiful flower beds,

In which flowers are colorful and blooming.

We can pick them as we wish,

Because we have time!

On an afternoon, Xinyun was studying in her room, and Dahu and Boping were kicking a ball in the yard. Suddenly, the ball flew through the grape trellis and hit the window in front of Xinyun. With a loud clatter, broken glass fell on Xinyun's desk.

Xinyun ran out and shouted, "Who did it?"

Boping mumbled, "I kicked the ball but Dahu did not catch it."

Dahu retorted, "You kicked in the wrong direction."

"It's your fault!"

"Your fault!"

"Don't quarrel. Please say what you are going to do."

Boping drew a long face and said, "If my father knows this, he will beat me."

The three kids became quiet. After quite a while, Xinyun said, "OK, I will say I broke the glass carelessly. My father does not beat me."

Dahu said, "You can say I did it, and I will ask my mother to not tell my father."

Boping shook his head, "No, no. I'm the culprit. I can't have you bear the responsibilities."

Xinyun said, "Don't argue now. Let's decide this with our rule – palm and back." She raise her right hand. And the other two kids looked at each other and raised their right hands as well. All three shouted together, "Misfortune falls on the different."

The result was that only Xinyun showed the back of her hand. She said solemnly, "It's settled now."

Dahu was still worried. He asked, "You don't kick, how will you say you broke the window?"

"Don't worry about it. I have my own method." Having said this, Xinyun went back into her room.

The adults went home one after another from work. When Xinyun's mother saw the window glass was broken, she asked what happened. While picking up glass fragments from the desk, Xinyun said, "Mom, I made trouble. When I was doing homework, a fly came. It was disgusting and flew around me. Then it landed on the window. I hit it with this book, but I used too much force and broke the glass."

"Look at yourself. You are a girl, but you are so short-tempered."

At this moment, Han Wenbo came back and looked around in the room. With a smile, he asked, "What are you doing here? You broke the window while cleaning the room?"

"Your daughter did it. She is skillful now. She could break the window while hitting a fly. Let me see how you will sleep tonight."

"Hit a fly? Xinyun, how did you hit it?"

"I used this book to hit it, but with too much force. Dad, I'm sorry."

"It's not what happened. You hit from inside, but why didn't the glass fragments fall on the outside? Instead, they fell on the desk inside. Xinyun, I have told you before that no matter what mistake you made, you should admit it bravely and tell the truth."

"I..." Xinyun was unable to respond.

At this moment, Xia Yongxiang took Dahu by the hand and went inside. "Mr. Han, I'm sorry. My son broke your glass. I have taught him a lesson already."

Han Wenbo looked at Dahu, who had tears in his eyes, and said kindly, "It doesn't matter, Dahu. How did you break the glass?"

Dahu glanced at Xinyun and said, "I kicked the ball to the glass by mistake. Uncle, I'm sorry."

Han Wenbo also glanced at Xinyun and was about to say something when Lu Xirui took his son by the hand and came in. Lu said with a smile, "Mr. Han, my son Boping said he broke your glass. I'd like to apologize for his mistake, and tomorrow I will buy a pane of glass and installed it for you. Is it alright?"

Han Wenbo said, "Mr. Lu, it doesn't matter. It's just a pane of glass, a trifle. But this is indeed strange." Han Wenbo glanced at the three children's faces and said seriously, "Xinyun, Dahu, and Boping each broke a pane, there should be three broken panes of glass. Right? But there was only one. What happened?"

Boping said in a hurry, "I kicked the ball."

Dahu said, "It was my mistake, because I failed to guard it."

"Guard what?" Han Wenbo asked.

"Guard the gate. Boping was shooting. So it was my mistake, not his."

"Ah, now I understand. Boping was the forward, Dahu was the goalkeeper, and Xinyun was the audience. And the forward shot the ball to the auditorium. OK, things are clear now. We won't blame you. But this yard is so small and cannot be used as a football pitch. You can't kick balls in this yard anymore. Do you understand?"

"Yes, I do." Two boys replied.

Lu Xirui said, "Mr. Han, so I will buy glass tomorrow morning."

Han Wenbo replied, "No, I have two panes of glass in my small room. They were small, but may fit in."

Xia Yongxiang said, "Let me do the installation work. I have a glass cutter and putty. It takes only a little while to install the glass."

"Thank you, Mr. Xia." Han Wenbo thought for a moment and said, "I have an idea. The children like playing sports. It's a good thing. I have an unused bed board, which can be made into a ping-pong table. It can be placed right under the south wall. I have to ask for your help in this matter."

"No problem. I'm good at wood work."

"That's great!" The three kids jumped.

"Be patient. I have one more question to ask you, and you have to be honest and cannot tell lies." Han Wenbo took back his smile and asked seriously, "Did you have breakfast together this morning?"

"Yes." All three kids replied with one voice.

"Did you eat the same thing?"

"Yes, the same."

"Good. You need to tell me what you ate."

"Baked food."

"Pancake."

"Fried sugar cake."

They gave different answers this time, and then looked at each other in despair. And other adults looked at Han Wenbo in confusion. Han continued, "You didn't have breakfast at all, right?"

The three kids lowered their heads.

"You didn't have breakfast all these days, right? I said you should be honest, but why don't you tell the truth?"

Dahu raised his head and said, "Sorry, uncle, it was my idea. Our classmate Yang Zhendong's father was put in jail, and his mother makes matchboxes for the subdistrict office to make a living. They are very poor. Last week his mother was sick, and they did not have money to buy food. So I discussed with Boping and Xinyun, and then we saved our breakfast money and gave it to him."

"It's good. Dahu is acting as a responsible class monitor." Han Wenbo smiled again, "I came across your teacher Miss Tang after work today, and she told us this. You are good kids, but you can't live without eating breakfast."

Dahu said, "We are not hungry."

"I'm hungry." Boping mumbled.

"Haha, Boping told the truth."

The adults laughed. Han Wenbo took out a 5 yuan RMB note from his pocket and gave it to Dahu. He said, "Little class monitor, you can give the money to Miss Tang, and she will pass it to Yang Zhendong's family in the name of the class."

"Wow, it's a lot of money." Dahu took the money and made a face to Xinyun.

As they grew up, a vague barrier was formed between boys and girls. Xinyun seldom played with Dahu and Boping now, and even when they spoke, they maintained a distance.

In the spring of their final year in primary school, their class went on an spring outing together. They would row on Kunming Lake. Miss Tang mixed boys and girls together in a group. Dahu and Xinyun were assigned to the same boat. Xinyun was afraid of water, so she did not get on the boat until the students encouraged her. Dahu was the rower, and he tried to row the boat quickly and steadily. He asked Xinyun to sit securely now and then and not to look at the water. Xinyun was very nervous in the beginning, but then she relaxed herself. When the boat was near the mid-lake island, she finally agreed to row. Dahu and her stood up to switch positions. The boat was shaking, and Xinyun's hand touched Dahu's arm, so she instinctively dodged backwards. As a result, she fell into the water. Without hesitation, Dahu jumped into the water. He practiced in the swimming training class of Shichahai Sports School before, so he swam very well and quickly lifted Xinyun, who was struggling in water, out of the water surface. He asked her to grasp the ship's side, and with other students' help, she climbed onto the boat. Xinyun was terrified. She was still trembling even after getting on the shore. The teacher asked two girl students to send her home.

On an afternoon a few days later, Dahu went to the grain shop to buy flour. When he arrived at the shop door, he saw Xinyun running to him from behind. With redness on her face, she handed him a paper slip folded in the shape of a pigeon and said gently, "Thank you." And then she went back quickly.

When he exited the shop, he hurriedly opened the paper slip and saw a few lines of graceful little words:

> *Bathed in bright sunshine was the Kunming Lake,*
>
> *Ripples came and breezes swept;*
>
> *Laughter, songs, and voices were reverberating,*
>
> *Leaves and flowers were dancing gracefully.*
>
> *Panicking Xinyun fell out of the boat,*
>
> *Desperate Dahu jumped over the side;*
>
> *Raise two hearts with both hands,*
>
> *And let revolutionary friendship live forever.*

Dahu read it several times. He was so excited that he forgot the grain book and change on the counter after buying flour in the grain shop, which caused the salesperson to chase him for quite a while. He felt very happy.

But shortly afterwards, Dahu's happy feeling was gone.

The "cultural revolution" swept across China, and "red rebels" were all over Beijing.

On this day, Dahu and Boping went back from school and found their yard was turned upside down — clove flowers fell on the ground, the grape trellis collapsed to one side, and the doors and windows of the north house were covered with the slogan "Strike down the reactionary capitalist academic authority Han Wenbo". The yard was deserted. They wanted to take a look in the north house, but their mothers pulled them back home.

A few days later, Han's family was evicted from the yard, and Xinyun also left school.

Later, Dahu joined the "red guards".

In the autumn of that year, dead leaves fell all over the street.

On one morning, Dahu's red guard squad received a "revolutionary task" – to criticize and punish the anti-revolutionary with the rebels of a factory. They started off immediately and came to a factory out of Andingmen. They saw some workers with red armbands standing in front of an office, so they ran there. Since there were many people in the room, Dahu was left outside. He stood at the door and felt unhappy. When he heard the loud shouts and the sounds of whipping a human in the room, how could he not be excited? He could not hold this emotions anymore; he wanted to join the revolution. Therefore, he untied his army belt, shouted slogans, and squeezed into the room.

A man with grey hair was lying in prone position in the center of the ground. Several red guards were questioning and whipping him. Dahu thought of the well-known landlord and bully Huang Shiren...Without hesitation, he wielded his belt and whipped the body which was already not reactive.

Suddenly, some shouts came from outside. Next, a middle-aged woman and a girl ran into the room. They pushed people away madly and rushed in without giving a second thought. When they saw the person lying on the ground, the girl called, "Father!" and threw herself on him.

Dahu was stunned – they were Xinyun and her mother! He bent down and checked the person beaten by them, who was turned over by the mother and daughter, and he saw a familiar face with blood and dirt.

At this moment, Xinyun lifted her head and shouted with tears on her face, "Why do you beat my father? He is a good person. I can take the beat on behalf of him..." With half-open mouth, she stopped unnaturally, and her vision was fixed on Dahu's face.

Dahu's heart shook suddenly, and his belt fell onto the ground. However, he had no courage to pick it up. Instead, he fled out of the room.

Dahu ran into the grove beside Tucheng without a stop. He wanted to find a place where no person or voice was around, but Xinyun's wails and shouts kept coming into his ears, and uncle Han's miserable face kept appearing in front of his eyes. He stood in a forest of short trees and cried at a loss. At dusk, he went home in horror.

After a painful and sleepless night, Dahu felt he grew up. Maybe all people were like this. After something happened in their lives, they suddenly found they had grown into adults.

Because he fled from the scene, his comrades laughed at him, and his red guard armband was taken away. He did not go to school anymore. Instead, he wandered on the streets all day. He heard from a neighbor that Han's family moved near Caishikou, so he went there often and hoped he could come across Xinyun on the street.However, he did not know why he was doing this.

Nothing was impossible for a willing heart. On one evening, he finally saw Xinyun at the door of the department store in Caishikou. He caught up with her quietly. After Xinyun finished shopping and went out of the store, he plucked up his courage and ran to her while calling, "Xinyun! Xinyun!"

Xinyun stopped and looked back. When she saw it was Dahu, she was surprised for a moment, but then continued to walk forward.

Dahu ran ahead of Xinyun and blocked her way. He said with a blush, "Xinyun, you can curse me; you can beat me. I..."

Xinyun's eyes brimmed with tears. She bit her lips, as if she was afraid something would come out of her mouth. Suddenly, she turned around and went towards the opposite side of the road.

"Xinyun..." Dahu was about to chase her when he noticed there was something black on her arm. He fixed his eyes upon it and found it was a black armband! He was shocked and stopped all movements.

Spring came after winter. Dahu did not wander in Caishikou anymore. Certainly, he did not forget the incident. He could only bury it deeply in his heart.

At noon, he was back from school to have lunch. When he saw her mother's face had traces of tears, he asked what happened.

His mother said, "Your aunt Lee came here just now. She said Xinyun's mother also left her."

"What? Her mother was gone?" Dahu put down his rice bowl, which he just lifted, and asked, "Where did she go?"

"Go? She was dead!"

"Dead? How?"

"Ah, she could not take the torture, so she hanged herself. Xinyun is indeed a miserable child."

"How did aunt Lee know this?"

"She came across Xinyun at the crematory."

"How about Xinyun? Did aunt Lee ask where she lived?" Dahu asked anxiously.

"No. In these days who dare care about such a family? Her family is avoided at all costs."

"Even if Xinyun's father is guilty, she is a child that can be reformed." Having said this, Dahu started going out.

"Dahu, where are you going?"

"I will find her."

"You don't know where she lives. Beijing is so big, how can you find her?"

Dahu rejected his mother's advice. He rode on his bicycle and headed to Caishikou. But when he arrived in there, he realized the meaning of his mother's words. He traveled through the alleys of Caishikou and asked around, "Is there any family nearby which had a deceased member recently?" However, the area was too large. He searched until sunset, but couldn't get even a clue, and he was given cold shoulders many times. He thought of a few girl students who were on good terms with Han Xinyun, so he asked them one by one, but they all lost their contact with her.

The evening swallowed the last sunset cloud. Dim street lamps were lit up on the streets, and people on the roads were fewer and fewer.

Dahu had traveled from the southwest corner to the northeast corner of Beijing. He was hungry, and he felt as if he was carrying heavy sandbags on his legs. But he was intensely searching with his eyes. He really hoped he could see her familiar figure in front of a shop door, under a bus stop board, or anywhere. Several times his eyes cheated him and brought him fleeting happiness, but then left him heavier clouds of disappointment.

He did not know where to head for next, so he aimlessly made a turn from Beixinqiao and rode west. When he passed Jiaodaokou and saw the drum tower in front, which appeared dark in the evening, he cried in his heart, "Xinyun, where are you?"

Suddenly, an idea occurred to him — maybe Xinyun was already back to the yard where they lived. Sure, when she lost all her relatives, where could she go except for seeking help from the old neighbors whom she lived together with for many years? Thinking of this, Dahu felt as if he saw a little light after groping in a dark cave for three days, and he would run to the light at any risk.

To reach home quickly, he turned onto the small road on the southeast of Shichahai and rode fast. The cool evening wind was blowing through his shirt, which had been soaked in sweat several times. He felt a little chilly, but he disregarded it, because he had hope in his heart.

The small road was very quiet. The street lamps far away were giving out dim light. The lake water now appeared black. And the lights on the other side were projected on the ripples, thus creating white light on the water surface. When the breezes swept over, the surface shadows were transformed into all kinds of bizarre shapes, as if many fairies were swimming in water.

Xia Dahu was riding fast when a splashing sound came from ahead. And a woman screamed, "Help! Someone jumped in the water. Help!..."

Dahu rode to the spot quickly. He jumped off the bicycle and saw two people on the bank. One was shouting and the other was taking off her coat. He looked at the water surface in the light from the other side and saw a head floating upwards and downwards in water. Without thinking much, he took off his shoes and jumped into the water. He quickly swam to the drowning person and dragged her back to the shore. With the help of the two women, he carried the drowning person onto the bank.

When Dahu got onto the bank himself, he saw the two women untied the belt of the drowning person and hung it on the back rack of his bicycle. Then the women performed water control and artificial respiration for the drowning person.

Dahu asked anxiously while putting on his shoes, "How's it going? Is she OK?"

"She's OK. She will recover soon." The woman doing artificial respiration said.

It was very dark there. Dahu could not see their faces clearly, but he felt the one who spoke was a middle-aged woman. At this moment, another woman said, "Please rest assured, my mother is a doctor."

"She coughed out the water and will wake up soon." The mother said.

Dahu put on his shoes, went close to them and asked, "How did she fall into the water?"

The daughter said, "We are not together. Just now when my mother and I were going on our way home, we saw someone standing under the tree. We felt strange. It was late now, why was she standing beside the river? In a few moments, we heard a splashing sound. She must have jumped into the water herself."

The mother said, "The water is so cold. Ah, she is a girl. She will wake up soon. We will move her to our home. There are a lot of such incidents in these days."

"Do you need my help?" Dahu asked.

"No. You are wet all over. Just go back and change clothes. We are not far from here. Honestly, we are fortunate to have you here, otherwise we don't know how to help her." said the mother.

Xia Dahu was thinking about Han Xinyun, so he rode on his bicycle and got away quickly. The daughter called from behind, "Sir, what's your name? Where can she say 'thank you' to you after she wakes up?"

"Just let her thank Chairman Mao." Dahu answered without even looking back.

He came to the back gate of Beihai, then turned onto the street and rode even more quickly westwards. After a while, he suddenly heard something falling onto the road. He put on the brake, got off his bicycle, and went back to check. It was a belt. He thought it must be the belt of the drowning person, so he picked it up. He was hesitating whether he should send it back, but suddenly he felt the dark red belt was familiar. He checked it under the street lamp but was stunned – it was his own belt. And he found his name on the back side of it. He used this belt to whip Han Xinyun's father, and dropped it in the office. How could it be here? At this moment, the mother's words flashed in his mind – the drowning person was a young girl!

He rode on his bicycle and rushed back. But when he reached the small road beside Shichahai, everybody had left.

He shouted, "Xinyun! Xinyun!"

His shouts swept over the silent water surface and flew towards the dark night sky. He looked for them along the small road, but still could not find them. At last, he went back home with frustration and regret.

On the morning of the next day, Xia Dahu went to Shichahai again and asked around, but in the chaotic age, his search was futile. And in the end, he lost all hope.

And later, he went to the Great Northern Wilderness.

He hadn't seen Han Xinyun since, but he kept the belt with him as a precious item...

Chapter 35 – One Phoenix and Three Dragons

Hong Jun left Meihu Decoration Company and drove back to Friendship Hotel. After entering his office, he make a call to Sheila's suite, but no one answered. Then he called the service counter in the front hall of Shangri-La Hotel, and they said Mrs. Sullivan had departed for the airport. Having heard this, Hong Jun got on his car right away and drove to the airport. When he arrived in the hall at the 2nd floor of Beijing Capital International Airport, the boarding procedure had been started for the plane to America. He saw Sheila and Chen Jingyi among the crowd, so he went to them quickly.

"Sheila!" Hong Jun called out.

Sheila looked back and saw Hong Jun. She frowned slightly but smiled, "Hey, Jon, are you seeing someone off in the airport?"

"Yes, I'm seeing you off, but I didn't expect you left without saying goodbye."

"Because I don't want an unhappy parting. I have been cherishing our relationship."

"Were you afraid that I didn't allow you to go?"

"You wouldn't do that. Even if you would, you had no right to."

"Exactly."

Sheila looked at her watch and said, "Sorry, Jon, I have to go."

"Take it easy. I have something important to show you! Sheila, it's noisy here, can we move aside? Just 10 minutes?"

Sheila went with Hong Jun to a quiet place nearby and asked, "What do you want me to see?"

Hong Jun took out the red waist belt from his backpack and handed it to Sheila.

Sheila took the belt, frowned and examined it carefully. She saw three characters on the back of the belt beside the metal buckle – Xia Dahu. Her hand trembled and the belt fell onto the floor. She bent over and picked it up. Then she raised her head and asked in confusion, "Where did you get this?"

Hong Jun was observing Sheila's expression. Now he said solemnly, "Xia Dahu asked me to give it to you."

"Where did he find this waist belt?"

"It was a long story." Hong Jun tried to put it simply. "It was the autumn of 1968. When he heard your mother died, he rode on his bicycle to search for you everywhere and wanted you to stay in his family. He did not find you, but saved a drowning young girl near Shichahai. A mother and her daughter were there at that time. The belt was the young girl's, but it was hung on his bicycle after she was lifted from water. On his way home, he discovered this belt, so he rushed back to look for them, but they left already. He searched on the next day and asked about the mother and daughter, but could not find them. He kept this belt with him all these years."

"What? Is it real?" Sheila widely opened her eyes.

"Xia Dahu said this, and I think it's real. And he asked me to tell you, when he took part in the criticism and punishment activity in those days, he did not know the person was your father. He really regretted what he did."

"Is it real? Is it real?" Sheila murmured, as if this was the only sentence in her mind.

Chen Jingyi went to them swiftly and said, "Madam, it's late. We should go now. We need to go through the security and customs procedure."

Sheila looked at Chen Jingyi and tried her best to control her emotions, and said to Hong Jun, "We have to go now. Thank you!"

"Sheila, I have a letter for you. Xia Zhe asked me to give it to you."

"Who is Xia Zhe?"

"Xia Dahu's son."

"It's him? I did not see him before. Why did he write me a letter?"

"I'm just entrusted to give it to you. As to why he wrote this, I don't know." While saying this, Hong Jun took out Xia Zhe's letter from his bag and gave it to Sheila.

Maybe in an attempt to adjust her mood, Sheila said with English, "Sorry, Jon, I have to board. Please wish me a safe journey."

Jon said with English, too, "I remember an English saying, 'Death may find us at any moment.' So I can only say, 'God bless you.'"

Sheila said with excitement, "Jon, are you really wishing me to die? I know you hate me and consider me as the worst woman in the world, but you don't understand me. You have not experienced that age, so you can't know who I really am."

Hong Jun apologized sincerely, "Sorry, Sheila, I don't mean it. I don't hate you at all, indeed."

"You can curse me. It's fine. I'm an atheist, anyway. I don't believe in death. I only believe 'the matter does not die'. OK, if I won't encounter death this time, I'll wait for you to swear at me in America."

"I wish you a safe journey!"

The plane took off. Sheila sat on her wide chair in the first-class cabin and fixed her vision on the red belt. Just now, her mind was in a mess and she did not have time to recall the past and to think. But at this moment, the unforgettable past events appeared in her mind.

...She had a happy childhood. So she once believed the purpose of human existence was to love, including loving others and receiving other people's love. But later, her kindly father was beaten to death, and her good-hearted mother left the world. How could she, a helpless and weak girl, face a hazardous life ahead?

On a night after her mother's body was cremated, she came to Shichahai. She was afraid of water since she was small, but she had to jump into the water. She wanted to die and let go of all suffering, but she was saved. She was very grateful for the mother, the daughter, and the unknown lad who saved her life. One who had never experienced death would not know the horror of it. She knew it now, so she decided to live no matter what came upon her. There was a saying, "Better is a bad life than a good death", and she thought it truly made sense.

Life was hard in those days. She was alone and did not have income, so she had to make a living by selling items in her home. In order to sustain life longer, she had to live frugally. Sometimes she had only one meal per day, the simplest kind of meal. Except for hunger, she was often assaulted. There were several times when young men stopped her on her way home and tried to take her away. If she did not go with them, they would beat her. She had no other choice but to run and cry. Society in those days was in total chaos. Girls in other families had mothers, fathers, brothers, and sisters to protect them. But she was alone. Who would protect her?

On an afternoon, she was stopped by two men. They stopped her before, and once again, they asked her to go with them to Taoranting Park. She didn't go, so a man beat her on the face and pulled her. She held a tree and cried loudly. People passed by, but no one cared.

At this moment, a young man came. He was riding on a Manganese Steel Model 13 bicycle and wearing a veteran suit, which was an indication of high social status in those days. The young man parked the bicycle and took out a spring lock from it. He held the spring lock in his hand, went to them and said, "What are you doing? Two men bullying a woman?"

The man who stopped her said, "Who are you? Mind your own business!"

The young man said, "Who am I? I belong here! Just ask around, who didn't know Dalong from Qianmen?"

When the two men heard "Dalong from Qianmen", their voices became weak. They apologized and ran away.

She thanked Dalong.

Dalong said, "You look good, no wonder they would assault you. Where do you live? I can send you home."

Dalong had white skin and didn't look like a bad guy, so she agreed to let him send her home. On the way, Dalong treated her to a fried stuffed bun meal in a Shanghai restaurant in Caishikou. She had not eaten delicious food like this for a long time, so she ate 1/4 kilograms. Dalong sent her home, sat inside for a while and left.

A few days later, Dalong came to visit her. They spent the day playing in Zhongshan Park. At noon, they ate preserved vegetable bun in a restaurant named Lai Jin Yu Xuan and drank wine. It was her first time to drink wine. She found that she could drink a lot. She drank half a bottle of kirsch without getting drunk. Dalong was the son of a senior government official. He liked fighting but was not rough like those scoundrels.

After coming out from Zhongshan Park, Dalong brought her to his home. He lived in a yard which was apparently luxurious. His parents went to the official school, so he lived there with his sister. At night, Dalong said he loved her and asked her to be his girlfriend. She did not know much about him, but she was safe with him, so she agreed. Actually, she liked him, too. Then he wanted to sleep with her. Initially she disagreed, but when he insisted, she did not resist anymore. When it was over, she was a bit aggrieved, but not too sad. She decided to treat him nicely to repay him. Since then, she often spent time with Dalong, and sometimes lived at his home, so she got to know some of his friends, including Erlong and Sanlong. They practiced martial arts and boxing every day. No one was at Dalong's home in the day, so they practiced in the yard. And there were stone dumbbells and sandbags made by themselves. She practiced along with them.

On one morning when she came to Dalong's home, Erlong and Sanlong also arrived. They three men imitated the "Oath of the Peach Garden" in *Romance of the Three Kingdoms* and became sworn brothers. At noon, they drank and ate lunch together. All three got drunk. Dalong said to her, "Erlong, Sanlong and I are sworn brothers. We swore to share happiness and hardship together. I'm the eldest, and I shouldn't enjoy a girlfriend alone. I'll let them enjoy you as well." When she heard this, she was worried and said, "Are you crazy? How can you share me with others?" Dalong stared at her and said, "I'm a man of my word. You must submit to us no matter what you think."

Then they stripped her naked and had sex with her in turn. They raped her for the entire afternoon. In the beginning she resisted and cried, but later she became insensitive and lost all tears. She felt she was like a public toilet which everyone could use.

After putting on her clothes, she gulped down half a bottle of wine. She could not remember how she went back to her small room. She was drunk and slept till the afternoon of the next day. When she woke up, her head still hurt, so she kept lying on her bed. She felt she was changed into a different person in terms of body and soul.

Since then, she did not view the relationship between a man and a woman like she did before. She found that as long as she gave up shame and guilt, it became a pleasant experience, a kind of intoxicating enjoyment. She even believed that they were not playing her; instead, she was playing them. And she could use this relationship to make them serve her and satisfy her needs.

She admitted she degraded herself, but she would enjoy the degradation. She called it "matriarchal society" or "polyandry". The establishment of this sexual attitude enabled her to break moral limits and do bad things with peace of mind. She cheated and robbed, but did not steal, because the former was a manifestation of wisdom or power, but the latter would only lower her social status.

In those days, they often fought. Normally she did not fight by herself, unless the opposite party had a woman. She benefited from practicing martial arts with Dalong and his friends, so ordinary women could not defeat her. But when she stabbed a person for the first time, her hand trembled. Later, she became more and more courageous and experienced, and she dare fight against men. She knew the key to winning a fight was cruelty and striking first. In this way, she got the nickname "Phoenix", and the four of them were the "Three Dragons and One Phoenix", who were feared by all in the southern part of the city. And in her words, they were "One Phoenix and Three Dragons"...

The airplane's jolt interrupted her reminiscence. All these years, hatred had become the cornerstone of her belief, and taking revenge had become her life's goal. However, the enemy who killed her father and whom she made every endeavor to take revenge on was exactly her life savior she was seeking for. Her spiritual pillar suddenly collapsed, and her heart was deeply pulled into pain and confusion.

Suddenly, she remembered the letter of Xia Zhe and took it out.

Sheila:

Please allow me to call you this name for the last time, although it left me a memory that I can't face directly. I'm writing you this letter in a mood of atonement, and I hope you will forgive me for cheating and hurting you.

I'm not the "Jon" whom you know, neither am I "She Guo". I'm the son of Xia Dahu. Now you know why I came to you. Indeed, I hated you and tried to take vengeance for my father. I thought of hurting you when I made love with you, but I couldn't do it, probably because of your charisma. In our first meeting, I felt you were not so evil as I thought. Apparently you were a capable woman, but you had an affectionate heart. And I felt that severe pain was hiding deep down in you. Whenever I thought of this, I was guilty because I used a very mean method to hurt your body and mind. I'm ashamed for what I did.

Now I'm a person who might be sentenced to death, and I sincerely ask for your forgiveness. Meanwhile, I hope you can treat my father with your sympathetic heart. He is a good person.

Xia Zhe

May 15, 1995

The writing paper was shaking in Sheila's hand and producing a rustling sound. She searched in the vast area above the ocean of clouds, but did not see anything. Finally, tears blurred her vision...

Chapter 36 – The Court Investigation

Hong Jun strode into the court with confident steps.

The court was not large. A national emblem of People's Republic of China hung above the judge seats in the front. The left side was the public prosecutor seats, the right side was the defender seats, and directly opposite the judge seats were the defendant seats and hearer seats. The judges and procurators had not arrived, but the hearer seats were fully occupied. Most of the hearers were stock investors who were concerned about the case.

Hong Jun glanced at the hearer seats. He saw Bai Mei and Lu Ting in the middle of the front row. He took a defender seat, then took out relevant materials from his briefcase, put them on the table and started reading.

The procurators and judges went into the court one after another. There were two procurators, one male and one female. The male procurator was in his 40s, and the female one was in her 20s. There were three judges, including the chief judge Qian Tuliang. And there was also a female court clerk.

Hong Jun stood up and greeted Judge Qian, who smiled and said, "Mr. Hong needed to read materials now?"

Hong Jun said, "I'm sharpening my spear just before going into battle. It may not be sharp, but it will be smooth."

"Does a lawyer like yourself need to sharp the spear before a battle?"

"To tell you the truth, each time I appear in court, I'm nervous just like my first time."

"I hope every lawyer can be as conscientious as you. Well, let me introduce them to you. They both are judges of our court, and you saw them before, Zhang and Chen. And this is the procurator Zhong Guoxin. And this is the procurator Ren Minqing."

Hong Jun shook hands with everyone and said, "I'm a newbie, I should learn from you."

Procurator Zhong said, "No, you are a foreign PhD. You have knowledge. I haven't graduated from university yet. We should learn from you."

Judge Qian said to Hong Jun, "Zhong is studying correspondence courses in China University of Political Science and Law, but it has been more than 10 years since he was transferred to civilian work in the procuratorate. He is a public prosecution expert. And the female procurator is a graduate from China University of Political Science and Law. Ah, the trial today is interesting. Mr. Hong is from Renmin University of China, which is the people's university. the procurators are from China University of Political Science and Law, which is the university of law, and I'm from Beijing University. Let me see which one is dominant, the people or the law."

Procurator Zhong thought for a moment and said in earnest, "In China, surely the people prevail."

Mr. Hong said earnestly, too, "But from the perspective of development, the law should prevail."

"You guys started debating." Judge Qian looked at the hearer seats and then his watch. "Many people came to hear the trial, we should have a good court session. I have an idea. The *Criminal Procedure Law* is under modification, and it's said that we will learn the adversary procedure used by the UK and USA. And the judge leaders encouraged us to make a bold attempt. And in this trial, I allow you to play leading roles. You can ask whatever questions you have in mind and say whatever you want to say. Debate sufficiently, just don't quarrel."

At this moment, Liang Gao hurriedly came in. He greeted the judges and procurators with an apologetic expression and said that Lu Boping could not appear in court because of some temporary tasks to handle, and that he would represent Hongyuan Securities in court.

At 9 o'clock in the morning, the three judges sat properly under the national emblem. The chief judge Qian Tuliang solemnly announced the opening of court session to publicly try Xia Zhe's fraud and negligent homicide according to law. Since both cases have the same defendant and were connected, they were tried together.

Two court policemen took Xia Zhe from the side door into the court and led him to the defendant seat. Without any facial expression, Xia Zhe sat on the chair facing the judge.

Chief Judge Qian first asked the defendant about his name, age and other basic details, and the time of arrest and whether he received the indictment, then announced the names of the collegiate bench members, court clerks, public prosecutors, and the defender, and then informed the defendant of his rights to apply for withdrawal, defend himself, inquire of a witness, apply for evidence collection, and make a final statement. After confirming that the defendant knew his above rights and did not request for withdrawal, the chief judge added that if the defender would apply to ask new witnesses to come to court or obtain new physical or documentary evidence, or redo inspection and authentication, such procedures should be carried out under the court's approval.

After announcing the start of court investigation, Chief Judge Qian first asked the public prosecutor to read out the indictment. Procurator Ren stood up and read out the indictment accurately. In the indictment, the public prosecutor charged the defendant with several basic criminal facts: First, the defendant Xia Zhe falsely claimed his account balance to cheat a large sum of money from Hongyuan Securities. He traded stocks by malicious overdraft and caused huge loss to national property. Second, the defendant Xia Zhe should have foreseen the possible death of the victim Fang Qiong while holding the gun, but he failed to foresee the result and caused the death of the victim. The public prosecutor considered that the defendant's behavior had violated Article 152 of the *Criminal Law* in relation to fraud and Article 133 of the said law in relation to negligent homicide; therefore, the defendant should be subject to criminal punishment.

Then, Chief Judge Qian asked the defendant to represent the facts. He emphasized faithfulness of representation and informed the defendant that according to Article 35 of the *Criminal Procedure Law*, if no evidence existed despite the defendant's confession, the defendant should not be considered guilty or given punishment; but if the defendant refused to make a confession despite the existence of conclusive and sufficient evidence, the defendant should be considered guilty and given punishment. The court would consider the defendant's faithful representation of criminal facts as a criterion for measurement of penalty.

Xia Zhe briefly recounted the whole story of overdraft stock trading and accidental gun discharge, and repeatedly emphasized that he did not have the motivation to cheat or kill anyone. At last, he said he was innocent.

Chief Judge Qian verified a few details and confirmed that the defendant had no objection to the interrogation record in the case files. Then he asked Judge Chen to read out in summary the inquiry records of the witnesses, including Liang Gao, Lu Boping, and Lu Ting. He presented documentary evidence including stock trading records of Hongyuan Securities, and the site survey record, forensic autopsy report, authentication of fingerprints on the gun, and relevant photos in Fang Qiong's murder.

After confirming that the defendant had heard clearly the details of the above evidence and had no objection to them, Chief Judge Qian asked the public prosecutor to question the defendant.

Procurator Zhong stood up and asked in a calm voice, "The defendant, how many times did you buy Shanghai Yansheng stock?"

"Only once. I was trying to sell in the second transaction." Xia Zhe answered carefully.

"Maybe it's not the fact. Think again."

"Are you asking about previous transactions?"

"All of them."

"I did it twice, maybe three times before the incident."

"What time?"

"One at the beginning of this year, and the other two last year."

"You liked Shanghai Yansheng very much?"

"I have been paying attention to the trend of this stock"

"You traded 10,000 shares in each of those three transactions, right? Why did you buy 100,000 shares at that time?"

"I was optimistic about this stock and thought it would go a long way up."

"It seems you liked to trade big, so you bought another 100,000 shares at the second time, right?"

"No, I was selling at the second time."

"You were selling it? But didn't you think it would go a long way up?"

"In the long run, it was a prospective stock, but I was overdrawing, so I couldn't do long-term trading. Besides, it was falling at the time."

"Did you write the signature on the authorization sheet?"

"Yes, but I did not see the content."

"The transaction was millions in amount, but you signed without looking at the content. Do you believe what you are saying?"

"I was careless at that time."

"So you are a man who makes mistakes easily, right?"

"I didn't expect the clerk would make such a mistake."

"The clerk's mistake caused a huge loss to you, so you hate her, right?"

"It's not like this, because she might have been used by someone. I didn't want to shoot her."

"I didn't say you wanted to shoot her. I'm just asking whether you hate her."

"I don't hate her."

"Do you love her?"

"No."

"Xia Zhe, I hope you can tell the truth. Now I ask you again, did you say something like 'Fang Qiong is seeking death' after you picked up the gun the other night at Lu Boping's home?"

"I can't remember clearly."

"Did you speak the truth to the investigators?"

"I was telling the truth."

"Did the investigators beat you during interrogation?"

"No."

"No forced confession?"

"No, indeed."

"You are telling the truth now. Chief Judge, I have no other questions."

After Procurator Zhong took his seat, Chief Judge Qian asked the defender to ask questions.

Mr. Hong stood up and said, "Xia Zhe, please tell the story of the accidental gun discharge the other night once more."

Xia Zhe said, "On the other night, we were eating when Fang Qiong came in. After entering the room, she spoke few words before she took out a gun from her bag. We were startled at that time so we stepped back. Fang Qiong said she would shoot me, and then Lu Ting jumped on her and they wrestled with each other. I wanted to help Lu Ting but I was afraid of being shot. Then the gun fell onto the floor, and I picked it up. I pointed the gun to Fang Qiong and it seemed that I asked Lu Ting to stay away."

Mr. Hong interposed, "How far were you from Fang Qiong? What were the positions of all people? There was a dining table and chairs in the room, right?"

"Yes, when Fang Qiong took out the gun, both Lu Boping and I stepped back to a position behind the dining table. Later, when I picked up the gun beside the dining table, I went back one more step, and Fang Qiong went back, too. It seemed that she was standing beside the wall and we were separated by the dining table and chairs. Lu Boping was on my right side, and Lu Ting should be one my left. Our positions were presumably like this." While speaking, Xia Zhe used his hands to illustrate.

"Do you remember what clothes Fang Qiong was wearing on that day?"

"It was a pink short wind coat, the fashionable style. She wore it before."

"Did she take off the wind coat after coming in?"

"No, she was in the coat from beginning to end."

"Then...OK." It seemed Hong Jun wanted to ask something more, but he did not ask. He turned around and said to the judge, "Judge, I have no more questions, but I'd like the court to summon Xia Dahu to appear as a witness. I have submitted his written testimony to the court already."

Chief Judge Qian nodded as approval, and then asked the court police to summon Xia Dahu, who was in the waiting room, to appear as a witness.

Xia Dahu went into the court and sat on the witness seat under the direction of the court police. He looked at Hong Jun and the procurator, and then Bai Mei and Lu Ting on the hearer seats. Then his vision rested on the judge seat.

Chief Judge Qian asked Xia Dahu about his name, occupation, and other basic details, and informed him that he should provide faithful testimony, and that he would be held legally liable for purposely giving false testimony or hiding evidence of a crime.

Xia Dahu carefully read out the written testimony about the wood business and the safe burglary.

Then, Chief Judge Qian looked at both procurators and said, "We discussed Xia Dahu's testimony before court opening. Some people thought Xia Dahu's testimony was not connected to this case, but to ensure the defendant's right to defense, we respected the defender's opinion and allowed Xia Dahu to appear as a witness. As to whether the incident of safe burglary has anything to do with Xia Zhe's case, you can give your opinions during court debate. Now, public prosecutors, do you have any questions to ask the witness?"

"Yes, I have." Procurator Zhong stood up and asked, "Xia Dahu, how much money did you give Xia Zhe for him to trade stocks?"

Xia Dahu thought for a moment and said, "I remember I gave him 500,000 in the beginning."

"Did you give him 500,000 for stock trading, indeed?"

"He said he needed that much money for account opening."

"But why did you take away 400,000 one month after account opening and capital verification and did not give it back to him?"

"Because I asked him to trade stocks with 100,000..."

"Did you give him 500,000 or 100,000?"

"I only gave him 100,000, but it required 500,000 to open an account. And I agreed that if he lost, I could repay the money for him. However..."

"Did Xia Zhe know you gave him only 100,000 to trade stocks?"

"Hmm..."

"I hope you can give an honest answer."

"I think...he knew it. But I agreed that I could repay money for him when I was able to. Now he was not able to repay the money. It was my responsibility, not his. However, I have no way to help him, because I was cheated by someone. I think both Xia Zhe and I were cheated. It was a huge conspiracy."

"What conspiracy?"

"I can't tell clearly. You need to ask Mr. Hong."

"Did Mr. Hong teach you to speak these words?"

"No, these are what I want to say."

Procurator Zhong shook his head and didn't speak anymore.

Chief Judge Qian asked the defender whether he had any questions to ask.

Hong Jun stood up and asked, "Xia Dahu, when did you hear Xia Zhe shot someone dead?"

"The day following the incident."

"Who told you?"

"Bai Mei, my wife. She heard it from Lu Boping."

"What was your reaction when you heard it?"

"My reaction? I didn't believe it and thought my wife was fooling me."

"Why?"

"Because Xia Zhe could not possibly shoot anyone. He is not the type of person. He has been very kind since childhood. He liked helping others, and he liked animals, too. When I caught a dragonfly or locust for him, he was very happy, but a dragonfly would die very soon if it was kept, and he was very sad. Later, after I caught a dragonfly for him, he would play with it for a while and release it, because he did not want it die. So it's not possible for him to kill a person. It might be an accidental gun discharge."

"Thank you, the witness. I don't have any other questions."

After Mr. Hong took his seat, Chief Judge Qian said, "The words of the witness belong to the category of character evidence. Currently, the law of our country has not specified the use of character evidence, but from a legal perspective, the judge cannot directly use character evidence to prove whether the defendant performed the criminal act. As to the above evidence, the public prosecutors and the defender can state their opinions during court debate."

Procurator Zhong raised his hand in front of the judges because he wanted to speak again. After approval by the chief judge, he stood up again and asked, "Xia Dahu, you said the defendant is a kindhearted person. I don't object to it. I want to ask you, he is smart, but why wasn't he admitted to a university?"

Xia Dahu glanced at Xia Zhe and said with contracted eyebrows, "He liked playing and was careless in study, so he did not perform well in exams."

"You mean he is careless when he does things?"

"A little."

"OK, you said it was not possible for him to kill. You referred to intentional killing, right? But we are accusing him not of intentional killing, but of negligent killing. Do you think it was possible?"

"Isn't negligent killing the same as killing?"

"They are different. Negligent killing means the perpetrator did not have the intention to kill, but his negligence caused the victim's death. Currently, the criminal law of our country is under modification. An opinion is to change the name 'crime of negligent murder' to 'crime of negligent homicide'".

"I don't understand these legal terms. You'd better ask Mr. Hong."

"It seems Mr. Hong did not teach you how to answer this question."

Xia Dahu did not speak, and beads of sweat appeared on his bald head.

The procurator sat down, and the chief judge allowed the witness to quit. Xia Dahu went down from the witness seat as if he was relieved of a heavy load. At the doorway of the court, he turned around and glanced at Bai Mei.

Chief Judge Qian announced the end of court investigation. Now the court debate started. He asked the prosecuting party and defending party to provide their opinions on the accusation of fraud. And he first asked the public prosecutor to make a statement.

Procurator Zhong stood up and said confidently, "At the time of court opening, my colleague fully stated our prosecution opinions, and I only want to add some comments. As to fraud, I think although the defendant's act was not typical, it still can be determined as fraud. With the deepening of reform and the development of market economy, some new types of criminal acts emerged in socioeconomic life, including various criminal acts in stock trading. Honestly, the law of our country has a lot of loopholes in this respect. It indicates the lagging nature of laws and regulations. But we can't give up cracking down on those criminal acts just because of this fact. I know the

Standing Committee of the National People's Congress will recently issue a decision on punishing criminals who damage the financial order, which includes specific provisions on the crime of cheating loans from banks and other financial institutions. As far as this case is concerned, Xia Zhe took advantage of imperfection of laws governing stock trading on overdraft and provided false proof of fund in account. And he cheated a large sum of capital from Hongyuan Securities when he did not have the capacity to repay the money. Therefore, he caused a huge financial loss to the country. As to the amount in account, the witness Xia Dahu just admitted that he only gave 100,000 yuan to Xia Zhe for him to trade stocks, but Xia Zhe overdrew from the security company on a basis of 500,000 yuan while he clearly knew he only had 100,000 yuan capital. This fact fit the characteristic of fraud known as 'fabricating facts or hiding truths'. Therefore, both his behavior and its result justify our determination that Xia Zhe committed the crime of fraud. More importantly, such a determination will not only punish and educate the defendant, but also warn all those in society who attempt to take advantage of current law deficiency to reap undue profits. I request the court to fully consider possible social influence of the judgment of this case while assessing the fraud accusation."

After the procurator took his seat, Chief Judge Qian first asked the defendant whether he would defend himself. Xia Zhe had been lowering his head. When he heard the judge's question, he promptly raised his head and looked at Hong Jun. He did not know what to do. After the judge repeated the question, Xia Zhe shook his head absentmindedly.

Bai Mei's sigh and Lu Ting's sobs were heard from the hearer seats.

Chief Judge Qian asked the court clerk to record the defendant's reply. Then he asked the defender to provide defense opinions. At this moment, all people in court fixed their visions on Hong Jun.

Mr. Hong stood up and gave a solemn bow to the judges, then he said with a calm voice, "Dear judges, I think the crime of fraud which the defendant is charged with in the indictment is ill-founded."

Hong Jun's opening remark stirred up a small commotion in the court. When everyone became quiet, he continued, "Although there is no explicit provision in the law of our country regarding whether trading stocks on overdraft constitutes a fraud, according to Article 151 of the *Criminal Law*, the subject component of fraud is the intention to illegally taking possession of public or private property, and the objective component is the obtainment of public or private property by fabricating facts or hiding truths or other cheating methods. However, the defendant Xia Zhe only performed normal stock trading, including trading on overdraft. It was the drastic change of market quotations that caused him to lose the capital and be unable to repay his loan offered by the security company. Therefore, from the subjective perspective, he did not have the intention to illegally take possession of the property; and from the objective perspective, he did not perform the cheating acts. The public prosecutor emphasized that the defendant's act caused significant loss to the country, but I'd like to point out that the defendant only caused financial loss to Hongyuan Securities. Hongyuan Securities is a state-owned company, but we can't equate it with the country. Besides, Hongyuan Securities is undoubtedly liable for the process which caused the economic loss. First, all transactions of the defendant were entrusted to and operated by Hongyuan Securities. It means every transaction he made was known and permitted by Hongyuan Securities. Second, there is a very important issue. In the second transaction, the defendant entrusted Hongyuan Securities to trade 100,000 shares of Shanghai Yansheng, but was it a sell or a buy? The defendant said he authorized a sell, but Hongyuan Securities made it a buy. If the 100,000 shares were sold as instructed by the defendant, the huge economic loss should not have occurred. Therefore, this is the critical fact in this case, but the public prosecutor does not have sufficient evidence in this respect. Xia Zhe's statement was inconsistent with Fang Qiong's testimony and the authorization sheet bearing his own signature, but according to the stock market quotations at that time, Xia Zhe's statement was highly credible. In other words, the defendant's explanation was very reasonable, especially when his personality traits were considered. Just now when the witness Xia Dahu was questioned, the public prosecutor pointed out that the defendant was careless. I agree with this. Since the defendant was careless, he signed the authorization sheet without carefully reviewing its content. Certainly, these do not suffice to overthrow the fraud charge. In order to overthrow the charge, I have to start from the safe burglary case."

When Mr. Hong saw the three judges were looking at him with interest, he smiled satisfactorily. "I asked myself two questions when I looked at the scene of safe prying: the first was why the perpetrator pried the safe; the second was why the perpetrator tipped over the small safe. The first question was easily answered – the perpetrator wanted to steal the wood purchase contract. But the answer to the second question was hard to guess. I thought the perpetrator's overlooking the sound of tipping over the safe indicated he encountered insurmountable obstacle while achieving his purpose. What was the obstacle? In safe prying, obviously it should be difficulty of opening the door. But why didn't he come across any obstacle while opening the large safe? So I carefully examined the difference between the doors of both safes. I found they had exactly the same structures but different dimensions. Both doors were opened from left to right, and the handles were on the left side and a little below the middle. And the handles were pointing straight downwards. However, the large safe was 1.2 meters high, and the small one 1 meter high, so the handle of the large safe was slightly higher than that of the small one. What did it mean?"

Chief Judge Qian frowned and said loudly, "Defender, I want to remind you that this is not a place for you to teach classes."

Mr. Hong realized his "roll error", so he said in a hurry, "Sorry! Then let me first introduce how the perpetrator pried the safe. His method was special. He forcibly pushed the handle so that strip steel used to fix the lock body within the door was bent inwards, thus the lock tongue lost its function as the block pin. The perpetrator's arm could not possibly have such great strength, so he must have used some kind of tool to extend the arm of force, such as a tube. In this way, I understood why the perpetrator tipped over the small safe. I thought the sequence of his actions on site was – he first pried open the large safe with the tube, but did not find the contract, so he had to pry the small safe. But he encountered an insurmountable obstacle when he was putting the tube on the handle – the tube was longer than the distance from the lower end of the handle to the ground, so the tube could not be inserted. Having no alternatives, he had to tip over the safe and change the orientation of the handle to put on the tube and pry open the safe. And this was why he tipped over the small safe. Meanwhile, the above reasoning provided an important piece of information. It was the length of the tool. We know the lower end of the handle of the large safe was 43 cm to the ground, and the lower end of the handle of the small safe was 31 cm to the ground. So the tube should have a length between 30 cm and 45 cm. And this is very helpful for us to identify the perpetrator."

Chief Judge Qian interposed, "Defender, please make it simple."

Mr. Hong nodded. "OK, based on site survey, I thought of Lu Boping, who had served as the political instructor of a reconnaissance company and was familiar with safes, and his metal crutch, because the middle section of the crutch was a 40 cm tube when it was screwed off. Later, in order to prove his tube was the tool used in the crime, I used an excuse to appreciate the tube. I discovered that one end of the section was slightly deformed, which was obviously the result of forcible prying. Therefore, I think Lu Boping was the one who pried the safe."

A commotion took place in the court, and the chief judge asked the court police to maintain order.

When everyone quieted down, Mr. Hong continued, "Why did Lu Boping pry Xia Dahu's safe? Why did he steal the contract which he had absolutely nothing to do with? The contract was useless to him, so he should have been stealing for someone else. Then, who was worthy of the sacrifice of him, the great manager, in personally stealing things? My assistant discovered by chance that Lu Boping went to Room 1016 of Shangri-La Hotel to meet someone, and there lived Sheila Sullivan, who signed the contract with Xia Dahu but did not want the contract to remain in Xia's hand. I think Lu Boping went there to hand the stolen contract to Sullivan."

Chief Judge Qian asked, "What's the connection between this and our case?"

Mr. Hong said, "Please listen to my explanation. I carefully studied the wood purchase contract. I found that Sheila had established a condition on water content that Xia Dahu was not able to satisfy. In fact, the purpose of her entering into the contract with Xia Dahu was to cause him to become bankrupt. Besides, based on her mysterious relationship with Lu Boping, I think she was the chief plotter who framed the defendant Xia Zhe. In other words, under her arrangement, Lu Boping made use of his manager position in Hongyuan Securities to cause the false fraud charge against the son of Xia Dahu. Why did she do this? Later I found the answer – her original name was Han Xinyun."

The court was very quiet. It seemed all people were waiting.

Mr. Hong looked at the hearer seats, then turned back to the judge and continued, "Han Xinyun, Xia Dahu and Lu Boping were neighbors and classmates when they were small. This case involved their story in the cultural revolution, which could not be explained in a few words. Simply put, Han Xinyun thought Xia Dahu caused the death of her family, so she carefully designed the trap of wood purchase contract to take revenge on Xia Dahu. Meanwhile, she asked Lu Boping to frame Xia Zhe. Therefore, the defendant Xia Zhe was not a swindler; instead, he was the victim of a carefully designed revenge conspiracy. In conclusion, I think the fraud charge against Xia Zhe is ill-founded."

After Mr. Hong sat down, Chief Judge Qian leaned back his body, looked at the other two judges and said to the procurator, "Public prosecutor, do you have any comment on the defender's statement?"

Procurator Zhong slowly stood up and said sincerely, "I want to say, Mr. Hong is indeed very smart and the most careful and responsible lawyer I have seen. But Mr. Hong's defense opinions are mostly based on reasoning and lack evidence. I only give two examples. First, simply by analyzing the tube and the crutch, Mr. Hong determined that Lu Boping was the person who sneaked into Xia Dahu's office, pried open the safe, and stole the wood contract. There isn't sufficient evidence to support this conclusion. Second, Mr. Hong concluded that Mrs. Sullivan asked Lu Boping to frame the defendant Xia Zhe based on Lu Boping's relationship with Mrs. Sullivan. Such a conclusion not only lacks evidence, but was made in haste. Evidence is the most important thing in case handling. We rely on conclusive and sufficient evidence to determine facts in the case."

After obtaining the approval of the chief judge, Mr. Hong stood up and said, "I agree with the public prosecutor's opinion. My conclusions are mainly based on reasoning and lack sufficient evidence. However, I want to remind the public prosecutor that according to the principle of assignment of responsibilities of providing evidence in a criminal procedure, the public prosecutor should be responsible for proving the defendant's guilt. And the evidence provided by the public prosecutor should meet the standard called 'Facts are clear, and evidence is conclusive and sufficient'. The defendant party is generally not responsible for providing evidence. The defendant does not have the responsibility of proving his guilt or innocence. As long as the defendant party can provide reasonable doubt of the facts stated by the public prosecutor, the court should acquit the defendant of the crime, because this is the basic requirement of the principle of presumption of innocence in criminal procedures."

Procurator Zhong stood up just after sitting down, "The defender deserves to be called an American PhD. He delivered an American-style speech. But in China, we have to execute the procedure according to Chinese laws. I know, in American criminal procedure, an important principle is presumption of innocence, and their standard of proof is to eliminate reasonable doubts. But in China, the basic principle of criminal procedure is being true to facts. The determination of guilt or innocence is based on facts. We don't perform presumption of guilt or presumption of innocence. We are true to facts."

Mr. Hong did not sit down. He said, "I heard that the Legislative Affairs Commission of National People's Congress is organizing experts and scholars to discuss modification of the *Criminal Procedure Law*, and the revised draft includes the principle of presumption of innocence."

Procurator Zhong did not sit down, either. "I know it, but the modification is not completed yet, so we have to follow current laws. And what you said is the scholars' point of view, and we are not sure whether the principle of presumption of innocence can be put into law."

Mr. Hong turned his vision to the judge. "In order to ascertain the above facts, I request the court to summon Lu Boping to appear as a witness. And he is a key witness in another charge against the defendant. I hope the court can take effective measures to ensure the key witness will appear in court."

"We will consider this request of the defender." Chief Judge Qian looked at his watch and exchanged a few words with the other two judges, and then announced solemnly, "Time is up. The trial this morning shall end now. At 9 a.m. tomorrow, the court will continue to try this case."

People went out of the court one after another.

Chapter 37 – The Hallucination

After going out of the court, Liang hurriedly drove back to Hongyuan Securities and came to Lu Boping's office. After entering the room, he saw Lu Boping sorting files on the writing desk. He closed the door and said with heavy breath, "Mr. Lu, a disaster is imminent!"

Lu raised his head and glanced at Liang, then he continued to look at the files on the desk and said calmly, "You look anxious. What happened?"

Liang went close to the writing desk and lowered his voice, "This morning in the court, Mr. Hong overthrew Xia Zhe's case and said you framed Xia Zhe."

"It's a joke! How could I frame Xia Zhe?" Lu raised his head and looked at Liang Gao.

"Sure, it's far from the truth, but Mr. Hong provided convincing grounds. It seemed the judges believed his words."

"How did he say?"

"He said Mrs. Sullivan and you conspired together to frame Xia Zhe, and that Mrs. Sullivan's original name was Han so-and-so. She wanted to take revenge on Xia Dahu, so she asked you to frame Xia Zhe. And he said you stole a contract from Xia Dahu's office. He was skillful in speaking and his reasoning was persuasive, otherwise why did the judges keep nodding?"

"What was the result of the trial?"

"It hasn't finished. And the judge asked me to pass on the message to you that they request you to appear in court as a witness on behalf of Hongyuan Securities."

"I'll go on a business trip tomorrow."

"I'm just afraid the proceeding may work against you, so I hurried back to report it to you. Mr. Lu, what measures will you take? Do we need to invite the judges to our office?"

"It's not a economic case, why should we invite the judges?" Lu stood up and said with a smile, "This lawyer is indeed a careful person, but he only speaks and acts on hearsay evidence. Will the judges reach a decision on those absurd grounds of him? Ridiculous! As the saying goes, 'We can't stop planting crops simply because the mole cricket is chirping.' Leave him alone. Let's just do our work. By the way, I will go to Chengde tomorrow. Please ask someone to buy me a train ticket of tomorrow morning. I want a soft seat in No.11 train. It seems the train departs after 7 o'clock in the morning. Give me the ticket as soon as you get it. I have a business diner party tonight."

"Mr. Lu, as to this case..."

"What's more?"

"I mean...you looked after me nicely in these years. If you need me sometime, I will surely help you at any risk."

Lu stared at Liang's eyes for a while, then he said, "Good! Thank you for your loyalty! If I need you to do something, I will tell you. Please first buy a train ticket for me. Don't forget, tomorrow morning's train, No.11."

Liang went out.

Lu looked at Liang's back and an elusive smile appeared on his face.

After work, Lu Boping drove to Black Land Restaurant on the south of Hepingli. After entering the restaurant, he turned left to the quiet "Tiger Wood Yard" and sat beside a small table. He ordered cold vermicelli, pine nut tofu, stir-fried shredded potato, braised meat with vermicelli, braised chicken with mushrooms, dry fried roe deer meat, and two bowls of porridge. He asked the waitress to put two sets of tableware, and serve the dishes after the guest comes.

The restaurant had a unique decoration. A circle of protective board, which was half the height of a man, was installed on walls of all sides. But the board was different from the elaborate wooden board in a regular restaurant, because it was made up of wooden plates with coarse barks. Large windows were separated into small squares by thin sticks, and covered with not-so-white window paper. The dining tables and chairs were all made of wood, which appeared simple and unadorned. Furthermore, a sickle and a long shotgun were hanging on the clean white wall.

Lu Boping looked at the surroundings and felt as if he was back in the Great Northern Wilderness, which he did not aspire for but could not forget. Indeed, he only lived for two years in the black land, but it was his first step into society, and he left his purest and confused youth in there.

At 6 o'clock, Zhang Xiaolan went into the restaurant with hesitating steps. She was wearing a suitable western-style petticoat and had slight make-up on her face. When Lu saw Zhang, he stood up to greet her. The waitress served the dishes soon after they took the seats.

Lu looked at his ex-wife across the table and smelt the mixed smell of hospital lysol and perfume. He was a little touched. He made a cup of yogurt for his ex-wife, "Xiaolan, I know you don't like drinking sweet things. This is sugar-free yogurt. I wish you good health!"

"Thank you for remembering this." Zhang smiled.

"Xiaolan, you look healthy, but you are thin now. Many people try to lose weight nowadays, but different people have different regimens. You should be moderate. I find that some women are obsessed with weight loss when they are not fat at all. It's funny to see a thin person imitates the fat to lose weight. And some people say vegetarian lifestyle is fashionable among foreigners, but I want to ask, how long have the Chinese people had meat to eat? Isn't it crazy to follow the fashion and be vegetarians? Xiaolan, I know you like eating northeast dishes, so I ordered several authentic northeast dishes. You can taste them."

Zhang took a couple of bites of the dishes. When Lu became less passionate in speaking, she asked, "Why did you ask me to meet you here and order so many dishes?"

"If I say I want to recover our love, will you believe me?"

"Since I have come, I'm willing to believe what you say. Are you really thinking about it?"

"I thought about it, but I can't make up my mind. It's mainly because I'm afraid you still hate me."

"Are you officially asking about my opinion?"

"Yes, I am."

"I have to consider this carefully. Please give me three months." Zhang had prepared for this before she came. She had thought if Lu proposed a remarriage, she would delay an answer.

"It doesn't matter. No matter how long you consider, it's OK. Actually I invited you today to fulfill my promise."

"What promise?"

"I remember when we got married, I promised to visit the Great Northern Wilderness with you. But after we married, I had been busy and did not have time. Now I invited you to have a meal in this restaurant; and in this way, I fulfilled my wish."

"Do you need me to help you with anything?"

"Help? What are you thinking about? Xiaolan, I just want to sit together with you and have a meal."

"Boping, I know you. We have been a married couple for many years after all. If you have encountered any difficulty and need my help, I can help you. I heard that she's dead, right?"

"Who? Oh, you mean Fang Qiong. The unfortunate event was an accident, but it was a good conclusion. It seems you have great information channels."

"Ting told me. The incident was a shock to her. She was raised by me. I know she is strong in the outside but weak in the inside. When I came back the other day, she hid in her room and wept for a long time. In the beginning she did not say anything, but later she told me everything. But there is one thing I don't understand. How did Fang Qiong know Xia Zhe came to your home to have dinner?"

"Ah. It was my fault. You know I'm a confident person, but sometimes I have undue trust in my capability. It was a painful lesson. It seems certain things are hard to control."

"So you asked Fang Qiong to go to your home?"

"Yes, but I did not expect the later events."

"Why did you ask Fang Qiong to go to your home?"

"Actually this is what I want to tell you. But it's a long story. You know I was in a relationship with Bai Mei, but both you and I did not expect Xia Zhe is my son."

"What? Xia Zhe is the son of you and Bai Mei?"

"Yes, and I did not know it all these years. Two days before the incident, Bai Mei suddenly met me and told me Xia Zhe is my son. He is Ting's brother and therefore they can't be in love. Bai Mei asked me to think of a way to break them apart. I knew Xia Zhe pursued Fang Qiong before, so I thought of this method."

"Xia Zhe and Ting didn't know it, right?"

"After this incident, I asked Bai Mei to tell Xia Zhe. And maybe it's your duty to tell Ting."

"How shall I tell her?"

"You are Ting's mother and she trusts you. You are not involved in this incident, so it's better that you tell her."

Zhang pondered for a moment and nodded, "This seems to be the only way. But I'm afraid it's hard for Ting to accept the fact. You know she loves Xia Zhe and she is like me in this matter. I wish she were like you."

"What do you mean? OK, you have the right to say this." Lu suppressed his anger.

"I don't want to blame you, but this is too abrupt for Ting. I really don't know how to tell her."

"I believe you can handle this nicely. After the incident took place, Ting did not live in my place anymore. It seems she won't go to my place anymore.

Xiaolan, you should take care of her in future." Lu took out an envelope from his pocket and put it in front of Zhang, "Here is a bankbook in Ting's name. Please keep it for her."

"What do you mean?"

"Nothing. By the way, I'm asking you out today because I have one more sentence to say to you – I did not treat you well in the past. Please forgive me."

"Boping, why do you say this? It feels like..." Zhang looked at Lu with wide-open eyes.

"Don't think too much. I just feel I should say this to you. All the incidents that took place recently enabled me to think more and understand some truths. It's not easy to be a decent human." Lu shook his head with emotion.

After dinner, Lu proposed to drive Zhang back home, but Zhang did not agree. She rode a bicycle and got away.

Lu Boping returned to his home, parked his car and went into the building. The corridor was quiet, and the sounds of TV programs occasionally came out from some apartments. He felt he was making great sounds with his steps, as if he shook the entire building.

Since Fang Qiong's death, Lu always felt a kind of weird horror after entering his apartment. Although he wiped out all traces of blood on the floor, he would see a piece of bloodstain on the floor whenever he went to the toilet. Sometimes he woke up at midnight and heard indistinctly someone walking in the living room. There were a few times when he held the metal crutch to search for the "someone" in the apartment. He did not believe in ghosts or spirits, but the horror gripped him and caused his hallucination. He once read about visual and auditory hallucinations and he knew it was an indication of psychiatric disorders. He did not believe his nervous system was so fragile, but he was not willing to enter the apartment alone late at night.

Lu opened the security door and the inner door with his keys. The light was on in the room. He felt strange. Did he forget turning off the light in the morning? He shook his head with a bitter smile. Then he locked the door and went into the living room. He opened the TV, and packed his luggage while listening to the news.

Lu was in tension. He was afraid of insomnia, so he took a sleeping pill. Then he took a hot water shower, went into the bedroom, and prepared to turn off the light and go to sleep.

At this moment, the telephone rang. He picked up the microphone, and the caller wanted to talk with Miss Fang. He said there was no person named Fang here. The caller gave him a number, and he said the caller dialed the wrong number. The caller apologized politely and hung up.

Lu turned off the light, lay on the bed and closed his eyes. However, the call made him think of Fang Qiong in spite of him. He thought of their first meeting in the ballroom, the first time they slept together, and...and the last night – Fang Qiong's painful and resentful face before her death kept moving in front of his eyes. When he opened his eyes, the face disappeared, but as soon as his eyes were closed, it appeared again. He forced himself to count. For tomorrow's trip, he needed to have a good sleep. Maybe the drug inside his body was taking effect, for he started feeling sleepy at last.

However, the telephone rang again. He picked up the microphone impatiently, but the caller hung up before he could speak. He stared blankly for a moment before he put back the microphone. But after more than 10 minutes, the telephone rang again. He angrily picked up the microphone, but the caller hung up silently. He thought for a while and did not put back the microphone. Instead, he put it on the bedside table beside him.

All was quiet in the dead of night. Suddenly, indistinct rustling was heard from outside the bedroom door, which sounded like someone walking stealthily in the next room. Lu sobered up immediately. He pinched his leg and made sure he was not in a dream. Thus, all his hair stood up.

He told himself to stay calm. Then he gently got off bed, picked up his crutch beside the bedside table, and went out of the bedroom quietly. He followed the sound to the door of Lu Ting's room. He suddenly pushed open the door and turned on the light, but no one was in the empty room. He gasped and swore. However, the rustling was there indeed, right under Lu Ting's bed. Years of military service made him think of a time bomb first. He went back into his own bedroom and brought a emergency light. He lay on his stomach on the carpet beside Lu Ting's bed and looked under the bed. He saw a shoe box, and the sound came out from the inside of the box. He thought for a moment, then he stood up, and moved the bed slightly aside. He carefully uncovered the box and saw a telephone recorder rustling.

Lu collapsed on the carpet.

Chapter 38 – The Tracking by the Outside Investigator

After the end of the morning trial, Hong Jun ate a simple lunch, and then went to the regulatory authority of Hongyuan Securities to learn about facts. When he was back to Friendship Hotel, it was getting dark. He went into the office and read the correspondence of the day. Then he took out Xia Zhe's case materials, sorted them out, and prepared the next day's court debate. Although he was confident that he would win, he should prepare for every possible scenario. Meanwhile, he was waiting for Song Jia to bring news from the police.

It was dark, and Song Jia hurried in. She said right after her entrance, "It made me so anxious. There was a car crash near Zhongzhou Road, which was followed by a severe traffic jam. I took the bypass through Anzhen Bridge. Mr. Hong, did I delay your going back home?"

"Returning is not delayed, but you delayed my dinner party." Hong Jun said with contracted eyebrows.

"Oops, what shall we do?"

"What shall we do? You should have dinner with me." Hong Jun stood up proudly.

"Hey, look at your tiny capability. Honestly I'm not afraid of such a task. Not to mention eating, I can even accompany you to..." Song Jia suddenly stopped.

"Accompany me to do what? You dare not say?" Hong Jun laughed.

"Certainly I dare say. I can even accompany you to go to America." Song Jia flushed.

Now the telephone rang. Hong Jun picked up the phone and said, "Hello!"

"Hello! May I speak to Mr. Hong, please?"

"This is Hong Jun. What's the matter?"

"I have a very important thing to tell you!"

"Please speak."

"Lu Boping will go to Chengde tomorrow morning. He already bought the train ticket of No.11 tourist train."

"Why do you tell me this?"

"I think you must be interested in it."

"May I know who you are?"

"This is not important to you. Don't forget, No.11 to Chengde tomorrow morning."

"Hello! Hello!" Hong Jun wanted to ask something more, but the called already hung up. Hong Jun looked at the phone in his hand, and looked at Song Jia. He made a helpless gesture and hung up.

Song Jia asked, "What did the person tell you?"

"He said Lu Boping will take No.11 train to Chengde tomorrow morning. Please check when No.11 train departs."

Sone Jia went out and returned quickly. "The train departs from Beijing Railway Station at 7:17 in the morning, and arrives in Chengde at 11:51 at noon. What is he going to do in Chengde?"

"I don't know. But what interests me now is not why Lu Boping will go to Chengde, but why the caller told me this."

"Obviously he wants you to know Lu's whereabouts. Maybe he feels Lu Boping is on the run."

"What does that mean?"

"Ah..." Song Jia could not guess the answer.

Hong Jun went around the writing desk in a circle and said, "It means the caller knows what I said in the court this morning, or he is one of the persons who sat in the court. Who is he?" Hong Jun looked at Song Jia and said to himself, "The judges and procurators won't do this. Xia Zhe is locked up.

Liang Gao? Is it him? The voice was similar to Liang's, although he purposely changed his tone."

"Liang Gao? Why did he do this?"

"Maybe he wants a promotion."

"Promotion? Promotion to what?"

"From the deputy manager to the manager."

"Oh, he is a bad bad man."

"In the first meeting, I just felt this person harbored evil intentions. Don't look down upon him! In our present society, such a person often achieves great success. I can predict that Liang Gao will probably become the manager of Hongyuan Securities."

"But you don't wish your prediction to come true, right?"

"So you have developed the habit of psychological analysis."

"One is influenced by close association." Song Jia laughed playfully.

"What if I'm a bad associate?" Hong Jun also talked a lot when he was happy.

"If so, I should have stayed away from you already."

"So you are wiser than me."

"Teacher, I dare not."

"Didn't you dare to do anything?"

"I dare not say 'doing better than my teacher'."

"Why?"

"I'm afraid you'll hold grudges and use an official excuse to fire me."

"Look at your mouth!" Hong Jun shook his head resignedly.

"What's wrong. It does not look good?" Song Jia tilted her head.

"It looks good, but harsh words come out of it sometimes."

"How is it at other times?"

"What other times?"

"Ah, are there moments of sweetness?"

"Sweet words? Very few!"

"I thought Mr. Hong does not like sweet words. If I had known you like them, I would have prepared them for you. Except for sweet words, I also have sugar-coated bullets."

"Just keep them to yourself. Don't frighten anyone."

"Didn't you say since the 'black bear hole' experience, you are not afraid of anything? Why are you afraid of my sugar-coated bullets?"

"They are different?"

"How come?"

"What if it is a sugar-coated atomic bomb? Then everything will be purged."

"If I really had an atomic bomb, would it be necessary for me to work day and night in your place, and in fear?"

"Why are you working in fear?"

"I'm afraid of being fired by the boss. It's not easy for female workers like me. Ah, I'm so hungry, but I have to stand here and have an idle chat with the boss!"

"Oops, I almost forgot this. Let's go to have dinner."

Hong Jun and Song Jia came to Friendship Restaurant and found a quiet table. After ordering the dishes, Hong Jun asked about the work.

"How was your visit to the police station today?"

"I don't think they had an active attitude. I told them about your analyses, but they asserted that they could not take compulsory measures against Lu Boping based on your analyses. They said Lu Boping is not an ordinary person, and they must be very careful before taking measures against him. However, they agreed to further investigate and verify the information we provided, and to send their people to monitor Lu's activities."

"It seems you have to run some errands tomorrow morning."

"For what?"

"Lu Boping is going to Chengde, you know."

"You want me to be an outside investigator again? Mr. Hong, are we trying to interfere with other people's business?"

"Lu Boping is an important witness of our case, and we discovered his problem while handling the case. As citizens, we should help the judicial authorities, right?"

"If an election of 'best citizen' is held sometime, I will surely vote for you."

"You will rank higher than me. I'm just giving orders, but you are doing the work."

"Oops, I'm lost. No wonder people say, women are destined to toil. As long as the man speaks some sweet words, the woman is willing to do all the hard labor for him."

"Don't make it so tragic. Just consider this task as an opportunity to enjoy driving."

"You want me to enjoy driving at five in the morning? I think I must be a car fan."

"You see those Qigong practicers and dancers. They went to the park as early as five in the morning."

"OK, OK. I guess I'd better not sleep at all."

"Sleep is necessary. There is a saying – people who don't rest cannot do a good job. If a person keeps working and does not take a break, he must be a robot." Again, Hong Jun said with a tone that is used by teachers to instruct students.

"The answer is simple, but the principle is profound." Song Jia imitated Hong Jun's tone.

"A philosopher said, when the woman becomes thoughtful, the man can do nothing but sleep."

"You might as well say directly that I should pay the bill."

After dinner, Song Jia drove Hong Jun to his residence. Hong Jun got off the car, and hummed a tune while walking to the building entrance. When Song Jia saw Hong Jun went into the entrance, she drove away.

Song Jia got up before sunrise the next day. After washing herself, she quickly had breakfast and drove to the building in Asian Sports Village where Lu Boping lived. She parked the car at roadside, shut down the engine, and waited. It was quiet in the community. There were only a few people doing morning exercise in the small garden.

Near 6 o'clock, Song Jia saw Lu Boping carry a travel suitcase and a briefcase and walk out of the building entrance. The briefcase and his metal crutch were held in one hand. Lu Boping went to a black Audi car, put both boxes in the trunk, and then opened the door and sat inside. The Audi ran southeast along the small winding road.

Just after starting the engine, Song Jia saw a young man, who was practicing Tai-Chi, ran to her car and knocked on the car window in a hurry. Song Jia rolled down the window and asked what was the matter. The man said he was a policeman on an urgent duty and needed to take a ride. Song Jia smiled and opened the door to let him in. The young man showed his police ID and asked her to follow the Audi in front.

The Audi ran out of the community onto the North 4th Ring Road, and west to Anhui Bridge, and then it headed south. There were few cars on the road, but the Audi's speed was sometimes quick and sometimes slow. Fortunately, Song Jia was driving a Santana with such good acceleration performance that it could maintain a suitable tracking distance. Song Jia noticed the young man kept turning his head and looking at her, and for a few times he tried to speak but held back. She was a little surprised. While driving, she used her corner vision to watch the man's behavior.

The young man finally opened his mouth, "Miss, did you graduate from the police academy?"

"Why are you asking this?" Song Jia glanced at him.

"Nothing. Is your name Song Jia?" The young man asked again.

"Yes, how do you know that?" Song Jia glanced at him once more.

"I felt you were familiar when I got on your car. I graduated from the police academy, too. My name is Qin Zhigang."

"Really? So we are schoolmates."

"You went into business?"

"I'm working now in a law firm."

"You are a lawyer? This is your car?"

"No, I'm working for my boss. My boss' car."

"Whatever job you do outside is better than the police work."

"Not necessarily."

"Why? You were in the police and you know the inner secrets. Outsiders think we are awesome, but we are doing tiring jobs with low payment. Take my errand today for example, they asked me to be the only outside investigator but did not give me a car. Do you know how I felt when I was asking drivers for a ride on the street? I couldn't wear the police uniform, thus, I was given cold shoulders. I'm clear in my mind. The leaders don't take the case seriously. Just now when the target moved, I planned that if I could not get a ride, I would call my team and go back home to sleep. Who cares? But by accident, I met you, my schoolmate. You support the work of us. Fine. It's my misfortune to do hard labor and practice my skills."

"We did not meet by chance, because I know who you are tracking. He is Lu Boping."

"Didn't you leave the police?" Qin Zhigang looked at her with doubt, "Do you know Lu Boping?"

"Of course I know him. To tell you the truth, your errand this morning was recommended by me yesterday to your leader."

"No wonder you picked me up so easily without asking anything. We are doing the same task."

"Don't misunderstand. I'm just fulfilling my obligations."

Song Jia followed the black Audi through Anzhen Bridge, and turned onto 2nd Ring Road on the Andingmen overpass, and then headed east. Now more cars appeared on the road, but they were running fast. There were always a couple of cars between the Santana and Audi.

The sun rose in the east. The pinnacle of Yonghe Lama Temple was reflecting brilliant golden light. The car passed the viaduct behind the temple, and then turned south along a curve outside the Russian embassy. After they passed the Jianguomen overpass, Song Jia shifted to the right track and prepared to head for Beijing Railway Station, but the Audi in front of them did not change track. Instead, it continued running south. Song Jia followed hastily and asked herself in the mind: "Where will this guy go?"

The Audi passed under the Dongbianmen overpass and ran fast south along the moat. Song Jia changed back to the fast track and followed. After they passed two overpasses, the road turned southwest on the east of Longtanhu Park which was shadowed by lush trees. The Audi shifted to the middle track as if to overtake, but a taxi blocked its way, so it had to slow down. In this way, the cars on the fast track overtook the Audi. Song Jia decelerated, but the cars behind her were sounding horns. She could not be too obvious in tracking the Audi, so she had to overtake it on the left. At this moment, Audi suddenly shifted to the right track and squeezed through the gaps to the exit of Zuo'anmen Bridge. It was too late for Song Jia to shift track, so she had to drove past the overpass from below.

Qin Zhigang was worried and said, "Now we are done for. When we turn back at the overpass ahead, we can't find him anymore. Your technique sucks."

Song Jia gave him a cold stare and did not speak. She drove fast. When they reached Yuting Bridge, they turned back and headed north on the original road. Qin Zhigang gripped on to the handrail above the car door. He looked at Song Jia and asked, "Why are you still chasing madly? He is nowhere to be found. We'd better stop chasing and park at one side."

"Cut the crap!" Song Jia shouted and stared at the road ahead. The Santana kept overtaking and then turned south at Jianguomen overpass. Then it entered the parking lot in front of Beijing Railway Station.

At this moment, Qin Zhigang seemed to understand. After the car stopped, he asked Song Jia, "Do you think he is catching the train?"

Song Jia did not answer. She got out of her car and searched among the cars which were parked there. Qin Zhigang followed her and looked at black Audi cars. He pointed to the license plate of one Audi car and said to Song Jia, "It can't be wrong. This is the car. I remember the license plate number."

Song Jia went to the car head and looked into the cab through the window. She saw Lu Boping's metal crutch on the seat next to the driver's seat. She nodded, "Yes, this one is his car."

Qin Zhigang said, "I didn't know you are so capable. I failed to recognize your capacity and spoke carelessly, please don't mind."

Song Jia said, "I don't have time to chat with you. Let me tell you, Lu Boping will take No.11 train of 7:17 to Chengde. What will you do? You still have time to get into the station."

"Sure! I have followed him to this place already. I must do my work from beginning to end. It's OK for me to go to Chengde. But I hope you can call my team and ask them to contact the railway police and Chengde Police Station, so that they can assist me with my work when necessary. Thank you! Goodbye!"

Qin Zhigang crossed the iron fence of the parking lot and ran to the hall of railway station.

The melodious bell of the big clock of Beijing Railway Station reverberated in the square of the station.

Song Jia looked at Qin Zhigang's back and felt relieved. A happy smile appeared on her face. To be honest, she did everything for Hong Jun. She thought she could take credit and seek rewards from Mr. Hong today. She did not expect much. As long as she could spend an enjoyable evening with him, whether eating, playing bowling, or dancing, or just having an idle chat, she would be fully satisfied.

Song Jia drove away from the railway station. She joined the commuting traffic and drove slowly. After going into the office in Friendship Hotel, she called the police station, and then started doing her routine work. But, her mind had flown to the court.

Chapter 39 – The Court Debate

Hong Jun sat on the defender seat, put relevant materials orderly on the table, and then he lifted his head and looked at people on hearer seats. Xia Dahu, Bai Mei, and Lu Ting sat in the front row. Xia Dahu looked blankly at the national emblem over the judge seats. Bai Mei's anxious vision alternated between Hong Jun and the court entrance. While Lu Ting lowered her head and folded a piece of paper again and again.

Liang sat there in a relaxed manner as if he was a spectator who had nothing to do with this case. Hong Jun looked at Liang's face for a moment and wanted to see his reactions, but his head was always turned sideways.

The judges and procurators went into the court and sat on their respective positions.

The court police took Xia Zhe to the defendant seat.

The chief judge Qian Tuliang announced the opening of court and continuation of court debate. He first asked the public prosecutor to give his opinions on the negligent homicide.

Procurator Zhong Guoxin stood up and said, "Chief judge, I'd like to ask the defendant a few questions."

Chief Judge Qian nodded.

Procurator Zhong turned towards Xia Zhe and asked, "Defendant Xia Zhe, do you know Mrs. Sullivan?"

Xia Zhe thought for a moment and said, "I heard of her from my father."

"Did you ever see her?"

Xia Zhe hesitated and shook his head, "No."

"Xia Zhe, I told you yesterday that you should tell the truth. Lying in court is very harmful to you. But you are a dishonest person. OK, let me remind you. Did you go to Shangri-La to meet Mrs. Sullivan?"

Xia Zhe lowered his head and did not answer.

Procurator Zhong turned towards the judges and said, "Yesterday afternoon, we did an investigation in Shangri-La Hotel. Two clerks of the hotel recognized the defendant Xia Zhe in the photos we presented. They said this young man visited Mrs. Sullivan more than once in the hotel, and it seemed they had an intimate relationship. Mrs. Sullivan hired a car to go to Shidu to have fun, and this young man accompanied her. Chief Judge, this is our written record of our inquiry from hotel clerks yesterday, including the photo recognition record. We request the court to consider the above record as supplemental evidence in this case."

While Procurator Ren Minqing stood up and presented the inquiry record to the judges, a commotion appeared among the hearers. All people, including Xia Zhe, turned their visions to the hearer seats.

They saw Xia Dahu tried to stand up, but Bai Mei was pulling and stopping him. And both persons were arguing in low voices. Suddenly, Xia Dahu spoke in a loud voice, "I said he is an ungrateful rascal, so what? I brought him up, but he betrayed me. He is an ungrateful rascal!"

Chief Judge Qian stood up and said loudly, "Quiet! Xia Dahu, you are hearing the trial as the defendant's family. You must observe court orders. According to the *Criminal Procedure Law*, if the hearer damages court order, the chief judge should warn and stop him, and if the hearer continues the violation, he should be taken out of the court by force. If the violation is severe, he might be fined or detained. Now I formally warn you. If you don't listen, I will ask the court police to take you out."

Xia Dahu sat on the chair and panted heavily.

Bai Mei kept bowing to the judges.

Lu Ting lowered her head and covered her face with hands.

Xia Zhe turned around and bit his lips. Tears rolled out from his eyes.

When the court quieted down, Chief Judge Qian asked the public prosecutor whether he had any more questions. Procurator Zhong shook his head and sat down.

Chief Judge Qian asked whether the defender had any questions. But now Mr. Hong was in a trance. He only heard the question when the chief judge asked for a second time, and he waved his hand.

The sudden event created a heavy atmosphere in the court.

After exchanging a few words with other two judges, Chief Judge Qian declared that court debate should go on and asked the public prosecutor to give his opinions.

Procurator Zhong stood up, cleared his throat, and said calmly, "To clarify the negligent homicide, we should first know how on earth the victim Fang Qiong died. She was shot, no doubt. But who shot her and in what way did he shoot her? This question is not easy to answer. We know there were four people on the scene, but the only one who was willing to give a faithful representation could not speak anymore. And the remaining three people did not want to tell the truth. In the beginning, they acted in collusion to fabricate a myth of Fang Qiong's committing suicide. But a myth would prove to be a myth in the end, just like the lie told by the defendant that he did not see Mrs. Sullivan. Our investigators are experts in lie identification. Therefore, during interrogation, the defendant had to admit the fact that he shot Fang Qiong. And the witnesses Lu Boping and Lu Ting admitted Fang Qiong's death was not a suicide. However, the defendant has been claiming that he did not have the intention to murder Fang Qiong and her death was an accident. Actually, in the indictment, we did not accuse the defendant of having the intention to murder Fang Qiong, but of course, we can not accept it was an accident. The key issue is the defendant's psychology at the moment. If the defendant could tell the truth, the answer would not be difficult to find. But as we saw just now, the defendant is not an honest person. But, even if he does not tell the truth, he cannot hinder our determination of the facts. We think the victim Fang Qiong's death was neither an accident nor intentional homicide. It should be negligent homicide, or negligence which caused the victim's death."

Procurator Zhong looked at his speech outline on the desk and continued, "I have to explain that when the case was transferred from the police station for prosecution, it was deemed as intentional homicide. But after our comprehensive review of the evidence, especially after we fully considered the defendant's explanation, we thought the defendant should be prosecuted for negligent homicide. Although some evidence in this case could prove Xia Zhe had the intention and purpose to kill Fang Qiong; for example, Hongyuan Securities' deputy manager Liang Gao's testimony can prove that Xia Zhe hates Fang Qiong because of his failed pursuit for her and the stock trading fraud. But after analyzing carefully and studying the exact situation when the case took place, we considered that the defendant did not have the intention to kill Fang Qiong at the moment. Instead, he killed her due to negligence. That means, when he pointed the gun to Fang Qiong, he should have predicted the possible result, but he didn't, and his carelessness caused the victim's death. I'd like to remind everyone that the defendant's father admitted the defendant is a careless person. While we were discussing the case, some people agreed with the police's opinion that the killing was 'indirectly intentional', which means a subjective attitude of knowing the harmful result but allowing it to happen. But we comprehensively considered the situation of the defendant and followed the principle of 'taking the lighter' in an environment of controversy. Therefore, our prosecution on the ground of negligent homicide was brought prudently and had a solid basis. It satisfies the requirements of judicial justice, namely, the requirements to consider not only the evidence to prove the defendant's guilt and grave crime, but also the evidence to prove his innocence and minor crime. I think the defense lawyer will not object to our opinion, right?"

Procurator Zhong looked at Mr. Hong, but the lawyer was just listening and did not have any reactions. The procurator concluded, "At last, I want to remind the court that although the defendant Xia Zhe denied his guilt, he confessed the basic facts of this case. In conclusion, we determine that there are sufficient grounds and evidence to prove that Xia Zhe committed the crime of negligent homicide."

Next, Chief Judge Qian asked the defender to give his opinions, but he reminded Mr. Hong to put it in simple language, because the court was not a classroom.

Mr. Hong stood up and came straight to the point, "I think the accusation of negligent homicide can't be established, either. First, I agree with the public prosecutor's basic judgment that Fang Qiong's death was not an incident of accidental discharge. But I don't agree with his saying of negligent homicide, because I think this is a case of intentional homicide." Mr. Hong paused to see people's reactions. Indeed, now many people had a surprised expression.

Chief Judge Qian said loudly, "Defender, please repeat your words just now, because your words will be put on record."

Mr. Hong smiled and said, "I think this is a case of intentional homicide. Certainly, the murderer is not the defendant Xia Zhe. Once again, he became the sacrificial lamb in an evil conspiracy without knowing it. To explain this, we need to review the events which took place the other night. Lu Boping asked his daughter to invite Xia Zhe to his home to have dinner. Fang Qiong appeared suddenly and used a gun to threaten Xia Zhe. Lu Ting tried to prevent her and the gun fell to the floor. Xia Zhe picked up the gun and pointed it to Fang Qiong. A shot rang out and Fang Qiong fell. Xia Zhe and Lu Ting escaped from the scene under the order of Lu Boping, and returned after about 30 minutes. Lu Boping made up a story of suicide and called the police. You must think this incident was so coincidental. It looked like a play written and directed ahead of time. That's right! It was a play!"

Mr. Hong paused for a moment to sort his thoughts; then he continued, "This play had an ingenious design, but there were a few flaws. We could also call them doubts. First, after Fang Qiong fell, Lu Boping immediately asked Xia Zhe and Lu Ting to flee from site. This was abnormal. In an accidental discharge, what people generally do is to first check the vital signs of the injured and consider sending the injured to the hospital or discuss solutions. But Lu Boping's reaction looked like he was prepared for the whole thing. Was it weird? Second, Xia Zhe and Lu Ting left the site and returned after about 30 minutes, what did Lu Boping do in such a long time? Was he just sitting beside Fang Qiong? Third, why did Fang Qiong go to Lu Boping's home the other night? Was her intention truly the same as she said, which was to give a lesson to Xia Zhe? I think, based on her relationship with Lu Boping, even if she wanted to make trouble for Xia Zhe, she would not go to Lu Boping's home directly. Therefore, she must have obtained Lu Boping's permission, or Lu Boping asked her to go to his home. The next question is why did Lu Boping asked Fang Qiong to go to his home? Suppose Lu Boping just wanted Fang Qiong to break apart the relationship between Xia Zhe and Lu Ting, then why did Fang Qiong bring a gun? She did not need a gun to damage Xia Zhe and Lu Ting's relationship. But the problem is that Fang Qiong brought a gun, and the gun was real and loaded with bullets. This was indeed hard to understand. Finally, I figured it out. It must be the instruction of the 'play director', and the 'stage prop' was likely provided by the 'play director', because the 'play director' served in the military before. Then why did the 'play director' ask Fang Qiong to bring a gun? The answer is the 'play director' thought there must be a gun in the play – a real gun that can kill people. And the next question is more important but easy to answer: Who did the 'play director' want to kill? There were four people on site that night. Lu Boping would not kill himself, and he would not kill Lu Ting or Xia Zhe. The only person left was Fang Qiong. When all other possibilities are excluded, the remaining one should be the fact, even if it's hard to believe. Of course, the above analysis is just reasoning and cannot prove Lu Boping is the one who shot Fang Qiong. But I know where we can find the evidence. Now I'd like judges to look carefully at the photos of the scene, especially the photo of the wound in her body."

After the judges found the scene photos, Mr. Hong continued with his speech, "I discovered a very important phenomenon on the photo – the clothes had a large and irregular hole at the wound, and the edge of the hole had obvious traces of burning. I have consulted an expert in Renmin University of China. He told me it was the trace of gunshot residues left by close-range shooting. Gunshot residues are powder residues, metal chips, and other trace substances ejected from the barrel along with the bullet at the time of firing. Based on the arrangement of gunshot residues on Fang Qiong's body, the expert deduced that the muzzle was less than 10 cm from the body at the time of firing. I want to add that this is only the advisory opinion given by the expert based on the photo and is not a formal authentication conclusion. But in the autopsy report of this case, experts in the police department also said it was close-range shooting. It does not mean anything alone, but when it's combined with the information provided by the defendant and witnesses, it becomes significant. You surely remember the defendant said yesterday that he was separated from the victim by a dining table at the time of gunshot. The distance should be at least two meters. The testimony of Lu Boping and Lu Ting can prove this, too. Since the bullet that took Fang Qiong's life was shot from a distance less than 10 cm, and Xia Zhe was holding the gun in a position at least two meters from the victim at the time of gunshot, we can arrive at this conclusion: the fatal shot was not fired by the defendant Xia Zhe. Besides, according to the statements of the defendant Xia Zhe and the witness Lu Ting, the victim Fang Qiong was wearing a pink short wind coat the other night, but her bloodstained coat on the photo was a pink suit jacket. Judges can look at this. Is it weird? Did the short wind coat magically turn into a suit jacket? Impossible! I think the only reasonable explanation is that when Xia Zhe and Lu Ting left the site, Fang Qiong was in a short wind coat, but when they returned, Fang Qiong was in a suit jacket. They only remembered Fang Qiong's clothes when she was living, but did not remember her clothes after death. This is understandable. Their brains were occupied by the sudden gunshot, so they did not notice the change of her clothes. Then, why did Fang Qiong change clothes? The only reasonable answer is: When Xia Zhe and Lu Ting left the site, Fang Qiong was still living!"

People in court started talking with each other. Chief Judge Qian said, "Everyone, please keep quiet and listen to the defender's statement."

Mr. Hong said, "But Xia Zhe and Lu Ting saw with their own eyes that Fang Qiong bled in her chest and fell on the floor. How to explain this? I remember Fang Qiong once acted a girl student who was shot dead in a movie. Her acting was amazing! Of course, some stage props were required. A packet of explosive and a bag of red liquid should be installed under the actress' garment. When the actress 'was shot', she only needed to press the igniter to create the vivid effect. If we carefully examine the dead's clothes, we probably will find traces of the red liquid. Actually, when Xia Zhe pointed the gun to Fang Qiong the other night, Fang Qiong ignited the explosive, then a bang was heard and she pretended to fall. Then Lu Boping held Fang Qiong and asked Xia Zhe and Lu Ting to get out. He had two purposes in doing this: The first was to prevent Xia Zhe and Lu Ting from discovering Fang Qiong was not dead; The second was to continue to act in another play. Yes, the most important scene in the play just started. After Xia Zhe and Lu Ting left, Fang Qiong was back to life – she opened her eyes, stood up, and took off the bloodstained wind coat. Maybe she was laughing complacently. But at this moment, a bang rang out in the room – this was the real gunshot. Fang Qiong fell down again, but now it was real. Who fired the gun? The answer was obvious, for only Lu Boping was in the room. I guess that after killing Fang Qiong, Lu Boping rearranged the site and hid the wind coat with fake blood. Now Xia Zhe and Lu Ting came back. This plot was probably not written in Lu Boping's script, but Fang Qiong truly died, and this was the end that the 'play director' wanted. I believe this was the whole story on the other night."

Now Mr. Hong cleared his throat and slightly raised his voice, "For the murder case, the above evidence is indirect evidence, because it can't directly prove the major facts of this case in one step. Other evidence or reasoning is required to fully prove the facts. But when all pieces of evidence are combined together, they can sufficiently prove that the defendant Xia Zhe is not the murderer of Fang Qiong. Therefore, he is not responsible for Fang Qiong's death. These are my defense opinions. Thank you!"

After Mr. Hong took his seat, the court became silent, but people started talking very soon. The three judges, the two procurators, and people on the hearer seats were all conversing in low voices.

Xia Zhe turned around and looked at Bai Mei and Lu Ting on the hearer seats. His eyes contained tears.

Chief Judge Qian Tuliang stood up and said aloud, "Quiet! Quiet!" When people were quiet, he said, "Given the defender provided some new facts, the collegiate bench decided to adjourn the court and make a determination after discussing with different parties and investigating evidence."

Xia Zhe was taken away by the court police.

After the three judges retreated from court, both procurators walked to Hong Jun. Zhong Guoxin shook Hong Jun's hand firmly and said, "Good job!" Ren Minqing shook hands with Hong Jun, too, but he did not speak. The procurators went out of the court together.

Hong Jun stood up and went to the door, but Bai Mei stopped him.

Bei Mei said excitedly, "Mr. Hong, you are really competent. Thank you! Thank you!"

Hong Jun went out of the court quickly. Song Jia had been waiting for him, and she drove the car to him right away. Hong Jun happily sat in the car and said thank you to Song Jia.

Song Jia started the car and said, "You are so happy. You won the case for sure."

"I won the first battle, but the final victory or defeat depends on the court judgment."

"I heard that in a lawsuit, the victory or defeat happens in the court, but work is done out of the court. And some people say a lawsuit is not just a session, it's also a relationship task. Maybe we can do some activities?"

"My body is not strong, and I sprained my waist. So please wait. How was your task going?"

"I won the first battle, too, but Lu Boping was indeed sly. He almost got rid of me." Song Jia vividly described the process of tracking Lu Boping in the morning, and emphasized her resourcefulness and decisiveness at urgent situations.

After finishing, Song Jia looked at Hong Jun and expected his praise. But Hong Jun leaned on the chair back and combed his hair with fingers. Song Jia was a bit disappointed.

When they were back to the law firm, Hong Jun said to Song Jia, "You'd better call the police station. I calculate that Qin Zhigang is complaining that you made him run for nothing."

Hong Jun went into his office. He stood in front of the glass window and gazed at the tree leaves outside. Although the defense work for Xia Zhe's case was completed and he did quite a good job, he was not happy for his victory or success. Instead, he was absorbed in heavy thoughts about life. He seemed to have realized some truths about life, but when he thought carefully, he did not fully understand them.

Song Jia called his name twice before he turned around. Song Jia stared at him and asked, "What are you thinking? You are so absentminded."

Hong Jun did not answer. He just laughed and asked, "How was your phone call?"

"I'm indeed less capable than you. I have to admire you. Qin Zhigang wants to settle accounts with me. He thinks I made fun of him. And he asked me to treat him to a meal. Do you think I'm wronged?"

"I don't think you are wronged. Who let you assign a task to him anyway?"

"I thought Lu Boping would take the train. You see, we had the information given by Liang Gao, and Lu Boping made every effort to get rid of us and came to Beijing Railway Station. Everything matched. By the way, how did you know Lu Boping did not take the train?"

"You underestimated him. I'm responsible for the mistake, too. In these two days, I was focused on defending Xia Zhe and did not give much attention to Lu Boping. Actually, if we analyze carefully, we can discover some doubts about his travel to Chengde. First, how could Liang Gao know Lu was going to Chengde? Undoubtedly, Lu already knew he was in a precarious situation. He was a smart person, and he certainly knew well about Liang Gao's character. If he truly wanted to run, would he tell his plan to Liang Gao? I don't think so. Don't forget that Lu Boping once was a scout. It fit better with his personality to say he used an escape plan. Second, why did Lu leave his crutch in the car, and put it in an obvious position? We all know the crutch was his favorite item which was never separated from him. He endured the pain to part with it for a reason. Probably he was afraid the person tracking him did not remember his license plate number, so he used the crutch to mark his car. Certainly, there was a precondition; that was he did not need the crutch anymore, or he thought it was inconvenient to take it with him. Just think, if he really wanted to go to Chengde by train, would he do this? I think the answer is very clear.

"Yes! Your analysis is perfect and not difficult to understand. But why didn't I think of this?" Song Jia said with frustration.

"Reasoning is not just an ability; it is also a habit. In many cases, if people did not make a certain deduction, it's not because they were unable to do it; rather, it's because they did not form such a habit. Consequently, they neglected those phenomena which could cause the deduction. If you told them about these phenomena and asked them to reason, they probably would come to the same conclusion. The death of Fang Qiong is an example. If we asked the case personnel of the police station and the procuratorate to pay attention to the distance between Xia Zhe and Fang Qiong at the time of the incident and the trace of gunshot residues on the body, and to analyze the contradiction between the verbal evidence and inspection records, they probably would deduce that Xia Zhe was not the murderer, but the problem was they didn't think of analyzing the case from this angle of vision. Maybe they had the first impression that Xia Zhe was the murderer, or they were used to make judgments based on oral confessions. In many cases, people's erroneous judgment was not because they lacked the ability to analyze problems, but because of negligence or loss of certain important information. Therefore, when many people have heard others give the result of reasoning, they cannot help saying: 'Ah, it's so simple.' I think people's difference in reasoning capability is not reflected in whether they can see a certain fact, but in whether they can notice it; it is not reflected in whether they know a certain analysis method, but in whether they can consciously use the method. Do you understand?" Hong Jun involuntarily spoke in a teacher's tone.

"It's such a pity." Song Jia shook her head.

"What is a pity?" Hong Jun was confused.

"Such brilliant language, and such excellent performance, have only one audience, which is myself. Don't you think it's a pity?" Song Jia said in earnest.

"Ah, you are receiving a one-on-one education. To think higher, you are studying a PhD; lower, you are in a home school. I don't charge any tuition from you, but you are making a cynical remark and not knowing your happiness." Hong Jun pretended to be serious, too.

"Hey, so I owe you money when I work for you? You are worse than Huang Shiren."

"It is fair to charge tuition for teaching. If all people think as you do, our country's education can't be improved. No wonder our country has a budge shortage. I can tell you, since the age of Confucius, the student should send "Shuxiu" to the teacher, which was 10 strips of dried meat tied together. Do you know? Sending dried meat!"

"Dried meat? Is beef jerky OK?"

"Fine, as long it is meat."

"But if I tell the salesperson of the store that I will buy 10 packets of beef jerky as a gift, they will certainly think I will send them to a child. Does this damage the teacher's image?"

"It doesn't matter. The teacher loves it."

"Thank you for your guidance." Song Jia imitated the gesture in Peking Opera and saluted.

"Don't bother, just three times." Hong Jun said with the same tone.

Song Jia saluted another two times and said respectfully, "Teacher, I'm ignorant. There is one more thing that I don't understand. Please tell me."

"There is a saying: 'It is true wisdom to accept the known as known and unknown as unknown.' Please ask."

"I don't know where Lu Boping went after he freed himself from tracking. Please enlighten me." Song Jia looked at Hong Jun gladly.

"This..." Hong Jun took back his smile.

The doorbell rang. Song Jia curled her lips and said, "Whenever it arrives at the critical moment, someone comes to rescue you. I suspect you have some supernatural skill."

Hong Jun laughed again, "This is called 'The good are protected by Heaven.' But when the guest leaves, I will give you a satisfactory answer."

Song Jia turned around and went to the door with uncertainty. She opened the door and saw Lu Ting. She let her come into the hall and asked, "Are you coming for Mr. Hong?"

"No, Song Jia, I want to ask you something." Lu Ting seemed to be anxious.

"Then come into my office." Song Jia led Lu Ting to her office. While passing the door of Hong Jun's office, Lu Ting politely stopped, and greeted Hong Jun.

After entering the office, Song Jia closed the door, let Lu Ting sit on the chair, and asked, "Is there any urgent business? Why didn't you call first?"

"It's not an urgent business. I just felt it was inconvenient to talk on the phone. So I came here to trouble you. Sorry for that."

"That's all right. Just say."

"My mother went back home very late last night. She said my father asked her out to have dinner. Then she handed me a bankbook and said it was given by my father."

"How much is the money?"

"100,000 yuan."

"It's a lot of money. So your father loves you, but where did he get the money?"

"Yes, that's why I came to you. I heard Mr. Hong's presentation these two days, and felt my father's crime was not minor. I don't know where the money came from or whether I can keep it, so I'm asking you. Song Jia, recent events made me confused and disoriented. I don't know what to do. We haven't known each other for a long time, but I think you are an enthusiastic and goodhearted person, so I want to hear your opinions. Do you think I should hand in the bankbook?"

"It's easy to hand it in, but you should think whether it's necessary. I'm not sure about this. You'd better ask Mr Hong. He is a reliable person. There won't be any problem if you talk with him."

"I know Mr. Hong is a good person. But I don't know why I'm nervous whenever I talk with him. He is not scary, and he speaks gently, but he makes people nervous."

"I know. You always feel he is a great person worthy of your respect. So when you speak to him, you feel as if he is a senior official, and naturally you feel nervous. To tell you the truth, I was the same in the beginning. I felt he was much higher than me, and every time I spoke with him, I was very careful. Later I was able to let go. Wasn't I tired? He has his capacity and I have my own advantages. Guess what? When you feel you and he are on an equal position, you are not nervous anymore. Now I'm casual when I talk with him. And another thing..." Song Jia lowered her voice, "These men...if you don't treat him as anything great, he will not think he is great. Both men and women care about their images, but they do so from different angles. A woman is most concerned about whether she is beautiful and charming, but a man is most concerned about whether he can show his identity and status. This is the born difference. So when you talk with a man, no matter how high his social position or standing is, you should think of a way to pull him off his pedestal, especially the men you regularly contact or work together. If he puts on airs all day long, and you are nervous at the sight of him, both of you will be exhausted. On the contrary, if you joke with him or even argue with him, you can work pleasantly together. Of course, joking should not be excessive, and arguing should not be real. Being moderate is the key."

"Song Jia, you are great! Where did you learn all these?"

"I found out in practice. I have been working as a secretary for men these years. But you should judge the man's character. If he is a pervert who takes opportunity to harass you, then you can't joke with him. You should put on airs. Besides, as to those men you despise, no matter how high his position is, you don't need to treat him equally. The method I just told you only applies to the men you like."

"So Mr. Hong is the man you like, right?" Lu Ting laughed and said.

"Wow, you are taking advantage of the loophole." Song Jia pretended to be angry.

"Indeed, I admire you. You are capable and fortunate. I can see that Mr. Hong likes you."

"You don't know every person has his own problems. I'm a shadow in his eyes, a substitute at most." Song Jia said with emotion.

"Substitute? Whose substitute?"

"I can't say it in just a few words. Let's discuss your problem."

"Ah, I live a tragic life. My mother talked to me about Xia Zhe last night. I could see that she does not agree with my relationship with Xia Zhe now, and I felt that she held back some words. She said she wanted to take me to my hometown in Anhui and live there for a few days, on one hand to visit my grandfather, and on the other to talk with me. I guess she will talk about my relationship with Xia Zhe. Why did all unlucky things in the world come to me?" Lu Ting said with red eyes.

"Ting, don't be sad. You are a good girl. I believe you can find happiness in life. By the way, Mr. Hong will get busy soon. Let's go and ask him!"

Lu Ting nodded. She took out her handkerchief to wipe her eyes, and then followed Song Jia into Hong Jun's office.

Hong Jun warmly asked Lu Ting to sit on the sofa. Song Jia repeated Lu Ting's question. Hong Jun thought for a while and said, "I think you can wait. You can report it to the authority when your father is investigated. If the money is his legitimate income, surely you have the right to use it, but if the money is his illegal income, it becomes illicit money, and you can't use it or keep it. Just wait. If necessary, Miss Song and I can testify for you in future."

"Thank you, Mr. Hong!" Lu Ting stood up and took leave.

After sending Lu Ting out, Song Jia went back into Hong Jun's office.

Hong Jun said as if deep in thought, "It seems that Lu Ting does not know yet."

"What doesn't she know?"

"Her brother-sister relationship with Xia Zhe."

"What? Lu Ting and Xia Zhe are brother and sister? No wonder her mother will talk with her. This must be a shock for her. It's too cruel. I did not expect things in this case are so complicated."

"There are more complicated things."

"Hey, don't change the topic. I'm waiting for your answer."

"Take it easy. Let's listen again to the telephone conversation between Lu Boping and Fang Qiong." Hong Jun turned on the recorder.

……………………….

"Hello?"

"Hello! Boping, it's me."

"Oh, honey, what's the matter?"

"How was the thing going?"

"It's almost done. You can't be too anxious in this matter."

"But I'm worried. You know, Hong is hard to deal with. I'm worried not only this thing will fail, our other things will also…"

"Watch your words."

"I know, but I'm afraid."

"What are you afraid of? Even if the sky collapses, the taller people can support it on their heads. As long as you are patient, we can pass through this difficulty. OK, darkness will end and the dawn will come. Just wait for my good news."

……………………….

Hong Jun turned off the recorder and said while thinking, "This conversation at least gives us two clues: First, Lu Boping and Fang Qiong obviously did something illegal. 'This thing' which Fang Qiong referred to should be their behavior of framing Xia Zhe. And 'other things' should be the cause of Lu Boping's escape and the real cause of his murdering Fang Qiong."

"Do you mean Lu Boping set a trap to kill Fang Qiong not to frame Xia Zhe, but to keep her mouth shut?"

"Yes, to silence her by killing."

"Originally, I also thought the idea that Lu Boping killed Fang Qiong just to frame Xia Zhe was hard to believe."

"The second clue is the 'thing' which Fang Qiong hurried to ask about. Based on Lu Boping's answer, what do you think is the 'thing' Fang Qiong asked about?"

"Maybe it is some kind of procedure. I thought then that Fang Qiong was asking about marriage procedure. But now I think it probably is a passport or a visa, right?"

"Yes! I have investigated this matter. Lu has been to Hong Kong and he has a passport. He only needed to wait for a visa. As to Fang Qiong, she trusted an empty promise. In the course of handling the case, I thought of a question many times – Why did Lu help Sheila to take revenge on Xia Dahu? Why did he do this even after knowing Xia Zhe is his blood son? It's not possible for him to do this simply because he had a love dispute with Xia Dahu. A reasonable explanation is that he made a deal with Sheila. For example, he takes revenge for Sheila and Sheila helps him to go to America. But Sheila probably does not want to get Fang Qiong to America also. Therefore, when Lu said to Fang Qiong that they would go abroad together, it was a lie used to comfort her. Actually he only went through the formalities for himself."

"This guy is really, really bad."

"Let's get back to our question. If Lu's destination is America, he should go to the airport instead of the train station this morning. Yesterday afternoon, he purposely told Liang Gao a message that he would go to Chengde. He probably calculated that Liang Gao would inform against him and that someone would monitor him, so he led you to the train station this morning, and then went to the airport by taxi so that he could board the plane without disturbance."

"That's true! Mr. Hong, let's go to the airport now, or notify the police..."

"It's too late. I just called the airport. The airplane to America has taken off on time. If he has passed the customs, he should be near Tokyo now." Hong Jun said while looking at his watch.

"What can we do?" Song Jia was worried and regretful.

"You can call the police station and ask them to check whether Lu Boping is in the list of passengers who left the country this morning. I think he will not use a pseudonym."

Song Jia picked up the phone.

Chapter 40 – The Inside Dealing

The airplane slid on the runway slowly, paused for a moment and then ran ahead with high speed. When the tyres finally ended their friction against the ground, Lu Boping gave a gasp of relief and his hanging heart returned to its position. Through the window, he looked at the receding ground and said in his heart, "Goodbye, motherland! Goodbye, my past!"

The airplane penetrated the clouds, and chunks of grey fog flew backwards quickly out of the window. Houses and roads on the ground gradually faded away and at last disappeared under the clouds.

The airplane rose above the clouds. The sun was shining brightly outside, the blue sky was like a peaceful ocean, and the snow white clouds were like boundless relief. It seemed the vast area between heaven and earth was in perfect stillness, and only the slightly vibrating wings and the roaring of engine indicated the airplane was flying in high speed.

Lu Boping looked outside through the window and tried to think about his life plans after arrival in America, but his thoughts were pulled to the past by the bright world.

...His childhood life was brilliant. He was smart, diligent, and versatile. He got top scores in class and had outstanding performance in recreational and sports activities. Since the start of the cultural revolution, although he was not as fanatic as some students, he was also called by the communist ideal to actively participate in revolutionary movements. He joined the "red guards", and copied "big-character posters". Whenever a "supreme instruction" of Chairman Mao was issued, he would passionately parade on streets and shout slogans with students. In the year he graduated from junior middle school, he responded to the great leader's call, and voluntarily request that he "go to the mountainous areas and the countryside", and "accept reeducation tailored for the poor and lower-middle peasants in the vast land". In the Great Northern Wilderness, life was difficult and labor was heavy, but he thought he was making contribution to the realization of the communist dream of the humanity, and his dedication was great and noble. However, certain things that happened next extinguished his burning passion and transformed his once pure thoughts.

The 913 event in 1971 gave a heavy blow on his belief. Lin Biao, the No.2 idol in his heart, proved to be a traitor. The movement of criticizing Lin Biao and Confucius, which came next, made him confused. He was surprised that certain ideas advocated in the past were false. He had a feeling of being cheated and fooled. He thought "go to the mountainous areas and the countryside" and "stay at the borderland" are all deceptive slogans. What they were suffering there had nothing to do with the realization of communism. Besides, he found that some idols he originally adored were in fact not noble persons. For example, the leaders of the construction and production regiment were his idols, at least his life examples, but later he heard that a political commissar of a regiment and a political instructor of a company became criminals who raped young females.

His understanding of sexual love changed, too. Previously, he thought love was noble and sex was evil, at least sex belonged to the category of vulgar interests. And he thought sexual intercourse was torture and humiliation of a woman by a man, because once it was mentioned among people, vile words were used, such as fuck, play with, pollute, rape, and ravage. Therefore, noble men should not have sexual demands from women, even if the woman is his lover. He decided to follow the great leader's teaching, "Be a noble person, a true person, and a person who has broken away from vulgar interests". He once had a beautiful fantasy: He fell in love with a beautiful and kindhearted girl. After marriage, the girl voluntarily offered her body for him to play with because of her love, but he curbed his carnal desire because of his love and did not play with the girl. The girl was touched by his noble act, and he was touched by his own noble act, too. And this was the pure love he aspired for. But later he knew that the "vulgar interest" was an essential step to make babies. Therefore, all people who had kids had done this thing of "vulgar interest", including his parents and the great leader. And the great leader engaged in "vulgar interest" activities with both Yang Kaihui and Jiang

Qing. This once made him confused. Later, Bai Mei gave him the experience of "vulgar interest". He found it was a miraculous enjoyment for both men and women. Thus, nobleness of love was shattered in his heart.

After parting with false nobleness in politics and in life, he started thinking carefully about his life's goal. He had the desire to prevail over others, so he must stand out. In 1972, his competent father made use of his relationships to get him into the army, and he put on the "patriotic green" admired by all his peers. And now he started another journey of personal achievement. Hardships in the army broadened his life experience and cultivated his willpower. Later, in the brutal Sino-Vietnamese War, his heart changed a lot. While fighting against the Vietnamese in the jungle, he learned cruelty. He once asked himself, "I don't know these Vietnamese, why should I kill them? When he first saw people killed by himself, he was guilty. But in the dangerous battleground, he had no choice but to survive.

Once he led two soldiers to conduct reconnaissance. They were lost in the jungle, and encountered a small team of enemies. After courageous fighting, they annihilated the enemies and caught a wounded soldier. But both of his comrades died and his leg was injured. Then, the Vietnamese captive led him out of the jungle. He had decided to release the Vietnamese, but at the moment the person got away, he shot him dead, because he was worried the person would bring people to catch him and threaten his life. It was just a possibility, but for his own safety, he must be cruel and merciless.

After he was baptized in the fire of war and witnessed people's transition from life to death, and especially, after experiencing the power of bullets, he found that human life was fragile and short, and nothing would remain after death. Therefore, he thought the purpose of human life was to enjoy whatever fun life had to offer to the maximum extent while one was living, and how much fun one could enjoy was a criterion of his capability. He wanted to be a strong person in life, and the strong need not sympathize with the weak, because the weak should use their efforts to become the strong. Therefore, he used his intelligence to seize a position in society which provided him with opportunities of enjoyment.

However, with the improvement of social living standards, he became unsatisfied again. His security company had abundant financial resources, but money in his name was so little. Whenever he saw the VIPs who got rich in the stock market squandered money in entertainment venues and said proudly they did not want invoices, he would envy them. Every time he asked the service staff to provide an invoice, he felt like doing it in a stealthy way. Therefore, he made a decision to increase his personal wealth. After careful thinking, he chose the method of "inside dealing". He selected some reliable VIPs to cooperate with him. He provided "information", the VIPs invested, and profit was shared out equally. To avoid suspicion, he assigned Fang Qiong to work in the VIP room of the security company. All activities were carried out by Fang Qiong, and he gave instructions behind the scenes. Over several years, he obtained a huge sum of money which was even inconceivable to himself. And he converted most of the money into US dollars and deposited it in overseas banks. With the increase of personal wealth, he had an increasingly strong desire to enjoy it. But he knew he could not enjoy the ill-gotten wealth in China, so he looked for the chance to go abroad...

The plane landed in Narita Airport, Tokyo, Japan. Lu Boping got off the plane with other passengers. He spent nearly two hours in the airport and then boarded the plane to San Francisco. After dinner, an American movie was shown in the cabin, but his English level was low and he could not understand. So he cast his vision to the black blue night sky outside the window, but his mind was involuntarily focused on the woman he was about to meet. He thought Han Xinyun was indeed a strange and mysterious woman. She was both lovely and scary. Therefore, the scene of 20 years ago appeared before his eyes...

"Next stop – back door of Beihai, please be prepared to get off." The female conductor used the least strength to make a soft and long sentence. He hurried to the bus door.

The bus slowed down sharply. The brake pad produced an acute and annoying friction sound, and an unseen force gently but persistently pushed passengers forward. When the bus fully stopped, Lu Boping went off with the passengers, crossed the street and went towards Shichahai Ice Stadium.

The ice stadium had not opened yet, and many young people carried skating shoes on their shoulders or in their hands and stood outside the entrance. In the 1970s, skating was a fashionable sport of Beijing people. Lu Boping was skillful in stating, so he became the regular customer of the ice stadium during his family visit in Beijing. He stood at one side of the road, lit up a cigarette, and admired the clothing of the skaters, especially the girls. And this was his hobby.

At this moment, a girl crossing from the other side of the road attracted his attention. She was wearing an overcoat, and her neck was surrounded by a red scarf. Her hair was curled on her head in a loose manner, which appeared noble and elegant. Her face was covered by a white mask, and only her long, thin eyebrows and good looking eyes could be seen. Her tiny half-high-heel leather boots on her feet made clear rattling sounds on the ground.

When the girl's eyes met Lu Boping's, she stopped for a moment, but soon went to the roadside with head up and stood under a tree nearby.

Lu Boping felt this girl was familiar, but did not remember where he met her. However, he had experience of picking up girls, so he went to her and said, "Hey, you look pretty. Alone?"

The girl raised her eyebrows and looked at him. She did not answer his question, and asked him instead, "Don't you know me?"

Lu Boping was embarrassed when he heard this, so he said, "I feel you are familiar, but I can't remember you now."

"Did I really change a lot?" The girl took off one side of the mask with her fingers and exposed the lower half of her face.

"Han Xinyun! I didn't expect you became so..." Lu Boping could not find the right word.

"What did I become?"

"You became wild!" Lu Boping smoked the cigarette and breathed out a large smoke circle. Then he took out a box of red peony cigarettes from the pocket of his woolen coat. He lifted one cigarette with his finger and brought the box to Han Xinyun. Han Xinyun smiled and picked out the cigarette with her slender fingers, and then held it in her mouth. Lu Boping took out the lighter and lit up for her. Han Xinyun smoked it deeply and breathed out a small and round smoke circle skillfully.

"What are you doing all these years?" Lu Boping asked.

"I'm free. I'm doing whatever I want. How about you? You went to the countryside?"

"Yes, I've been there, but later I became a soldier. You see, my military uniform changed into the four-pocket type."

"You are promoted? Well done!"

The ice stadium opened and people flocked in. Lu Boping and Han Xinyun followed. When they put on skating shoes, deposited their clothes and came to the ice stadium, many people were already staking. They joined side by side in the people flow which was moving in circles.

It was getting dark, and more people came into the ice stadium. Bright light illuminated the stadium and made it as bright as daytime, as if darkness was barred out by the fence. Different people slid in the light back and forth. Noise of mixed frequencies was shaking cold air and disturbing the silent night sky.

At about 7 o'clock, Lu Boping and Han Xinyun went out of the ice stadium. They were tired but felt very relaxed.

Han Xinyun said, "Soldier, it's time for dinner. I'm hungry."

"OK, you choose the place. I'll treat you."

"Let's eat in Cuihualou."

They went to the west entrance of the lantern market by trolleybus, and then they went for a few minutes to Cuihualou Restaurant. Since the peak hours of dining had passed, they easily found seats after entering the restaurant.

Lu Boping ordered four hot dishes. Then he went to a shop and bought a plate of assorted cold food and a bottle of Chinese red wine. He filled two glasses with wine and raised one of them, "We came together by predestination. Cheers!" He drank up.

"You want to make me drunk? I think you are up to no good. Soldier, don't forget No.7 point of your 'Three Rules of Discipline and Eight Points for Attention' – Do not take liberties with women." But she also drank up, and said, "Don't look down upon me. I'm not the girl you originally knew."

"I saw it." Lu Boping took out his cigarette box and picked one cigarette. Then he put the box on the table.

Han Xinyun also lit up a cigarette, smoked it, and asked with a squint, "Have you heard of 'Three Dragons and One Phoenix' in the southern part of Beijing?"

"Yes, I heard of them. Are you the phoenix?"

"Yes, I am."

"So you had a huge influence in Beijing those years."

"In the southern part, no gangster dare act against me."

"How about you now?"

"Just mess about."

"Didn't you find a job?"

"I put my name in a subdistrict factory. I work there when I'm happy."

"What if you are unhappy?"

"I take sick leave at home."

"What illness do you have?"

"I can have whatever illness I want. I have connections in the hospital. It's so easy to get sick leave notes. To tell you the truth, I have blank sick leave notes with me. Do you want one?"

"I don't need that stuff."

"If your friend needs it, you can ask him to meet me. Two yuan for one note!"

"You are making money this way?"

"I have a lot of ways. I can only get money for cigarettes by doing this."

"What other ways do you have?"

"It depends on what you need!"

"You are quite conceited in saying this."

"I can tell you, if I agree to do something for you, I can find ways right away."

"Are you indeed so capable?"

"Believe it or not!"

Lu Boping and Han Xinyun ate and chatted until the waitresses started sweeping floor and putting chairs upside down on the table. They went out of Cuihualou Restaurant.

Lu Boping sent Han Xinyun home and entered her small room which had simple furnishings and was very tidy. After entrance, Han Xinyun took off her overcoat, poked the fire with a hook, and sat on the bedside. Lu Boping sat on the only wooden chair in the room.

Han Xinyun's heart throbbed. He took off his coat, too, and said, "It's warm in your room."

"You have a fire in your heart." Han Xinyun spoke softly, but her words aroused Lu Boping. Lu Boping did not speak, so she asked, "What's wrong? You don't want to go home? I know you men are all like this. When you come into my room, your feet are immobilized. Soldier, did you have a taste of women?"

Lu Boping shook his head against his will.

Han Xinyun bolted the door, drew the curtain and said with a more tender voice, "I'll let you enjoy once."

……………………………

Lu Boping and Han Xinyun lay on the bed side by side. In darkness, each of them knew the other was awake, but they did not speak. Maybe they were a little ashamed in the heart. Maybe their body contact just now made them reluctant to say those insincere words. And maybe they were guessing each other's mind.

At last, Han Xinyun broke the silence. She said, "Is this your first time to spend the night outside? What are you thinking? Do you think I'm too bad now?" She was speaking in a gentle voice, and the artificial tone disappeared.

Lu Boping said, "No, I'm thinking everyone changes, and it's hard to say for better or for worse. Maybe life is like this."

"Actually, I'm surprised of my own change sometimes. How could I become such a woman? But, this is not something I can decide. If you know my experience, you won't feel strange."

"I heard your father and mother died miserably."

"That's just the start of the tragedy. You don't know and will never know what happened next."

"You just said you were 'Three Dragons and One Phoenix'. Where did the 'Three Dragons' go in the end?"

"Dalong died for me in Shidu. He was stabbed to death. Erlong went to Shanxi, and Sanlong joined the northeast corps."

"Do you contact each other?"

"It's a farce originally. When the play is over, who can remember anyone?"

Lu Boping and Han Xinyun were lost in thought.

A few days later, Lu Boping returned to the army. After that, he wrote two letters to Han Xinyun, but she only replied one letter, and there was only one blank sheet of paper in the envelope.

Two years later when Lu Boping was back to Beijing, he went to the room to see Han Xinyun, but she moved out already. And the neighbors did not know her whereabouts. Lu Boping was sad, but he forgot this with time.

In the beginning of 1994, Lu Boping saw a Chinese-American woman in a diner party hosted by a friend. Her name was Sheila Sullivan. He heard Mrs.

Sullivan had tens of millions of dollars, so he came to her and introduced himself.

After looking at his business card, Mrs. Sullivan took off her large sunglasses and said with a smile, "Mr. Lu, you don't know me again?"

"You are familiar, but I can't remember where I met you. I'm sorry."

"Do you remember Shichahai Ice Stadium and Cuihualou Restaurant 20 years ago?"

"You are Han Xinyun?"

"I'm honored that you still remember my name."

"I didn't expect you changed so much these years." Lu Boping said with emotion.

"Even at 20 years ago, you were surprised at my change. But I think my change this time is not greater than the last time."

"I think you changed more than last time."

"That's because I grew old and ugly."

"No, I don't mean that. You don't look like a woman in her 40s. At most you look like a woman a little older than 30 years. And you are more charismatic than before."

"Thank you!"

"The change I referred to is your identity. How did you go to America?"

"After the collage entrance examination was resumed, I was admitted to a university and studied English. Our country was bringing order out of chaos, and I mended my ways. After graduation, I worked for two years, and then I was admitted to a graduate program in America, so I came to the other continent."

"But how did you..." Lu Boping looked at the business card in his hand and did not know how to ask.

Han Xinyun smiled, "Do you want to ask how I got rich? I made it by personal effort and luck."

"I believe you are an outstanding person among overseas Chinese. I admire your career success."

"You also made great achievement in your career, Mr. Lu."

"Nothing. Nothing. And I may need your help in future."

On the morning of the next day, Lu Boping received Han Xinyun's call. She asked him to eat dinner with her in Shangri-La Hotel. Lu Boping was very happy, because he was considering how to use Han Xinyun to realize his dream of living abroad."

At the dinner meeting, Han Xinyun said happily, "Mr. Lu, I remember you treated me 20 years ago. I don't want to owe things to people, so I treat you today. I'm returning the favor."

Lu Boping said politely, "Thank you for your invitation, Mr. Sullivan. But to speak of owing favors, I owe more favor to Mrs. Sullivan." The favor Lu Boping referred to was the favor of friendship.

Han Xinyun smiled and said, "We are old friends. You don't need to care much about etiquette. Mr. Lu, can I still call you Boping?"

"Sure! Of course you can! So can I call you Xinyun?"

"My current name is Sheila. If you prefer, just call me Sheila."

"Ah, this name is beautiful. It seems the wife of United States president has the same name."

"Her name is Hillary."

"Foreign names are hard to distinguish. By the way, why didn't your husband come with you?" Lu Boping asked carefully.

"Ah, he went to see God. Amen." Han Xinyun habitually made a cross in front of her chest with her right hand.

"I'm really sorry! I should not make you sad."

"Sad? Why? I'm good now. Or in the words of mainland people, I'm natural and unrestrained, right?" Han Xinyun looked at Lu Boping in earnest.

"Yes! It seems you are familiar with the situation in China mainland."

"It's my motherland, anyway."

When the alcohol and dishes were served, Lu Boping clinked glasses with Han Xinyun and celebrated the reunion. Then he asked, "Sheila, do you have children?"

"Why are you so interested in my family? You are up to no good again. Haha. Don't flush. We had close contact before, don't be shy. As to children, I'm destined to live my life alone. It's the will of God. Amen." Han Xinyun made another cross.

"You will not be lonely."

"Why? How do you know?"

"Such a smart and pretty woman like you can't be lonely."

"And I have a lot of money, right?" Before Lu Boping could answer, Han Xinyun said again, "Ah, I forgot. Mainland people don't talk about money, even if they want it in the worst way. OK, let's talk about something else; for example, your family."

"I married before and have a daughter."

"Why did you say 'married before'? Your wife went to see God? No, went to see Carl Marx."

"No, we divorced."

"That's a tragedy."

"It's a kind of liberation."

"I agree. No matter what the cause is, if both persons can't live together, they'd better not torture each other with a dead marriage anymore. It's indeed a liberation. How long have you been liberated?"

"The year before last."

"I guess you have a new girlfriend? I remember you are not comfortable with yourself."

"Hey, it's not so easy. It's difficult for people to find an intimate friend since the ancient times." Lu Boping raised his glass and drank up.

Han Xinyun looked at Lu Boping and smiled with contempt. She raised her glass, too, but only took a sip. Then she changed the subject, "How is Xia Dahu?"

"Dahu? Ah, he's doing good. He ran an interior decoration company and made some money."

"Is he married?"

"Yes, and he has a son. His son is trading stocks in my company. We are old friends, so I take care of his son." Lu Boping knew Han Xinyun and Xia Dahu once got along very well in school, so he added, "Dahu is a hen-pecked husband, do you know what it means?"

"He is afraid of his wife."

"Do you want to meet him?"

"It's not necessary. He has a happy family and a successful career. Why should I bother him? Don't mention me in front of him. I hope he forgets me completely." Han Xinyun said as if deep in thought.

"I will absolutely not mention you in front of him. Let the past be the past."

Han Xinyun snorted and did not speak.

After dinner, Lu Boping politely sent Han Xinyun to her room. At the doorway, Lu Boping asked, "Can I sit inside for a while?"

Han Xinyun laughed, "Your bad habit has not changed." But she allowed Lu Boping into her room.

After closing the door, Han Xinyun took off her coat and went into the bedroom. Lu Boping followed her. He suddenly embraced Han Xinyun and said rapidly, "Honey, I love you! Do you know? When I received your blank letter that year, my heart was broken. I know you don't like me, but I'm not reconciled to it. I tried to visit you when I was back in Beijing, but you moved away. No one knew your whereabouts. Do you know how painful I was? I have been thinking about you these years. My marriage broke because you were a shadow in my heart. I love you, and you are the real intimate friend in my life. Now destiny put us together. Honey, please give me another chance. I will accompany you forever, wherever you are. Honey, I hope you can say yes."

Han Xinyun did not speak. She closed her eyes and allowed Lu Boping's mouth to kiss her face, and his hands to move all over her body. Lu Boping understood her consent and carried her to the bed.

…………………………

When they got up from bed, Han Xinyun took a shower and sat on the couch in her nightgown.

Lu Boping sat beside Han Xinyun and said affectionately, "Honey, thank you for giving me so much happiness. And thank you for your trust. I will not let you down. I will make you happy. Honey, for God's sake, let's get married."

Han Xinyun smiled and said, "You can say whatever except God, because cheating God is the severest sin."

"What? You don't believe my love for you? Honey, I I really want to take my heart out and show it to you."

"Don't be so bloody. I know everyone's heart is red, because there is blood on it."

"I really love you. I can prove my love for you with my acts. I…"

"Aren't you tired? It's hard for you. You are old and have a high social status, but you have to play a role that even a young man finds difficult."

"Honey, you can't say that. I…"

"Call me Sheila. When the play is over, it's awkward to use the address in the play. Actually I was acting in the play. I closed my eyes and imagined you are my lover who waited for me for 20 years, so that I could experience the happiest feeling. Now the happy moments have passed. Let's talk frankly." Han Xinyun stood up and sat on the couch opposite Lu Boping. She said calmly, "You just said you can accompany me wherever I am. You don't want to be the manager anymore?"

"What aspect of the manager job is attractive to me? No matter how hard I work, I'm working for someone else. The money I earn with hard labor will be taken away if my leaders so asked. They will use the money for their personal enjoyment. I have wanted to quit much earlier." Lu Boping said emotionally.

"Then why do you want to marry me? For my money?"

"Money? I don't lack money. I love you from my heart. How can you say my love is money-oriented? To be honest, I have a large deposit in a bank in Hong Kong. It's not as much as yours, but it's enough for me to use. I can assure you that after marriage, I won't take a penny from you. We can sign a contract before marriage – the property of the husband and wife is not shared. My only wish is to make you live a happy life with my love, and protect and comfort your scarred heart. Maybe I'm too impulsive today, but I'm not that bad as you think. And what you said just now was an insult to my character. But I'm not angry with you and I understand your feelings, because you were hurt so much before. If you think I hurt you once again, I sincerely beg your forgiveness. Good night!" Lu Boping stood up and strode out of Han Xinyun's room.

Two days later, Lu Boping received Han Xinyun's call again, and came to her room.

After entrance, Lu found that Han Xinyun dressed up solemnly. It seemed she was going to take part in an important social activity. So he asked, "Sheila, are you going out? If you have any important activity, I can come someday later."

Han Xinyun smiled, "Yes, there is an important activity, but you are one of the participants."

"What activity?"

"Sit down and talk." Han Xinyun asked Lu to sit on the couch and she sat opposite him. "I think we should carefully discuss our deal. If everything is smooth, we can reach an agreement."

"Do you mean a marriage agreement?" Lu Boping was overjoyed.

"You can call it this way, but its content is much broader than an ordinary marriage agreement."

"I know. And I promise to accept all of your conditions."

"Don't make promise so early. You can tell me how you think after hearing my conditions."

"OK, honey, I'll listen with respectful attention."

"This is a serious negotiation. Please watch your words."

"You are different from others in doing things."

"What surprise you will come next. OK, let's return to the subject." Han Xinyun moved her body backwards and said, "If I'm right, your purpose of marrying me is to go to America."

"No. No. I..."

"Mr. Lu, don't interrupt me. We are formally negotiating, and I will patiently listen to your statement after I finish. Besides, I want to remind you that if you can't speak frankly and sincerely, cooperation will be very difficult. This is the precondition, can you accept it?" Han Xinyun looked at Lu Boping seriously.

Lu Boping hesitated and nodded resignedly.

Han Xinyun continued, "You want to go to America to escape punishment. There is no doubt about this. You said you have a large deposit in a Hong Kong bank. You are the manager of a state-owned company. With a limited salary, how can you get a large deposit? Your money must be illegal income obtained probably by corruption and accepting bribes. Don't be afraid! I have neither obligation nor interest to help Chinese judicial authorities to investigate your crime, and I will fulfill your wish, if you can do me a favor."

"How can I help you?" Lu Boping took back his smile. He thought this woman was indeed intelligent, and he was analyzing what she probably would threaten him to do by using this knowledge.

"Last time you said Xia Dahu's son was trading stocks in your place. I think it's easy for you to use your power to punish him."

"Why do you want to punish him?" Lu Boping let out a sigh of relief.

"Because I hate Xia Dahu. He beat my father to death. I'll take revenge. I'll make both Xia Dahu and his son repay the debt." Han Xinyun was not speaking loudly, but her face got red.

"Xia Dahu beat your father to death? Why didn't I know it? It must be your misunderstanding. He has always been good to you. How can he beat your father?"

"I saw it with my own eyes. There were other rebels, but he was in front of them and beat my father in the most ruthless manner. Initially I could not accept this fact and tried to find excuse for him. I thought he was forced and it was a misunderstanding. I was too young and kindhearted. After all these years' tribulation, I gained a deeper understanding of human nature. Under the urge of selfish desire, people can do the cruelest thing. Xia Dahu pursued me before. And when our family moved away, he was searching for me, but I could not meet him. He must have thought my father placed obstacles in the way, so he took the opportunity to beat my poor father. So it was me who caused my father's death."

"Really? No wonder Xia Dahu never mentioned this to me." Lu Boping muttered.

"How could he tell you the bad things he did? He is a narrow-minded man who seeks to prevail over others. Whatever the reason was, my father was beaten to death by him. And that was the cause of my miserable life. Therefore, I'll take revenge on him and his son."

"How do you want me to take revenge on his son? Beat him up or kill him?"

"I'm not crazy. I won't let you do such a stupid thing. Besides, doing so would only prove my incapability. I will use legal means to ruin his family. Let him helplessly taste the bitter fruit he planted. First, you should cause Xia Dahu's son to lose all money in the stock market, preferably putting him into debt; then you should speak sarcastically to him and cause him to commit suicide or put him into prison. You should let him know he is paying debt for his father and let him hate his father. As to Xia Dahu, I'll trick him by myself." Han Xinyun said the final sentences with hatred.

Lu Boping calmed down at this moment. He thought he had taken initiative in this life combat. He said slowly, "This is not difficult, but how about myself?"

Han Xinyun said, "I have thought for you already. You have two ways ahead: One is to get married and then go abroad. The other is to first go abroad, and then marry. By the first method, you can directly apply for immigration. It seems to be a shortcut, but haste makes waste and it's risky. You probably know that you have to stand in a queue to apply for immigration visa. Even if you meet all the conditions, you have to wait for the quota assigned to China mainland by the USCIS, and there must be many people queuing before you. More importantly, if you apply to go abroad after marriage, you might be suspected by the relevant authorities in China. If you are caught, all your efforts will be wasted. So I advise you to take two steps. First, you should go abroad. This is not difficult and you can hide your intention easily. I can invite you to do business investigation in America in the name of my company. As long as you can get a passport, the American visa can be obtained secretly, and you don't need to alarm your superiors and colleagues. Obviously this is better for you. The second step is marriage and the immigration procedure. When you arrive in America, I promise to marry you and help you go through immigration procedure. Certainly, our marriage is temporary. Once you get your status, our marriage shall end. And we shall be financially independent from each other during marriage and after divorce. The above are my conditions. How long do you need to give me a reply?"

"Hmm...I have another question."

"Please ask."

"When will you send me the invitation?"

"This is an important question indeed. I think, based on my conditions, I need to see the initial result of your work before I can send you the invitation. Particularly, I need to see you make Xia Dahu's son bankrupt, because only by doing this can you show me your sincerity of cooperation. You won't object to this, I believe?"

Lu Boping had to admire in his heart Han Xinyun's shrewdness and eloquence. He thought for a while and understood the wisest choice for him was to accept all the conditions. He said, "You are really an extraordinary woman. I totally accept your conditions. But I hope you can change your mind before you cancel our marriage at last."

Han Xinyun smiled gracefully, "It depends on your capability. Some people say woman are wantons. But it's not easy to change their mind when they have made a decision. I can only say good luck."

Han Xinyun went back to America soon after parting with him.

After careful consideration, Lu Boping started to implement his action plan. Based on internal situations he knew of, he used Fang Qiong to put Xia Zhe into prison. He felt at ease because he was always unhappy about Xia Dahu and Bai Mei's union. Of course, he was not a person who constantly held grudges. He valued tomorrow instead of yesterday. As long as his future life was not obstructed, he could live on friendly terms with Xia Dahu's family. He had been doing so in these years.

Han Xinyun sent him the invitation letter as agreed.

However, things were not going as smoothly as he expected. But he found that he had to keep going after stepping on this road, and his destiny gradually fell into Han Xinyun's hands.

Han Xinyun made new requests. She first asked Lu Boping to steal a contract from Xia Dahu's office, and then frame Xia Zhe once more when the trial progress was too slow. The first request was not difficult for Lu Boping. He was familiar with Xia Dahu's office and had good knowledge of safes. So he finished the task easily. But the second request was an awkward matter, because he already knew Xia Zhe was his blood son.

Lu Boping was not a person who did not value kinship. Actually he thought blood relationship was the most cherished relationship between humans. He was guilty that he hurt his son when he did not know the truth, how can he hurt him again? Over the years, it was the first time for him to worry about another human's happiness and destiny. However, he couldn't only consider Xia Zhe's destiny, and he must consider his own. And he was accustomed to put his destiny in front of others. Now he felt the threat – from the lawyer Mr.

Hong, who was hard to deal with, and from Fang Qiong, who was infatuated with him.

He knew Fang Qiong's love for him was genuine, and she was willing to go through all difficulties for love. Therefore, he placed Fang Qiong in the security company to directly operated those "inside dealings". To deceive the public, they pretended to not have any personal relations in the company. He promised to take her to America, get married, and share the money. And Fang Qiong was self-studying English diligently. In fact, he wanted to take Fang Qiong to America, but he knew Han Xinyun would not agree. And he couldn't leave her alone in China, because she knew too much of his secrets. He was distressed about this, but he had to first protect himself. At last, he carefully designed an action plan which could kill two birds with one arrow – to keep Fang Qiong's mouth shut and satisfy Han Xinyun's requirements. Sometimes he was guilty and felt sorry for Fang Qiong. Fang Qiong loved him wholeheartedly, and obeyed all his orders and arrangements, but he betrayed and killed her. Her resentful look before death was like two swords penetrating into his heart. However, he had no choice, just like he shot the wounded soldier in Vietnamese battlefield.

The only person who suffered from injustice was his son. But he found an excuse to maintain his psychological balance – on one hand, he prevented the marriage between his son and daughter; on the other hand, he could compensate for his son's loss. As long as he was safe, his son could share his wealth. He could get his son to America and give him a great fortune. He promised to send him to study in the University of Hong Kong, or Harvard University in America. But could his son pass the trial? Maybe...

Thinking of this, Lu Boping let out a sigh.

Since the plane flew from west to east, night passed quickly. At about 10 o'clock of local time, the plane landed in San Francisco Airport. Now he was on the land of America; he was excited, but was somewhat upset, because this was a new country for him, and his did not understand people's language. He did not know what was awaiting him.

After picking up the checked luggage, Lu Boping pushed a luggage trolley and went to the customs exit. There was a long queue in front. He waited for 40 minutes until his turn to go through the procedure. He went to the window of a square glass room and handed in his passport and relevant documents. A middle-aged woman in uniform was sitting inside. She examined Lu Boping's passport carefully and asked him something, but he could not understand. He involuntarily nodded and shook his head. The female officer turned around and exchanged a few sentences with a man behind her. Then the man went out and asked Lu Boping to follow him. Lu Boping pushed the luggage trolley and went into an office with him.

After more than 10 minutes, a Chinese translator came in. With the help of the translator, the customs officer said to him, "Mr. Lu, I regret to tell you that you can't enter America."

"What?" Lu Boping virtually could not believe his ears.

"You can't enter America."

"Why? I have the visa of U.S. Embassy."

"Getting a visa of the embassy does not guarantee entrance. It shall be determined by the customs officer."

"But I have an invitation letter and financial guarantee. You can't be unreasonable."

"We have reasons to do this, because the person who sent you the invitation has asked us to cancel her invitation letter and financial guarantee."

"What? It's her!" Lu Boping felt he was cheated and fooled. He tried his best to keep calm and said, "I will ask for political asylum".

"Political asylum? What's the reason? You are not persecuted. So your claim is ill-founded."

"Then...because of family planning. I can't stand the family planning policy of Chinese government. It violates human rights."

"But the form you filled out says you are 42 years old and unmarried. Mr. Lu, I formally order you to take the next plane and go back to China."

Lu Boping suddenly felt it was destiny's arrangement. His leg became soft and he collapsed onto the floor...

The Epilogue

Hong Jun sat in front of computer and looked at lines of characters on the screen. He made a fist with the right hand and moved it in two circles, and then tapped the keys to give the printing command. Thus, the printer connected to the computer produced a rhythmical sizzling sound. Hong Jun stood up, went to the pergola beside the door and leisurely appreciated the soothing water drops on monstera deliciosa leaves.

Suddenly, Song Jia's teasing voice came into his ears – "Mr. Hong, what are you thinking? Be careful, because I might tell Xiao Xue. Seriously, why don't you get married now?"

Hong Jun looked at Song Jia and asked her calmly, "Why are you in a hurry?"

"Who are in a hurry? I just want to know when I can attend your wedding ceremony."

"You should ask Xiao Xue. Even if I'm eager to marry her, it's useless. I have proposed to her twice, but she said she would consider it."

"You always boast that you understand psychology, but you don't understand a woman's psychology at all. Let me teach you today." Song Jia sat on the chair proudly.

Hong Jun looked at Song Jia with interest and asked, "How will you guide me?"

"Let me ask you first. Do you call her every day?"

"Not that frequent, I call her twice or three times in a week."

"No wonder the telephone bill of our firm is so high, but it's your own money, anyway. I mean you can't always call her. You should let her call you."

"How to tell her this? Say 'You call me and I save money'?"

"Not to save money."

"Then what should I say? 'Works is busy'?"

"You don't need to say anything. You refrain from calling her for a week, and see if she will call you."

"What if she does not call?"

"Then you call her once and say you are busy, and talk about your cases at hand. Don't always say you miss her. Do you know?"

"Then?"

"Then refrain from calling her for two weeks, and see her reactions. I calculate that even if she does not call you for the first week, this time she will call you. You must be patient. Do it twice or three times, and propose to her again, then she will agree."

"You are young but you have so much experience."

"Don't forget that I studied psychology. I'm professional on this matter."

"Does it work? Don't mess things up."

"Rest assured. Do as I said, and you won't mess things up."

"What if she uses this as an excuse and refuses to marry me?"

"If that happens, it means she does not want to marry you in the first place. Then don't wait. Move on."

"Move on to what?"

"Move on to your case. If you have time, you can write your thesis. I think you are overly energetic. You have a lot of cases at hand, but you are writing this kind of thesis." She picked up the article printed by the computer just now. The title of the article was *The Black Holes in Life*.

Hong Jun laughed, "I wrote this based on my inspiration."

"You are really learned. You dare study the universe. I read your great work, but I still don't understand what a black hole is."

"That's natural, because humans are still not able to understand black holes in the universe. The scientists have speculated its existence, but cannot describe the form and cause of its existence accurately. Some people say a black hole is a special star which does not give out light. Some people say a black hole is the remains of a huge star at the end of decay process. Some people say a black hole contains nothing. Some people say a black hole is filled with highly condensed matter. Some people say a black hole is the unavoidable end result of a star's self development. And some people say black holes are products of the Big Bang and the birth of the universe ten billion years ago. But scientists agree with each other on one thing – black holes have inconceivable, tremendous attractive force, and the entire universe will ultimately disappear in the black holes. Maybe this is the ultimate fate of humanity."

"I think you must be very tired. Why do you always study those crazy things?"

"I like it. The more profound and difficult the problem is, the more I'm interested in it."

"You are sick. If I work together with you for a long time, I will get sick, too."

"But what really interests me is not the black holes in the universe, but the black holes in life. Black holes in the universe are very far from us in time and space, but black holes in life live by our sides."

"This is interesting. But what is a black hole in life?"

"This is also a question that humans are unable to answer. At least I think so. If the line from life's beginning to its end is called 'life path', then what determines a person's life path? No doubt, the life paths of Han Xinyun, Xia Dahu, and Lu Boping have similarities and differences, but are these determined by their life characteristics or some non-living or super-living power? There are some 'deviation points' in their life paths. And what is the basis of these deviations? Are there any intrinsic laws behind these deviations? Maybe Newton's law of universal gravitation and law of motion similarly apply to the determination of life path. Then, based on the 'law of universal gravitation for life', all lives in society attract other lives, and the attraction is proportional to the product of the 'masses' of both lives, and inversely proportional to the product of the 'distances' of both lives. Based on the 'law of motion for life', first, if a life is in uniform linear motion, as long as there isn't an external force, it will continue with the motion by inertia; second, attraction can modify the moving speed and direction of a life; finally, the forces between two lives are always equal in magnitude and opposite in direction. But the above laws can only explain an ordinary life path. How to explain the life paths which have significant deviations, especially group deviations? I think this is the effect of black holes, because their inconceivable attractions significantly twisted the life paths of a group, and their mystic power caused a small or large number of miserable lives. Where does the strong attraction come from? From the special events? Or from those people who made special events? Or from the desire and energy which are driving those people? I don't know, because we can only see the effects of black holes, but can't see the black holes themselves."

"What can be the title of this scientific research achievement of you? Ah, 'law of universal gravitation for life'. You can apply for the Nobel prize! But I don't know which discipline it belongs to. Medicine? Chemistry? Physics? None of these seems suitable. I think only the prize in literature fits it."

"Are you mocking me?"

"No, I just feel you are so imaginative! And this theory is too profound for ordinary people to understand. Can you describe it in a simple way?"

"This theory is difficult to be described simply. You know, once I was a college teacher, and a basic skill of college teachers is to make simple problems complex to show they are learned. But you want me to do the opposite, to make complex problems simple. This is difficult. I can give you an example, but it may not be accurate. Cultural revolution in China changed the life paths of thousands of people, so it seemed to be a black hole effect. But what is the black hole? We can't see it or describe it. Of course, if we can see it, it's not called a black hole anymore. Do you understand?"

Song Jia did not answer, because she was carefully thinking about the meanings of Hong Jun's words. She seemed to understand some truths, but also seemed to know nothing. She looked at Hong Jun, who was absorbed in thoughts, and became speechless.

The telephone ring broke the silence in the room. As if relieved of a heavy load, Song Jia picked up the microphone, "Hello! This is Hong Jun Law Firm. What can I do for you?"

"Hello, is that Song Jia? I'm Xia Zhe."

"Hi, Xia Zhe. How are you? Back to the stock market?"

"I pick up from where I left off. If I give up because of setbacks, I will be called a coward. Is it right?"

"Good for you. By the way, how is Lu Ting?"

"She is good."

"How about your relationship?"

"You surely know we are brother and sister. In the beginning, she could not accept this, and she fell sick. Later she understood it was the arrangement of heaven. Now she focuses on her study, and I'm studying, too. Our goal is to go to college together next year. She will study medicine and I will study finance. Don't worry. I can take care of my sister this life."

"I believe you. By the way, how is your father?"

"Which father? Now I have two fathers – Xia and Lu."

"Of course I mean Mr. Xia."

"He is miserable. All his assets which he built up for many years were lost, and the company closed down. He was ill. And we know things about Mrs. Sullivan now, but we can't comfort him. Now he either strolls in Shichahai or drinks alcohol at home. For the entire day, he does not speak. I know he is vexed, and I'm afraid lose faith in life."

"It might not be so serious. How about your Mr. Lu?"

"He is more miserable. I'm calling you for him. I want to ask Mr. Hong to defend him."

Hong Jun took the microphone from Song Jia, "Hello, Xia Zhe."

"Mr. Hong, Lu Boping was formally prosecuted by the procuratorate. I heard that his crime warrants a death sentence. I want you to be his defender and I will pay for it."

"There may be conflict of interest in the defense. You know, on the murder of Fang Qiong, my reasoning proved your innocence, but was very unfavorable to him. If I become his defense lawyer, I will advise him to use reasonable explanations to overthrow my reasoning, at least to prove that my reasoning and those indirect evidence cannot sufficiently and conclusively prove he shot Fang Qiong. On this matter, your interest and his interest conflict with each other, so I can't be the defense lawyer for both of you."

"He voluntarily surrendered himself after coming back from America. He confessed to the murder of Fang Qiong, which was exactly the same as you deduced. And he admitted that Sheila asked him to frame me. If he hadn't admitted all these things voluntarily, I could not have been released so soon. I think he did this for me."

"If so, I have no reason to refuse. Because of my feelings, I don't want to defend him , but as a lawyer, I have the obligation. I hate this person, but I have to respect his right to defense. However, I have to tell you first that you can't have too much hope."

"I know. I just want to help him and let life give him another chance, because he is my biological father."

Hong Jun put down the microphone and looked at Song Jia. He found Song Jia's eyes contained tears. He asked in confusion, "What's the matter? What made you so sad?"

Tears finally rolled out of her eyes. She said with sobs, "I'm not sure. After knowing the truth of this case, I just want to cry. I think these women lived a miserable life. Not to mention Sheila, even Lu Ting, Bai Mei, Lu Ting's mother and Fang Qiong were not happy. Although Fang Qiong was a disgusting home-wrecker, she was miserable, too. She was infatuated with Lu Boping, but died in his hand. Maybe this is women's destiny."

"I heard that the existence of tears is meant to prove sadness is not an illusion." Hong Jun said in earnest.

"Up yours!" Song Jia laughed.

Hong Jun looked at her, smiled, and said with a contented expression, "I also heard people's real meanings are somewhat different from the original meanings of the language they use. When we studied English, the teacher taught us about this. When a diplomat says 'yes', he means 'maybe', and when he says 'maybe', he means 'no', and when he says 'no', he is no longer a diplomat. On the contrary, if a girl says 'no', she means 'maybe', and when she says 'maybe', she means 'yes', and when she says 'yes', she is no longer a girl. Similarly, when a woman says 'up yours' to a man, it means she likes him."

Song Jia frowned and looked at Hong Jun, and then nodded, "You should change your name to 'Qiu Gao' (vast sky in autumn)."

"This is a good name. It's pleasant to hear, but why should I change?" Hong Jun was confused.

"Because my name is 'Qi Shuang' (cool weather in autumn)." Song Jia laughed complacently.

One year later, Hong Jun went to Chicago, USA to attend the alumni gathering of the law school of Northwest University. While standing beside the boundless Lake Michigan and overlooked the magnificent tall buildings, he was full of emotions. When he studied and lived here, he saw these things every day but did not feel their beauty and magnificence. But when he visited the place again after a long time, his love for the city was awakened.

It was five years after graduation, and the students seemed to have changed a lot. When they met, they talked about themselves and people they knew. From the words of the schoolmates, Hong Jun knew Sheila attended the alumni gathering every year and was an active participant. Thus, every time he attended the gathering, he searched for Sheila but could not find her. He asked his schoolmates, but they did not see her, either. And he checked the alumni donation record and did not find Sheila's name on it.

After an inner struggle, he dialed the number on Sheila's business card, but no one received the call. The monotonous beep sound threw him into disappointment and confusion. He finally understood he had a latent desire in the heart – to see Sheila again.

One day before his return, Hong Jun decided to not wait anymore and to find Sheila. He took the subway to the Chinatown at the south of Chicago, and found Hongya Co. Ltd. with the address on the business card. It was a two-story building with Chinese characteristics and style. With the help of the staff, he came to the office of the chairman of the board located on the 2nd floor and handed the business card to the female secretary. He said he wanted to meet the chairman of the board. The female secretary said the chairman was having a conversation and asked him to wait in the reception room.

Hong Jun sat on the couch in the reception room and looked at the Chinese calligraphy and paintings on the wall. He was thinking about the imminent meeting with Sheila. And he seemed to have a lot to say, but did not know where to start. Start from the past or the present? China or America? Xia Dahu or Lu Boping? The case or the waist belt?

The female secretary interrupted his thoughts and brought him into the office of the chairman of the board. He was surprised because the chairman was a middle-aged man.

The chairman smiled and said in Mandarin with a Cantonese accent, "Are you Mr. Hong? How can I help you?"

Hong Jun said with embarrassment, "I think I got the wrong person. I'm coming for Mrs. Sullivan. Isn't she the chairman of the board of Hongya Comany?

"Ah, you are asking for Sheila? She used to be the chairman of the board of our company, but she has resigned from his position half a year ago."

"Why?"

"Seemed to be because of health. I remember she was ill for a long time after she came back from China." The chairman looked Hong Jun up and down, and then asked, "Are you from Beijing?"

"Yes, I come to this city to attend the alumni gathering of Northwest University. Sheila and I are schoolmates."

"Ah, you finally appeared." The chairman looked excited.

"What do you mean?" Hong Jun was confused.

"When Sheila left the company, she left something for you. She asked me to pass it on to a lawyer from Beijing and said he was her old schoolmate." The chairman opened a cabinet and fetched a delicate gift bag; then he gave it to Hong Jun, "This must be for you."

Hong Jun opened the paper bag. There was an envelope and a cassette in it. He opened the envelope and saw a bank draft of one million USD. The beneficiary was Xia Dahu. He nodded and checked the inside and outside of the paper bag, but did not find any written word. He raised his head and said with contracted eyebrows, "You said Sheila left the company, but isn't she still the shareholder of the company?"

"She donated all of her property to the church."

"Do you know where she is, or how I can find her?"

The chairman shook his head and said, "I don't know, either, because she does not contact us. We wanted her to be the honorary chairman, but we didn't have her contact information and could not find her. I remember she talked about Beijing many times in her last conversation with me. It seemed she missed Beijing very much. I guess she went back to China."

Hong Jun pondered for a moment and asked, "Is Miss Chen Jingyi in your company now?"

"She left, too. It seemed she went back to Taiwan."

"They all left!" Hong Jun nodded as if he understood something. And he asked, "Do you have a recorder here? I want to listen to this tape."

"No problem!" The chairman brought a small recorder and put it on the table. He said, "Sorry, I have something to deal with. Please help yourself." The chairman closed the door when he went out.

Hong Jun held the tape in his hand and looked at it carefully. Then he put it into the recorder and pressed the play button. Soft singing with a little sadness came out from the speaker.

Let bygones be bygones,

Since life is always filled with ups and downs.

I try hard not to recall the past,

But all emotions hover over me like a blast.

Bid farewell to the old days,

Abiding tomorrow to be on its way,

And let me loose so that not a thing of mine is here to stay.

Love is a riddle,

Making us puzzle and hustle,

Painful memories might even be erased but never will your shadow.

You were never anywhere far away,

For you are lingering in my heart forever and a day.

My love for you will never sway,

But there's nothing I can do to keep myself awake.

I still harbor dreams deep inside,

Never being able to take you out of my mind.

I will turn blue when thinking about the old good times,

With my heart throbbing with unquenchable pang.

So let go of every romantic episode from the past,

Try not to suffer from nostalgia,

Never question whether and when we will meet again,

And never try to test whether I mean what I said.

Pain and love are inseparable peers,

That's something you should always remember.

So you'll find out that your life is all the same with my absence someday in the future.

Life will forever carry on with haste,

And I fear to face the coming years with so many tears to taste.

Just forget me to get rid of the pain,

Leave the long-past love blown and gone with the wind.

The singing ended. Hong Jun pressed the fast forward button to search the tape, but there was only the song *Love Long Past* sang by the popular singer Zhang Guorong. There weren't other words. He replayed the song and tasted the meanings of the lyrics. Why did Sheila leave this song to him? It seemed Sheila believed he would look for her. Then, what was the meaning of "Love" in "Love Long Past"? Love for him or Xia Dahu? Or it was an abstract love in life. He thought hard but could not understand.

The singing knocked on Hong Jun's heart. He knew Sheila was gone. She came into his life in a mysterious way, and also vanished in a mysterious way. Maybe Sheila was an arcane book for him forever.

After leaving Chinatown, Hong Jun took the subway to the downtown area. He walked on the street with a vacant mind and looked at the people, cars, and buildings. His vision and mind wandered aimlessly. Suddenly, the two cloud-kissing poles at the top of Sears Tower captured his vision and mind. Memories of ascending the tower with Sheila occurred to him.

He went into Sears Tower, bought the sightseeing ticket and went to the top floor by elevator. He walked around slowly along the edge of indoor sightseeing platform from north to east, and south to west, and had a full view of the city of Chicago. At last, he stopped. Facing the sunset, he remembered the poem Sheila recited that year – "People say the sunset is the end of the world; you can see the end of the world, but you can't see your home."

Did Sheila find her home? Maybe she found the home of life.

A feeling of self-reproach arose in his heart. Again, Zhang Guorong's singing appeared in his ears.

Let bygones be bygones,

Since life is always filled with ups and downs.

I try hard not to recall the past,

But all emotions hover over me like a blast.

Bid farewell to the old days,

Abiding tomorrow to be on its way,

And let me loose so that not a thing of mine is here to stay.

....

Pain and love are inseparable peers,

That's something you should always remember.

So you'll find out that your life is all the same with my absence someday in the future.

Life will forever carry on with haste,

And I fear to face the coming years with so many tears to taste.

Just forget me to get rid of the pain,

Leave the long-past love blown and gone with the wind.

Clear was the blue sky and splendid was the evening sunset. Life was like a dream, and destiny went up and down. The scene made him cry. The same night, Hong Jun dreamed of Sheila...

On the next morning, Hong Jun went to the O'Hare International Airport on the southwest of Chicago by taxi. After going through the boarding procedure, he went to the security checkpoint with regret.

Suddenly, he saw a woman in black nun robe standing beside the checkpoint and looking at him. It was Sheila! He called her name happily and went to her with quick steps.

Sheila took off her hat and exposed the grey hair curled on her head. She did not make up and appeared much older.

Hong Jun didn't expect Sheila's appearance changed so much. He nearly greeted her but took back his words.

They looked at each other silently.

Hong Jun finally found words to say to her, "Sheila, I'm very happy to see you again."

Sheila just gave a faint smile, "Jon, I'm seeing you off this time. This is what I owe you. But I want to tell you one thing – I believe in God now!"

The Afterword

I

Whenever sex is mentioned, what people first think of is having intercourse, also called making love. Sex has been a taboo for Chinese people. They think sex is vulgar, obscene, and even dirty or evil, and that sex pollutes one's heart and influences the fortune of the family or even the country. People will have sex when they reach a certain age, and any normal couple will make love, but this is something people can do but cannot say, can sense but cannot speak of.

When I was young, the cultural tradition of sex taboo went to extremes due to the propaganda work of red revolution. Both sex and love were taboos. Therefore, our generation developed a "sex language disorder". Even after many years of sex life, they felt difficult to talk about sex, except when they swore at people – they didn't talk about sex with the loved one, but talked about it without restraint to other women. Under the influence of sex criticism culture, I was biased in novel writing. It appeared that only the negative characters could have sex, and the love lives of positive characters should be invariably asexual. So much so that some readers criticized my novels as being unreal. For example, the well-known jurist and professor Zhang Weiping said my novel was "too clean". The well-known writer Mr. Mo Yan said my leading characters were "too hypocritical". Later I did careful introspection, and my European tour this summer "brainwashed" me.

I had a wonderful summer holiday this year. On the invitation of the International Criminal Law Sub-Institute of Max Planck Institute, I came to Freiburg im Breisgau in Germany to give lectures and do academic exchange. Freiburg is on the south of Germany and borders France and Switzerland. The city is not large and has a population of 200,000. It is in the famous Schwarzwald area in Germany with beautiful scenery and a pleasant climate.

417

During two months, I enjoyed the leisure of holiday without disturbance, appreciated the exotic landscapes, wrote study tour notes, and even read novels in a beautiful natural environment and a relaxed living atmosphere.

I read the novel *Der Vorleser* written by the German author Bernhard Schlink (I read the English version with the title *The Reader*). The main reason was that the book's author was a writer and jurist, which was the same as my status. It was said that the novel was translated into 35 languages and made into a movie in Hollywood. It had a huge influence in the world. However, my reading did not have an easy start, because the detailed descriptions of the cradle snatching romance between the leading characters Hanna and Michael in the beginning of the novel triggered my instinctive aversion. But as the plot unfolded, I was gradually attracted to the story, and the descriptions of sex were natural and beautiful, and did not affect my understanding of the novel's profound subject in any way. I realized that a serious literature work is not necessarily free from sex. Therefore, I wanted to exchange my realizations with Mr. Schlink. By friend introduction, I made an appointment to have lunch with Mr. Schlink in Berlin on July 14, but later the meeting was canceled because of my business in Freiburg. And this was a matter for regret in my European journey.

During my first month in Germany, my wife and I lived in the Haizi Park near the downtown area of Freiburg. Our room was at the corner of the 6th floor of an apartment building. One side of the balcony faced southwest, and the other side faced northwest. On the southwest were the building block and streets, and on the northwest were luxuriant trees. Some light yellow small flowers were scattered on the crowns of the trees. A path passed under the trees and led to a medium lake nearby. Tall aspens as high as six to seven floors of building were standing erect beside the lake. Behind the aspens was a winding and long wooden bridge crossing one corner of the lake, which was built on a few large blue floating balls. The bridge was eye-catching. On the east of the lake was a vast area of mountain slopes covered by green grass. On the north of the lake were dark green woods embedded in the light green grassland. And a wooden color watchtower and the pinnacle of a white church were hidden deep in the green woods. The west side of the lake was covered by the woods, and only some blue and white buildings can be seen indistinctly. Far from the back side of the lake area were rolling green mountains. At about 5 o'clock in the afternoon, my wife and I would go jogging along the lakeside path for one round, and every time we saw some men and women bathing naked in the sun on the grassland of a hill. At first I would turn away my vision due to embarrassment, but later I was accustomed to it, and I ran past them casually. Afterwards, we saw a larger scale of naked bathing.

During the second month, my wife and I went on a tour to France, Austria, Switzerland, and other cities of Germany for sightseeing in my spare time between lectures. We traveled by train just like Europeans. In Munich, we visited the Englischer Garten, which was known as the largest park in Europe. We entered the park from the Chinese Tower, went into the forest along an earth road, and soon got the feeling of staying away from the world. We saw a creek, so we went against the current and found our way out of the forest. Standing beside the woods, we were stunned by what we saw – numerous people in swimsuit or short trousers were lying on the back, on the stomach, sitting, or playing on the wide grassland on both sides of the creek. In my impression, such a scene can only be seen on the sand beach of Beidaihe in summer. We walked and looked, and saw some people who were thoroughly enjoying the sunshine. Under a beautiful willow, I took photos of my wife. Of course I had to keep the lens away from the completely naked persons. A girl in bikini walked to me. I thought she would stop us from taking photos, but she smiled and offered to take a family photo for us. Her facial expression was very natural, which made myself feel unnatural.

We passed by crowds of people who loved sunshine. I discovered that all people on the east side of the river, which we were at, wore clothes, even if some people wore very little. While completely naked people were on the west side, most of whom were middle-aged or old men and women. However, I also saw some young men and women, hand in hand, crawled to the bank from water, and the only clothing they had on them was the shoes. What made me surprised was that both they and people around them looked natural. Maybe seeing naked private parts and seeing naked non-private parts made no difference to them, and they would not have any "thoughts". The scene confused me for a while. Maybe they were the real decent humans, but we were persons of indecency or faked decency. Maybe humans should be like this way, like ducks on the banks and fish in water.

I heard that in ancient Greece, the housemaids in noble families were naked all day because they had no clothes to wear, but the male hosts were not sexually interested in them. Instead, the fully clothed madams and Misses could turn them on. They pursued these women to get the right to make love with them.

I asked myself: "Is sex beautiful or ugly? Is sexual behavior an act of kindness or evil?" After careful consideration, I thought sex is natural and beautiful and sexual behavior is an act of kindness, like food. Later, the social values centering on family needed to restrict sexual behavior, and thus mystified and smeared it. The sexual cultures and concepts today were developed in this way. And people have different or totally different sexual cultures and concepts in different societies and at different times.

After the European journey, I purposely added descriptions of sex while revising the novel *The Black Holes in Life – Evil Behind the Stock Market*, including the positive and beautiful descriptions to make characters in the book more rich and the story more real. But these were mainly sex lives in the 1970s and 1980s and affected by the age. Young people today might find some plots unbelievable, but these were reflections of the real world. Compared with people today, the sex lives of the people of that generation were feudal and outdated, but there was also a lot of beauty and kindness in them.

In the eyes of children, the father and mother are serious adults, and even old Ultramans. However, they all lived through innocent periods of youth, and the romantic seasons of first love. Moving on is the rule of life. The elder generation cannot have the ages of their sons and daughters again, but the sons and daughters will surely reach their elder generation's ages. When the happy youths have turned into deep or shallow memories, the past events can only be exchanged into faint smiles or soft sighs. The past is gone.

In the past 20 years, a lot of changes took place in Chinese society, including changes in sexual concepts and sexual behavior patterns, and changes in economic and legal systems. For example, in the 1997 revision of the *Criminal Law*, the "crime of negligent murder" was changed into "crime of negligent homicide", and eight "crimes of financial fraud" were explicitly explained. For another example, in 1996, China Securities Regulatory Commission explicitly prohibited the brokers from providing overdraft to customers for stock purchase; thus, the once prevalent "stock trading on overdraft" gradually disappeared. In conclusion, the novel depicts the social lives at that time. I think Chinese society and the Chinese ethnic peoples should keep such memories.

II

Sex is good and beautiful, not evil or ugly. Therefore, sex itself is sinless. However, for higher animals like us, the beauty of sex lies in its combination with love and observance of social behavior rules and moral standards; otherwise it will become evil. And sexual morality has an important position in the human morality system. A person who breaks through the sexual morality bottom line will easily break through the morality bottom lines of other aspects. Thus, sexual misconduct leads to other types of misconduct. A perfect example is that the degradation of many corrupt officials in China started from casual sex. Therefore, many crimes in human society can be traced back to sexual misconduct. These crimes seem to be derived from human nature, but also seem to be the overthrowing power against human nature.

Therefore, my thought entered into another level of meaning of sex. It is human nature, or humanity. In *The Evil in Blood*, I explored good and evil of human nature, but analyses were mainly conducted on individuals. But in this book, I continued to explore good and evil of human nature, and did so from the perspective of group and society. Actually, the evil in the characters is more or less within each of us as well.

To discuss good and evil of human nature, we should first clearly understand what is good and evil. In Chinese language, "good" means goodness, including friendliness, kindness, and amity; "evil" means badness, including evilness, ugliness, and malevolence. However, good, bad, and evil are relative. Good is required for bad and evil to exist. Certain things may be good for you but bad for me, may be good here but bad there. Therefore, we should understand the linguistic meanings of good and evil as well as their judgment criteria.

What are the judgment criteria of good and evil? First, these standards should be standards of conduct, instead of standards of thoughts. Indeed, the origin of good and evil is thoughts, but thoughts are hidden; if they are not shown in one's conduct, no one can know them. Even those thoughts shown in conduct cannot be accurately judged. For example, a wealthy person donates for the poor, and an official does good for the people. These are acts of goodness, but we cannot tell whether they do this for the people or themselves. I think we don't need to get to the bottom of their minds to know whether they are thinking about personal reputation or political achievement. As long as they are doing good, that is goodness. Second, the judgment criteria shall be group criteria instead of individual criteria. Humans are social animals. In a society, individuals are connected, and good and evil are manifest in the relationship between individuals. Since individual interests are different and even conflict with each other, individual interests cannot be used as judgment criteria of good and evil. Only group interests can be used. Conduct that is beneficial to group interests is goodness, and that damages group interests is evil. For individuals, the group interests often require their conduct to be altruistic instead of self-interested. Therefore we can say: self-interest leads to evil, and altruism leads to good; harming others to benefit oneself is typical evil, and sacrificing one's own interests for the sake of others is typical good.

Now that we know the behavioral standards of good and evil, let's discuss the influence of human nature on conduct. Human life has both individuality and the group nature. After eons of evolution and inheritance, the two natures have become the origin of human conduct that was melted in the blood. On one hand, to maintain the individual life, one should try his best to satisfy his own needs, even at the cost of others' and the group's interests. On the other hand, in order to live in a group, one must satisfy the group's needs and consider others' interests, especially those who have special relations with us. For example, the parents can sacrifice their personal interests for the children; the lover can sacrifice her own interests for the loved. Therefore, both self-interest and altruism are human nature. In other words, both good and evil exist in a human. Individuality of life is the origin of evil, but the group nature of living is the start of good. This is the manifestation of the nature's law of survival in humanity.

No doubt, crimes are the most typical evil in human conduct. But why are there crimes in human society? Scholars who believe in original goodness assert that crimes are caused by acquired factors, namely the defects in social system, culture, morality, and environment. For example, crimes of property violation are mainly because of injustice in social distribution system, huge gap of wealth, and lack or failure of education. But the viewpoint of this school of criminal sociology cannot fully explain the criminal phenomena in society. Why do some people commit crimes and others don't in the same social environment? And why are there criminals and law-abiding citizens even among people who grow up in the same social class or family environment? Therefore, some scholars explore the causes of crimes based on the differences of inborn physiology and psychology between humans. And this is as good as admitting the viewpoint of original evil, at least it admitted some people have the origin of evil in them since they were born. I think the origins of good and evil co-exist in human nature. In other words, human nature is originally both good and evil.

III

On December 13, 2009, I watched an American science fiction movie in the hotel during my lecture tour in Mianyang, Sichuan before I returned to Beijing. I missed the start and end of the movie, so I did not know its title, but the part of story interested me. In the movie, a fat scientist with superior intelligence invented a technology to trim genes and restore people's youth. Meanwhile, he discovered there was a fragment of evil DNA strand in his own genes, which manifested at critical moments to destroy his love life. Therefore, he used his technology to identify the position of the evil gene and did a surgery to cut and seal it. In this way, he parted with evil, but lost his intelligence...Maybe this was only an allegory.

Origins of both good and evil co-exist in human genes, but in some people's genes, there are more evil than good. Such people have more potential social harmfulness than others. If they are ordinary people, they may become murderers or robbers; if they are government officials, they may become evil officials or corrupt officials; if they hold national power, they may become cruel governors or tyrants. Suppose one day humans can recognize the origin of evil in their genes and have the technology to trim the malignant DNA fragment, then it will be possible for humans to eliminate crimes from the root, and realize the dream of "let the world be full of love". This is similar to our dream to use gene surgery to cure cancer once and for all. Of course, crimes are different from cancer. Even if humans have this technology, they may not widely use it, because it violates human rights and has the risk of changing humans to idiots.

I think the realization that human nature is originally both good and evil has practical significance. Since origins of evil and good co-exist in human nature, the social environment has become the factor determining the good and evil of people's conduct. If the social environment cultivates goodness, more and more people will do good, but if the social environment cultivates evil, more and more people will become evil. In modern China, people often complain that good people are so few. Why? Because the current Chinese social environment does not cultivate good persons. In a society which encourages people, in both material and spiritual aspects, to engage in cut-throat competition to become the strong, people won't be kind. In a society which allows people, on both moral and cultural levels, to practice fraud and swindle others to obtain personal interests, people won't be righteous alone. Therefore, in the political circle, business world, and workplaces of all walks of life, people try hard to use evil in them to counteract and overcome the evil of others. Some parents even try every means to cultivate their children into "wolves", because they are afraid their children will become "sheep" in a "wolf pack". Some corrupt officials justify their evil behavior by saying they have "difficulties that are hard to mention"; some unscrupulous merchants justify their notorious behavior by saying they "have no other choice"; and even some foreign businessmen offer bribes or cheat in China while saying "do in Rome as Rome does". And some people stand for "use evil to punish evil", and "use violence to eliminate violence". For example, some law enforcement officers use the excuse that the object of law enforcement is "an evil person", or "a cunning person", and therefore use malignant law enforcement methods, such as violent law enforcement, extorting confessions by torture, and brutal eviction. But using evil to punish evil will only make people eviler, and further deteriorate the social environment, because in the world of "wolves", no one wants to be the "sheep".

To create a social environment which cultivates good, there must be someone who does good first.. Then who should be the first? I think the powerful group should do good first, because this is fair. If we ask the weak group to do good first, they will become weaker, and this is not beneficial for justice, righteousness, harmony, and stability of society. And this rule is in line with the powerful group's interests, because they most need social harmony and stability. The so-called powerful group means the people who hold power or wealth. To keep the acquired power and wealth, they need the society to be stable and harmonious. If the society is unstable and disharmonious , their power or wealth will be threatened. The history of mankind has proved this rule of social reform for numerous times. Therefore, the powerful group should be prepared for the unexpected, and take measures to prevent them. We should stop the bad and advocate the good through actions in order to avoid trouble.

Democracy and rule of law should be taken as the basic guideline to build a social environment that stops the bad and advocates the good. System construction is the key. In modern China, the establishment of a system has to be approved by government officials. Therefore, the decision-making officials are the key to building a system that stops the bad and advocates the good. The government officials must sacrifice some personal interests for the sake of the people. For example, building a real official property declaration system is an effective measure to prevent corruption, and it is also an exemplary system that stops the bad and advocates the good, but it will damage the officials' privacy to some extent. If the decision-making officials can help the public at their own expense, it will be great goodness. Besides, as to the important issue of building an official property declaration system, which concerns the interests of the people, disclosing the decision-making process as well as the decision-making result is also an institutional progress in the effort to stop the bad and advocate the good. As to how to disclose them, I have once put forward a simple suggestion: Live broadcast across the country the discussion in the meeting and request every decision-maker to show his attitude with real name. Indeed, such a system will be hard for the decision-makers, and it's them who will make trouble for themselves. But if they can make trouble for themselves for the interests of the people, they are actually doing an act of ultimate goodness.

The Chinese ethnic peoples are facing an unprecedented crisis. It is the Great Depression of Spirit which has come together with material abundance. Every ethnic people needs a spirit to support its soul. Every age needs a spirit to respond to the transition of history. In the face of the crisis, we need not teachings and arguments, but bravery and conscience.

IV

In *The Evil in Sex*, Han Xinyun, Lu Boping and Xia Dahu used to be good persons, but the wicked social environment caused them to go astray and give up good for evil. Therefore, people's goodness and evil are affect by the social environment, and the social system is an important component of social environment. Under a good social system, people's conduct will be inclined to goodness.

If there is indeed a heaven on earth, and if humans can build a communist society, I believe all people living in the society will surely be good, because the system can help people develop good habits. However, our current social system doesn't have such a function. Therefore, to make people do good, we must improve our social system.

Similar to people, systems are also inherited. At the time of regime change, the new rulers often claim to build a brand new social system, but the genes of the old system will be subtly inherited. After the foundation of new China, we claimed ambitiously to "smash the old world", and even to "destroy the four stereotypes" at any risk, but our social system still carried the genes from the past, including the bad genes, such as rule of man, dictatorship, privileges, and uncivilized political struggles. In other words, Chinese social system lacks the genes of democracy, rule of law, and equality, as well as civilized genes of respecting and tolerating political opponents. Therefore, our political struggle must be that "the winner becomes the king, and the loser becomes the bandit." Politicians of different factions must fight in a life-and-death struggle and they often use hidden weapons. In such a system, being evil corresponds with the natural law that the strong survives, but does not agree with the common interests of human society.

How to improve the genes of Chinese social system? I think we should take the gradual approach, starting from small systems by changing them into good genes, and then push forward the improvement of large systems. For example, I once proposed to build an official promotion system with balanced sense of achievement to reduce the allure of official positions, i.e. promotion without raise of salary. Specifically, raise of the salary and level of civil servants should depend on their qualifications and merit ratings. As long as they can complete their own work according to the assessment criteria, their level and salary can be raised on time. But the raise of position should have no connection with the salary level. And after each raise of position, the raise of salary level should stop once. In other words, if they want a promotion, they have to give up salary raise. Although such a system cannot thoroughly discourage civil servants' pursuit for promotion, it helps achieve the balance of sense of achievement in the political circle, and helps reduce contradiction between supply and demand of official positions, and reduces the phenomena of buying and selling of official positions to some extent.

Additionally, I once proposed to change the standards of electing NPC members and CPPCC members. Currently, most of the representative members of NPC and CPPCC on various levels in China are senior government officials, business elites, celebrities, and stars of recreational and sports activities. All of them are socially successful persons in the "power standard" and "wealth standard". Therefore, NPC and CPPCC are like a large gathering of high-end people in society. Actually, these people cannot represent public opinions which should be represented; nor can they really supervise the government. Besides, these people already have high social honor or reputation, and there is no need to give them the honor of being representative members of NPC and CPPCC to enhance their sense of achievement and enlarge the gap between their achievement and common people's, which makes most people feel uneasy. Sense of achievement in society should be balanced, and only balance can lead to harmony. Therefore, I once proposed that government officials should not act as representatives or members of NPC or CPPCC. And high-end persons in other industries should be denied the position of a representative or a member of NPC and CPPCC, too. So that NPC and CPPCC can be the representative meeting for low-end public opinions in society. And "goodness standard" should be adhered to as the election standard. No matter in what industry or circle, only people who do good and care about public welfare can become the representatives and members of NPC and CPPCC.

I'm not an alien, although some of my thoughts are alien-like. I think the above small systems might be first set up in certain districts and departments in China. When the small systems increase in number, they can improve the genes of Chinese social system and make more and more people think good and do good. Besides, as genes, they can influence our offspring, so that the children and grandchildren of Han Xinyun, Lu Boping, and Xia Dahu will not step on the old way from purity to evil.

Actually, it was not my original intention to discuss the good or evil of human nature. So many knowledgeable "masters" from ancient to modern, and in China and foreign countries, cannot give a conclusion about this, how can I, a small scholar of tiny brain, tell the fact clearly? What I want to say and see are the tangible and genuine goodness, the goodness that can be passed on to our descendants.

When there is more goodness, sex will be sinless.

He Jiahong

Written in Chixingzhai, The Century City, Beijing in 2010.

www.ingramcontent.com/pod-product-compliance
Lightning Source LLC
Chambersburg PA
CBHW080730250626
47170CB00011B/2895